To Barbara,
Welcome to Chincoteague!
I hope you love the
story & learn to stay out
of the onesies.

Stuck in the Onesies

Diana

Diana McDonough

7/5/17

To my mom, the original queen of the Tensies and the best Redskins fan ever. If there is a choice of crowns in heaven, hers is a Redskins headdress. HTTR!

Contents

Acknowledgments

I want to thank all my friends and family for encouraging to me to pursue my dream to publish *Stuck in the Onesies*. Many have listened, encouraged, and probably rolled their eyes behind my back, but no more than I did. A big hug in heaven for my husband, Jeff, who gave me the support, space, and time to write on weekends while I worked my day job all those years ago.

My dear friends, Susan Walker, Shelley Cummings, and Cindi Krempel trudged through the initial manuscript and gave me the honest truth. Back to the drawing board I went. I can't thank you all enough. A big thanks to my cousin, Norma King, for her creativity on my website. It's a big plus to have a millennial in your corner when it comes to the techy part.

I love my sister, Tracy Cox, for telling me to quit beating around the bush and write the truth, so I did. In the process, I discovered there is no more ugly truth than racism.

Most of all, I want to thank God for the passion He instilled in me for the written word as well as the drive and ability to pursue my dream. Without Him, I am nothing.

CHAPTER 1

Barb
You Are My Sunshine

I beg you to speak of Woman as you do of the Negro, speak of her as a human being, as a citizen of the United States, as a half of the people in whose hands lies the destiny of this nation.

—Susan B. Anthony

Jake and I drove over the Chesapeake Bay Bridge in our pink Chevy two-door sedan, listening to Chubby Checker sing "The Twist," one of last year's top tunes. I stared at the water and the Eastern Shore and realized it hadn't been one of those days when I'd been tempted to flee. Some days, I just wanted to duck out the back door and keep on running. Taking off had been a routine part of my daydreams before we'd married, if for no other reason than I had been tired of ducking the Old Man's advances.

It turned out that the leap from childhood to adulthood at seventeen was more of a belly flop than the anticipated swan dive. However, I must admit that I do resemble a swan, beautiful with the facade of gracefulness until I get up and walk around. And, like the swan, if provoked or threatened, I can pack a wallop, a survival technique learned from growing up with two brothers and a lecherous father.

I sometimes wonder what Jake really thought of what he'd gotten himself into. Supporting two kids and a wife had to be a big task for a guy who's little more than a kid himself.

Jake, the kids, and I drove an hour and a half from our little apartment in the Washington, DC, suburbs over the Chesapeake Bay to Cambridge, Maryland, on the Eastern Shore. Well, actually, Jake drove, as I didn't have a license. He'd given me a few lessons, but he hadn't been that great a teacher, or I'd been a poor student. He claimed the latter.

We were going to visit Will Reilly, Jake's coworker and our weekday roommate. Will's family lived in Cambridge, and he went home on weekends. Jake and Will were best buds, and they were determined that Ellie and I would be, too.

Now, I was a friendly enough person, I just didn't have that many friends. Motherhood with two kids can be a lonely profession. After Jay was born, I had decided to stay home, since the cost of a sitter versus my meager salary as a secretary left us in the hole. I'd come to realize that I enjoyed my own company much more than that of any other person I knew anyway. I'd wanted to just stay home that day, and I'd pleaded my case for Jake to make the trip alone, or maybe just take Karen, our five-year-old along, but he insisted that we all go. Meeting new people has never been my strong suit, but he reminded me that I had been talking on the phone some with Ellie, so he built his case that it really wouldn't be that bad.

It took us about an hour to get to Cambridge once we crossed the Bay Bridge. Jake took a right off the highway, and the road followed along the Choptank River. He stopped the car as we waited for a drawbridge to go back down. There was a police car with its lights flashing on the other side of the bridge, and the cop was pushing someone around, a black man wearing a baseball cap and blue jeans.

"Is that a bad man, Daddy?" Karen asked as the bridge came down and we drove past.

"Must be, hon." He tossed his cigarette butt out the window and rolled it up the rest of the way. The cop shoved the man into the backseat of the cruiser and slammed the door shut.

"You'd better get outta here, or I'll lock the rest of you up!" the cop yelled at the small group of onlookers. They began to disperse and head their separate ways. Jake continued past the cop car, and I pulled the "take a left, take a right" directions from Will out of my purse and read them aloud.

"Where is the policeman taking that man, Daddy?"

"Leave Daddy alone right now, hon." I held up the directions. "We're trying to find Ginger's house."

She sat back down in the seat.

Jake pulled our pink Chevy into the gravel driveway of the little shingled cottage, the fifth in a row of look-alike homes. I grabbed baby Jay's tote, and Jake opened the door for Karen. We walked toward the backyard, where Will stood up from working on his lawn mower, and a freckled red-haired boy about Karen's age peeked around his dad to check us out.

"Jake, Barb, how was the trip?" Will said, shaking hands with Jake.

"Not too bad. The baby slept most of the way," Jake said, looking down at Jay. "And this must be Scott."

"Sure is," Will said as the boy reached out and shook Jake's hand. He looked sideways at Karen and whispered, "Hi."

"Come on in. Ellie's been cooking all morning." Will waved a follow-me hand over his shoulder, and we walked behind him through the screen door to the back porch. The aroma of bacon filled the air.

The music from the kitchen window swelled, and it was evident that more voices than just that of the Kingston Trio were singing the old version of "The Lion Sleeps Tonight." Will opened the kitchen door and stopped short to eavesdrop.

A strawberry blonde who I assumed must be Ellie stood with her back to us wearing a flowered housedress. The extra weight tried but couldn't hide how pretty she was. The dress was loose-fitting, and though she was big through the middle, her legs were slender and curvy. A little girl, about four years old, who I assumed was Ginger, leaned close to her side, singing into a wooden spoon. "A wheema whack, a wheema whack, a wheema whack!"

Will started to interrupt them, but I motioned him to let the show go on.

They swayed back and forth as one, oblivious to their talent-show-crashing audience. Ellie sang the lyrics, "In the jungle, the quiet jungle, the lion sleeps tonight," in a pretty, lilting voice, and the little girl chimed in on the chorus.

"A wheema whack, a wheema whack!"

The music faded, and the top-ten hit came to an end.

3

Will cleared his throat. I put the baby's tote down on the floor, and we applauded.

Ellie wheeled around. The little girl hid behind her mom and giggled. Ellie's eyes widened, and her hand flew to cover her mouth as she tried to stifle a laugh.

We introduced ourselves between chuckles. Will shook his head in embarrassment at his wife's inhibitions, but I was impressed.

"We were just practicing for our talent show," Ellie said. "Have to be ready for our weekend matinees, you know."

"We've heard about those shows, and we just got a sneak preview. When's the real show?" Jake asked and set the suitcase down.

"Oh, stay tuned. You just never know," Ellie said and smoothed her hair down with her hands.

We hugged hello, and thanks to our more and more frequent phone conversations while Will was staying with us during the week—as well as her singing debut—I was relieved to feel at home right away. Small talk has never been my strong suit.

Karen pulled her shy routine even though everyone was so friendly. Since the idea was for her to stay and visit for the week and make Will and Ellie's little girl, Ginger, her new best friend, the pressure was on.

"This is my Ginger." Ellie nudged the little girl toward Karen. She had bright-red curly hair and was freckled like Scott. Only Roger, their eight-year-old son, who had walked in from the other room, looked like Will with dark hair and an olive complexion.

Ellie took Karen by the hand and introduced her to each of the kids, as well as Charlie Brown, the family boxer dog from the front porch.

"Why don't you take Karen out back, Ging?" Ellie said. The little girl crooked her finger at Karen for her to follow. They walked through the kitchen and headed out the door to the backyard.

"I don't know which one of them is shier," I said as I picked up baby Jay.

"They'll be okay," Ellie said as she cleared a spot at the kitchen table. "Ginger couldn't wait for y'all to get here."

The guys walked to the living room with a couple of beers and sat down in front of the TV to watch whatever was on that involved a ball and keeping score. Ellie and I landed at the kitchen table. She warmed up Jay's next bottle for me in a pan of water on the stove as I jostled him back and forth, trying to keep him happy until his meal was ready. It wasn't helping much, and he began his midmorning tirade, screaming for food. Ellie wrist-checked the milk from the bottle and handed it to me.

As I fed Jay, he quieted down, grabbing hard onto the sides of the bottle. By the time he drained it, he was snoozing again.

"Just like his daddy, his eyelids clamp shut as soon as his belly is full," I said as I eased him back into his tote. "But don't worry; unlike his daddy, it won't last long!"

Ellie motioned for me to follow her to the back porch, and I tiptoed past the baby. She held her finger to her lips and walked over to eavesdrop on the girls. Karen and Ginger were sitting on the steps of the back porch looking at the chickens in the yard next door. Karen was amused with the backyard barnyard.

"Does he cry all the time?" Ginger asked and handed Karen one of the two dolls that sat on the back porch.

"Yeah, most of the time. Sometimes we have to drive him around in the car to get him to stop." She held the doll and touched the dress with lace on the hem. "This is really pretty."

"My mom makes all my doll clothes. She even made me a dress to match that one," Ginger said.

Great. She sings, sews, and according to Will, cooks and who knows what else.

Ellie opened the back door, and we walked out to join the girls.

"Why is it so quiet back here, y'all? Ginger, you're usually talking my ear off!"

They both shrugged. Ellie reached in her pocket and handed me a handful of jacks and a little red ball. Karen and Ginger's faces lit up.

I picked up the ball, tossed the jacks on the floor, and started to practice while Ellie cleared a bigger spot for all of us to play. One by one, I picked up the jacks as I tossed and bounced the ball. I got all the way to foursies before I had to stop for the real challenge to begin.

"Okay, girls, let's start with Karen since she's company." Ellie sat down, pulling her dress over her knees, and I handed the jacks to Karen.

Karen dropped the jacks onto the linoleum porch floor. She tossed the ball in the air and bounced it once on the floor, swooped in with the same hand, and picked up the jacks one at a time without moving any of the others. She got halfway through her twosies before she fumbled.

And the competition began. Karen and Ginger got on to twosies, but I had a lousy throw and got stuck in the onesies.

Getting stuck in onesies is lethal to a jacks player. It's considered the easiest step, and if you don't sail right through it the first time, you play catch-up for the rest of the game.

"Stuck in the onesies, huh?" Ellie asked.

"Yeah, kinda like getting behind in the laundry. You go one day without hanging something on the line, and you're forever playing catch-up." I scooped up the rest of the jacks and handed them to Ellie.

"Yeah, I know what you mean. The last time I caught up on laundry, I think Truman was still president."

Ellie uncrossed her legs and knelt down on the floor. She sailed through the onesies and got all the way to fivesies before she goofed. In no time, she'd whooped us all. I was determined to learn to be as coordinated as her, but it was apparent that it was going to take some practice.

"You're the champ for now," I said. "But just wait until Karen and I get some practice under our belts." I tossed the jacks to take a practice turn.

It had been a long time since Karen and I had sat on the kitchen floor to play. I made a private promise to myself to spend more time just playing with her. Since Jay had come along, there just never seemed to be enough time. Not that I'd been all that good about getting down on her level before that. I promised myself I'd do better.

My worries about spending the weekend with the Reillys and leaving Karen behind for a week dissolved as the hours passed. Ellie was so genuine, and I soon discovered that laughter was never in short supply when she was around. Everything had an upside, a positive spin. She'd been married a few years longer than I had, but already we'd discovered that we had more than a few things in common.

We talked and laughed while we peeled potatoes for salad and took care of the kids' needs in between. The guys decided to take the boys and drive to the local marina to watch the boats bring in the daily catch while Ellie and I finished getting dinner ready. I had corn-shucking duty as I rocked Jay's baby seat with one foot.

Rosemary Clooney crooned from the record player in the living room as Ginger and Karen played in the backyard, chasing the neighbors' chickens.

"My mom was a big Rosemary Clooney fan," Ellie said as she refilled the saltshaker. "She sang back up with her until my brother and I came along."

"Wow, now I know where you got your voice."

Ellie smiled in response.

The phone rang. She walked over to the kitchen wall and picked up the black receiver.

"Hello? You did? That's great!" She looked at me wide-eyed. "I'll get the pot cooking, and it'll be ready to go when you get here. Hold on a minute; I think I might need Old Bay." She let the receiver hang from its cord and opened the cabinet above the stove. She shuffled around bottles and jars until she came out with a yellow can and a bottle of vinegar.

"Never mind, we're in good shape, but pick up some rock salt to mix it with." She hung up the phone.

"What was that all about?" I asked and put the last shucked ear on top of the corn pile.

"Will said they got a bushel of crabs for ten bucks right off the boat and they're all jimmies."

I could hardly hear her. The clanging avalanche of pots and pans hit the floor as she pulled out a big black pot from the bottom of the kitchen pantry. The baby startled. I rocked him with my foot, and he settled back down to his nap, sucking hard on his pacifier.

"Sorry!" Ellie squinted and shrugged.

"Makes me feel right at home. I can't open a cabinet without taking two steps back!" I continued rocking Jay with my foot. "Anyway, what's this about crabs? They got a whole bushel? How many is that, and who is Jimmy?"

Ellie giggled at my lack of crab-savvy. "A jimmy's a male crab; they're better tasting than the females. There might be five or six dozen in a bushel, depending on how big they are."

"Wow, can you all eat that many?"

"It's a social event. We'll be chowing down on them for at least two hours. Don't you eat them?"

"Just the claws. I've started picking them for Karen. Haven't found the nerve to go any further."

"Man, you don't know what you're missing. More for me, I guess."

Ellie put the large black pot on the stove, added water and vinegar, getting ready for the crabs. The girls walked into the kitchen, and Ginger's eyes grew wide.

"We're having crabs!" She clapped her hands together at the sight of the black pot. Ellie grabbed a stack of old newspapers from the bottom of the pantry.

"Yep, Dad and Mr. Kincaid are bringing us a bushel. Here, girls, let's go out back and cover the picnic table."

Ellie scooped up the newspapers, and we followed her out the back door. We layered the papers over the top of the wooden picnic table and taped them down with a roll of black electrical tape.

"You're never caught without a roll of black electrical tape when you're married to an electrician, are you?" I said and held up the roll of tape.

"That's true; I've wrapped more than one birthday present with it, too," Ellie answered, and I smiled in agreement.

We looked toward the driveway when we heard the wheels of our pink Chevy pull onto the gravel driveway. Charlie Brown barked to make sure we knew they were home, and we walked to the driveway to see the crabs.

"How'd you get him to buy a pink car anyway?" Ellie elbowed me.

"I won a bet," I said and winked at her. "Or lost, depending on how you look at it."

Jake pulled the wooden bushel basket out of the trunk. Crab legs poked out around the sides of the slats. The kids walked alongside as Ellie held the door open to the back porch. Jake lugged it inside and plopped the basket down on a stack of newspapers Ellie had put down in front of the stove. Chesapeake Bay blue crabs were supposed to be the best in the world.

"Where's the tongs, El?" Will bent down the metal hasp, and eased the wooden lid from the basket. The blue crabs wiggled a little, wondering why their world had changed so fast. No water to swim around in. Not yet, anyway.

"Here." She fished them out of a drawer and handed them to him. "Wow! Look at those guys. They're nice. You only paid ten bucks?"

"Yeah," Will answered. "Bucky pulled up right after we got to the pier. He had a good day and was going to just give them to me when I promised to help him wire his shed, but Jake insisted on paying him the ten bucks."

That's my boy, the big spender.

"Mr. Bucky said that the Chesapeake Bay stands for 'great shellfish bay,'" Scott piped up.

"Really?" I looked down at the six-year-old.

"Yep, and did you know that they only swim or walk sideways?" the Howdy Doody look-alike asked.

"Wow, that must be hard." I grinned and tousled his carrot top.

We backed up to watch Will reach into the pile of crabs with the tongs and select the first of many unlucky winners. Ellie put the lid back down on the basket to confine the other death-row inhabitants.

"Okay, I'll ask a dumb question." I picked up the baby's tote and put him on the table, just in case somebody escaped on his way from the basket to the pot. "Why don't you kill them first? Wouldn't that be a lot easier than fighting with these guys?"

"You have to cook the crabs while they're still alive. Once they die, germs begin to grow and can cause you to get really sick," Jake said as he reached down to pat Karen on the head. She shrank back behind his pant legs when Will reached for another crab.

The crab woke up fast, and his legs and claws grasped the air and reached for the tongs as Will dropped him into the pot. Jimmy scattered around the bottom of the pot, his claws and legs clanging in desperation. I shivered and backed up a little further as Ellie lifted the lid and Will reached in and grabbed another crab. This guy was smarter than the last. He grabbed onto his neighbor with his claw, pulling him along. He wasn't going down alone. The other crabs started to wake up and jostle for position away from the tongs.

"Buy one, get one free," Ellie said as Will dropped them into the pot.

"Yeah, just like a good red-dot sale at Hecht's!" I took hold of each of the girls' hands.

"Boy, what I wouldn't give to go to one of those." Ellie sighed.

"Stick with me; you'll get there yet!" I said.

"Yeah, Barb rarely misses one of those. I'll be glad when you get there, El, and I won't have to take her," Jake said. He lifted the lid of the basket. Will reached in and grabbed a crab with the tongs.

Ellie lifted the lid of the black pot for Will.

El looked at me. "You have a pink car and you don't drive?"

"No, not yet. Jake's tried to teach me, but…" I looked at him.

"She's not the most coordinated when it comes to a clutch." Jake put the lid back on the basket, but not before a few crabs made the great escape and flopped over the edge to the floor. We all took a step backward.

"Well, we'll fix that. Sounds like it's time for an automatic. You can learn in my car." Ellie scooted back, and the crabs tried to make their way under the stove. "Uh oh."

"*You're* going to teach Barb to drive?" Will looked up from his crab slaying, eyebrows raised. Nobody took the bait.

Ginger and Karen shrieked, and we all stepped back to avoid the pinch of their claws, swinging back and forth, daring anyone to come near. Will turned to see the two escapees scurrying along the wall next to the stove. He snatched up one of the runaways before the other disappeared under the stove.

"Don't worry. We'll get him out later. Put some Old Bay on these before I put more in," Will said. Ellie grabbed the yellow can, poured the orange spice onto their shells, and added the rock salt. Will kept reaching back in the basket with the tongs until the pot was full, and Ellie sprinkled on more Old Bay and salt. Jake put the lid back on the basket.

"Whew! That was fun!" Karen giggled from the doorway of the kitchen. She and Ginger had all but exited trying to keep a safe distance during the crabs' getaway.

"Hope he doesn't decide to die under there. Could get a little stinky," Ellie said.

"He'll get hungry before that happens," Jake said as he headed out the back door. He pulled his cigarettes out from the sleeve of his T-shirt, where they had been rolled up for safekeeping.

The guys agreed to make a Pepsi run to the store while the crabs steamed. I resumed my hamburger patty molding, and the girls went outside to finish their game of jacks.

"I'm amazed Jay didn't wake up during all that commotion," El said as she sat down at the kitchen table with me.

"Yeah, he's just waiting for the crabs to be done cooking. He's got incredible timing for a four-month-old," I said. "I can't remember the last time I ate a meal with two hands."

"Must be how you stay so skinny. By the way," she added, reaching down as if to swat a fly from her leg, "when do you…" She frowned, looked down, and tried to swat the pesky fly again. Her eyes flew open, along with her mouth, and she let out a yelp. "Oh no!" She jumped up, pushing the kitchen chair back until it toppled over onto the floor.

It wasn't a fly but a crab that had crawled back under her chair, and in an attempt at mountain climbing, he'd reached up and clamped his claw on the hem of her dress. This time, Jay didn't sleep through the ruckus, waking with a start and a scream of his own.

Any other time, the sight of a clawed creature latching onto anyone would send me running out the door, but the sight of the blue crab dangling from the hem of her dress was more than I could take. I started laughing, and in a brief flash of motherly instinct, picked up the baby and backed up. Ellie danced around the kitchen, holding her dress away from her body, trying to shake the crab loose, and at the same time working to dodge his free claw.

"It's not funny. He's trying to eat me!"

"Where'd he come from? I thought they got him from under the stove."

"Who cares where he came from? He thinks he's gonna have me for his last meal!"

"Don't worry, it'll only take one bite, and he'll be begging for one of my burgers." I giggled and sat the baby in his tote on the top of the table and popped his pacifier back in his mouth.

"Now, from what you've told me, that'd be enough to make him go outta here hungry," she said as I was squatting down laughing, holding on to the edge of the table. It was all I could do not to pee my pants.

"Geez oh flip, Barb! What should I do? Get rid of the crab! For crying out loud, help me out here," she begged, her eyes bugging out of her head while she tiptoed around the kitchen in a panic. I tried to regain some composure, thinking that if I didn't, she might just pass out in the middle of the kitchen with the blue crab still intact. Maybe he'd let go then.

"Be still and take off your dress."

"But he'll bite me," she argued, holding her dress away from her body. She stood on her tiptoes, going from foot to foot as if she could dance away from him, but it didn't help. Jimmy was clamped on tight, swinging his other claw, but so far, catching nothing but air. She reached into a drawer with her free hand and grabbed a pair of scissors. "Here, cut him loose."

I grabbed the scissors, took one look at the crab holding on to her dress, and tried to figure how I'd start cutting. Unable to control myself, I started giggling again. "El, I'd have to cut your dress in half, and he'll just bite me instead of you."

"So?" she asked, wide-eyed, and we both cracked up.

I reached over and grabbed the tongs. "Turn around a little," I instructed, and she turned sideways. I reached down and grabbed the crab's body from behind with the tongs. I slapped his clamped claw with the scissors in my other hand in an effort to get him to loosen his grip.

"Boy, he must think you taste pretty good. He doesn't want to let go." I hit his claw five or six times before he loosened his grip enough for me to pull him away.

"Hurry, pick up the lid," I said, holding the crab at the end of my outstretched arm. She opened the bushel, and I dropped the crabby little bugger in the basket. She plopped the lid back on, and we just looked at each other. Her hair was sticking out as if she'd short-circuited, but her dress was in one piece.

We started laughing, this time unable to control the guffaws until we plopped on the floor, eye level with the crabs in the basket.

"You should've seen yourself dancing around holding your dress like a curtsy, with a crab hanging off." I held my stomach, hurting from the laughter. "Bet the Queen of England's never seen a crabby curtsy like that before."

"Yeah, and thank goodness he wasn't able to take that first bite 'cause you were laughing so hard he would have been ready for dessert before you figured out what to do."

"I couldn't help it. You just kept hollering and dancing. Hey, maybe you ought to put that act in the talent show."

"Yeah, and if anybody gets the crabs, we'll just send you with some scissors and tongs." With that visual, our bladders got the better of us. We jumped up and raced to the bathroom. I won, and she stood in the doorway and laughed some more.

Nothing seals a friendship like doing the cross-legged ballet together trying to hold your bladders at bay. The feeling of success when you don't wet your pants and the look of horror on your face when you do is a great way to bond. I made it; she didn't.

"I think I'd better take a shower," El said as she wiped up the floor beneath her with a towel.

"Yeah, and I'd better go check on Jay," I answered as I washed my hands. "It's way too quiet in there."

Back in the kitchen, Karen and Ginger sat next to Jay, keeping him entertained as best they could. I warmed up a new bottle, and by the time it was ready, so were Ellie and the crabs, and the guys were back from town.

"Told you he had great timing," I said as I handed Jay his bottle.

We loaded the now orange crabs onto a tray and began the exercise of channeling the next batch into the pot. Jake and Will returned with the Pepsi, and we tried to fill the guys in on Ellie's crab dance.

"I guess it lost something in the translation," I said, when they didn't fall over laughing like we did. Just describing the scene had El and me giggling again. Jake dumped the crabs off the tray onto the newspaper-lined picnic table. The steam rose from the once-blue, now-orange crabs, and the smell of Old Bay made my mouth water. I sat the tray down with the dinner knives and wooden hammers that we'd use to crack open their claws, a stack of napkins, vinegar, Old Bay, and melted butter.

Before the afternoon was over, I was hooked on more than just the claw meat. I started out picking the crab for Karen, but with some coaxing from Ellie, I took a bite of the sweet white meat, and one was all it took.

My Alabaman southern belle mother would disown me for taking part in such an animalistic ritual.

"There's only one thing better and that's chocolate." I licked my fingers and reached for another napkin. "At least I don't have to worry about getting fat off crabs. I wonder who was the first person to ever eat one. They had to be starving to even touch one of these mean little buggers." I reached for another one.

"Yeah, he must've had a wife that couldn't cook," Will said.

Jake opened his mouth to say something.

"Don't even go there," I said before he could get his foot in his mouth.

"You're right, hon," Jake said. "Besides, Kraft macaroni and cheese is a great way to keep me from getting too hungry."

"That's right, and lucky for you that I don't have to cook from scratch," I said. "You just name the dish, and I'll find the box or can at the grocery store."

The kids filled up on hamburgers and corn and gave up on the crab picking. The chickens from next door wandered over for some crumb snatching, and the kids burned off energy trying to herd them back to their own yard.

"Nothing like a little chicken chasing to top off the day." I shook my head and looked up from my crab.

"Yeah, we're really gonna miss that when we move," Ellie said and rolled her eyes.

"Hey, did Jake tell you we saw some cop stuffing a nigger in a police car when we drove through town?" I asked Will.

"Yeah, he did. Sorry Karen had to see that," Will said.

"I wonder what he did." I picked out another crab.

"Probably looked at the cop cross-eyed." Ellie said. She frowned as she took a drink of Pepsi. "It doesn't take much to get 'stuck in the onesies' if you're a colored person in this town."

I looked at her and could see the disapproval on her face. Whoops, don't look now, but I think my foot's in my mouth.

"Stuck in the what?" Will asked, and Ellie explained our newly coined phrase and went on.

"Gloria told me that Joe had to walk a mile out of his way on his way home from the docks to steer clear of the Barker family reunion last weekend," Ellie said. She had mentioned her friend, Gloria, earlier in the day, but I hadn't realized that Gloria was colored.

"What do you mean?" I asked.

"Well, because he's colored and they're white, he wasn't allowed to walk down their street while they were having their celebration," she said.

"You mean the cops stood watch over a family reunion?" I was dumbfounded.

"Nope, don't have to. Joe just knew better, that's all." She went on. "After a lifetime of rules, they tend to figure them out." I just let that sink in and grabbed another crab, hoping I could pull my foot out and put it back on the ground without too much fanfare.

"I hear unemployment is really bad among the coloreds here," Jake said.

"Yeah, when the Phillips Packinghouse opened back up, they managed to exclude coloreds from being hired there," Will explained. "That's one of the reasons I ended up working in DC. The jobs just aren't here like they used to be, and I really didn't want to work in a factory anyway."

"I guess the union did its job," Jake replied and looked up as Roger ran toward us.

"Mom, I almost caught him!" Roger said, wide-eyed and out of breath from chasing the rooster.

"You sure did." Ellie wiped her hands on a napkin.

"If I can catch him, we'll have him for dinner tomorrow," Roger offered as he stopped to explain his hot pursuit. The poor rooster took the opportunity to hide under the house.

Ellie laughed. "Honey, Momma was just kidding about wringing Rooster's neck. He just wakes us up too early, but that's his job."

Roger looked confused.

"You gave him a run for his money though. Let the poor guy off the hook this time." The eight-year-old shook his head, picked up a stray basketball, and headed for the driveway.

"So, what are you thinking about this election, Ellie?" I asked.

Before she could answer, Will jumped in. "She thinks Kennedy is a sure thing," he answered. "But politics ain't exactly her cup of tea, right, El?"

Ellie looked from Will to me and took a deep breath. "That's a dicey thing to say to a woman with a hammer in one hand and a knife in the other, Will." She knocked the shell off a claw with the hammer. "I've been reading up on it and saw where Eisenhower just signed the Civil Rights Act of 1960, which is gonna help to make sure that coloreds and Mexicans can vote this time." She ate the claw meat and continued. "You just might be surprised, Will."

"Sounds to me like you know plenty about politics." I grabbed more napkins and wiped the Old Bay from my hands as best I could. "More than me, that's for sure."

Jake had to jump in with his two cents about how women only wanted to vote for Kennedy because he was good looking. Well, there's no denying where my vote was going, good looking or not.

We sat for two hours picking, eating, drinking, and then topping it all off with a watermelon that Ellie cut into pieces and doled out to everyone. When we were finished, we fished out the dinner knives and hammers from the piles of empty crab shells. It was a joint effort as we rolled the shells and napkins up in the newspaper and dumped everything into the metal trash can in the backyard. Back in the kitchen, Ellie washed and I dried the crab pot and the few knives and glasses.

"Boy, wouldn't it be nice if we could just roll up the tablecloth and throw everything away at the end of every meal?" I said. I still felt pretty crummy about my foot-in-mouth experience and wondered how to redeem myself.

"Yeah, we could get rich if we could figure out how to make that happen."

I decided to take the plunge into humility. "El, I'm really sorry if I offended you earlier," I said as I hung the dish towel up to dry.

"Whadya mean?" she asked.

"When I referred to the coloreds as 'niggers.' I could tell you didn't like it much."

She turned back toward me. "It's okay. It happens all the time. It's just that Gloria and Joe are good friends." She touched my shoulder. "They help me out a lot when Will's not home." She wrapped her arms around me in a big hug. "Thanks, but don't give it a second thought."

"It's strange that things are so different here than just over the bridge, closer to DC." I picked up a glass and started drying it with the dish towel. "Like someone turned back the clock."

Ellie nodded. "Sometimes it feels like we're in Alabama and not Maryland." She turned around and kept washing dishes. "People in this town are so stuck in the onesies in more ways than one." Ellie shook her head.

"I've heard there are protests happening at Glen Echo near DC." I continued my dish drying.

"What's Glen Echo?" Ellie put another glass in the dish drainer.

"It's an amusement park, and they don't allow coloreds," I explained. "I save up my Pepsi caps, and they weigh them and give you free tickets for rides when you turn them in once a year on Pepsi Day."

"Sounds like I can hook you up with a bunch more. I'll start saving them for you." Ellie reached in and pulled the plug to the sink drain. I handed her the towel to dry her hands.

"Save 'em, and when you move to DC, we'll take the kids." We were making lots of plans for their move to the Western Shore.

By the end of the weekend, I felt as if I'd known Ellie forever. I had never been very close to my own sister, Charlotte. She'd gotten married a few years before me and had gone from dodging our father to living with an alcoholic husband. "It's gonna be great having you guys live so close when your house is finished." I handed her the last of the dried dishes to put in the cupboard.

"Yeah, it sure will." She leaned over and whispered, "But having a full-time husband will probably be my biggest challenge."

"Yeah, the everyday-sex thing can be enough to put me over the edge," I said.

"I can handle that part. I'm looking forward to not having to wait for a weekend."

Now I was baffled but didn't admit it.

"Did you see the movie *The Misfits* yet?" I asked as we sat down at the kitchen table and put our feet up on the empty chairs. "I'm a big Marilyn Monroe fan."

"Nope, there's only a drive-in here in Cambridge, and it seems that they are two years late with most every movie that comes out."

"Maybe we can go when you guys come next weekend. We'll get a sitter." I took a sip of Pepsi, and she nodded.

There was something about Ellie that I knew mirrored a part of me, a part of me that I didn't know existed until that weekend. We'd discovered similarities during our long talks about our childhoods. She brought out the loose-lipped Barb that, until now, had been a stranger, even to me.

When we arrived in Cambridge less than two days earlier, I would have bet that Karen wouldn't stay behind when we left, but by Sunday evening, she proved me wrong. She even helped us load our suitcase into the car. She reached up and gave Jake and me a kiss and a hug, and we said our good-byes.

Karen grabbed Ginger and Ellie's hands as we backed out of the driveway. *Hey, what about me? Why can't I stay and send the baby home with Jake?*

As we drove home through Cambridge, the sun began to set over the Choptank. The sky turned orange, purple, and pink as a cloud drifted over to hide the sun before it ducked below the tree line.

"Why don't we pull over and watch the sunset? Jay's snoozing," I said. It surprised me when Jake agreed and slowed down to pull over. We slid out of the front seat, trying not to wake the baby. I grabbed an open pack of crackers from the dashboard to feed the birds.

The marina was a soft, easy-going place with lots of seagulls gliding over the water. I was in no hurry to get back to the hustle of the DC suburbs. The gulls circled and called out to us as we stood next to the car by the dock. Jake slipped his arm around my waist.

I tossed a cracker in the air. The gulls began circling and diving for their dinner.

"Don't do that, Barb. One of those rats with wings is liable to—"

He didn't get to finish before a gull showed him that if you can't say something nice, don't say anything at all, leaving a nice deposit on his shoulder. The boy needed to start living right. Even Jake had to laugh at the gull's timing, but not until he cleaned up with Jay's burp cloth and I dug an extra T-shirt out of the trunk.

"So much for our romantic sunset," I said, shutting the car door. "If it's not a kid, it's a bird."

We headed west over the Chesapeake Bay Bridge toward home. Now that we were closer to the city, Jake tuned in the radio to WPGC and did his Elvis impersonation. I hummed along, thinking about the weekend and that maybe, just maybe, with Ellie as my sidekick, I wouldn't be so tempted to flee and was sure I wouldn't be stuck in the onesies for long.

CHAPTER 2

Ellie
Save the Last Dance for Me

Author James Michener recalled feeling quite startled when guests at publisher Bennett Cerf's early 1960 dinner party challenged John F. Kennedy's presidential candidacy on religious grounds.

—Thomas Carty, A Catholic in the White House?

I've lived in Cambridge for eight years now, eight long years. How I ever let Will talk me into this, I can't figure. The first few years were full of babies and bottles and learning how to be a mom. I think once I got the basics down—diapering, bottles, and no sleep—the rest was a piece of cake. As the dust settled from having kids (and it settled on my house, all over my house), it dawned on me that I needed to get out of here. Only problem was, by then I was stuck in the onesies, big time.

Stuck, as in, I didn't have any money to move us anywhere and I couldn't get a job because a sitter cost too much and I wouldn't want to leave my kids for that long anyway.

All Will would say was "We can't afford it," and what was a girl to say to that? All I knew was he'd been playing the weekend husband and dad gig for two years, and if he could afford to live in DC, then we could, too. Ultimatums are a girl's best friend.

The good thing about the way things are now is that Will's gone Monday through Friday. The bad thing is that he's gone Monday through Friday. Now, don't get me wrong; it's not that I don't like Will, but there are some perks to the weekend marriage thing. Like, it allows me to get away with leaving the housework until Fridays. There are not a lot of things I might not do very well, but housework is definitely at the top of my list. Dusting and picking up is supposed to be what I do best, and Will and his mother aren't shy about reminding me. Have I told you about his mother yet? Let's save it for a rainy day, 'cause it will take that long.

Life with the kids is just one big party until Will comes home on Fridays. Then we have to straighten up our act and behave. It's not that Will's not fun—he can be a thrill under the sheets—but he's just not a kid kinda guy.

It intrigued me when he came home talking about his new buddy, Jake. Not that I find my husband's friends interesting, it's just that he never had any before. I don't think he ever had a good friend in school. His mother was not the type to encourage relationships outside her little world. I think Will's best friend was always his dad, and that didn't make the old biddy, I mean lady, happy either since she kicked him to the curb. You can only imagine what she had to say when he brought me home.

I'd met Jake a few times before when he'd come down to go fishing with Will, but I just met Barb this past weekend. Will said she was pretty, but he neglected to mention that she was cover-girl gorgeous, with long wavy black hair and dark eyes to match. She could be on the cover of a magazine with her slender figure. She looks a little like Jackie Kennedy, the wife of that Catholic senator who wants to be president someday. Just my luck.

Just when I made up my mind I wasn't gonna like her, she turned out to be a real gem. Her down-to-earth ways were not what I'd come up against in the past with women of beauty that matched my own. I must say that I do manage to hide my not-so-bad looks with this ghastly weight I've gained since moving here to this godforsaken place. I learned to cook since coming here, and hey, it wouldn't be fair to use the kids for total guinea pigs without trying some of it myself.

Barb was impressed with my cooking and sewing abilities. Evidently, it doesn't take much. Geez, what else is there to do around here? She even suggested that I give her a few lessons after we move up her way. They can't finish that house quick enough to suit me.

The one drawback to moving back to the Western Shore is Will's mother, Sylvia. She lives just a few miles from where our new house will be. She's definitely where Will gets his dark side from. She doesn't like me, but then again, I don't think Ava Gardner would have been good enough for her only child. Can't we just move back and forget to tell her? Just for a decade or so?

We'd had a great weekend, and Barb and I had become fast friends. I hated to see them leave. An hour or so later, Will climbed into his black sedan, throwing his suitcase in the backseat. I leaned in the window and kissed him on the cheek. That's us, Ozzie and Harriet. He rolled up his window and waved good-bye as he pulled out of the driveway. Karen and Ginger were each holding my hand with one hand and waving good-bye with the other.

I'd promised the kids we could camp out on the back porch after their dad left, and they didn't waste any time reminding me.

"It's fun time!" Ginger said, jumping up and down as Will's car headed down the road.

I shushed her, afraid that Karen would think they didn't like their dad.

"But it is! Remember you said we could camp out tonight?" Scott tugged on my arm.

"Okay, go get the sleeping bags and pillows."

"What's camping out? Like on *Gunsmoke?*" Karen asked Ginger.

"Kind of, only we just camp out on the back porch," Ginger said. Karen followed her to the bedroom to gather our camping gear.

The boys arranged our homemade tents from one end of the screened-in porch to the other using blankets and clothespins. They made separate bedrooms for the girls and boys. We used flashlights to create enough light to eat the hot dogs and later on roasted marshmallows cooked over the gas flame on the kitchen stove.

We taught Karen our camping songs. "You Are My Sunshine" was the all-time favorite. Scott and Roger told ghost stories about the cemetery across the street.

"And old lady Barker still walks down our street looking for her lost dog whenever there's a full moon." Scott held the flashlight under his chin and did his best to scare us.

"Oh, don't look now, but there's a full moon!" Roger pointed to the sky. Ginger and Karen huddled closer to me.

We fell asleep on the back porch in our makeshift sleeping bags. I woke to the sound of the neighbor's rooster crowing. "I should have let the boys catch him." I thought once more about wringing the neck of that crowing cock-a-doodle-doo. It's only fittin.' Never liked an alarm clock anyway, dead or alive. I rolled over and tried to go back to sleep, but no luck. I slipped out of the covers and started to make breakfast. The smell of bacon and eggs cooking bribed them out of their tents, and one by one, they filtered into the kitchen.

"Get the porch cleaned up. After breakfast, you can go out and play while I get the house straightened," I said.

They played with Donna from next door in the backyard, which gave me the chance to catch up on the housework. I tried to get it all done on Monday mornings so we could hit the beach every day. At least, we call it a beach.

The Choptank River sits at the mouth of the Chesapeake Bay. The town of Cambridge has fashioned a sandy spot alongside the bridge on Route 50 for beachgoers like us. It's the one thing I'll miss when we move.

We piled into my blue Ford station wagon that the kids and I affectionately called Betsy and drove down to the edge of the Choptank River for a day at the beach.

"Who's Betsy?" Karen asked.

"Betsy's our car's name. What's yours called?" Ginger asked, as if everyone had a name for his or her car.

"I think it's 'Damn It,'" Karen said.

I looked up and laughed. "Why do you think that, Karen?"

"Every time Mom says it's time to make the car payment, that's what Dad says." *How do you get your husband to buy a pink car anyway?*

Betsy turned into a Sinclair gas station to put a dollar's worth of gas in the tank. I opened the glove box and pulled out my booklet with S&H green stamps all over it. As the attendant handed me two more stamps, Ginger was tickled that she would finally have filled up the book enough to trade for Dino. Dino was a large inflatable green dinosaur suitable for floating one large kid at a time. We filled Dino with air from the tire pump, being careful not to pop him. It was a bigger challenge to load him into Betsy's wayback without killing him before we got to the beach. His face smooshed up against the glass; he looked like a prisoner begging for mercy.

I always loved to see the look on kids' faces when they see sand and water for the first time, but I'd never seen one more fascinated than Karen. She just lived in the water all week long and turned out to be a beach rat, just like the rest of us. Even though it was only the Choptank River, you would have thought it was the Riviera.

I promised Ginger she could ride Dino first as he popped out of the car when I opened the door. The boys complained, but with four kids in tow, it was first come, first served, and besides, she did put the stamps in the book all by herself.

The beach wasn't far from the marina, and we could see the watermen coming back after working on the water since before dawn. Baskets full of Maryland blue crabs and some fish to boot were the popular catch of the skipjacks. The watermen waved and hollered, "Ahoy!" from the boat, to the kids' and my delight.

After a lunch of peanut butter and jelly sandwiches, I made the kids take a break and get some rest on the beach. To kill time, we lay on the blanket and stared at the clouds "making skies." We created pictures in our minds.

"There's Mickey Mouse!" Ginger tugged on my arm.

"Where? I don't see him." Scott squinted and searched the sky.

"Right there." She pointed. "See his ears there and his smile?"

"I see it!" Karen said, and Scott nodded.

Oh yeah, did I mention that I'm also the best sand castle contractor east of the Chesapeake Bay? We built a castle with Dino sitting in the middle, guarding the princess.

"That's the prettiest castle I've ever seen, Mrs. B," Karen said as she pushed her wet and sandy bangs out of her face. I hugged her and kissed her on the head.

I doled out saltine crackers as a reward for their artsy efforts. It doesn't take much to make this crew feel special. I had them believing saltines were what royalty ate as a snack.

"You guys had better not go past that fence post. There's quicksand on the other side!" I lied, again.

They tended to believe me since they never strayed too far.

My theory was that God allowed minor white lies when it came to motherhood. I doubted He even called these lies, more like "Momma-fibs." After all, He gave us these little creatures to care for, and He knows better than anyone how hard they are to keep track of. Sometimes the quicksand theory wears thin, and I switch to the seaweed scenario.

"The seaweed monster will stick to you and give you a fungus." Momma-fib number two.

"And then there will be a fungus among us!" Scott laughed. Don't roll your eyes; it works.

"Look, Mrs. Reilly! It's a watermelon!" Karen pointed to the shoreline.

Sure enough, a watermelon had washed up on the shore, an escapee from someone's picnic, no doubt. Roger ran over and picked it up.

"Neat! Can we keep it, Mom?" Roger asked.

"I don't see why not. It doesn't appear to belong to anyone here but us. But how are we gonna cut it?"

I'd no sooner said the words than I spied an oyster shell.

"This might work." I cut the melon open with the shell, slicing clear through to the bright redness inside. We were all impressed with my ingenuity and chowed down on the fruit. Boy, saltines and watermelon all in the same day. We were sure it didn't get any better than that.

It seemed that Cambridge natives didn't see the benefits of hanging at the beach and, as a result, we had it to ourselves most days. It was nice, but sometimes it would have been great to have someone else to talk to besides kids ages ten and under. I have one good friend here, and that's Gloria. She lives next door. She's colored and is one of the nicest people I've ever met. Living in Washington, DC, when I was growing up, I didn't know any colored people personally, so getting to know Gloria was something new for me. Of course, Will didn't approve, so our friendship was pretty much a Monday-through-Friday thing.

It was after three o'clock and time to leave, but after a lot of begging, I agreed to drop the kids off at the park with Roger in charge while I ran to the grocery store to pick up something for dinner.

When I left for Acme, the girls were taking turns pushing each other on the metal merry-go-round. Scott and Roger headed for the creek in search of turtles and whatever critters they could find to use for torture tools on the girls.

I hurried to Acme and skimmed the aisles, grabbing necessities. I scanned the meats for yet more hamburger and wondered what I'd do to it this time to make it resemble something other than what it was. Burgers, sloppy joes, meat-loaf, and spaghetti were just about my entire repertoire, but then I saw a nice steak and I slowed down.

"This one steak would be enough to feed all four of us tonight," I said to myself, but at two dollars, I couldn't justify the cost.

I looked behind me and to both sides and made sure the butcher behind the two-way mirror was turned the other way. My heart beat fast as I slid the packaged meat into my purse. Thank goodness for big pocketbooks. I pulled my wallet out at the same time so I wouldn't have to open my purse in front of the checkout girl and finished up my shopping.

I guess I should feel guilty about my little indiscretions in the grocery store, but first of all, Will doesn't give me enough money to properly feed us when he's gone, and secondly, the grocer doesn't miss one little steak now and then.

Halfway through checking out, I could see through the plate-glass window dark clouds and large raindrops splattering on the ground. A loud thunderclap boomed overhead and a bolt of lightning streaked across the sky. I asked the cashier to hurry, and I got soaked as I threw the paper bags full of groceries in Betsy's wayback. I jumped in and drove as fast as I could back to the park.

I shuddered at the thought of telling Barb I'd left her little girl out in a thunderstorm. I finally found a friend, and now I'd killed her kid, not to mention my own. Visions of explaining my lack of parenting skills to Barb and the cops ran through my head as I broke the speed limits through town.

I parked Betsy (at least I kind of parked her) and ran toward the park. The rain was coming down harder. Without warning, two thunderclaps hit as if cannons had been shot. I jumped out and heard the kids shriek in between the kabooms. I ran as fast as I could, my Keds splashing through instant puddles. I didn't see any of them on the jungle gym equipment and hoped they hadn't looked for shelter under the trees in this lightning.

"Please, God, let them be all right," I said out loud as I ran toward the park.

I spotted Roger and Scott inside a telephone booth and ran toward the park, relieved until I saw that Ginger and Karen were outside the booth, banging on the door, begging them to open up and let them in.

The boys were laughing and taunting.

"The dead bodies come out of the cemetery when lightning strikes! They're coming to take you away in a flying saucer!" The little buggers belly laughed as they terrorized the girls.

I screamed for them to head my way, but the sound of the storm drowned my voice. A clap of thunder struck, and the girls shrieked again.

"We can't let you in 'cause then they'd get us, too!" Roger tormented the girls. He shut up fast when he saw me running toward them. The door opened, and the excuses began.

Ginger and Karen clung to me while the boys begged forgiveness. We all ran back to Betsy and were soaked by the time we piled in. I put Karen and Ginger in the front seat and banished Roger and Scott to the back.

"Geez-oh-flip, you guys are gonna get it," I said and pulled out the sucker-punch part. "Wait till your father gets home!"

That dreaded threat, but the boys knew they had several days before they would even see their dad, and my angst would be but a faint memory, but I wasn't above torturing them in the meantime. Who knows, I might even get some clean bedrooms out of the deal.

I sent them to their rooms with instructions to change their clothes and get ready for dinner. I remembered the steak in my purse and pulled it out and put it on the broiler pan of the stove.

Once the delinquents were fed and tucked in, the girls and I sat in the living room, eating our dinner on TV trays, and enjoyed the leftover runaway watermelon for dessert.

Ginger and Karen drifted off in my bed listening to stories about me when I was their age.

"My momma was a show girl." I laced my fingers behind my head between the two girls. "She performed on the big stage in New York and Washington, DC."

Well, there *are* different definitions for the word "stage." Just because it wasn't Broadway doesn't mean it's not "the stage." She could sing like a bird, was a dancer, and even subbed for the Rockettes a few times. She taught me to perform in our little kitchen, using my old standby, a wooden spoon, as my microphone.

Momma tried to make up for Daddy leaving when I was three. She did her best to give Ernie and me everything we needed. Fun and laughter were her cure-alls for most everything that went wrong.

"When I was little, I didn't get to see my momma perform too much, only once in a while. I had to go to school early in the mornings, and her performances were late at night."

I was thirteen before I realized what Momma's real profession was, and where. And until then, I'd thought that poles had just been for firemen.

"Is that where you learned to sing so pretty, Mrs. Reilly?" Karen asked. This kid's good; her brownie points were piling up.

"Why don't you be a show girl, too, Momma?" Sometimes I asked myself the same question. I grew up thinking I'd be the next Rita Hayworth. We red-heads gotta stick together.

"Because I want to be home and take care of you instead." Well, it was kind of the truth. "When are you going to show Karen how to put on a talent show, Ginger?" Kids give you lots of practice when it comes to changing the subject.

Ginger's eyes lit up at the thought.

"Yeah, we'll do it tomorrow. I'll show ya," Ginger said as she patted Karen on the shoulder.

They dozed as I wove a story about me as a show girl on the stage, singing my heart out and wearing fancy outfits. Of course, Ginger and Karen were standing backstage waiting to join me to sing back up on "The Lion Sleeps Tonight." Somebody had to do the wheema whacks. As the girls drifted off to sleep, I lay in bed remembering growing up with Momma.

❧

"Look, Momma, that one looks like my daddy. He's got a hammer in his hand. See?" I pointed to the clouds in the sky. I could still feel her hug like it was yesterday as Momma's gentle arm reached around me and pulled me close.

"Yeah, baby, I see," she said as the bus pulled up in front of us, hiding him from my view.

I never did meet my father again, and Momma died when I was fifteen years old. She came down with a bad cold that turned into pneumonia and never recovered. I was devastated, and since I'd never known my dad, I was left alone except for my older brother, Ernie. We moved in with Momma's sister, Aunt Muriel, who lived in northeast DC, just a few blocks from our apartment. We continued in the same school and pretty much took care of ourselves while Auntie M worked two waitressing jobs.

I'd had dreams of going to art school after graduation. I planned to save up money over the summer for tuition. I graduated high school and started working full-time as a waitress in the same coffee shop as Auntie M.

Six months after Momma died, I met Will while picnicking near the Tidal Basin. My girlfriend and I noticed him sitting on a wall, looking at us. He was a dark-haired good-looking Italian boy, tall and gawky, but I thought he was gorgeous. His shy manner attracted me, and I figured I had enough sense of humor for the both of us.

He lived a few blocks away with his mother, and we spent every free moment together. We'd talk for hours in person or on the phone for as long as our party line partners would allow. Will explained that his parents separated when he was nine. His mother was a government secretary and his father, a carpenter.

"My parents are just so different from each other. My mother's a staunch Catholic and refuses to give Pop a divorce. He's a carpenter and moved back to Cambridge when they broke up," he'd said.

"Wow, they sound very different," I'd said.

"Yeah, I don't know how they ever ended up together, but she won't divorce him, so he lives with Beth, his longtime girlfriend," he'd said, looking down at the table.

I had reached over and latched on to his hand. It was cold, too cold for this warm autumn day. We sat in the booth of a little coffee shop on M Street.

People whizzed by outside the plate-glass window. The first leaves of fall floated down to the sidewalk. He stared straight ahead as if he didn't see anyone or anything. The waitress walked over to see if we wanted refills, but I shook my head and she walked away.

We dated for nine months before I ever met his mother, Sylvia. As I fell in love with Will, I began to have dreams of finding a surrogate mom. That's when I found out that dreams are not always visions; sometimes they're nightmares.

We walked down the sidewalk holding hands. My heart beat in anticipation as Will opened the door to their first-floor Georgetown apartment. I walked into the living room, which looked more like a shrine. Pictures of Will were on every wall along with every ribbon and trophy he'd ever won.

"Wow, I didn't know you were such an athlete," I said as I picked up a baseball trophy.

"I'm not really. Mom just signed me up for every team in the neighborhood." He took the trophy from my hand and quickly put it back on the shelf.

"Oh, hi, Mother," Will said as a tall woman with reddish-brown hair and a large nose walked into the room. He made the normal introductions, and Sylvia motioned for us to sit down. I found myself sitting in a wingback chair across the room from Will and his mother. I crossed and uncrossed my legs and wished I had worn my brown dress instead of the colorful flowing skirt of blues and purples.

Sylvia wore rhinestone glasses and a stylish tweed suit with matching spiked heels. The seam on her nylons ran straight as an arrow up the back of her legs. I wondered how she managed such perfection.

"So, Ellie, what kind of work did your parents do?" Sylvia asked.

"My momma was in show business until she died last year." I swallowed hard as it dawned on me that this was not going to be fun. "I never knew my dad. He left when I was three," I said.

"Oh, really? Then your dad could be living right down the street and you wouldn't know it? Isn't that interesting?" Sylvia's eyes widened as she turned and looked at Will.

He started sinking low into the couch next to her.

"Was your mother an actress, Ellie?"

"Well, not exactly. She was a singer and a dancer." I squirmed.

"Ellie's got a beautiful singing voice, too," Will said. We stumbled through the rest of the inquisition before Will whisked me out the door and down the street.

"I told you meeting my mother wasn't such a good idea." We walked back to Auntie M's apartment. The moon lit our path in front of the row houses on the street.

"Oh, don't worry about it, Will." I interlocked our fingers. I tried not to show how disappointed I was. Sylvia had taken the knife that had been sticking in my heart since Momma died and twisted it a little deeper, but I didn't want him to know.

He stopped, pulled me toward him, and wrapped me in his arms. My head rested on his chest and unannounced tears slid down my cheeks. I cried like I hadn't since Momma died. I wasn't sure if I was crying because I missed Momma or because I felt sorry for Will. Having a mother like he had was worse than having none at all. I felt the warmth and protection of him. I felt safe for the first time in a year.

"Ellie, let's get married."

"Married? When?"

"As soon as we can." I grabbed onto him as if my life depended on him, and at that moment, I was sure it did.

"I think Auntie M might sign for me, and we can just elope."

And so it went. We stood in front of the justice of the peace in the downtown courthouse, and Auntie M and Ernie stood up for us. We celebrated with a lavish dinner at the diner and headed back to our furnished apartment as husband and wife.

Sylvia came unglued when she discovered her little boy had gone behind her back and tied the knot to something other than her apron strings. She threw a red ashtray against the wall. It shattered all over her shiny hardwood floor.

"She's nothing but a tramp, Will! Her mother was a stripper, nothing but a harlot!"

"Mother, what are you talking about?" Chills ran up my spine. This woman was as wicked as I'd feared.

31

Surely he'll tell her to kiss off, I thought.

"You heard me!" She smashed another dish against the paneled wall, leaving a dent. I was sure she would have hurled me next if she could have. "Her mother wasn't an actress or a singer. She worked at Chancey's, a strip club, Will!"

Without realizing it, I backed up to the front door of the apartment. I never had anyone kick me in the stomach before, but now I knew how it felt. I turned on my heel and walked out of her house, down the steps, and over to the bench at the bus stop. I thought I was going to be sick; my head hurt and my mouth was watering. I shivered with shock and waited for what seemed like forever until Will came out and sat down beside me. He was quiet and just held my hand as we waited for the bus to take us back to our new furnished apartment. He withdrew and didn't talk much for several days.

Will went to work, and I left for school every morning that week. I kept busy on the weekend waiting tables at the diner. Our time together was strained, and I wondered how I could get out of this mess. The more I tried to get him to talk, the more he clammed up.

I'd never felt so alone in my life. When my period was late, I was afraid to share the news. I think I hoped that if I didn't say it out loud, it wouldn't be true. I waited until I was almost a month overdue before I told him. He didn't react much either way. The promise of a new baby in our lives seemed to seal both our fates.

It became quite clear that Will married me to get away from Sylvia. Now the question was, how did he get away from me *and a baby*? And how did I get away from her? But as the weeks passed, I realized that I was no longer in this alone. The little creature growing inside of me was in it for the long haul, too. The baby was a gift from God, and it was up to me to bring the sunshine. My baby didn't ask to come here and didn't sign up for a life of quiet denial. I'd see to it that it was anything but quiet.

❖

I hugged Ginger tighter, as if squeezing her would make my sadness leave. I'd learned that nothing makes the sadness leave. I'd just learned to make it take a seat, way in the back. Sometimes it listened; sometimes it didn't.

I tiptoed out to the living room and flipped the TV on to channel four to catch Jack Paar's monologue and fell asleep in Will's recliner. That's another advantage to living alone. I could sleep wherever I wanted.

As soon as their feet hit the floor the next morning, the girls headed for the linen closet, grabbing the biggest sheets they could find. Scott and Roger helped (in a not so subtle attempt to achieve amnesty), and they installed a stage curtain across the back porch. The girls began rehearsals as I fixed breakfast. It was raining, so there'd be no beach today. The sound of their voices singing, "You are my sunshine, my only sunshine," poured a sunny glow on my mood this rainy morning. I smiled to myself as I scraped the scrambled eggs onto a platter and called them in to eat. I had to promise I'd sit in on their dress rehearsal after breakfast to get them to eat.

We finished breakfast and hustled back to the porch and took our seats. The boys and I sat on the floor of the back porch as Ginger made the intros to her audience.

"For their first act, Ginger the Lovely and Karen the Delightful will perform 'You Are My Sunshine.'" Ginger curtsied, reached up, and pulled the curtain aside.

Karen was nervous at first, but Ginger carried the act like she'd done it a thousand times before, and she probably had. The audience responded with applause, and they continued the performance with "Twinkle, Twinkle, Little Star" and wrapped it up with a few choruses of "wheema whack." Scott and Roger behaved, holding back their normal taunts and jeers, little suck-ups trying to get back into my good graces.

That afternoon, the rain had finally backed off, and we were able to get outside again. As one last painful jab at the boys for scaring the crap out of the girls, I banished them to extra chores while the girls and I drove into town. Roger promised they would behave in an effort to get out of jail early.

"I smell a french fry!" Ginger squealed. I put Betsy into drive, and we were off to the corner drugstore for fries and a Pepsi. That was our secret code for a special treat whenever I managed to find alone time with any one of the kids. Each of them was sure it was his or her own special secret, and so far, each had kept it.

The neighborhood where we lived was only a few years old even though it was still a dirt road. Cambridge was a poor town, full of watermen who fished the seas early in the morning and chicken farmers. Yes, "chicken farmers." I've often wondered how you plant a chicken, feet up or down? I'll bet it's up.

We had initially relocated here from DC so Will could take a job at the factory in town. Neither of us said it out loud, but the prospect of adding a hundred miles between Sylvia and us was a bonus, but within six months of moving to Cambridge, the factory laid off a bunch of workers and Will was out of a job. With Sylvia's help, Will applied for a federal government job and was hired. By then, we already had the house and nothing was selling in Cambridge, so Will began to commute, coming home on the weekends.

"Whoops, wrong turn," I muttered to myself. Have I ever been behind the wheel of a car without saying that at least once? Don't think so. I can't find my way out of a paper bag, let alone all the way across town.

We reached Race Street, and I parked the car (well, kind of) and walked across to Woolworth's. I did love this little store. You know, the kind with hardwood floors and a soda fountain surrounded with mirrors looking back at you. Paper-Hat Bob behind the counter knows Ginger by name. I'm sure it's hard to forget her curly red locks and freckled nose, but I really think he lusts after me, truth be known.

"I think she smells a french fry, Bob!"

"By George, I think you're right!" Paper-Hat Bob headed back to drop the basket in the oil. He was my accomplice in making each sibling think he or she was the only one to ever "smell a french fry."

"Pepsi?" he asked me.

"No, today I think I'll try that new drink, Sprite, that you mentioned last week, but I think the girls still want Pepsi." I was right.

I took a taste of the Sprite. "Mmm, good. Tastes a lot like 7-Up!"

"Who's your friend?" He turned back around, and Ginger introduced Karen as her new best friend.

"Best friend? If she's your best friend, who's your worst friend?" Bob teased, but Ginger took him seriously. She leaned her chin on her hand and gave it some thought.

"Hmm, I think Roger and Scott are my worst friends! They tried to kill us yesterday, you know." She filled him in on my latest blunder as a mom. Paper-Hat Bob's eyes grew wide as Ginger told him about the thunderstorm. I grinned and shrugged as he looked my way during her story.

Bob looked over my shoulder as someone walked up to the counter. I looked over and discovered it was Gloria. "Hey there!" I slid over to the next stool to make room for her to sit.

"No, that's okay," she said and looked at Bob. "Can I have a BLT on toast to go, Bob?"

"Sure thing," he replied, and turned to drop the bread in the toaster.

"Come on, join us." I pointed to the stool, but Gloria just stood there.

"It's not Wednesday," she reminded me, and nodded toward the sign.

"No coloreds permitted at counter except on Wednesday" read the black handwritten words on a piece of white paper taped to the wall. Get me outta here.

I shook my head in apology to Gloria.

"That's okay, my friend." She patted me on the back. She was trying to make me feel better. Go figure.

Bob wrapped up the BLT in white paper and handed it to her. He rang up the sale, and she handed him fifty cents. He gave her the change. Gloria leaned over and gave me a hug before she turned and left the store.

The girls had fun playing grown-up, sipping on their Pepsis and watching the fries bubble in the oil. Bob served them up on green plastic plates. We added salt, pepper, and ketchup and dug in. As we finished up our drinks, we giggled about ways to tease the boys about their punishment when we got home. We filled Paper-Hat Bob in on our new home in the DC suburbs.

"I'm going to miss you, Ginger. Nobody 'smells a french fry' like you." He winked at me. "And your mom, too." Don't look now, but I'm pretty sure that Paper-Hat Bob was flirting with me. We finished our fries and Pepsis and said our good-byes, promising to come back before the move.

The girls jumped off their stools, and we walked out of the drugstore and headed back toward Betsy after a stop at the bank. As we walked down the sidewalk, two colored ladies and a young boy walked in our direction. When they saw us, they crossed the street to the other side. I didn't think I'd ever get used to that. Walking on separate sides of the street, using different bathrooms, riding in the back of the bus, not able to dine together in a coffee shop, the list goes on.

That town was like living in the Middle Ages. These people needed to cross over the Chesapeake once in a while. I never could understand what entitled me or anyone else to discriminate against someone because of the color of his or her skin. Gloria would do anything for me, and I felt the same about her. None of it made any sense. It's no wonder the coloreds were getting restless and resentful.

The girls and I piled back in Betsy and headed back to the house to see what damage the boys had done while we were gone. The house was intact, and we settled in after a few jabs about french fries and Pepsis from the girls.

The week went by and the weather cooperated, enabling the kids to play outside, and we hit the beach daily.

Friday afternoon when we returned from the beach, we began to pack up our stuff for the weekend. I put on Rosemary Clooney's album and she started singing "This Ole House." We'd been talking about leaving this house and moving into the new one, so the kids and I started singing along.

"Ain't a gonna need this house no longer!

Ain't a gonna need this house no more!

Ain't got time to fix the shingles,

Ain't got time to fix the floor."

Karen and Ginger folded blankets and sheets on the back porch, hips a-swinging, singing their little hearts out. The boys even joined in to reap extra amnesty points. I gave them credit for "time served" and agreed to keep their phone booth escapade just between us. When the song ended, I hurried to the record player and picked up the needle and put it back at the beginning of the song, over and over until we were done.

"I ain't got time to oil the hinges,

Or to mend the windowpanes.

Ain't gonna need this house no longer,

I'm a-getting ready to meet the saints!"

By the time the house was clean and we were packed up, we could sing it a cappella, no problem.

"Hey, you guys could put this song into your lineup for the talent show this weekend," I suggested to the kids.

"Yeah, my mom will like that one," Karen agreed.

Saturday morning, the kids and I piled into Betsy and headed for the Western Shore. I was concerned about finding my way without getting lost. My kids call me "Mrs. Wrong Way," and not because I hadn't earned it. I knew I had to get on Route 50 west, but after that, I wasn't so sure…

I shouldn't have worried. Sure, we got lost (I always build in extra time for that), but believe it or not, a five-year-old guided us all the way there. Karen kept telling me, "I know where we are, Mrs. Reilly. Don't worry, Mrs. Reilly!" Me, worry? It takes more than getting lost to do that.

The sad part was, I was so lost at that point that I gave in and followed her directions. She took us down back roads with nothing but trees on both sides for miles. If we had run out of gas or broken down, I knew we'd all be killed or maimed.

It didn't make me feel much better when she tried to ease my concern saying that her dad's gun club was in the area, and she had been there many times. Gun club?

I had no choice but to put my trust in her navigational abilities. She didn't let us down. I'm convinced this little girl has a built-in radar system. Not only did she get us to the right part of town but she directed me right to the front door of her house. I wondered if Barb would just let me keep her.

CHAPTER 3

Barb
I'm into Something Good

Castro Offers Peace to US on His Terms
Havana, January 21, 1961 (AP)—*Fidel Castro offered last night
to "begin anew" a quest for peace with President Kennedy's adminis-
tration. But the Cuban Prime Minister made clear it would be strictly
on his own terms.*
*The main condition for reconciliation was a total change in what he
labeled a "mistaken and absurd" policy of the United States toward his
Communist-oriented revolutionary regime.*

*S*ummer in the DC suburbs can be a challenge when the steamy air
makes you want to open the freezer door and climb on in. Visions of
Jake finding me freezer burned around the edges was enough to bring on the
hunt for central air conditioning.

A few months after Will and Ellie moved into their new home, I convinced
Jake that it was time for us to make the leap into home ownership. It took me a few
years to catch on to the art of getting his buy-in on major issues. I realized that if
Jake thought I was trying to talk him into something, he would go on the defensive.
I decided it was going to take a little adjusting on my part, so I learned how to plant a
seed and back off. A little water, a little sunshine in the form of a promising kiss now
and then, and before you know it, ladies, voilà! It was all his idea.

Now, some might say that I was being manipulative. I'd like to think of it
as persuasive in a quiet kinda way. I was figuring out the art of negotiations.

Negotiating isn't about getting into a big argument; it's about compromise, and compromise is made up of two words: "come" and "promise." Come, let me know what you think, and I promise to make it all your idea if you go along with it.

Jake's dad helped us with the down payment, and we bought a three-story town house in the Maryland suburbs of DC. The kids each had their own bedrooms, and at least Karen was getting some sleep with Jay in his own room.

Ellie's new house was about five miles from ours, but we managed. When we didn't have a car, we just burned up the phone line. Will's so cheap he insisted they get a party line to save two dollars a month. I'm not sure how I dodged that bullet and got a private line, but I'll go with the flow on that one.

Ellie's enough to make the biggest hermit break the rule against having any friends. I'd laughed more in that past year than I had in my entire life and shared things with her I'd never told Jake. Not that I'm a hermit, but if it hadn't been for Jake and the kids, I would have considered it as a career option.

Jake and Will carpooled to work, so that left one of us with a car. That's the good news. The bad news was I didn't have a driver's license. Jake had tried to teach me, but forget that. Let's just say I'm not the dumbest person in the world, and he's not the most patient. Sometimes we're just not a good combination.

Darn clutches. I kept getting my feet mixed up and giving us both whiplash. Ellie gave me a few lessons while the guys were at work, but talk about the blind leading the blind. She has trouble just finding her way out of the parking lot. I told Ellie I decided to save up my babysitting income to pay for driving lessons. That's our little secret.

I was babysitting two kids, ages two and four, two little boys who lived up the street from us. I made an extra twenty-five dollars a week. Ellie sat for two little boys also. Don't know how she did it with all those kids. She had nerves of steel and a heart of gold, that girl.

An old acquaintance of mine from school, Roberta Bennett, moved in up the street two days after us. Her last name is White now. She got married right about the same time I did and had two kids, a boy and a girl. I'd known Roberta since junior high school. We were never close friends, and I only knew her by "reputation"—and I don't use the word lightly. I know. Momma always said, "If u can't say anything nice, don't say anything at all." I'll shut up; well, I should nut up, but let me just make one little comment…the girl was no lady.

Jake wondered if her name was still written on the phone booth next to the school. He confided that "For a good time, call" was written in the boy's bathroom with Roberta in mind more than once.

"Two kids and a husband can do a lot to change a girl, Jake," I reminded him.

"It did for you!" he said with a wink and a pat on my butt.

The heat and humidity were making everyone cranky, so Ellie and I took the kids on a picnic the previous week (or as she liked to call them, "picka-nickas"). I made the macaroni salad, and she fried up the chicken. We all piled into Betsy and took off for Patuxent River State Park, just west of Baltimore. I navigated and she drove, which worked out pretty well, except that she had a hard time telling left from right, so I learned to give hand signals while directing her. We always factored in extra gas and time for U-turns.

Ellie had a great way to take the kids' minds off of how long it would take us to get somewhere. She got them singing "You Are My Sunshine" or her latest new "favorite," "Zip-a-Dee-Doo-Dah," and they didn't even notice the circles we made. The little buggers were too busy laughing at me trying to carry a tune.

Ellie sings like a bird, and me, I sing like a bird, too. A rooster's a bird, right? As a result, I've learned to hum instead of sing, at least in public. When I'm alone I don't sound so bad. I can even qualify for a microphone if I let my imagination go, but when there's anyone else around, I'm the best hummer in the crowd.

The kids tormented one another for a few hours on the playground equipment and played in the river. Jake and Will came out and joined us after their rifle match. Now there's a male activity that bears psychological investigation. What is it about shooting at a target all day long that keeps them going? Well, it must increase the appetite because they finished up the food, and we packed up and headed home.

The activity of the picka-nicka was not enough to put Jay to sleep in the car, so I dropped him in the stroller while Jake unloaded the car. I headed up the street, hoping the baby would conk out.

"Did you see the new Good Humor man?" Roberta asked as I stopped the stroller in front of her house to chat. Her chestnut brown hair was pulled back into a ponytail.

"No, we just got home. Guess I missed him," I answered.

"What a cutie, blond hair and dark tan." Roberta sighed.

"Looks like you'll be loading up on chocolate éclairs this summer."

"Yeah, I won't be sending the kids to run him down, that's for sure," she said, patting her three-months-from-being-due-with-the-third-kid belly. "My cravings just went from peanut butter to Popsicles; you can bet on that!"

I repeated the conversation to El on the phone the next morning.

"She's got to be the horniest woman I know," I said, checking first to be sure there were no kids close enough to hear. I didn't want to have to dole out that definition.

"Not so sure that it's the sex drive as much as the need for attention, and she did just that by raising your eyebrows!" El explained. Sometimes she surprised me with her wisdom in the middle of her wit.

That summer, the papers and television kept talking about Kennedy like he was the second coming or something. Someone needed to teach him that there's an *r* in the alphabet with that Boston accent, but he sure was easy on the eyes.

I didn't normally pay much attention to all the political stuff, and living right outside of DC, we heard it all, but that year it sounded more interesting to me than usual.

Jake and Will were as opposite in politics as they were in personality. Jake was a die-hard Republican, and Will was a liberal Democrat, so it was killing Jake that any of us even gave this guy Kennedy a glance. I'd say most men who differ as much as those two in views are rarely friends let alone safe going to rifle ranges together. Ellie and I hadn't decided what political affiliation we were yet, but my guess was that she would go with whomever Will didn't.

"Are you gonna watch the debate tonight?" Ellie asked over the phone.

I worked to untangle the cord from the kitchen stool. "I don't have to watch a debate; I live one every night," I answered.

"No, really, the presidential debate," El explained. "We really need to be informed voters, you know." And so I watched the first-ever televised presidential debate. I watched more than I listened, as Jake decided to debate JFK himself rather than listen to Nixon.

El signed us up to help with JFK's campaign, putting Jake into a tailspin.

"Barb, if this guy gets elected, I'll have to turn all my guns in. He hates the NRA and thinks if you own a gun, you'll shoot your neighbor the first time he lets the grass get too high," Jake ranted as he paced the living room. "And if he gets his way, they're going to do forced bussing of the kids, and we'll be sending them to Southeast DC to go to school!" he was pulling out all the stops. "Besides, how are you going to get there?"

Now, he had a point. Driving in Washington, DC, could be a challenge for a directionally competent driver, and El and I didn't fit in that category, but we decided that together we could do it. Two heads were better than one, in most cases.

"Well, you can give me directions," I answered. So, he did, and he did a pretty good job until it came to the circles. He told us to follow one road but failed to mention that there would be a circle or roundabout.

Ellie pulled to a stop at the light. "I thought you said go straight," she whined.

"That's what the directions say." I defended myself. "I think you just follow the circle and turn on the other side of it." I didn't sound real convincing.

You'd think if you entered a "circle" and came out on the opposite side of it, you'd be on the same road as when you started, right? Well, not in DC you wouldn't. Good thing we left an hour early.

I never thought I'd be stuffing envelopes or answering phones for a presidential candidate. Lucky for us, they weren't that picky when it came to "experience."

Friday was our first day in the campaign office. It was nice to wear something other than pedal pushers for a change. I orchestrated my usual assembly-line madness. Ellie folded, I stuffed, she sealed the envelopes, and I put on the stamps. We stuffed envelopes until we ran out of spit and supplies. We didn't see JFK, but we never gave up hope.

We headed home after five hours of envelope licking and paper cuts.

"Listen to that," Ellie said as she reached over and turned up the volume on Betsy's radio. It was a new rendition of "The Lion Sleeps Tonight."

"They've sure got the wheema whack down pat," I said, and we began to sing along. "In the jungle, the mighty jungle, the lion sleeps tonight!" Rocking through Southeast DC, a slight oversight on my part, I suppose.

You might say that my navigational skills let me down, but if you want the truth, when Ellie's singing, she can't tell her left from her right. When we ended up in Southeast DC, we decided it was no big deal. It turned out to be a more direct route to where we lived, but not the best of neighborhoods. We jammed to the radio, and Betsy's sputtering was our first clue that we were now going to take a hike. The car sputtered to a halt, and Ellie managed to steer it to the shoulder.

"I can't believe you didn't check the gas gauge, Ellie!" We both just stared at the arrow pointing to the E on Betsy's dash, as if staring might make a difference. I looked around at run-down apartment buildings and knee-high grass on the median strip. There were no neatly trimmed grass lawns surrounding the monuments in this part of DC.

"Don't worry, we'll be fine." Ellie tried to be reassuring, but the sound of her voice gave her away. I was no help.

"And just how do you define 'fine'? Being stuck in a nigger neighborhood with no transportation?" I asked, fearful of walking the two blocks to the gas station. My fear had overcome my sensitivity to using the n word in front of her. I knew she'd had colored friends and normally tried to clean up my act when it came to that subject, but my southern ancestry hung on tight, especially now.

"It'll be fine," she kept saying, as if trying to convince herself.

We looked around to determine if the coast was clear. I'm not sure what it was that we were looking for. Murderers, rapists, drug addicts. What do they look like? I'd always been led to believe any colored neighborhood was nothing but bad news. My adrenaline was in full throttle and I realized for the first time in years, I was scared.

"This feels weird," I said as we crossed the road as traffic whizzed by. We kept moving, not looking to our right or left.

"I know," she said.

"If we live to tell about this, we're not telling about this!" I grabbed her hand as if I was five years old, and we ran across the street.

"You don't have to worry about that." She pointed. "There's a gas station!"

We walked as fast as we could to the Esso station. Music blared from a radio inside the garage.

"Let's twist again, like we did last summer. Yeah, let's twist again, like we did last year. Do you remember when..." The colored gas station attendant sang along as he pumped gas into a customer's car.

"Excuse me, sir. Sorry to interrupt your concert!" Ellie said.

I nudged her with my elbow to shut up and get to the point.

"You ladies must be outta gas," he said with a southern drawl as he raised his eyebrows and adjusted his Washington Senators baseball cap.

"How'd you know?" I asked without thinking. When am I gonna learn to think?

"Most folks just drive up to the pump instead of walking up." He pulled the hose out of the gas tank. "And most folks around here don't look like you," he added.

Thanks for the reminder...

"Yeah, we noticed that, Mack." Ellie called him by the embroidered name on his green uniform shirt. "Can you help us out?"

"Where's your car?"

"Just down the street a few blocks," Ellie answered.

"Sure, just have a seat inside, and I'll get Gus to cover for me. We'll get you back on the road in no time." He pointed to the chairs in the gas station office.

We walked into the little glass-enclosed front office and sat down on the red vinyl chairs and waited. I pulled out a cigarette and lit up. Ellie picked up a magazine and thumbed through, trying to pass the time.

"Hey, look at this recipe for making homemade candles." El lifted up the magazine and turned it my way. There were big colorful candles, both round and square, some with glitter and some with a white topping on them th. looked like snow.

"Yeah, that's neat." I feigned interest.

"We could make these for Christmas presents," she whispered. Ellie looked around to see if anyone was looking and began to rip the pages from the magazine.

"Damn it, Ellie. What are you trying to do, get us killed?" I asked and snatched the magazine from her hands. She grabbed it back.

"I don't think they'll hang us for a few pages out of *Good Housekeeping*." She continued ripping as discretely as she could. I stood up and looked out the door, pretending to stretch my legs.

"I don't know, but the Klan hangs *them* for far less, that's for sure. Hurry up; he's coming!" I turned around, sat down, and snuffed out my cigarette in the tall one-legged metal ashtray. By then, she'd already folded up the pages and stuffed them in her purse in one swift movement.

Mack opened the door and walked inside.

"Well, ladies, Gus is watching over the pumps, so let's get you back to your car," He held the door open for us.

"We can just take the gas can back to the car. You don't have to leave the station, Mack," I said, thinking this might have been the first time I'd ever spoken to a colored man by name before. He really didn't seem all that different.

"No big deal. You don't want to be walking around unescorted in this neighborhood. Not on my watch, anyway." He opened the door to the Esso tow truck. We climbed inside and felt eyes staring us in the back of our heads as his coworkers and a few customers took note of the white ladies going for a ride with Mack. He put the red gas can in the back of the truck. I wondered if he was the serial rapist we'd been reading about, or maybe the drug dealer that hung out on the corner in his spare time.

"So, ladies, what brings you to this part of town?"

"Just taking a shortcut home. We've been working on JFK's campaign," Ellie answered.

"Wow, sounds important." Mack stopped at a red light. "That's that fancy senator from Boston, right?"

"Yeah, that's him," Ellie answered. "He's a big civil rights supporter."

"So I hear," Mack said as he crossed the intersection. "What do you ladies think will change if he's elected?"

"It depends on who you ask," I said. Where did that come from?

"What do you mean?" Mack asked. Ellie's elbow was now deep into my side.

"Just that it seems that some people are scared he's gonna change their way of life, like not being able to own a gun or our kids being able to go to a neighborhood school." I hoped that didn't sound too racist. Am I a racist? I decided to set that one aside for later.

"Fear is a sad thing." Reaching into his breast pocket, he pulled out some Wrigley's spearmint gum and gave us each a piece. "It's funny 'cause I just read a quote by Martin Luther King that said, 'The negro needs the white man to free him from his fears. The white man needs the negro to free him from his guilt.'"

"Hmm," I said as I chomped the gum down to chewing size. "Maybe we both need to be freed from fear," I thought out loud.

"Yeah, if we tell the white guys they're all guilty, well, that ain't gonna go anywhere, Mack," Ellie chimed in.

He chuckled. "Yeah, change is tough on everyone, and painful is the process. At least this time I can vote since they passed the Twenty-Third Amendment!"

The law had been ratified, giving DC residents the right to vote in the presidential election. Since it wasn't officially a "state," its rights had been limited.

"And now that the Senators moved to Minnesota, I sometimes wonder why I stay here, but voting is progress." He referred to the American League baseball team that packed up and left town.

"My father-in-law said we might get an expansion team next year." I offered up some hope.

"Sure hope so!" Mack said as we pulled up next to Betsy. Mack put his flashers on as we climbed out of the Esso tow truck.

He poured the red gas can of fuel into her tank. Ellie and I resumed our normal positions in the front seat, and when Mack gave the thumbs up sign, Ellie turned the ignition and Betsy started right up.

"Phew, music to my ears!" I said as I rolled my window down. Time for a cigarette.

"I'm right behind you." Ellie assured Mack and rolled up her window. We followed the tow truck back to the Esso station. Ellie pulled up to the pump and asked Mack to pump in a dollar of regular.

Mack cleaned Betsy's windshield, and Ellie and I scrounged around in our purses for extra change for a tip for Mack. We came up with a $1.45. Mack replaced the nozzle onto the pump and Ellie handed him $2.45 and told him to keep the change.

"Oh, no, I can't do that," he said.

"Sure you can. We really appreciate what you did for us." Ellie insisted, but Mack wouldn't have it. He handed the excess change back to her.

"Just doing my job and helping folks when I can. Thanks for the chance to bless you ladies. If my wife's ever stuck in your neighborhood, I hope you'll return the favor!" He walked away with a wave and a smile.

Ellie and I looked at each other.

"Wow" was all I could say. "Guess he's not a serial rapist or drug dealer after all."

"Huh?" she asked.

"Never mind."

She put Betsy in drive and honked the horn good-bye, and we drove away in silence.

"I don't get it." I broke the ice.

"Get what?"

"If they hate us so much, why would he help us like he did?"

"I don't think they hate us, Barb. I think both sides have been so afraid of each other for so long, we all tend to believe our own crap. It's nice to know it ain't necessarily so."

"Yeah, I guess it is." I still wasn't so sure but was less convinced of my bigotries than I had been an hour earlier.

❁

We continued to volunteer at JFK's headquarters throughout the fall and began to learn our way in and out of town. We even stopped at Mack's Esso station to gas up a few times and ran into him once.

"You ladies gonna make sure that Yankee gets elected, aren't ya?" Mack asked as he leaned in to collect our dollar.

"We're doing our best, Mack!" Ellie assured him, and we pulled away.

A few weeks later, John Fitzgerald Kennedy was elected president. Ellie and I toasted each other over the phone.

"Well, we did it!" she said as I answered.

"Yeah, my paper cuts aren't even healed yet," I said, stirring the boiling potatoes on the stove. All those hours of envelope stuffing had paid off.

"I'll keep watching the mail for our inaugural ball invitation," Ellie said.

"Yeah, we'd better start shopping for our gowns soon." We laughed and hung up so I could finish burning dinner and set the table.

"Momma called yesterday and asked if we'd like to come over for Thanksgiving dinner," I said at the dinner table. I was all for it as long as I didn't have to cook. Besides, I missed her.

"Uh huh," Jake said in between bites of mashed potatoes and pot roast. Sounded like a yes to me.

Mom and the Old Man lived about four miles from us, but we didn't see them too much. Momma and I talked on the phone a lot. She still worked as a secretary at the Pentagon. I was so glad to be out of that house. Getting married at sixteen saved me from the reaches of the Old Man, and I'd die making sure Karen never spent a minute alone with him.

Jake and Will's annual gun club dance was coming up, and Roberta and Dick were going, too. It wasn't the inaugural ball, as it was apparent that our invitations got lost in the mail, but we were excited anyway. We had sitters lined up, and Ellie was teaching me to sew. It seemed like she was always teaching me how to do something.

First it was driving (well, when all was said and done, maybe I ended up teaching her more about that than she did me) and then it was cooking (that lesson didn't take; we still eat spaghetti three times a week) and now sewing. She tried to tell me there was more to sex than I knew, but I managed to dodge that lesson.

The kids were outside. Jay was busy terrorizing Roberta, Karen was practicing with her baton, and I was jamming in the kitchen to "Everybody's

Somebody's Fool" by Connie Francis. Connie and I were old dancing and singing buddies.

"What are you doing?" El asked as she walked into my kitchen. I had the stereo blasting and was dancing while I cut potatoes for dinner. Many people are closet smokers; some are closet chocoholics. Me, I'm a closet kitchen dancer. I've just never done it in public until now. I knew she was coming. *Why did I let her catch me?*

"What are you doing sneaking up on me like that?" I threw the dish towel at her. I could feel my neck and cheeks blush.

"Don't worry; your secret's safe with me. Besides, there was no getting your attention, girl. You're a great singer and dancer; you never told me," she said. I wasn't sure if she meant it or was just being her usual pass-on-a-compliment self. "All I ever get to hear you do is hum a few bars," she said. "Here, I brought in your mail." She dropped several letters and ads on the counter.

"Sure, thanks." I continued to cut more potatoes into little cubes to boil for mashed potatoes. I dumped them into the pot and turned up the flame.

"No, I mean it. Show me what that little dippy thing was you had going on." She pulled me back into the middle of the kitchen. The stereo continued playing, with the arm going up and back automatically on the 45-rpm record so that Connie sang her song over and over again.

I gave in, and we headed into the living room, where there was more space, and started dancing until we were out of breath and I could smell the potatoes cooking. I ran back in the kitchen to turn down the flame.

The phone rang, and I reached around the kitchen doorway and picked it up.

"Hello?" It was Roberta.

I covered the receiver and hollered, "Jay, shut the door! You're letting flies in!" and returned to the phone. "Yeah, he's home now and Ellie just got here," I said. The door banged, then landed open, and I reached over and pulled it closed, stretching the phone cord across the room. "Yeah, I've got some. Send him on down." I hung up the receiver and reached over to flip through the mail.

I pulled out an envelope with the return address of 1600 Pennsylvania Avenue. "What's this?" I wondered aloud, and grabbed a knife to open the nvelope. El walked over and took a peek. "Well, look at this!" I opened the gold embossed card with a handwritten note inside: "Thank you so much for your hard work on our campaign for president. Your hard work has paid off! Sincerely, Jackie Kennedy."

"I wonder if I got one, too." Ellie snatched the card out of my hand.

"I'm sure you did. Wish this was an invitation to the ball, but I'll take it!" I laughed. "Pretty cool, handwritten by Jackie herself." I turned and headed to the dining room.

Ellie had created a sewing fiend when she taught me how to sew. It seemed like I'd have one project just finished, another just started, and a new one going in my head at any given time. I'd convinced myself that I was saving money, too.

"Was that Roberta?" Ellie asked.

"Yeah, she needs to borrow a stick of butter."

"Hey, it looks great," she said while she held the half-sewn dress up to me.

"I'm about halfway through the blue pattern, the one that Jackie wore when he won the election," I said.

"Slip it on so I can mark the hem," El instructed. I slipped out of my shorts and top and into the skeleton of a dress.

"Looks great, just like Jackie's little sister."

"Yeah, well, Lee's got better teeth than me, not to mention jewelry!" I'd read up on the silver-spoon upbringing of Jackie and her little sister, Lee Radziwell.

"But she doesn't have an original like this one," El said.

"No kidding, and as long as I don't raise my arms too high, nobody will see where I had to rip out the seam and start over," I said.

Ellie knelt down to mark the hem length with straight pins, holding them between her teeth. "Don't worry; it'll be fine," she said with straight pins hanging out of her mouth.

"So, Roberta and Dick are going to the dance, too, I hear."

"Yeah, I guess so." I turned as she pinned the hem. "What's she wearing?"

"Not sure, something flowing, I'll bet. Gotta cover that tummy. She's getting bigger by the minute." She stood up, examining the hemline. "Think she's having twins?"

"Nah, probably just too many visits from the Good Humor man!"

We giggled at the thought of our pregnant buddy flirting with Mr. Popsicle

"So, did you get her to start giving you her empty milk cartons for candles?" Ellie asked as she plopped into a dining room chair and leaned her head on her hand.

"Yeah, but it wasn't that simple. I had to talk her into buying milk at the store instead of from Mike the milkman since he only delivers glass bottles." I slipped back into the bathroom for a quick change back into my clothes, talking louder so she could hear me. "Flirting with him was sometimes the highlight of her week, you know."

"Oh well, it's for a worthy cause. Santa will appreciate it," Ellie said.

"Do you really think we can make any money selling candles?" I hollered through the bathroom door and before she answered, opened the door and walked back to the kitchen while pulling down my blouse.

"It'll be easy. Our only overhead is wax, food coloring, and a little bit of glitter."

"Okay, but we're gonna mess up your kitchen, not mine." I reached over to the stove and turned off the flame on the potatoes.

"Hey, what's a little bit of wax gonna do?" She mumbled something else that I couldn't make out as I walked back into the dining room and hung the dress over the sewing machine cabinet.

"What was that?" I asked and sat down across from her.

She ran her hand through her red hair and shook her head. "Nothing. It's just the usual 'day in the life of the Reillys.' Will's his normal charming self again today. Fussing about the kids eating all his potato chips while he wasn't looking." She stretched her hands above her head as if trying to excise him from her thoughts. "I'd like to tell him where to stick his potato chips. And his beer. And his television, and his car. It's all 'his,' you know." She shook her head.

Before I could respond, she waved her hand and said, "Enough! I'm not gonna wallow in misery. While he's at work, at least I can have some peace." She slouched further down in the chair.

"I didn't really mean we couldn't do it here, El. If it's easier…"

"Nope, nothin' doin'. My idea, my house. But I get all the credit when we make a million!"

I turned off the potatoes and stuck them in the fridge for later. Roberta's son, Bobby, came to the door, and I gave him a stick of butter for his mom. She walked me through the tough part of the dress pattern, and I continued sewing while we chatted. I tried to steer clear of any topics that included Will. It wasn't like El to complain or go into detail about their fights, but it was obvious that lately there were more and more of them. Living together full-time had proven to be a bigger adjustment than either of them had thought.

The dress turned out pretty good, and we had a great time at the dance. After a few drinks, even Will managed a slow dance or two with Ellie. Roberta managed a few waddles on the dance floor, and my dancing lessons in the living room with Connie Francis had paid off. Jake and I were the hit of the evening, twirling and gliding across the floor.

After Thanksgiving came and went, we started the candle manufacturing. It turned out we didn't sell any, and we weren't too keen on giving them to people we knew as gifts, at least not to people we liked. The article she ripped out of *Good Housekeeping* that day at Mack's gas station was a little lacking on details. Like how long it took to cool a large candle (and most important, how to keep kids away from it during the cooling process), how to make the foamy wax for the decoration on the candle without splattering wax all over half of the house with your mixer, and that you need to clean the wax off the beaters and out of the pan *before* it cools off. Is that enough of a visual?

It looks like we'll be painting her dining room next, right after we figure out how to get the waxy stains off the walls. It might take a couple of coats to cover that up.

I'm sure the author of the candle recipe didn't have six kids underfoot, spilling everything on the dining room carpet when the kitchen wasn't big enough for the assembly line. With our mass production, Ellie ended up having candles cooling off in every room of the house by the time we were done. Poor kids, we warned them that Santa would fly right over their house if we found one more fingerprint on the side of one more candle.

"We'll just have to let them cool and set up. Will's gonna hate it, but what else can we do?"

"We should have done this at my house. I could have dead cats sitting all over the house and Jake would never notice!"

And then there's the few "drips" of wax on the carpet in the dining room. Paint definitely won't fix that.

"Don't worry. I read in *Hints from Heloise* how to get waxy stuff out of fabrics with a hot steam iron and a paper bag," Ellie said. I argued with her but lost the battle.

She grabbed the iron out of the utility room and plugged it into the wall. I ran out to check on the boys while the iron heated up. Seeing that they were playing in the sandbox in the backyard and hadn't burned anything down, I headed back into the house. El was on her knees holding the iron on top of the paper bag and carpet.

"I'll fix us a Pepsi," I said and headed for the kitchen.

"Oh my God!" she cried.

I turned on my heel as my heart skipped a beat, that old familiar feeling that comes from hanging with Ellie. There she was, on her knees, eyes bugged out, strawberry blonde hair askew, and holding the iron in the air.

"What?" I looked down at the carpet where she raised up the iron and paper bag. There were remnants of the wax on the bag and a nice imprint of her iron on the carpet.

"I burned the carpet up!" She stood up, one hand flying to cover her mouth and the other waving the iron in the air.

"Hold on, there," I said as I grabbed the iron from her hand. "You're gonna brand me, too, if you're not careful!"

She stood staring at the carpet in disbelief. "Heloise didn't say anything about burning the carpet. Will's gonna kill me! Do you think we can cover it with anything?"

"El, it's in the middle of the pathway around the table. There's no way we can cover this up," I said as I stooped to inspect the carpet. "Hey, maybe it's not burned; maybe it's just still hot. Could be when it cools off, it'll lighten up," I hoped out loud.

And we knelt there staring at the ground.

"You think it would help if we prayed?" Ellie asked.

"You think God's gonna waste a miracle on your carpet? When's the last time you went to church?" I looked back down at the waxy dots on the carpet. The way I saw it, you needed to make a deposit before you could withdraw anything when it came to prayer requests. We were both overdrawn, if that were the case. I shook my head, and seeing the desperate look in her eyes, I added, "Go ahead. It can't hurt, I guess."

By this time, she already had her eyes closed, logging in her need. I wondered if prayers have to get in line in order of importance or time requirements. If it was importance, we were out of luck. If it's time sensitive, we just went to the head of the line. The guys would be home in about twenty minutes according to the kitchen clock. Ellie opened one eye and found me peeking.

"You've got to close your eyes, Barb!"

I complied and tried to bite my lip on the excuse. "Just checking the clock to see how much time He has to make this happen." I bowed my head.

Thirty seconds later, we opened our eyes and found the iron imprint gone, along with the waxy stains.

"See! Our prayers were answered," Ellie said.

I wasn't sure if it was coincidence or divine guidance, but who was I to argue? I think that time, we just got lucky, but Ellie was convinced the kneeling was what did it.

"Here, let's move the finished candles into the living room," Ellie said. Ginger and Karen walked in the front door right on time. "Ginger, you're in charge of lining up the cartons. Karen, you've gotta hold the wicks in place while Ginger moves them."

"I told you we should've stayed after school," Ginger said to Karen. They shrugged, but not before they got in a good eye roll to each other that said, "Here we go again," and got to work.

Sure enough, Will blew a cork when he saw the state of the house. Milk cartons, pans of wax, and candles on every flat surface in sight. Put that in *Good Housekeeping*, why don't ya? We ended up putting two kids on "chisel out the wax from the inside of this pot" duty on the back porch when Will not-so-delicately suggested we just heat the pan up again to melt the wax. Ellie and I just looked at each other and shrugged.

"Guess we could do that," I said.

"How long are we going to be living in a candle factory, Ellie?" he asked, and she pretended not to hear.

"Look at it this way, Will. You're gonna have all these beautiful candles to enjoy."

"I thought they were for selling…or gifts."

"Would you buy one?" I asked, eyebrows arched. His gaze shifted back to the still-warm candles, some of which looked like they'd partied all night, leaning, trying hard to stand up straight. A few of them appeared to be trying to hide behind the other to escape Will's glare.

The look in his eyes was enough of an answer when he said, "Only if there was an impending hurricane and I needed them for some light." He laughed at his own sarcasm.

It took a few weeks, and we didn't end up making any money for Christmas cash, but every person we know is now the proud owner of an original "Barbellie" candle. We can only hope that they talk to us again.

❧

Go ahead, shake my hand. I got my driver's license! It was no easy feat, let me tell you. After disastrous lessons from both Jake and Ellie, I was able to save enough of my babysitting money to pay for the driving class.

Ellie drove me to school every day and took the kids to the park while I was in class. She even passed me on the road one day while I was in the "Caution, Student Driver" car.

"Why did you beep at me?" I asked when I jumped back into Betsy.

"I wanted to make sure you saw us."

"Betsy's pretty hard to miss with five kids hanging out the windows. Not to mention Charlie Brown barking, with boogers trailing down the roadway."

Telling Jake that I'd gotten my license, now that was something I would have rather skipped. I wasn't sure how to go about it, so I just took the plunge.

"You did *what*? Without telling me?" He ran his hand through his hair. Not a good sign. "Where'd you get the money?"

"If I'd told ya, you would've insisted on teaching me yourself, and we've ried that before, Jake. I saved the money from watching the boys. Don't worry; I didn't spend a dime of yours." I slammed the ketchup bottle down on the dining room table.

I have to say, we don't fight that much, but when we do, it can get loud. Nothing more than that, but Jake has a booming voice that can rattle windows, and there's no getting around his reactions sometimes.

At first, he told me that since I had gone behind his back, I couldn't drive his car.

"What is it with you men? Does everything belong to you because of a paycheck?" I ranted. "Never mind, I don't think you'd better answer that!" Okay, time for a different approach. Don't give him time to reload.

"I thought I'd better learn to drive so I don't have to worry the next time you've had too many beers. The cop that stopped me on the way home from Colonial Beach was nice enough to let me keep on going, but we're lucky we didn't both end up in jail!" Good work, put him back on his heels. Put him on the defensive. Now for the "aren't you grateful?" approach.

"Besides, think of all the driving I'll save you. I can drive Karen to majorettes and do the grocery shopping on my own."

With that, he shut up and headed to the basement to work on his precious gun collection, slamming the door behind him.

The silent war went on for a few days, but as always, makeup sex glossed over the harsh words. We'd had a major argument over my license, but once the light bulb of good sense went off, it occurred to him how this would make his life easier. Now I could be the one to drive the kids around, do the grocery shopping, and go to Hecht's red-dot sale alone when Ellie couldn't go (I should have neglected to mention that one). There's a lot to be said for freedom. Let it ring.

"Hey, did you see that cartoon show that was just on?" Ellie asked me over the phone.

"No, why?" I folded another towel and added to the already leaning pile.

"I think you need to watch it."

"I'm not big on cartoons." The pile gave in to gravity and fell across the bed.

"You will love this one. It's like somebody's been looking through you window."

"What are you talking about?" I rolled my eyes.

"Fred Flintstone is the spitting image of Jake—big guy, booming voice, and unknowingly controlled by his wife. Will and I howled through the entire half-hour show."

"What's the wife like?" and before she could answer I added, "No, let me guess, she must be a beauty."

"Pretty, good body, and quite a manipulator. She has a partner-in-crime best friend named Betty. Not as pretty as me, but I can live with it."

That Thursday night, we sat down to watch the show at Ellie's house after she served up a dinner of hot dogs and beans. She was right. It was as if they'd peeked in our windows.

"Yabba dabba doo!" Fred Flintstone hollered on the TV.

"Sounds enough like Jake," Will said. "He's got the bellowing part down pat!"

"Yeah, well I'm not so sure I'd fit into that skimpy little dress." I trolled for compliments and Jake took the bait.

"You would make her look bad, Babe." Jake stood up and patted me on the butt. "Yabba dabba doo!" He laughed at his own joke and headed towards the kitchen for another beer.

"Keep your hands to yourself, Fred or I'll 'Yabba dabba doo you!" I said.

"That's what he's counting on!" Will said as he followed Jake out of the room.

I pretended to model the outfit that Wilma wore.

"I wonder what kinda animal pelt it's made from," I said to Ellie.

"Can't be rabbit, doesn't look furry enough," she said. "Although rabbits are dropping like flies around here these days." It took a second for the meaning of her comment to knock me upside my head. I looked down at her sitting on the couch.

"Really, El?" My heart sank to my knees knowing it was true. "You're pregnant? How do you know?"

"Really?" she said. I shook my head and pulled my foot out of my mouth yet again.

She looked around the room to be sure the guys were out of earshot.

"Yeah, I'm a month behind. I made an appointment with Dr. Reardon for Tuesday to double-check." She sighed, her head bowed down and shoulders slumped. I sat down next to her and put my arm around her shoulder.

"Does Will know?"

"Not yet. Can't bring myself to ruin his good mood." She winked at me. *She's the one with another kid on the way and is trying to make me feel better?*

"Maybe you should serve up some rabbit for dinner tomorrow!"

"I would, but we can only have fish on Fridays!" She stood up and I followed suit. "I'm gonna tell him when the kids go to bed tonight." I hugged her hard. We walked into the dining room where the guys were polishing off their drinks.

"I'll drive." I took the keys out of Jake's hand referring to the three beers he'd had. "Bet you're glad I have my license now." He grinned in agreement. We pulled on our coats, single filed out of the house and into the car. I drove us home with Ellie's dilemma swirling in my thoughts.

Lying in bed after a little cave man activity and a few "Yabba dabba doos" from Jake, I filled him in.

"Ellie's pregnant with kid number four?" Jake propped himself up on his elbow and looked down at me.

"Yep, poor thing. Just when she was getting a little freedom, here she goes again."

"Man, Will's gonna blow a cork." He shook his head, kissed me on the cheek and rolled over. I laid there feeling sorry for my friend.

I don't know how she does it, living with Will. I like to think that our friendship has been as good for her as it's been for me. Still, if I were her, I think I'd jump—ship, that is.

It had been weeks since I'd had a waking-up-slowly kind of day, but it looked like I was getting lucky that Saturday morning. Jake had left at 6:00 a.m. for a side job, and I was in "rollover stage two" after he leaned over to give me a good-bye kiss on the cheek.

In professional terms, I was snoozing.

Bang! Bang! Bang! Something pounded on my bedroom door.

"Give me my baton, you brat!" Karen yelled.

I hollered for them to knock it off, threw off the covers, jumped out bed, and opened the door to see the baton coming my way. The next coheren memory I had was Roberta kneeling over top of me with a bag of ice wrapped in a towel, shoving it into my face.

"Barb, can you hear me?" she asked, stroking my forehead, pushing my hair back so she could put the ice over the bridge of my nose.

"Uh huh," I answered, trying to remember what happened. I turned my head to find Karen and Jay huddled behind her. Jay was crying, and Karen was about to. *The baton. You opened the door, you idiot!*

"It's okay," I said, lifting my head up. *So, this is what it's like to see stars...*

"Mom's gonna be just fine, guys. Karen, why don't you take Jay back downstairs and fix some toast for breakfast?" Roberta said.

"Okay, Mrs. White," Karen said and took Jay by the hand. He seemed to feel better knowing it was okay to eat.

Roberta helped me sit up. My head felt sore, but I thought I was okay.

"Here, take these," Roberta said as she handed me a couple of aspirin. I washed them down with the water she had in the other hand.

"What the heck happened, Barb?"

"I was sleeping." My hand covered my eyes, as it hurt to open them. "I heard this loud banging on the door and Karen was fussing at Jay to give her the baton and the next thing I knew, I opened the door, not realizing." I put the ice back on my nose with my other hand. I stood up and walked over to the mirror. Big mistake.

"Oh my God!" I cried. "Roberta, look at me!" I turned around from the dresser with two of the biggest shiners you've ever seen. I looked like I'd been in a prizefight and lost.

Roberta joined me at the dresser, and I must say, the girl had tremendous restraint. I don't know if I would've had the same kind of control if the tables had been turned.

"Oh, hon, it'll be all right. It'll go away in a few weeks."

Somehow the thought of looking like this for a few weeks was more than I could take. Even a trip to the grocery store proved traumatic.

"What happened to you? Did Jake get mad about something?" my neighbor, Becky, asked as we stood in line at Kroger's.

"Nope, Jay got me with Karen's baton," I said, not wanting to go into detail in front of everyone in the grocery store line. I promised her an explanation later.

"I swear, El, I'm not going anywhere until these bruises are gone. People think Jay's the demon seed every time I tell the story. Either that or they don't believe it at all, and I'm not sure which is worse," I whined.

I stayed home for almost two weeks before venturing out again. I hadn't had cabin fever that bad since Jay was a baby.

I often wondered what Jackie would've done if she'd had a Jay instead of a John-John. I doubted there was a nanny out there you could have paid enough to keep up with him, and just to think—I did it for free. There was no way he would've sat still for the White House photo ops we saw in the *Post* all the time.

Sometimes Jay's temper or lack of self-control worried me. His outbursts were frequent and unpredictable.

"Jay, no!" I fussed as I took away the knife he'd pulled off the kitchen counter.

"No!" he stamped his almost three-year-old foot and reached for the knife, but I put it in the sink out of his reach. He stood on his tiptoes and tried to peek over the counter's edge into the sink. When he realized he'd been outsmarted, he plopped down onto the kitchen floor.

"Mom, can you help me with this top button?" Karen asked as she walked into the kitchen. She turned around and held up her hair. I stepped over Jay to button her dress.

Thump, thump, thump!

"He's doing it again." Karen pointed at Jay. There he was, on his hands and knees, thumping his little head on the floor. We'd caught him doing it a few times before.

"Jay, stop that!" I bent over and picked him up and put him on my hip. I kissed his little forehead and rocked back and forth fast. Sometimes it slowed him down and sometimes not.

Before the day was over, I managed to get a "Calgon, Take Me Away" moment and headed out the door. Jake and Will were good with staying with the boys while Ellie and I escaped to Hecht's with Karen and Ginger. The Hecht Company is a quality department store—one that, even on a good day, we wouldn't be able to afford except for the red-dot sales and dollar day in the bargain basement.

Ellie and I combed the racks on the main level just to look at the fall fashions before heading for the bargain basement. The girls played hide-and-seek among the aisles of clothes to keep themselves occupied. I fussed at them to stay close by.

"Why are you so worked up?" Ellie asked, and I glanced toward the men in black suits standing here and there throughout the women's department. It just seemed strange. My head nodded in reply, leaning toward the suits.

"Let's just keep them close. Seems weird." I grabbed a hold of Karen's hand. I noticed there didn't seem to be many people in the store.

Karen sat on a chair for a few minutes until she became bored once again and got up to see where Ginger had gone. I saw the clothes move in a nearby rack and was sure it was Ginger or Karen hiding from me. As I came closer, I crouched down to jump out and say, "Gotcha!" But it was not Ginger or Karen. My almost-victim was a little girl of about five years old with straight brown hair and tears streaming down her face.

"I want my mommy," the little girl cried. I walked over closer to her, stooped down, and brushed her hair from her face.

"It's okay. Where is your mommy?"

"I don't know. She was trying on clothes." She rubbed tears from her eyes with the backs of her hands.

"Come on, I'll help you find her." I took her damp little hand in mine. "Don't worry, I remember when I lost my mom when I was smaller than you. I know it's scary, but I think I know where she is. What's your name?"

She sniffled. "Caroline."

"Well, Caroline, just hold my hand, and we'll find your mom soon. I promise."

Caroline seemed to relax a little, and I led her back to the dressing room. The men in the black suits were still there. They were standing in a circle with a woman who was near hysteria.

"How could you let this happen?" The woman was fussing at the men. She wore a white linen blouse and blue skirt, with a Jackie Kennedy hairstyle.

Another man spoke into a radio. "I know I told those idiots to block all exits. Just make sure they did!" he barked into the speaker.

I held onto Caroline's hand as we approached the dressing room, where Ellie and the girls were staring wide-eyed. When Caroline saw the men in black suits, she broke free of my hand and ran toward them.

"Mommy!" The woman whirled around to see us coming down the aisle behind her. There was a ring of familiarity when I saw the lady's face, but I was sure I was wrong.

"Darling, thank heaven you're all right!" the lady cried. They hugged each other tight.

Darling? Who in the world calls their kid "darling?" One of the men in the black suits approached, asking where I had found her.

"Over there." I pointed toward the clearance rack. Caroline should've known better than to look for Mom in the clearance section. "She was crying, and I was trying to help her find her mother." I said as Ellie looked up and headed over from a few racks away to see what all the commotion was about.

"What'd you do, lift something?" Ellie whispered in my ear.

"Shhh!" was all I could manage in reply.

By this time, store management personnel were gathered around us. *Jackie Kennedy*? No, it couldn't be. The mother of the little girl walked over to us.

"Thank you so much for looking after my Caroline." The woman extended her hand. She had neatly cropped black hair and manicured hands. My reaction was to hide my chipped red fingernails, but I reached out and shook her hand anyway and glanced at Ellie and the girls.

The woman looked at Ellie, who, before this very moment, had never been rendered speechless. I figured her wheels were turning like mine. If this was who I thought it was, well, that would explain the men in the black suits.

"How do you do? I'm Jackie Kennedy," the woman said. "I would so like to thank you and your daughter for your kindness in looking after Caroline."

How do you do? Now there's a catch phrase not from Radiant Valley if ever heard one.

I gathered what little composure I had and answered, "I'm Barb Kincaid, and this is my daughter, Karen." Ellie's hip gave me a not-so-gentle nudge. "And this is my friend Ellie Reilly and her daughter, Ginger."

"Well, Mrs. Kincaid, I am so very grateful for your thoughtfulness toward Caroline. I was just frantic when I couldn't find her. I just wanted to do a little shopping and pick something out on my own for a change," the First Lady said. Did I say "First Lady"? *Somebody pinch me...*

"I know what you mean, and please, call me Barb." One of the men in the black suits prompted her that it was time to go.

"I'm sorry to leave so soon, ladies. Perhaps we will meet again," she said as the Secret Service agents escorted them both away. Caroline left, holding onto her mother's hand, looking back over her shoulder with a little wave. Yeah, we'll meet again all right. See ya next week at bingo.

We waved back, still stunned that we'd just met the First Lady of the United States as well as her famous little girl. We all stood looking at one another, wondering what just happened.

"I can't believe we just met Jackie!" Ellie said.

"I know."

"Where's John-John?" Ginger asked, and we all just looked at each other.

The store manager, Bob Cooper (according to his plastic name badge), walked up and thanked us for being there. "I suppose we can unblock the doors now," he instructed one of his employees. Beads of sweat glistened on his balding head, and he struggled to re-tuck his white shirt and straighten up his disheveled black tie. Once he was put back together, Bob took down my name, address, and phone number.

"Just in case I need to reach you, but I don't know why I would, except it's not every day that the president's kid gets lost in my store."

Some Secret Service heads were sure to roll tonight.

"What in the world was Jackie Kennedy doing shopping for clothes in Hecht's?" Ellie asked the manager. "Doesn't she have a dress designer of her very own?"

"Yeah, I think his name is Butterick." I laughed.

Bob looked at Ellie. "I don't know for sure. All I know is that they called about an hour ago to say that she was coming in a few minutes to look at women's clothes." He wiped his head with a handkerchief. "We had selected some things in her size, and she was trying them on when we realized Caroline had disappeared."

The small crowd that had gathered lost interest and moved away from us. We picked up our on-sale selections and headed for the cash register. "Here, let me take care of this for you. These are on the house." Bob took the clothes from us.

Realizing that the clothing was for the adults, he added, "And you girls may have any toy you want today." He looked at Ginger and Karen.

"We must be living right!" Ellie said in my ear.

The sales girl bagged up our selections, and we headed home quite pleased with ourselves.

"I had just started putting things back on the racks in my usual 'you don't really need that' routine." I laughed as we headed to the car. "Too bad I had already put back that purple dress!"

Even the mess in the living room that had accumulated to Jake's oblivion while we were gone didn't let the air out of my balloon.

"Yeah, Jackie and I are on a first-name basis," I said.

"Hmm, when are we going to the Hamptons?" Jake asked. I punched him on the arm in response.

Roberta was green with jealousy that she'd missed meeting Jackie. "That's the last time I miss a red-dot sale! How did she wear her makeup? What did she have on?" she asked without taking a breath.

"Impeccable makeup and a blue and white linen outfit."

Roberta had popped out a baby boy just weeks before and was working on getting her figure back on a steady diet of hard boiled eggs and lettuce. Why she'd given the little boy the name of Wallace, I couldn't figure. Something about a family name. I think I'd have to change families.

A few days later, Karen met the mailman as he walked up the steps to the house. She handed the pile of bills and advertisements to me.

I took my foot off the pedal of the Kenmore sewing machine and put the fabric down. I sifted through what I thought was nothing more than more bills to try and figure out how to pay when I spotted a fancy white envelope. The blue and gold imprinted return address read "1600 Pennsylvania Avenue, Washington, DC."

"Geez oh flip, no way!"

Karen rushed over to see. "What, Mom?" I opened the envelope with a dinner knife, making a mental note to buy a letter opener, trying not to rip it too much, and read aloud the note that was in an impeccable handwritten script.

> *Dear Mrs. Kincaid,*
>
> *I would love to properly thank you for the act of kindness that you so graciously extended to Caroline and me. Words cannot express the gratitude I felt when you returned my precious daughter safe and sound.*
>
> *I hope that you will accept my invitation to visit us at 1600 Pennsylvania Avenue. It may be presumptuous of me, but I would like to have my driver pick you up as well as your daughter, Karen, and your friends, Ellie and Ginger Reilly on Saturday, December 15th at 2:30 p.m.*
>
> *Please call and RSVP at 202-555-1600. Assuming that this invitation fits into your social plans, my driver will pick you up at two o'clock p.m. on December 15th. I hope you will permit me to reciprocate your kindness in this small way.*
>
> *Sincerely,*
>
> *Jackie Kennedy*

I read the note over and over again before I was sure it was for real.

"Quit pulling my leg, Barb. Nice joke, but enough already!" Ellie fussed over the phone. Yeah, it would've been a good prank, but not this time.

"No, El, it's for real!"

"Yeah, they must've heard that we stuffed envelopes for the campaign and realized the oversight of the never-sent inauguration invitations."

"Okay, I'll just call and tell her you're not coming."

That was enough to make her jump in Betsy, and she drove over to see for herself. Fifteen minutes later, Ellie barged into the dining room half out of breath with excitement. She picked up the invitation from the table and ran her finger over and over the gold embossed lettering.

"Wow, I can't believe they're sending a limo to pick us up. It's not that far; maybe we should tell her we'll drive ourselves," Ellie suggested.

"You are kidding, right?" I asked, not believing my ears, and added, "Yeah, with you driving and me navigating, we'll only be a day or two late."

"You're right. We'll take the limo."

What does one wear for tea at the White House? I guess I'll just check with my social secretary now that I've cleared my calendar. Should I wear one of my Butterick Jackie knock-offs or just splurge and buy something new? Forget it; what's to decide? If I'm going to the White House, I'm going in style. We unearthed the Hecht's company credit cards we'd earned by filling out an application a few months ago, and Jake didn't even object. I don't think Ellie told Will.

Karen and Ginger practiced walking with books on their heads. Ellie checked out *Etiquette* by Emily Post, and we all took a crash course in social graces.

We laughed until our sides hurt when Jake demonstrated the proper curtsy, pretending to pull his skirt out on each side as he crossed one big foot behind the other. Even Will couldn't help giving into a belly laugh at the sight of Jake's hairy crisscrossed legs. The guys were helpful with suggestions on how to irritate the president.

"Why don't you try to find out what in the world JFK is thinking when he talks about the desegregation of schools?" Jake asked and went on to irritate me more. "And ask him if he'll be sending Caroline to school on a bus to Southeast DC."

I have to admit, I just can't believe the government would even think of bussing our kids to distant schools to try and achieve racial equality. They're talking a twenty- or thirty-mile school bus ride instead of the normal three or four. After-school activities would be almost out of the question, and no doubt, Jake would have a coronary if the kids were to bring home a colored kid as a new best friend.

"Yeah, and see how much longer we'll be able to own a gun." Will looked up from his newspaper. I looked at Ellie, and she rolled her eyes.

"Geez, just think of all the extra money we'd have if you stopped buying new guns, Will," she said. Will had blown a cork when she modeled the new dress she'd bought at Hecht's. He burst her bubble of excitement good for spending a measly seven bucks.

December 15 arrived quickly. Roberta came down while we were getting ready. She was openly jealous that she couldn't have tea with Jackie, too, but she was nice enough to offer to sit with Jay and Ellie's boys during the visit, which freed Jake and Will for a trip to the rifle range. The guys decided to wait and check out the limo before they left.

Ellie had hairdo patrol and took charge of everyone's hairstyle for the day. She even managed to get some curl out of Karen's poker-straight hair. You have to love that Aqua Net.

Our new outfits, complete with white gloves, were so pretty, freshly ironed, and starched. I wouldn't sit down for fear of wrinkling. "You're gonna have to sit down in the car," Ellie said.

"You can go looking like a refugee from a dryer, but I'm not." I took one last look in the mirror.

We were all ready forty-five minutes before the driver was scheduled to arrive. "You did call and RSVP, didn't you?" Ellie asked.

"No, Ellie, I thought I'd let her guess if we would show up. Of course I did." We were all getting a little more edgy with every passing minute.

"Jake, you have the camera ready?" I checked with Jake for the third time.

"Wow! Get a load of that car!" Karen said, pulling back the homemade red drapes in the living room. We all peered out from behind her to see a long black limousine pull up in front of our little townhouse.

"Geez, Louise!" Ellie said as she peered over my shoulder. We gathered our purses and headed for the door. The neighbors had all stopped dead in their tracks, looking to see what important person was tooling around in their neighborhood. They were even more shocked to see the four of us come out of the house and get in the car. Roberta and her neighbor, Polly, stood next to us on he sidewalk. They were happy to let the rest of the neighbors know what was going on.

The driver wore a black suit and hat and stood holding the door as we all climbed inside. I had only seen these cars on television pulling up at the White House or traveling down the Baltimore-Washington Parkway, certainly not in our neighborhood.

Inside the limo, we all looked around in amazement. Black leather seats, air-conditioning controls, and even a bar! All four of us were speechless as we pointed from one gadget to another. The windows were tinted, and it wasn't long before the girls realized they could make faces at the neighbors without being seen.

The chauffer was very polite but quiet, as I'm sure he wondered what in the world these rednecks were doing in his car. We rode down the familiar streets of our town, leaving Maryland and heading through Southeast DC and right past Mack's Esso station. Ellie and I just looked at each other.

We passed the same boarded-up row houses with waist-high grass and an old liquor store on practically every corner. It amazed me that just a few short miles from here stood the White House and all the monuments that honored our history.

"Look! That's where Grandad works!" Karen pointed out the window. We passed Union Station and drove down Fourteenth Street toward Pennsylvania Avenue.

"Look, Mom! It's the Willard Hotel!" Karen, our little tour guide, pointed out. "Isn't that the hotel that Aunt Frances is named after?"

"Yes, it sure is," I said and stared at the hotel while we sat at the stoplight.

"What's she talking about?" Ellie asked.

I explained to Ellie and Ginger that we'd learned from Jake's aunts that their ancestors were the original owners of the Willard, a famous meeting place for presidents and political powers from around the world since pre–Civil War days and the same place where Julia Ward Howe authored "The Battle Hymn of the Republic."

"Aunt Frances was named after Frances Willard, a famous temperance speaker and sister of the original hotel owners." It was Jake's aunt's theory that someone in our family lost it in a poker game somewhere along the way.

"I knew I was supposed to be born rich or at least marry into money. Jus think about it. I'd be Jackie's next-door neighbor."

"Wow, there's the White House!" Ginger said. We looked across the street to see the white mansion of modern day Camelot.

"And this time, we're going inside instead of just seeing it on the TV," Ellie said. Our little group fell quiet and just a little unnerved as the limo pulled inside the wrought iron gate.

"Girls, remember what we talked about. Don't speak unless spoken to. Mind your manners. 'Please,' and 'thank you' for everything," Emily Post Junior reminded us. The car stopped, and the driver got out and opened our door. We all pulled up our white gloves and straightened our skirts as we exited the limo. We walked up the front steps, and I wasn't sure if it was the chill of the December air or the sight of Jackie and Caroline standing on the front porch that caused my knees to shake.

"Welcome! I'm so glad you could come visit us today," she said in that gracious ladylike tone that was unique to the First Lady, at least in our world. She shook hands with Ellie and me and bent over to hug Ginger and Karen. Caroline stood next to her mom but this time greeted us with a familiar smile, reaching out to shake our hands.

Jackie wore her hair down and tucked under, just like the last time we'd seen her. Her suit was pink with soft orange flowers around the hem. She'd been criticized in the media for mixing pink and orange but at the same time had created a new craze by mixing the two pastels.

"Come on in, ladies. Would you like to take a quick tour before we have tea?" Jackie asked as she turned, indicating that we were to follow.

"We'd love it!" I answered, looking at Ellie for approval. She was too busy gawking at the cathedral ceilings and ornate staircase to care.

As we walked through the lower level of the White House, there were painters and drop cloths along the walls of the Blue Room. They unveiled the presidential seal above the door as we walked past.

"Be careful, ladies. As I'm sure you've heard, we're in the midst of some renovations, and it's easy to mess up your clothes if you don't watch where you're going," Jackie said. The painters continued their work as if they didn't even notice that the queen of the free world just walked by.

I'd seen on the news where she'd begun restoration the day she'd moved into the presidential palace. The media said she'd gone through the budget for the remodeling within weeks of moving in. That hadn't deterred her, as she'd formed the White House Fine Arts Committee of friends that had gone to work raising money for the project. From the looks of things, they had been raising plenty.

"How is the fund raising going?" Ellie asked.

"Oh, quite well. Thank you for asking." That famous Jackie smile swept across her face again. "We are developing a White House guidebook to help raise more money, and people have been so generous donating some of the furnishings." She walked us into the newly renovated Red Room.

The smooth dark-red walls outlined in white were incredible, with paintings hanging on every wall.

"Who's that?" Karen asked, looking at the woman in the painting above the mantle.

"That is Angelica Singleton Van Buren, daughter-in-law of President Martin Van Buren," Jackie answered. "It was painted in 1842."

"Wow, that's old, like my granny's clock," Karen said, and Jackie grinned and continued the tour of the ground level of the White House before taking us to her private residence on the second floor.

"We decorated it in American Empire," she explained, and I nodded like I knew what she was talking about.

I gawked at the chandeliers in Cross Hall, consciously trying to keep my mouth from hanging open. The opulence swallowed me up with sights I'd only read about in the *Style* section of the *Post*.

"I thought it would be nice to have our tea in the Green Room today." She motioned for us to follow her. "It's much cozier, and we just finished the remodeling in there."

The Green Room was just that. Green wallpaper and draperies with white and gold for accents. The tapestry carpet was amazing, almost a starburst effect, and was just daring one of the girls to spill something. The chandelier dazzled as the focal point of the room. Jackie had a right to be proud. I'd seen pictures before, and it had looked like an old tattered parlor. Now it had a taste of elegance.

The girls sat at the table, and we joined Jackie on white sofas facing one another with a table in between. The butler came in on queue and sat the silver teapot and tray on the table alongside the tiered tray of scones and cookies. Together with the pink and white china place settings, it looked like something out of a magazine.

I looked around, and from the faces of Ellie and the girls, I could tell we were all thinking the same thing. Today was a day of firsts, in more ways than one.

"So, girls," Jackie said, addressing Ginger and Karen as she handed each of us our teacups. "What kind of things do you like to do with your summer vacation?" Jackie stood next to their table, looking down on them.

Ginger and Karen looked at each other. Ginger gave Karen an elbow, encouraging her to give the answer.

"We like to go to the beach the best. Ginger and I have an awesome shell collection." Karen looked up into the First Lady's eyes.

"Really, where do you go to enjoy the beach?" she asked as she squatted down to Karen's level. The First Lady squats? Karen looked over at me, hoping for some help.

"We sometimes go to Sandy Point and Chesapeake Beach, which are both on the Chesapeake Bay," I said. "A few times a year, we try to take a trip to Ocean City to enjoy the ocean."

"Mrs. Reilly took me to the beach in Cambridge when I was little." Karen was getting more comfortable and was now on a roll. What happened to my shy little girl?

"That was my favorite beach!" Ginger added.

"Cambridge, Massachusetts?" Jackie asked, eyebrows raised, and looked at Ellie.

"No, Cambridge, Maryland," Ellie answered. "Just over the Chesapeake Bay Bridge going toward Ocean City."

"The Reillys used to live there, and I spent a whole week at their house one time," Karen added, forgetting our "don't speak unless spoken to" rule of the day. "We used to spend the whole day at the beach, playing with all the other kids until it got dark."

Ellie squirmed, and it became evident that she wasn't happy to have her roots exposed (and this time, it wasn't her hair).

"I'm sure it's not as nice as the beaches you are used to," Ellie said. "I've seen the pictures in *Look Magazine*. Nantucket looks wonderful. Not so many people and a lot more private."

"That's true—it's private—but I don't think I've ever seen a beach that wasn't beautiful." Jackie sighed. "But I must say, I do envy you being able to share your lives with strangers and just anyone you choose. Sometimes Nantucket can be too quiet." She had a look in her eyes that suggested just maybe she was a tad bit envious of our freedom, but I was sure that's where any type of envy would have come to a screeching halt.

"Maybe you and Caroline and John-John could come to the beach with us!" Ginger said, and we all smiled, not wanting to burst her bubble.

"Would you like to see Caroline's pony?" Jackie asked, looking at Ginger and Karen.

"Macaroni? Yes, please!" Karen answered, without hesitation. "I've seen him on TV. He looks just like Misty of Chincoteague!" If a horse had four legs, it looked just like Misty to her.

Karen's always loved horses and ponies, ever since she saw *Misty of Chincoteague* at the drive-in with the Reillys in Cambridge. She'd had no chance to be around any horses or ponies other than an occasional ride at the carnival or fair. Even when she was small, I couldn't get past the mechanical pony at the grocery store without giving up a dime.

"So, how do you like having a pony around? Didn't the vice president give that to her?" Ellie asked Jackie.

Being the lady that she was, she just grinned. It was well known that there was very little love lost between her husband and Vice President Johnson.

"Yes, he did, and it was quite a surprise!" Her arm indicated that we should sit down at the table. "I do love horses and riding, but it can be a challenge with little children. Caroline wants to ride all the time, but Macaroni's not always here at the White House." Jackie put her napkin in her lap, and we followed suit. "However, we made sure they brought him here just to meet you ladies."

After the girls had their tea and at least one bite of a sandwich, Jackie suggested that Caroline show the girls her pony, and a lady I assumed was her nanny joined them on the way out the door. Caroline grabbed the nanny's hand.

"Ladies, I'd like to introduce you to Miss Shaw." Jackie nodded in the nanny's direction. "She will look after the girls so we can finish our tea." Ellie and I nodded, and I silently prayed for good behavior, theirs and mine.

"Is it all right if the girls ride Macaroni at little bit after we moms finish our tea?" The girls squealed and lost all self-control at the thought. The strangeness of the First Lady calling herself a mom didn't escape me.

"Can we, Mom?" Karen asked, wide-eyed.

"But you're wearing a dress." The mother in me popped out.

"That's no problem. We have all kinds of extra riding habits," Jackie said. She softly laid her hand on my arm. "If that's okay, I don't mean to be presumptuous." *The First Lady is asking me for permission?*

"No, that's perfectly fine," I assured her, and the girls jumped up and down with excitement. They followed Miss Shaw to go change their clothes.

After tea and scones (I always wondered what they were, and now I knew), we headed down the hallway, the sound of our heels echoed on the marble floors. Jackie opened the door towards the Rose Garden. The girls stood outside the horse trailer as the stable boy walked Macaroni down the ramp. He was a dapple brown on his body with a brown face and black mane.

Miss Shaw walked the girls over to us as they modeled their riding habits.

"What do you think, Mom?" Ginger asked Ellie as she twirled around.

"I think you look like a real equestrian!" Ellie patted her on top of her helmet that crushed her perfectly red curls. So much for Aqua Net.

"They got rid of the stables after President Taft said they were no longer needed," Jackie explained. "I suppose the horseless carriage took over." She stooped down and fastened Caroline's helmet under her chin. "I decided not to ask the committee to try and raise funds for that, so Macaroni lives in his temporary quarters here when he's not at Camp David." She stood and waved her hand letting Caroline know she was free to share her pony with the girls. They ran over to the pony and we followed.

Caroline's shyness left her when she handled Macaroni. Her springer spaniels, Clipper and Pushinka, ran out to greet us. The black-and-white dogs circled and yapped at our heels. Jackie was impressed that we knew the dogs' names.

"Mom and Mrs. Kincaid made us play a White House Concentration game until we knew everything by heart." Ginger ratted us out.

Jackie laughed. "Caroline, why don't you show your friends the best way to ride Macaroni?"

Caroline took charge of her pony, walking him around on the lawn otherwise known as the Rose Garden. Karen and Ginger followed at her side. The stable boy placed a box on the ground. Caroline walked the pony over next to it and stood on the box. "You just put your foot in the stirrup like this and swing your other leg over his back." She demonstrated and ended up on the back of the pony. Caroline circled the Rose Garden and pulled back up next to the box and dismounted. The girls took turns riding as I ran around with my Kodak snapping pictures. Jackie and Ellie walked the perimeter of the grounds.

Caroline coached them as they made beginner mistakes. She came out of her shell, giggling at their novice attempts to ride. It was evident that Macaroni was well trained and used to inexperience riders.

After a half hour or so, the girls went back to the dressing room with Miss Shaw and put their Sunday best back on. We walked back inside and continued our tour. Jackie was the master of small talk and made me feel comfortable in the unusual surroundings and almost made me forget I was in the White House.

Almost, except for the fancy dishes and lacy cloth napkins. Almost, except for the manicured lawn and white marble surroundings. Almost, except for everything I laid my eyes on.

"You ladies are doing such a wonderful job raising your girls," Jackie said.

"Why, thank you. It's a challenge sometimes, as I'm sure you know," I said.

"We've thought about getting jobs to help out with finances, but when you weigh the pros and cons, staying home with them seems to win out." Ellie said. She pulled out a comb and ran it through Ginger's hair trying to bring back the curls.

"I couldn't agree more. If you bungle raising your children, I don't think whatever else you do well matters very much," Jackie said. "I've always said I'll be a wife and mother first, then First Lady when there's time."

"Yeah, and Mom's having another baby too!" Ginger said. Ellie's shoulders drooped.

Jackie's eyes lit up. "That's marvelous, Ellie!" she said.

"Well, I wasn't so sure about that at first, but I'm getting used to the idea." Ellie looked at the First Lady.

"I know what you mean." Jackie walked over and gave Ellie a hug. "Sometimes the surprises life dishes out to us turn out to be the best blessings ever."

"Yeah, and maybe I'll get a little sister!" Ginger said.

"Daddy!" We all looked her way as Caroline squealed and ran toward a man in a suit standing in the doorway. He stooped down, and she ran into his arms. "When did you get home?" Boy, Jake doesn't get quite the ovation that Caroline's daddy does, but then again, he's home a lot more.

"Just a few minutes ago, Pumpkin." The handsome man looked our way.

Jackie stood up and walked over to the president.

"Holy cow, it's him!" Ellie blurted out. Jackie pretended not to hear. What a lady. *She must be wondering what rock she found us under.* Jackie hugged the president and turned back to us to make the introductions.

"Ladies, I'd like to introduce you to my husband, Jack."

Ellie and I just stood there, forgetting all our Emily Post lessons.

Ginger bailed us out. "How do you do, Mr. President?" she said out of nowhere. *Who is this kid anyhow?* She shook his hand and then curtsied, her crown of red curls bouncing. Well, the rest of us cracked under the pressure, but Ginger had saved the day doing a great imitation of a well-bred DC suburbanite. Maybe we had a few silver spoons hidden in the kitchen drawers after all.

"I'm doing very well now that I'm home and find the house filled with beautiful women." His blue eyes twinkled.

The rest of us shook his hand and blushed. My heart pounded so hard I was afraid it showed.

"So, you're the ladies who saved my damsel in distress at the shopping center." We all nodded like mute bobblehead dolls.

"Well, I know you all are anxious to have your family time together. I think we'd better be going now," I said, not knowing a better way to make a graceful exit.

"It has certainly been a pleasure getting to know you ladies better. Perhaps we can do this again sometime," Jackie said, letting us know in a polite way that the tea party was over.

"That would be wonderful," Ellie answered, with a twinkle in her eye. Oh no, there's that look. Knowing her as I did, I knew she was up to something; I just didn't know what.

I tried to look at the president when he wasn't looking at me, hoping he didn't notice the stare, but I supposed he was used to that. He seemed even more presidential in person, yet normal. He wore a suit, and that I wasn't used to. Jake was a "blue-collar" worker. The only time Jake wore a suit was when we dug it out of the closet and dusted it off for a wedding or funeral. It was obvious that the president was glad to be home, if you could call this castle a "home."

We said our good-byes, shaking hands, and Jackie stooped down to kiss Ginger and Karen on the cheek. Our chauffer was waiting for us. We slowly piled back into the big black limousine again, trying our best to prolong the visit. We just stared out the tinted windows, watching the White House fade in the distance.

Breaking the silence, in all seriousness, Ellie looked at me and asked, "Do you think I should give this back?" She pulled a shiny black object out of her purse.

"What in the world is that?" I asked, realizing that she'd lifted it from Camelot.

"It's a paperweight. It says '1600 Pennsylvania Avenue' on the top," she said.

"Ellie, I can't believe you stole a paperweight!" I whispered, trying not to let the girls hear. I was mortified, at least at first.

"Well, I did get two, one for me and one for you," she whispered back as she reached in her purse and pulled out a replica of the first.

"Give me that!" I grabbed my stolen treasure from Ellie's hand, and after a quick exam, put it in my purse, pretending to be interested in looking out the window. I don't think Emily Post would approve. Maybe this was how Ma Barker got started. Stealing from Camelot—well, we might as well start big.

CHAPTER 4

Ellie
Break It to Me Gently

I have a dream that one day this nation will rise up and live out the true meaning of its creed: 'We hold these truths to be self-evident, that all men are created equal.'

—*Martin Luther King Jr.*

*I*t's hard to believe I've been back on this side of the bridge for more than two years already. I try to say a little prayer of thanks every day for my being back in civilization, whether I'm on my knees or not…

Call it superstition, call it being religious—doesn't matter to me—but I'm convinced that prayer works, and when I'm on my knees, it works even better. I'm not a churchgoer. I figure Will does enough of that for both of us, but I know God's around. I can "feel" Him, know what I mean? Watching a seagull soar over the water or a baby grab onto your finger. There's no denying a presence greater than me. I can create lots of things—candles, clothes, and a good casserole—but when it comes to the real thing, that's His gig.

Who would've believed we would end up at the White House for even the guided tour, let alone a tea party?

I loved being back on the Western Shore; although, I must admit, I missed living near the water, and not to mention living with Will full-time could be more than I bargained for.

Visit the Stuck in the
Onesies Facebook page!

Diana McDonough

Stuck in the Onesies

Diana McDonough

Sign up for Diana's blog at
www.dianamcdonough.com and
receive updates on the sequel to
"Stuck in the Onesies."

Please leave a customer review on
Amazon (even if you didn't buy it
there) when you finish reading
"Stuck in the Onesies."

I hope you enjoy reading "Stuck in the Onesies" as much as I did writing it. I sure do miss those characters. If you find you come to love Barb and Ellie as much as I think you will, please take a moment and leave a review on Amazon after you've read the book. Just go to www.amazon.com, search "Stuck in the Onesies" and drill into the book. Tap "Customer Reviews" and then "Leave a Customer Review." Reviews help SITO to gain more exposure. Thanks in advance for your support!

Don't miss the sequel to "Stuck in the Onesies." Sign up for Diana's blog and receive updates at www.dianamcdonough.com.

We lived at least an hour from the nearest coastline—saltwater coastline anyway—pools, and rivers notwithstanding. The Chesapeake Bay has a few little beaches we like to haunt, and Barb and I took the kids every chance we got. It was a carload of kids, food, and all the fun we could handle.

Having a good friend like Barb has been the best gift a girl could ever want, other than a big diamond, of course, but let's face it, that's more than a prayer away.

Money is our biggest issue. Will was always saying we can't afford this, we can't afford that, but I'd have to be a moron not to see that there are always funds available when he wants something.

He's such a cheapskate that when he and Jake discovered they'd save five bucks a month if they shared a checking account, they decided to pool their resources. I thought Barb was going to blow a fuse. Every month the guys get together to reconcile the account and figure out how much money is left and whom it belongs to.

After listening to their arguing during their monthly reconciliations, Barb and I finally wised up and just made that our girls' night. Those two are like two little old men. At first, I thought it would be worth the five bucks to be done with the wailing and gnashing of teeth every month, but I'd pay ten to keep our girls' night out going. Whatever he saves, I spend on my night out. Makes sense, right?

Miser is Will's middle name, and he lives up to it by squirreling away money until he finds a perk he can't live without. It made no sense that we were the first family in Radiant Valley to own a color television, the family with four kids and holes in their shoes. It just didn't add up when there was "no money in the budget" for a tent or bikes for the kids but plenty for him to watch the NBC peacock in living color, not to mention *Bonanza*. But now that I've had time to think about it, Little Joe's blue eyes do look kinda nice…

Barb and I still babysit for our mad money. Getting a job at this point doesn't make sense when we factor in the cost of a sitter. I'm still the world's worst when it comes to saving money though. There's always something on a shelf somewhere calling my name.

The kids are growing up so fast. Ginger and Karen are inseparable, and Scott's mission in life is to torment them at every opportunity, but the girls have learned to hold their own with him.

"Here's your milk," I said to Scott as he grabbed his sandwich with his left hand and took the milk with his right.

"Thanks," he said and headed toward his seat in the dining room. Ginger and Karen walked in. Karen carried her baton in one hand, and he sneered at her.

"Watch out, Mom, she'll hit you over the head with that weapon if you cross her," he said.

He went to sit down at the dining room table, still holding the sandwich in one hand and the glass of milk in the other.

Karen reached behind him and slid his chair back as he went to sit down. He missed the chair and landed on the floor.

"Geez oh flip!" I gasped, and the girls broke into laughter. He'd plopped onto the floor, the sandwich had flown to the other side of the room, but he'd managed to hold the glass upright and not spill the milk. Charlie Brown was on top of his game and gobbled up the baloney and cheese sandwich.

Scott looked around and tried to figure out how he'd missed his target. Once he realized he'd been had, he struggled to his feet. The girls stopped laughing and exited stage right, shrieking as they ran out the door and down the street. Roger just watched from the other room, smarter than to get involved.

And so it goes.

Living full-time with Will has its ups and downs. Let's leave the ups out of it, mostly because I can't remember any. Sometimes I can't believe I married him, but the babies just keep on coming. So, what's a girl to do? Have another brownie.

I do like sex though. I think if it hadn't been for that, I would have had to leave. He can be so mean with the things he says; it really cuts to the core of me. Then he'll come back later and act like nothing happened. It isn't hard to figure out that he thinks he's smarter than me, and maybe he is, but I've found ways to survive despite this lousy relationship.

Oh yeah, did I mention I'm pregnant?

"How'd you let that happen?" Will asked when I broke the news.

"Gee, let me think." I rolled my eyes.

"How are we going to afford another kid, Ellie?" he asked. My heart hit the floor, and I just stared at him. He turned and walked out of the bedroom and back to his *Washington Post* in the living room. I sat down on the edge of the bed and the loneliness that always sat in the back of my bus threatened to move to the front seat again.

Ginger came out of her bedroom and saw me sitting there.

"Hey, Mom. Can we join the pool this summer?" she asked. I gathered my composure as quick as I could. Doctor bills trump pool memberships.

"I don't know, hon. It costs a lot of money, you know," I said.

"Yeah, I know, but Tammy's going to join, and if she's at the pool all the time, who will I hang out with?" Oh, to have the problems of a ten-year-old again.

"Well, we'll do our best, how about that?" I grabbed her hand, and she sat down next to me. "Guess what?"

"What" she asked.

"We're going to have a new baby."

Her eyes flew open. "Wow! Really?"

"Yep, how do you feel about that?"

"It's great! Tammy had a new little sister last year, and she got to feed her all the time."

I hadn't had time to think that Ginger might actually be some help this time. This might just work out after all.

"That would be awesome if you would help me out like that."

"And I won't be the youngest anymore either." She pulled her feet up on the bed and laid her head in my lap. I stroked her red-almost-auburn hair and leaned down and planted a kiss. What is it about kids that enable them to set you straight when you're feeling all crooked?

Yep, number four is on his or her little way. I've decided a summer baby is a good thing. I won't have to worry about wrapping the little bundle of joy up to hit a sale. The somewhat suicidal thoughts subsided once Ginger set me straight, but the thought of putting off my job-seeking plans still haunted me.

It looked like Barb will beat me to the first real paycheck and I was still stuck in the onesies on this one. Maybe I should just join that new organization, the Peace Corps, and see the world. Wonder if they take kids instead of extra baggage, or maybe that's one in the same.

Jackie was right with what she said about raising kids, but I've decided she didn't have all the facts. Let's face it, we're not all able to live in the White House with butlers and nannies to pick up the slack. A dual-income household sometimes has to be in the cards if you want to do anything other than watch soap operas and raise the next-door neighbor's kids for cash.

"What kind of job do you want to get?" I asked Barb over the phone while we both stirred our respective pots on our stoves.

"It doesn't matter, just one that keeps me off my feet, pays well, and is only part time."

"I think prostitution is still illegal, sweetie."

"Now sex for pay, that's a novel idea. But come to think of it, Jake's been 'paying' for years; it just hasn't dawned on him. I need to raise my rates though." Barb laughed.

The guys run a little electrical side business and work lots of weekends. When they aren't doing that, they're most likely at the rifle range or heading to a Redskins game on Sundays.

Barb and I made a day trip with the kids to Ocean City, Maryland, last summer. We left the house at 6:00 a.m. and were on the beach by ten o'clock (allowing time for a few wrong turns). It was great; the water wasn't too rough, and I rode the canvas raft all day. We parked in the inlet parking lot, and the kids enjoyed a few rides on the boardwalk. We treated ourselves to some Thrasher's french fries, and the kids all had soft ice cream. Comatose and ready to puke, we loaded everyone back into Betsy.

We decided to figure out a way that we could take the kids down for an entire week. We knew there was no way we could afford a hotel or apartment, but someone on the boardwalk had filled us in on a campground on the beach that wasn't too far away. Before we headed home, we turned left off of Route 50 and headed down to Assateague Island.

We drove over the bridge that crossed the water to the barrier island. Ponies that lived on the island grazed in the salt grasses, and the blue sky and sand dunes made us gasp. The arthritic arch of the treetops showed the footprint left behind by Old Man Winter.

"Wow," was all I could say.

"Yeah, it's pretty here," Barb said.

"Look at the ponies!" Ginger said.

"And the water," Karen said.

The campground consisted of tents and campers, the pull-behind and drive-it-yourself models. Since a camper was not in the budget, it looked like we'd be members of the tent community. We headed toward home and made plans along the way.

Barb and I decided we'd buy a big tent together. The way we figured it, we could afford to take the kids to the beach for a week or two in the summer.

Now several months later, with my new baby on the horizon, I was having second thoughts but didn't let on.

"Ellie, I don't know if I can go camping," Barb said, looking at me out of the corner of her eye. We'd pulled into the drive-in part of the Hot Shoppe restaurant in the plaza parking lot on our way home from a bingo game. I rolled down my window and pushed in the little black button on the gray speaker hanging next to the menu sign.

"What do you mean you can't go? Jake's got no problem with it," I said, eyebrows raised. "And if I can take an infant, you can surely deal with a little dirt!"

"El, I can't stand to have dirty hands, and camping means getting dirty from head to toe, and then there are the bugs. I just don't know if I can do it for a whole week. You know I can't stand getting dirty." She threw her head back and stared at the ceiling.

"Barb, we're not going to camp in dirt, remember? Assateague Island is just that, an island. No dirt, just sand. Sand isn't so bad." I tried to sound like I believed it, too. I knew that without camping, our having an entire week at the beach wasn't going to happen.

"Well, maybe," she faltered.

"Really, think of sand as 'happy dirt.' The wash and wear kind. Looks like dirt, acts like dirt, gets on you, but doesn't stick like dirt!" I was on a roll now. I hit the speaker button again and turned up the volume, thinking I just didn't hear them answer me the first time.

"Well, I guess you're right. Sand isn't quite as bad when I think about it, but what about the bugs?" She pulled out her purse. "I'll have a Mighty Mo, onion rings, and a Pepsi." She pulled out two dollars.

"Yeah, if they ever decide to answer us." I hit the button again, this time a little harder.

"Can I take your order?" the garbled loud speaker screamed at full volume, sounding like someone just stepped on a monster's toe. I screamed and threw my hands in the air, dropping all the money on Betsy's front seat and floor.

Barb jumped, and her head almost hit the ceiling of the car. We both looked at each other and started laughing.

"Can I take your order?" the grainy loudspeaker repeated when I reached over and lowered the volume. We just kept on giggling.

"You should've seen—" I pointed at her face.

"Yeah, well, you acted like someone was gonna reach out of that speaker and grab you by the neck!" The sound of roller skates on concrete brought us to our semi-senses, as two skate-clad waitresses appeared to find out what was going on.

They looked at us two "old ladies," whispered, and shook their heads. When we realized they were waiting for us, we straightened up and gave them the order in person.

"Two Mighty Mos, one onion ring, one french fry, and two Pepsis, please," I said to the blonde after I had tried to explain what happened, and they disappeared on their skates back into the kitchen. Munching on Mighty Mos in the front seat, nothing better.

I walked in the living room as Jack Paar finished up his monologue on Will's color television. The kids slept in various positions on the couch and floor, and Will sat with his legs propped up in his recliner.

"Hey, have fun?" he asked.

"Yeah, didn't win though." I lifted Scott's legs up from the couch and sat down, laying his feet on my protruding tummy.

"Jake and I were talking about us all taking a vacation together this summer."

"Really?" I was stunned as he filled me in on their plan.

I'm sure it was no coincidence that when I started talking about buying a tent and taking the kids to Ocean City, Will started throwing the word vacation around. Of course, it was in conjunction with a rifle match, but I'm all for it if there's sand and water in the mix.

He went on to explain that the National Rifle Matches were at Camp Perry, Ohio, an army base right on Lake Erie. We'd go and rent a little cabin (otherwise known as unoccupied barracks belonging to deployed soldiers now in Vietnam, no doubt) and Barb and I could go to the beach with the kids during the day while the guys went to their matches. As long as he was buying and Barb was going, I decided I was in. Before the next commercial, Will was asleep in his recliner. I covered the kids up with my crocheted Afghans, turned off the TV, and headed to bed.

Before my first cup of coffee, Sylvia showed up for her Saturday morning care-package delivery.

"Well, Ellie, it looks like you've put on a few pounds. You must be eating all these goodies I bring over all by yourself." What a gal.

"Sylvia, even I couldn't eat that junk. What day-old bakery did you buy them from anyway?" Time for the one-two punch, but I was still in denial and couldn't drop the "I'm pregnant with baby number four" bomb quite yet, so I just stood there.

It was enough to shut the old broad up. She crossed her arms, harrumphed, and exited stage right. Just can't figure out why the two of us don't get along. Why did we have to tell her we moved back here anyway? Too bad she left so soon; I was looking forward to making Will tell her that I was pregnant again. I think every time she thought she could have her little boy back, the rabbit would die again. Just call me the "rabbit slayer." Elmer Fudd and me.

Summer in DC is a hot, humid, and miserable experience. It's the only time of year that I remotely miss Cambridge, or more specifically, our little beach. The poor kids resort to playing in the sprinkler in the backyard. I had the pool membership on the top of my wish list but couldn't get Will to bite. He wouldn't go to the pool if we did join, so he doesn't see the need.

I'd started saving money to buy the membership myself, and for someone with a perpetual hole in her pocket, it's quite an accomplishment for me. I've never saved a dime in my life. Summer will be half over before I have enough, but what the heck.

I've gained forty pounds with this pregnancy, and unless I give birth to a thirty-pound bundle of joy, the excess weight will still be here after he or she pops out. Guess I should skip the Mighty Mo next time—or not.

It was a hot, sticky afternoon, and I was desperate for some air conditioning that worked. My stomach was huge with this baby, and my feet were swollen to the point of ridiculous.

"Come on, let's go to Super Giant and go shopping. At least it's air conditioned there," Barb said, probably tired of my whining by now. Money or no money in my pocket, I was ready to escape for a few hours.

I did some grocery shopping, and after we'd stowed the bags away in Betsy, we headed for home. Ginger and Karen joined the radio with their rendition of "Doo-Wah-Diddy." "There she was, just a-walking down the street singing, 'Doo-wah-diddy-diddy-dum-diddy-doo!'"

I made my normal U-turn on Defense Highway and reached down to push the button on Betsy's console for the three-point turn. Her gearshift wasn't the normal stick that came out from the steering wheel column. She had these big buttons on the console for park, reverse, and drive. Whenever I would shift gears, I'd just reach down and push in the correct button. Most of the time.

I went to hit the button and couldn't believe my eyes. When Betsy just sat there, I looked at the gearshift to see what was wrong, only to see nothing but four empty holes. I'm not kidding; they disappeared, went away, hocus-pocus, see ya later, vanished.

"Geez oh flip, the button's gone!" I stared down at the console.

There we were, stuck in the middle of the median during rush hour. The doo-wah-diddying in the backseat stopped.

"Now's not the time to be worrying about your wardrobe, Ellie. There's cars coming, and this is my bleeding side," she said as the oncoming traffic headed for her door.

"No, the gear shift button's gone. Look." There were four holes bigger than life in the middle of the console.

"Holy crap. What'd you do?" Barb's eyes were popping out of her head as she looked down at the console and back up again at the oncoming traffic.

"Nothing, just hit the button like always. You think those cars will stop?"

"Geez, I hope so."

We were the cause of a major traffic jam, and it must have been all those dirty looks and shaking heads that threw the bad karma our way. If it did, I was doomed for at least the next five years or so. The cops came and called a tow truck. They seemed pretty annoyed with us. We must have interrupted their coffee break.

"Mom, you peed your pants!" Ginger laughed and pointed at me. I looked down, and sure enough, I was standing in a puddle, but it wasn't pee, not this time.

"Oh crap, Barb, my water broke!"

This wasn't good. I could cook dinner for five in less time than it took for me to pop out a bundle of joy. By the time I explained that I'd not peed my pants, Barb was already bringing the craggy cop up to speed.

"You'd better put her in that cruiser and get moving. This is number four, and that's her lucky number."

"Oh no! I need to push!" I knew it was too soon for that, unless I wanted Barb to tie off the cord with her new scarf she'd bought that afternoon. "I'll just sit here and squeeze my legs together." I sank to the curb.

"You should've done that nine months ago." Barb tried to make me smile, and I managed a grin. She was having trouble getting the Menace, a.k.a. Jay, to sit still curbside.

"Geez, Barb," I said between contractions. "Go ahead, let him play in the traffic. How many chances you think he'll get to have four lanes at one time?" I did a nice imitation of a smile, but a contraction-induced grimace took over.

"Well, I just hope he makes it to lane number two," she hollered as the cars and trucks kept whizzing by. She kept her left hand firmly planted on his arm and her right on mine. Like I was going somewhere.

Karen and Ginger were busy flirting with the boys in the parking lot of the nursery across the way. Cute, lots of sweat, lots of dirt. Just what girls like. No need to worry about them. They weren't about to go anywhere.

Officer Lackey looked up with eyebrows raised and picked up his radio and called for help. I don't think he wanted me leaking in the back of his cruiser. We waited for what seemed like forever.

"Look, here comes an ambulance." Karen pointed down the shoulder of the highway. The tow truck was right behind it.

"I can't believe they called an ambulance. All I need is a ride. Can't they just hook Betsy to the tow truck and we can all go together?" All of a sudden, I was scared. I didn't know if it was the sight of an ambulance at my service, or what. My stomach did a flip-flop or two, feeling like butterflies trying to get out.

"Barb, tell them you and the kids have to go with me. I can't get in that thing alone."

"El, think of it as a private limo." She put her arm across my shoulders and leaned forward to look me in the eye. "There's not enough room for all of us." But the look in my eyes must have told her I wasn't joking. I sank back down to the curb as the contraction doubled me over. She must have done some incredible double-talking.

The next thing I remembered was lying on a stretcher with Barb, Ginger, Karen, and Jay crowded around me inside the ambulance. Karen and Ginger took control of Jay. That was a full-time job just keeping his hands off the tubes and shiny instruments. Oh, the shiny instruments.

It was a good thing that Prince George's Hospital was only a five-minute ride in an ambulance. Lucky for me and lucky for the ambulance attendant who quickly figured out that it took more than five people to entertain Jay for very long. Once we pulled up and they wheeled me in on the stretcher, I could feel the baby's head peeking out. Yep, dinner would've been ready by now.

"Geez oh flip!" I lifted my head and looked down toward the bottom of the stretcher. "It's coming!"

"Get her to number five." The ER nurse ran my way, but my body couldn't hold the baby back any longer.

"You girls take Jay to the waiting room and stay put. I'll be right back," Barb instructed. The nurse took one look under the sheet and rushed back over to the desk, barking more orders.

"Barb, you'd better catch him!" I leaned up and pulled down the sheet to see for myself. Never mind that there was a host of onlookers getting a look at me.

Barb moved to the end of the stretcher and caught the little guy's head as he popped out.

"Somebody get over here! This kid's trying to make a swan dive off the bed!" she hollered. The nurse came over and with one more push, the black-haired, brown-eyed Italian Will clone greeted us with a serious howl. I looked up to see Karen and Ginger standing there with eyes as big as Peppermint Patties.

"Where's Jay?" Barb remembered. I glanced over to see the little guy shrunk down in a waiting room chair, scared by all the confusion.

The nurses whisked the baby off to the nursery and wheeled me away for the cleanup. Boy, could I use a nap. I had to admit, I was looking forward to a few days of having my meals brought to me on a tray and no piles of laundry that called my name.

We named baby number four after Will, William Reilly. I'd managed to avoid the "junior" thing with Scott and Roger, but Will's on this namesake kick. The poor kid would have to go by William to save the confusion 'cause I refused to saddle one of my kids with the name "Junior."

Betsy had to get a new transmission, and there went any thought of Will helping with the pool membership. I wasn't telling him about the money I have saved up. He'd just have to fork over the dough for Betsy's overhaul or let me drive the Cadillac. Donkeys would fly first. Did I tell you about his Cadillac?

William's not a good baby, but he isn't bad, not a crier like Jay was, but he's no sleeper either. I guess I was due since the others were so easy, but that philosophy doesn't do anything to fill in for the lack of sleep. Sleeper babies are great because you tend to think life is normal when the little guy is zonked out for hours at a time. William's a clingy little fellow and likes to nurse and nurse and nurse. Barb's still trying to talk me into bottle feeding, but to tell you the truth, I'm too lazy to deal with sterilizing all that stuff, and Will is definitely too cheap to fork over the money for formula.

"Why buy cans of milk when Ellie can crank it out for free?" he says to anyone who will listen. I'm thinking of pumping some out just to serve up with his Cheerios.

The kids are turning out to be a big help. I've decided that Ginger's old enough to babysit while Will watches TV, so Barb and I ducked out the door to the bingo hall for a girls' night out. Barb loved the gambling part of it, and I was excited just to get out of the house to somewhere besides a grocery store for a few hours.

"I can't believe Marilyn Monroe is gone!" Barb whined when she slid onto Betsy's front seat.

"I know. They say it was suicide. Hard to believe." I shook my head. Rumors of an affair between her and JFK still persisted. We'd enjoyed her movies and watched our husbands drool through *Some Like It Hot* and *The Seven Year Itch*. I supposed Will was gonna have to look for another hot blonde to fantasize about.

"Yeah, and now Johnny Carson's gonna take over for Jack Paar on *The Tonight Show*," Barb whined again. "Our world as we know it sure is changing, El."

We sat down with our bingo cards and plaster ice chips. Man, some of these people are serious about their bingo with their lucky charms and trolls lined up on the table in front of them. "I pity the fool who knocks one over." I elbowed Barb and nodded toward the troll table.

Barb giggled in response. "Should've brought my Campbell's soup cans." She'd been making fun of Andy Warhol's latest pop art craze all day. "If Andy can make all that money with a soup can label, maybe I can start a craze. I could keep my chips in the can for starters." I shook my head.

"I just hope you rinse them out first." I spread out my cards on the table, thinking a soup can would've worked well for a chip holder after all.

The games began, and I started putting my chips on the corresponding square. The evening wore on, and we hadn't won a game.

"If that lady wins one more time..." Barb complained about the lucky charm lady. It was the last game of the night, and the big cash prize was a hundred dollars. I was getting antsy, as I only needed B14 to win, and can you believe it? Bingo Man called my number!

"Bingo!" I hollered. "I can't believe it. Geez oh flip! Did I win?"

"You better have. I just cleared my card." Barb nudged me with her elbow.

Bingo Man read off my numbers. "B14, I25…"

Boy, the bad karma that gets thrown your way when you win a bingo game. I could feel the stares in the back of my head as my blue-haired competitors hoped I'd screwed up, but sorry to disappoint you, girls; I cashed in on the big game, and our pool membership just became a reality.

CHAPTER 5

Barb
Can't Get Used to Losing You

Don't let it be forgot, that once there was a spot, for one brief shining
moment, that was known as Camelot.

—Lerner and Loewe's *Camelot*

*L*iving in the shadow of Washington, DC, all my life had been my normal. Being the daughter of an Alabamian southern belle mother and
Georgia-born father instilled certain opinions in me. It wasn't until I met Ellie
that I realized that a colored person's "normal" was quite different from mine.
It was one of her missions in life to convince me that that wasn't necessarily a
good thing.

I looked out the living room window and noticed Jake was home from work,
standing on the sidewalk talking to Ted, our neighbor. I opened the storm door
and walked down the steps, crossed my arms, and tried to shake off the slight
October chill in the air.

"Yeah, he's got them pointed in our direction, that's for sure," Jake said to
Ted.

"How do we know that?" Ted asked.

"They're flying planes over Cuba every day, and don't worry; they just
know."

Jake had a tendency to get a little worked up over political stuff, but this
Castro thing really had his attention. I guess it came from working at the Naval

Ordinance Laboratory. He heard all the scuttlebutt from his fellow federal government coworkers. The government's heightened concern for the possibility of war due to the Russians planting missile sites in Cuba could prove to be enough to put him right over the top.

"Yeah, Jake's got the basement stocked with canned food and jugs of drinking water," I said and kissed him on the cheek. "I think it's the first time Jake's ever darkened the door of a grocery store." He draped his arm over my shoulder. "We've got walls and walls of canned corned beef hash, fruit cocktail, and tomatoes. Hey, as long as you have tomatoes, you've got a meal."

"Well, speaking of which, what's for dinner, hon?" Jake pulled me toward him. Man's gotta claim his woman, you know, mark his territory. With the promise of meat loaf, I was able to lure his attentions back toward the house and dinner. We said our good-byes to Ted as his kids rode up on their bikes.

For almost a week, Jake wouldn't let the kids play anywhere other than our own yard. The other neighborhood kids had to come to our house. He kept the news on day in and day out. I joked about setting a place at the table for Walter Cronkite.

With the construction of missiles within Cuba's borders, the politicians thought the communists were within striking distance of the nation's capital, and we were only a few short miles from there. If the bomb fell short, we'd be toast.

It wasn't until Jake was satisfied that the crisis was over that we were allowed to go back to our normal routine. Whew, a week of Jay confined to the yard; I was beginning to dream of sending a few missiles toward Castro myself if he didn't back off soon.

When you have kids, you have a built-in yardstick to measure the years as they go by. Birthdays, Christmas, Easter, walking among the cherry blossoms in DC, and summer days at the pool and beach came and went over and over, and before I knew it, August was here, and both my kids would soon be in school.

Ellie and I walked through Hecht's toward the elevator to the bargain basement. There were several black-and-white televisions turned on, but we gathered around the lone color TV in the electronics department, and the March on Washington was in full swing. They were expecting a quarter of a million people in town.

"I thought that would be over by now," I said. "We could get caught in major traffic going home," I mused, forever the optimist.

Martin Luther King walked up to the podium and began to speak. The crowd erupted. We stood and listened. I knew Walter Cronkite would give me a recap on the evening news, but I couldn't bring myself to leave. Fifteen minutes later, he was almost finished. "Even though we face the difficulties of today and tomorrow, I still have a dream," MLK went on as the crowd erupted again.

I didn't know what to think. I was torn between two worlds; the southern one I'd grown up with and the one that my heart told me was right. "Why does he have to sound so angry all the time?" I asked Ellie.

"I don't think it's anger so much. Kinda like the Baptist preacher that he is, he's just passionate about what he believes," she answered. "Ever heard one of those guys preach?" I shook my head as others gathered around the TV with us. When he finished, the crowd dispersed, and we caught the elevator to the basement for back-to-school shopping.

We rummaged through the sale bins and racks in our usual fashion.

"Whadya think?" Ellie asked. She held up a pink dress with flowing sleeves lined with sequins.

"I think Ginger would look kinda weird showing up to school in that," I answered, knowing that it was for her and not Ginger. She frowned, not seeing the humor in my sarcasm. Imagine.

"Actually, I think it's really pretty." I tried to redeem myself. "Looks like you're set for the gig in Atlantic City!" She tried it on, and the dress was perfect.

"I love the sleeves," El said as she held up her arm. It flared out at the elbow.

"I do too. You gotta get it!"

She did. We finished up, making sure all the kids had what they needed to start the school year.

"Guess you're right again," El said as I lit up yet another cigarette. We were now stuck in traffic on the beltway as the busloads of people from DC left the March on Washington. Bus after bus pulled onto Route 50 from New York Avenue in a slow crawl.

"Yeah, well this time I wish I wasn't," I admitted. "Jake's gonna be starved by the time I get home, and I haven't even thought about dinner." Then I remembered she'd been reading some women's libber book, *The Feminine Mystique*.

"Did you finish that book yet?"

"Nope, not yet." She put her turn signal on and squeezed into the left lane to let another bus in. "Some of what she says makes sense, but I gotta tell ya," she said as she giggled and shook her head, "chapter 11 talks about how housewives often seek validation in sex. She says that by doing that, we open ourselves to affairs by both partners."

"Doesn't add up to me." I blew the smoke out the cracked window. "Guess I'll have to be satisfied living here in the onesies."

"Yeah, I think we should leave 'validation' up to meter maids." She held up the parking ticket she'd just been awarded. "They're pretty good at what they do!"

The kids went back to school, and we gravitated back to the schedule of PTA, field trips, homework, and making cupcakes for classroom parties.

Karen flourished, and several of her teachers were impressed with her abilities. That plus the fact that she was so easygoing and never disrupted class put her in the front running for teacher's pet every year. My birthday had come and gone, and yes, I turned twenty-six. How did I get this old?

It was Friday, and I'd just coaxed Jay down for his nap and had settled on the couch to watch *Search for Tomorrow* and *The Guiding Light*. I turned the knob on the television and flipped to channel 4, but instead of learning what was up with Meta and Trudy, Walter Cronkite showed up. Not a good sign.

"Oh man! What now?" I said out loud. I wasn't happy that my soap was delayed, and I'd probably end up missing the showdown between my soap-sisters. Ellie and I had a bet as to what was going to happen that day, but it looked like we were going to have to wait, unless Cronkite got short-winded.

"Once again, ladies and gentlemen, in case you just tuned in..." The newscaster went on, and the phone rang.

I dragged myself off the couch and walked in the kitchen to pick up. I wondered who it could be because anyone that knew me knew better than to call during that one half hour on a weekday.

I picked up the wall phone receiver and checked out the nail I'd broken earlier in the morning.

"Hello," I said, running my finger over the ragged edge of my nail.

"Barb, is that you?" Jake asked. Knowing how unusual it was for him to call me in the middle of the workday, I frowned and looked away from my nail to Karen's spelling test that was stuck to the refrigerator with a bright red "100 percent" and a gold star posted on it.

"What's wrong, Jake?"

"Have you heard about Kennedy yet?"

"Heard what?"

"He was assassinated in Dallas this morning."

"What?" Assassinated? Doesn't that mean dead?

"He was in a parade, and someone shot him. They took him to the hospital, but he didn't make it."

I sat staring at my chipped nail's reflection in the toaster. My stomach hurt. My thoughts turned to Jackie as if we were on a first-name basis or something...

"Barb, hon, are you there?"

"Yeah, yeah, I'm here." I shook my head as if that would help me understand. "When did it happen? How'd you hear about it?" The questions kept coming out without waiting for answers. I walked back and forth in the kitchen, pacing and staring at the floor. There was a fresh spill of red Kool-Aid, but I just stared at it.

"Turn on the television. Hey, I'm sorry, but my phone's ringing again. I'll let you go. Call me later."

"Okay," I answered, not knowing what else to say except that I added, "I love you."

My thoughts turned to Jackie, and tears slid down my cheeks.

"I love you too, babe." Jake hung up. I sat there for a moment listening to the phone dial tone in the background, and then gathered my senses and hurried back in the living room.

I watched the horrible scene over and over again as Walter Cronkite narrated. He was having an awful time reporting the unthinkable. The tape showed the president slumping over into Jackie's lap.

Someone had shot him in Dallas, and he slumped into Jackie's lap. I'd never seen anyone get shot before, let alone killed, and here it was, someone I knew and had grown to love. Poor Jackie. What in the world was going on?

After I watched the horrible scene over and over again on the television, I picked up the phone to call Ellie.

She was crying on the other end, and we tried to talk, but neither of us made much sense.

"I need to go get Karen. She's gonna be in a tailspin when she hears the news," I said as soon as the thought touched my head.

I hung up the phone and ran upstairs to wake Jay, realizing at the same time that this was a first. I'd never intentionally awakened him from a nap. But this was evidently a day of firsts.

"We need to go to the school and pick up Karen," I explained to him as he rubbed his eyes, confused. I scooped him up, and we headed downstairs and out the door.

I held his hand, and we walked to the school, or should I say, I dragged him as I walked as fast as his little feet would take us. We found the front office and requested permission to take Karen home early. It turned out I wasn't the only parent concerned for their kid that day. There was a line of ten people in front of me, afraid of what might happen next.

Karen walked in and her eyes were red from crying. She ran to me and wrapped her arms around my hips. I bent over, stroked her head, and held her close. She pulled away and looked up at me.

"Mom, why'd that man kill Caroline's dad?" Today, we didn't think of him as the president of the United States but the father of her little friend who lived in a big white house and rode a pony in her backyard.

"I don't know, honey," I choked and crouched down to look her in the face, brushing her hair out of her brown eyes. All the teachers and staff were teary eyed and moving in slow motion. We were all in shock and didn't know which way to turn except home. Today, Dorothy was right more than usual—there was no place like home. I just wanted to click my heels and make everything all right again.

"Come on, Karen, let's go." She held my other hand tight, and the three of us headed out the door.

When Jake came home that afternoon, I got up off the couch, where I'd been glued watching the news. We hugged like we hadn't for a long time, and I started crying again. He held me tight and nuzzled my neck.

"I know, I know." He choked back a sob of his own.

"What about Jackie and the kids? What an awful thing for her to see her husband murdered." I cried. Although I'd only met her twice, I'd always felt that if I'd been born with my own silver spoon, we could've been friends. My heart broke for her over and over again. No silver spoon could make this any better for her.

I sat down, stared at the television, and watched pictures of Jackie standing next to LBJ while he was sworn in on Air Force One. There was blood on her suit since she'd refused to change it, wanting the world to see what some nutcase had done. Nothing could hide the look of numbness on her face. She stood not crying, not seeing, just being there. She must've been crying inside just thinking about having to tell Caroline…and I broke down again.

Looking up, I saw Jay sat next to me on the couch not knowing what to think. I grabbed onto him, and in a rare moment for this active little guy, he let me hold him. I held him and kissed his little head until he finally squirmed away and went outside to ride bikes with Bobby.

The news reported that school would close at its normal time today, but wouldn't reopen until further notice. The world seemed to stop for a few days. It would be a long time before anything seemed "normal" again.

"The kids and I walked down to Route 50 and sat on the hillside and watched the motorcade go by," Ellie said over the phone the next day.

"Really?" I sat down to fold the laundry in the basket. "Were there a lot of people there?"

"Probably thirty or so, sitting on the grass near us. Wasn't a dry eye to be found, men and women alike."

"Boy, makes me feel awful for envying her like I have over the years," I said.

"Envy? You call that envy? Let's try jealousy." Only Ellie could get away with that kind of criticism.

"Yeah, you can guilt me into owning up to that one." I folded the towels and put them one by one into the laundry basket as my sins piled up.

We went through the motions of a normal weekend with the awful thought of our president dead from an assassin's bullet. His wife and kids were facing a life alone, soon to be packing up to leave the White House. The television ran nonstop for days.

Karen and I shopped for a sympathy card, mine for Jackie and hers for Caroline. "What do you think, Mom?" she asked as she handed me her card of choice. It was not a sympathy card, but one with no words and the picture of a horse running in a meadow, representing Macaroni and our time with them. Tears stung my eyes.

"That's perfect, hon." I pulled her head into my side. "Much better than mine," which was a pink rose that reminded me of Jackie. We bought the cards and headed home.

The style section of the *Post* reported that protocol required soldiers, one from each branch of the military, to stand with their backs to his casket to watch over him. However, Jackie had requested that they face the coffin, afraid that Jack would feel too alone with their backs to him. We watched on television as the horse-drawn carriage rolled down Pennsylvania Avenue toward the Capitol. The riderless horse, Black Jack, gave the young soldier that was leading him a run for his money. It was as if Black Jack just didn't want to be there. Nobody did.

"Why is the horse named Black Jack, Daddy?" Karen asked Jake as he lay in his usual spot on the floor in front of the TV.

"Well, believe it or not, I just read that in the paper this morning." He turned and looked at her, propping his head up on his hand. "Black Jack was named after General John J. 'Blackjack' Pershing, who gained his nickname from his students at West Point from his tenure with the Tenth Calvary."

Karen slid closer to listen.

"They were a segregated African American unit in the post–Civil War era. Actually, they initially called him 'Nigger Jack,' he explained.

"Jake!" I admonished him. We'd agreed to try to quit using the *n* word in front of the kids.

"Sorry, dear." He raised his eyebrows and looked at me. "It was part of the history lesson!"

I shook my head. The more things changed, the more they stayed the same.

Ellie and I made plans to stand in line at the Capitol to pay our respects. The guys agreed to stay home with the kids. I put my coat on and headed out the door when El pulled up in Betsy. We didn't know how long it might take to get through the line, as the last report said it was over a mile long. We'd packed up a thermos of coffee and some sandwiches and traveled our old route toward the campaign office. Memories of paper cuts and Mack's Esso station tapped us on the shoulder.

We drove to Mack's Esso station to find a place to park, but he was closed. We both agreed he was probably standing in line, too. "Maybe he'll give us frontsies!" Ellie quipped. We left him a note on Betsy's windshield, hoping not to get towed.

The leafless trees reached for the sky in our nation's capital that day, as if searching for an answer that might never be given. Living near DC, we often took for granted what the rest of the country only saw on television. Camelot was who we were, and now that identity had been snatched away and was forever gone. We were wounded, but when one hurt, we all hurt. I learned that standing on the streets of DC that gray November day. We were all bare and exposed like the branches reaching for the sky. Only the hope of spring and knowing that life does indeed renew itself kept us moving forward.

We saw the line that seemed to go on forever, winding around the streets of the city. We walked what seemed like miles before finding the end and joining in the slow progression toward the Capitol. I heard on the TV later that the line had stretched for ten miles.

Thanks to Ellie having never met a stranger, we became fast friends with Freda and Bob, the couple in front of us. Bob had a transistor radio and kept it glued to his ear, much to his wife's chagrin. We began to chat only to discover that they lived just a few miles from us.

"Lee Harvey Oswald was shot!" Bob shouted, and looked at his wife, eyes wide open. The crowd gathered around us. We all recognized the name of the president's assassin.

"He's dead, too?" Ellie asked.

"That's what they just said on his radio," Freda answered. We all leaned in to hear, and the news report confirmed the murder. A man named Jack Ruby had gunned him down in the Dallas jail parking garage. Now what?

It was as if the world had gone mad. Nothing made sense anymore. The axis had tilted, and it didn't feel as though it would ever be straight again. A feeling of vulnerability grabbed me that day. I think it grabbed our entire country.

We cried and talked with strangers about the tragic past few days. That week, I saw how a common tragedy made a stranger a friend. We shared our coffee with Bob and Freda.

November can go either way in DC. For the most part, it's chilly and windy. That day, the wind was easy and the sun bright, lending its warmth until it started to dip below the horizon of the city's skyline into the hills of Virginia. Whatever warmth the sun had offered had left with the sunset. We pulled on our gloves and wrapped Ellie's hand-crocheted scarves around our necks.

"See, I told you they'd come in handy sometime," Ellie reminded me. I had teased her when she'd crocheted one with more holes in it than stitches.

"Touché! Brrr! It sure got cold fast," I whined and looked at my watch. The line still moved, but very slowly. "They said the rotunda is supposed to close at 9 o'clock p.m." I looked at El.

"Yeah, not so sure we're gonna make the cut, kiddo." She stepped up on her tiptoes to see how far it was to the steps of the Capitol. We were inching closer.

"They just said because of the crowd, they are going to leave it open possibly all night!" Bob reported as he pulled his transistor radio away from his ear.

"Well, that's the best news I've had in days!" I said and smiled for the first time in as many.

It turned out that we got to the Capitol right before nine, so we may have made it in time regardless. As we walked into the huge round room, we could see nothing at first except the huge painting on the wall as we walked in the door. The guards split us into twos to make things flow faster, and luckily Ellie and I were able to stay together. She grabbed my hand, and I gratefully hung onto hers. One could hear nothing except the sound of shoes shuffling over the marble floor and an occasional nose blow into a tissue.

Then, there it was; our Stars and Stripes draped over a casket. Something no one ever wants to see. My hand covered my mouth as if to keep the wailing sounds stuffed inside. Tears again flowed down both our cheeks. At first we didn't notice, but the line stopped moving. Ellie looked at me, and we shrugged at each other. The crowd started to murmur with wonder. People stepped back at the instruction of the soldiers, and Jackie and Bobby Kennedy entered the Rotunda once again. There was a collective gasp as we watched our First Lady and the president's brother walk in to join us. I now knew what it meant to be able to hear a pin drop.

I grabbed Ellie's arm as if to hold myself up, and she latched on to mine. Jackie walked within arm's reach of us, her lovely profile shadowed by the dark veil that tried but couldn't hide her despair. Our friend and First Lady was wounded and going through the motions of what must have been shock. The sound of her heels echoed in the Rotunda as she walked straight to the flagged coffin, reached out, and stroked it, shaking her head as if to deny its reality. She leaned her head back as if to stare into space for a second and just that fast, she took a deep breath, let out a heavy sigh, turned on her heel, and walked back out the door with Bobby again at her side.

I looked at Ellie. "I can't believe that just happened," I whispered, and she squeezed my hand.

The slow shuffle of feet began again as the crowd walked through the room, and within a few minutes, El and I walked slowly past his flag-draped casket. It didn't seem possible that he was really inside this ornate box. I held on to the velvet rope that lined the walkway. The same rope I'd watched little Caroline hold onto just this morning on TV in her light-blue coat and white gloves.

Memories of our white-gloved afternoon at the White House flooded me. El slipped her arm around my shoulder as we exited the Rotunda. We trudged what seemed like miles back to Betsy at Mack's Esso station in silence. The cold air tried to penetrate our thoughts, but this time even the wind couldn't make us whine. Mack left a note on the windshield, next to ours. "Ladies, I'm sorry I missed you. My parking lot is always here for you. Our world will never be the same. Mack."

We drove home and for another first didn't get lost or make one U-turn. We didn't turn on the radio this time. News was something we'd both had a belly full of by then and didn't relish any more surprises just yet. Not even a song. The Days of Camelot forever gone, our songbird was silenced, and we found ourselves stuck in the onesies again.

❄

Weeks went by, and Christmas came and went. Presents, food, desserts, and card games filled our days, and before we knew it, New Year's had come and gone, and it was time to take down the decorations. We were forced to move on in the wake of the rumors of who had killed the president and why. LBJ was now commander-in-chief. There was a new sheriff in town. Lady Bird would put her own touches on the White House now. Somehow, we didn't think we could wrangle another invitation.

Summer showed up, and I planned a baby shower for Ellie. Yeah, number five was on the way. She needed to quit drinking the water in Radiant Valley, or she'd end up with a dozen. Roberta was pregnant again, too. I decided that maybe I needed to quit drinking water all together.

"I don't need a baby shower, Barb. This is kid number five, after all."

"Hey, everyone deserves a shower, especially for number five."

"Why do I always have to be the showeree?"

"Better to be the showerer than the showeree, I always say." I then wished I had bit my tongue. She took it in stride, but only after she threw one of the couch pillows and hit me upside the head.

"Besides," I added, "entertaining is not my strong suit, but with a shower, all I have to do is bake some of my famous cookies, make some punch, and line up a few of those stupid games."

"Why do we have to play games anyway?" Ellie asked.

"Good point. Guys don't feel the need to giggle and play word scrambles when they get together. Who says we have to do it?"

"Yeah, right. I guess we could drink beer, pat each other on the butt, torture the cat, and have belching contests," Ellie said. "But too many of us are expecting at any given time to party like they do. Maybe we should just resort to playing cards."

"Hey, now there's something." I tossed the pillow back on the sofa. "Why not a poker shower?"

I could no longer say I couldn't entertain. Our poker shower was a big hit with the girls. We taught one another Five-Card Draw, Jacks or Better, and Blackjack, with Patsy Cline crooning on the stereo.

"Hey, you cheated, Ellie!" Roberta tossed her cards to the middle of the table.

"You gotta prove it first, girl." Ellie circled the chips with her arms and raked them into her lap. We mastered the art of gambling well into the night, a far cry from the word-scramble games we'd been cursed with in the past.

After my gambling partners left, I finished up the dishes and hung up the towel to dry. I tiptoed into the bedroom and slid into bed, trying not to stir Jake. I was too tired for even a quickie and tried to doze. I stared at the back of his head and wondered what my life would have been like if I hadn't married him, hadn't had two kids before I was twenty-two years old, and hadn't bought into the Donna Reed lifestyle. From what Ellie had told me, I didn't think Betty Friedan's book was the answer. At least not mine.

I closed my eyes and fantasized that I'd caught the eye of a handsome young congressman while I was waitressing at a private catered event in DC. He was smitten with me and whisked me away, but then I found out he was from South Dakota. "Forget that," I said half-awake, half-dreaming. "Too cold there." Jake moved, and I shushed myself.

Then I remembered that if I hadn't met Jake, gotten pregnant, and married before I was seventeen, I would have been fighting off the advances of the Old Man until I got out of school. I still managed to graduate from high school after I was married, so I had the credentials I needed to start a career, but wondered if the time would ever get there. I laid my arm over Jake's waist and decided there were worse things than living with limited choices as I drifted off to sleep.

The next afternoon, a knock on the door brought me out of my latest daydream and I opened the front door. I normally didn't talk to door-to-door salesmen, but this day, Mr. Electrolux showed up just as the smoke cleared from my suicidal $9.95 Eureka vacuum cleaner. I'd warned Jake that it was getting ready to die, but he'd so far managed to ignore the inevitable.

It was ninety degrees in the shade, with the typical DC 100 percent humidity. Mr. Electrolux looked as if he could use some air conditioning, and I decided I could use his vacuum. I let him in, and he wiped the sweat from his brow with a handkerchief and pushed his hair back on his almost baldhead.

He introduced himself as Homer Hooker, and he quickly convinced me of the superiority of his product.

"Mrs. Kincaid, I know you would never allow such dirt to enter this lovely room, but for the sake of demonstrating just how wonderful this Electrolux vacuum cleaner performs, I'll now show you how effective it really is! It's helped so many of your neighbors, and I'm sure it can help you, too." He went on with his pitch.

Homer took his little bag of dirt and dumped it in the middle of my living room. I gasped and started to object, but Homer waived me away. He quickly turned on the machine and started running the nozzle back and forth on the rug and left not a trace of dirt behind. I was amazed with the demonstration, and by the time Mr. Electrolux finished his pitch, I agreed to go into debt for the expensive but worthy machine. I offered Homer a second glass of Pepsi, but he was energized by his success and headed up the street to see Roberta next. He'd given me a free vacuum bag for every lead I could think of. As it turned out, I wouldn't have to buy bags for two months since I gave up every friend I had.

"You paid how much for a stinking vacuum cleaner?" Jake ranted. "Barb, I'm still trying to pay off Valley Dairy!" (Did I forget to mention the ninety-five-dollar milkman bill?) "Are you crazy?" The kids looked up from the other room. Things were getting loud.

"Jake, I'll pay for it with my own money. Calm down!"

"Oh, now it's your money, is it?"

Whoops, did I say that?

Before nightfall, the silver bullet of a vacuum found itself sleeping on the front porch. We argued, fussed, and I cut him off until the Electrolux gained a permanent spot in the front closet.

A girl's gotta do what a girl's gotta do.

Jay and I cleaned house on the buddy system. I had to take him with me from room to room so I could keep an eye on the little bugger. I couldn't let him out of my sight for a minute, and if I did, I lived to regret it. That afternoon, I was vacuuming the hallway when the phone rang. I turned the week-old Electrolux off and ran to the bedroom to answer the call.

"Hold on, Ellie, Jay's in the hallway, and he just turned the vacuum back on. Oh no!" I dropped the phone and ran to the hallway. Just that fast, he'd placed the end of the vacuum hose into the toilet and sucked up all the water. I turned the machine off and as quick as I could, pulled the saturated bag from my capital expenditure and threw it in the bathtub.

"I can't believe it. I almost had to move to a homeless shelter because of that Electrolux, and he's probably ruined it in ten seconds or less!" I cried over the phone to Ellie. "Let me call you back," I said and hung up without waiting for her to answer.

The vacuum must have been worth the extra money because it survived and somehow didn't electrocute Jay. If I ever needed a sedative, I think it was then.

I kept telling myself that Jay would get better when he got older. Jake tried signing him up for ankle-biter football, thinking that a team sport would help develop his attention span. It was great in theory, but he cried and begged to stop playing.

The kids are finding new friends in the neighborhood as more of the townhouses are finished and people are moving in. Jay found Roberta's son, who was a year older at the ripe old age of four. Bobby had the brains, and Jay had the lack of good sense to go along with whatever Bobby told him to do.

Yesterday, Roberta dropped by to return my mixer and let me know that Jay had been knocking on her door.

"He asked me quite nicely if I had a hammer he could borrow. I suggested he ask his mother if he could use hers, but he told me his mother wouldn't give it to him." That's why they call him the "Menace." Dennis could take some lessons from this kid.

"Yeah, I'm not quite sure what he had in mind, but I'm thinking it was a good idea to turn him down." We sat down at the dining room table with two glasses of Pepsi.

"How many caps do you have saved?" Roberta asked.

All year long, we saved up our Pepsi bottle caps and cashed them on "Pepsi Day" for a day of free rides at the Glen Echo amusement park.

"I've got three coffee cans full. Are we going next week?

"Check with Ellie and let me know what day." She tipped her glass and finished off her soda. "I'd better get back before the boys remodel my living room." She headed out the door.

The next Wednesday morning, we hauled our coffee cans full of caps up to the gate of Glen Echo. The kids stood there breathless while Mr. Carnival dumped the Pepsi caps on his scale and determined just how many ride tickets we had earned.

Roberta, Ellie, and I packed the customary picka-nicka lunch, and seven of the nine kids (Roger and Scott considered themselves too old to hang with us anymore) rode and ate until they either barfed or passed out exhausted.

"I finally found something that will tucker him out," I said. I carried Jay back to the car, passed out on my shoulder, as the evening sun dipped below the trees. A day of roller coasters, bumper cars, tilt-a-whirls, and Ferris wheels proved to be too much for the little guy.

"It seems like this is the only time I get to cuddle this little fella, when he's passed out and exhausted." We loaded El's and my kids back into Betsy and Roberta's crew got in her Falcon and drove away. It was quiet in the backseat as our crew followed Jay's lead and nodded off one by one.

"Let's take the new section of the beltway home. Will said it'll be a lot faster," Ellie said as she put Betsy into drive.

"Okay, but you're on your own with directions because I don't know where to go."

"No problem, he said to just follow the signs for 495." We followed the blue signs for 495 and before we knew it, we were getting close.

"Whoops, almost missed it!" Ellie said and made a sharp turn onto the ramp for the dual four-lane highway, and we were on our way, just like that.

"I thought this was one-way," Ellie said as she noticed oncoming vehicles.

I looked up from digging in my purse for a cigarette and saw the headlights coming our way. Something wasn't right.

"My God, Ellie, it is! You're going the wrong way on the beltway!"

"No way."

"Yes way! Get off on the shoulder right now!" The drill sergeant in me shoved her way forward. She steered Betsy, thankfully in between the oncoming traffic, to the shoulder with cars whizzing past, laying on their horns. Thank heaven the kids were all sleeping so there'd be no witnesses or extortion material threatening to retell this one.

"How'd that happen?" she asked.

I stared at her as if she had two heads.

"How'd that happen? How'd it happen that we didn't get killed, that's what I want to know!"

"Skillful driving, I guess." She leaned her head back in relief and giggled in self-defense, and I joined in.

"Yeah, skillful to the point of stupid!" We laughed.

"You should've seen your beady little eyes turn into saucers when you looked up!" She doubled over the steering wheel.

"Wish I could've, but I'm glad I looked at the road instead of the mirror." I gave myself a verbal pat on the back.

"Yeah, for once!" she shot back, and with that I crossed my legs and doubled over my knees.

"Stop! I gotta pee." I threatened.

"What's going on?" Karen asked, rubbing her eyes in the backseat.

Recovering as quickly as I could, the mom in me answered her, "Nothing, hon. Go on back to sleep." I reached over and patted Karen's knee and stifled a giggle. Thankfully she closed her eyes and leaned back on the window of the back door. Didn't need any witnesses to testify in front of Jake.

"We'd better get turned around before someone notices," El said. The words hadn't hit the windshield when we noticed the red, white, and blue lights pulling up in front of us.

"You should've turned off your lights so he couldn't see you," I said. You can't fix the stupid in either one of us.

"Now you tell me!" She shook her head.

Ellie cranked her window down, and I opened the glove box to find the registration while handing over her purse to retrieve her driver's license. This was a drill we had down pat.

"As often as you have to produce your driver's license, you'd think you'd just wear it around your neck!"

"Wow, cops just keep getting cuter and cuter," Ellie said as she looked in her mirror.

"What are we gonna do if he tows the car away, El? What will we do with the kids?" I asked with my normal trouble-borrowing pessimism.

El rolled her window down and looked up, "Hi, Officer, this must look pretty weird, huh?" Ellie asked.

"License and registration, please," the tall, good-looking cop answered. I leaned over Ellie's lap to get a look at him for myself. I've discovered that since I'm an old married lady, the only time I can really use my flirting skills is when El and I are in the weeds, so here I go again.

"Barb?" the cop asked. I narrowed my eyes to get a better look at him and realized he was my neighbor from across the street.

"Yeah, it's me, Derrick."

"You know him?" Ellie asked, eyebrows raised, and looked my way.

"Did Sue have her baby yet?" I asked him, ignoring her question. She could figure this one out for herself.

"Not yet. I'm waiting for them to call me on the radio any minute!" His chest puffed, and a grin appeared on his face.

"How in the world did this happen, ladies?"

It happened every day, right? Welcome to our world.

"Just one wrong turn and here we were!" Ellie answered.

Derrick shook his head and handed El back her license.

"Oh yeah, Derrick, meet Mrs. Wrong Way." I introduced Ellie. "El, this is Derrick, Sue's husband."

"Hey there. Oh yeah," she said, remembering. "I met Sue at the baby shower. She taught us how to play One-Eyed Jack and the Man with the Axe."

"The gambling shower." Derrick nodded and smiled. "I remember."

"We were just on our way back from a day at Glen Echo and got mixed up on the new road." Ellie babbled. "I'm sure it must happen a lot." My girl was serious.

"Well, not exactly," he answered. The sides of his grin threatened to betray him but his laughing blue eyes gave him away. "But I suspect it happens a good deal in your world." Derrick laughed. "Lucky for you it looks like the kids missed all the excitement." He checked out the brood in Betsy's wayback.

"Glen Echo exhaustion," I said. Derrick looked at the traffic lanes and decided on a plan for our escape from wrong way on a one-way.

"Let's wait for a big break in traffic. When I pull out and go, that means it's safe for you to pull out and turn around." He waited for us to nod in agreement and walked back to his cruiser.

"Whew, that was lucky!" Ellie said. She put Betsy in drive and waited for Derrick to pull out. As he pulled onto the highway, she punched the gas and made a U-turn, squealing wheels that woke up at least 50 percent of our groggy backseat occupants. I instinctively shushed them back to sleep back in my role as navigator and kid controller while El drove us home, this time in the right direction.

A few weeks later, as the spaghetti noodles were boiling on the stove, I heard Jake's car door close as he got home from work. When he didn't show up in the kitchen in his normal sixty to ninety seconds, I turned down the flame on the pasta and headed for the front door. My heart skipped a beat when I saw through the living room bay window that Jake was standing on the sidewalk talking to Derrick.

Geez, if he rats on us, there'll be no living this down.

I debated with myself. Should I go down and take a chance of walking in on the description of our wrong way on the beltway fiasco or just stand here and wait for the brow beating to begin?

I just stood with my feet planted, unable to walk into what could be disaster. After a few minutes that seemed like an hour, Jake turned and walked into the house.

"Hey, hon," I said as I did my Donna Reed greeting and kissed him on the cheek. "What did Derrick have to say?" Boy, when it comes to suspense, I just can't take it.

"Oh, not much." He put down his newspaper and flicked on the television. "He did say that he caught some woman driving the wrong way on the beltway last week!"

My stomach did a flip-flop. "Really?"

"Yeah, can you imagine anyone being stupid enough to drive up the exit ramp to a freeway and not realize it?"

Do I have to answer this question, or can I plead the Fifth?

"Hmm, how's spaghetti sound for dinner?" I asked. Nothing like food to get Jake to change the subject.

Now that both the kids were in school full time, I was able to convince Jake it was time for me to go back to work. I'd had to wait until Jay started school. Simply put, there's no way I could ever make enough money to pay someone to watch him full-time, but the poor teachers didn't have a choice.

I struggled with how to fill out the job application. When it came to listing past experience, I didn't think they'd want to hear about my schemes with Ellie or housekeeping and kid-chasing qualifications, so I just left it blank.

Jake suggested that I go to work at the school office since I seem to spend so much time there visiting the principal about behavior issues. I thought about it, *briefly*, but decided not.

I landed an interview at an auto repair shop, and thanks to Roberta's recommendation, I made out okay.

"Just wear a short skirt and plenty of lipstick, Barb. Smile pretty and cross your legs like this during the interview," she said as she demonstrated her sexy interview style.

Her suggestion must have worked because I got the job as a receptionist just a few miles from the house. We bought a cheap secondhand Corvair from Jake's cousin, Mike, the family connection car salesman, so I didn't have to walk to work.

Karen was old enough to watch Jay after school until I got home. I have her doing some chores every day, and it was a shock to her system, but a hike in her allowance helped lessen the sting.

The extra money I brought home was nice, and I think Jake was enjoying it, but he wouldn't admit it. I was beat by the end of the day, but I guess that's what happens when you're doing double duty. No more midafternoon naps for me. I had this theory that if I left the dust bunnies alone, they'd go away, but all that's done is given them license to move their relatives in.

Since I'm working now, I've decided to employ the services of the milkman again. Jay drinks milk like most people drink water, and I can get donuts and bread from the guy, too. I have my own little insulated metal box on the front stoop, and he just leaves my regular order each Tuesday since I'm at work when he comes by. He saves me a trip to the store midweek. I could get used to this. I wonder if he does laundry.

Nothing much has changed in Jake's world since I went to work. We eat dinner a little later than before, but that's about it. Life as a working mom isn't so bad. At least it wasn't until I drank the water that I knew was tainted.

I'd been back to work for about five weeks when I woke up with flu symptoms and had to call in sick for the first time, but by noon, I was feeling better. I cooked dinner and got everything ready for the next day, when I woke up sick again.

You guessed it; the rabbit died. Dang rabbits. You'd think after all these years, they'd be more resilient than that. Looks like Ellie and I are due about six weeks apart.

"How'd that happen?" El asked as I sat at her dining room table with my head lying on top of my hands. I picked my head up slowly and stared blankly up at her.

"Never mind, I'll make some tea." She patted my head and walked into the kitchen. Her tea always made things better.

"I can't believe I'm starting over with diapers and bottles, and now I'll have to quit my job!" I whined and added an extra self-pity teaspoon of sugar to my tea.

"You don't have to quit. I can babysit for you," she offered.

"You're the best friend a girl ever had, El." I considered the offer for a moment. "But with the piddly amount of money I make, you'd have to do it for free, and I doubt even you're that good a friend."

"Yeah, you're right. I'm not." She nodded and reached across the table and patted my hand.

"Yep, I'm kicked back to the onesies for now."

I worked until I was about seven months along before giving my notice. It was either that or just snooze between my desk and file cabinet come three in the afternoon. I don't think Bill would've cared much, but the customers would have a rough time waking me up just by walking through the door. Being the professional napper that I am, I can sleep through just about anything, especially when I'm pregnant.

I was sorry to leave the office. I'd enjoyed my brief career at Martin's Auto Body. I'd even learned how to type, sort of. I made a promise to myself that I'd go take a typing class in night school so that I'd be ready to start my career again when the time came.

Ellie was full-term and ready to pop out baby number five.

"This is it for me, too, no more kids. They're my sunshine, but I'm getting too old to put my body through much more of this," she complained. "My feet are swollen, and I think it's giving me varicose veins." She lifted up the hem of her housedress. She was getting a roadmap of blue veins on the side of her thigh.

"Yeah, and I don't think there's enough Slim Jims left on the East Coast to take care of my cravings until I squeeze this one out." I'd probably depleted the Slim Jim inventory of every 7-Eleven between DC and Baltimore since I'd been pregnant this time. "I'm going on the pill as soon as I can," I added.

"Me too," Ellie said.

"But you guys are Catholic. I thought it wasn't allowed."

"Will's Catholic. I'm not. If he can't keep it zipped, then I'm going on the pill. What he doesn't know won't hurt him," she declared.

Her delivery of number five, better known as Timmy, was much less dramatic than with William. Will called at seven the following Tuesday morning to let us know Ellie delivered in the middle of the night.

"Yeah, it was touch-and-go as to whether we would make it to the hospital in time, but we ended up with a half hour to spare," Will told me. "Tell Jake to let them know I won't be in today."

I offered to watch the kids so he could sleep, but he said he'd let Ginger stay home to keep an eye on William while he got some rest.

The remaining weeks of my pregnancy passed quickly, and when the time came, Kelly Lee popped out without much fanfare. We were a little older and a lot wiser this time around, and since the third time's the charm, we were sure we had the drill down pat.

The Beatles invaded the USA with their first appearance on *The Ed Sullivan Show*. Ellie and I talked on the phone and could hear Ginger and Karen swooning and singing in our respective living rooms.

"Yeah, this is starting to make me feel old," Ellie complained. "Beatles music is gonna take some getting used to."

"Yeah, I know, but that guy Paul is easy on the eyes, at least." I picked up the *Style* section from that day's *Post*. I looked at the picture of the band getting off the plane in New York. My eyes scanned the page and saw an article on the new DC beltway. "Hey, listen up. The beltway's ready to open next week," I said. Route 495 had been under construction for several years now and was nearing completion.

"That's great!" Ellie said. "Getting lost will be so much harder since it goes in a circle." And she was serious, folks.

CHAPTER 6

Ellie
What's New, Pussycat?

War Unconstitutional, Raskin Insists at Trial

Boston (AP)—*Marcus Raskin, the fourth defendant to testify in the antidraft conspiracy trial of Dr. Benjamin Spock and four others says he believes President Johnson and his top aides "abrogated to themselves power not given in the Constitution" when they widened the war in Vietnam in early 1965...They are accused of conspiring to aid, abet, and counsel young men to avoid the draft, a federal crime, which carries a maximum penalty of five years in jail and a $10,000 fine.*

—The *Evening Star,* Washington, DC, Thursday, June 6, 1968

I decided that if I get a choice for my next life, I'd come back as a man with a wife just like me. Not that I really believe we come back here again, but I thought I'd let it be known, just in case. Will and Jake are now proud owners of Redskins season tickets. Now, I don't begrudge the guys having their fun, and the added benefit of Will taking off for half the weekend could give a girl a much-needed break, but I have to ask, just how can we afford luxuries like that?

"Think about it, Ellie. They're at work all week, in front of the television and newspapers in the evenings, and weekends, whether it's a for-real side job or just an afternoon at the gun club, they're out having a grand old time," Barb said. "Now they're going to be gone just about every Sunday, and when they're not, they're glued to the TV set watching the games." My girl was on a roll.

This particular Saturday, Will and Jake had taken Betsy on their side job. It was no big deal; they needed to haul some long pipes to the jobsite, and it didn't look like I was going anywhere.

"Did you see the sale at the Hecht's in Tyson's Corner?" Barb asked without taking a breath. So that was the plan.

"No, what's the deal?"

"Red-dot sale, one day only, today."

"Come and get me. I just hit for twenty dollars at bingo last night. I didn't tell Will, so it's all mine."

"I can't; the car's got a flat. Will picked Jake up on his way out to work this morning."

"Red-dot sale, huh?" The wheels turned in my head and visions of Will's Cadillac parked in front of the house danced in my crazed mind. He'd always made it clear that he didn't want me to drive his car unless it was an emergency. Well, nothing better qualifies as an "emergency" as a red-dot sale.

"I've got the Cadillac. I'll pick you up in thirty minutes," I said and hung up the phone before I lost my nerve. I looked up and down for the spare Cadillac key. Of course, I didn't have one of my "very own" since Will looked at it as strictly his car. This time it was different. This time he was using Betsy, and well, I was entitled to four wheels and a key, right? You betcha. I found the key in his sock drawer, nicely tucked away in the back.

"Oh, Mom, I don't want to go!" Ginger argued since she and Karen were lying on the living room floor engrossed in *American Bandstand* after a sleepover.

We compromised, and they agreed to finish watching the show at Barb's and look after Timmy and Kelly since they were ready to be fed and put down for naps. I took William, thinking that Jay would behave better if he had a partner in crime. Nice strategy, but what was I thinking?

"Wow, you sure do look small driving up in this hearse," Barb said as she slid in next to me.

"Yeah, well, it might turn into a hearse if we don't get back before Will, so let's hit the road."

We managed to drive the forty-five minutes to Tyson's Corner without a U-turn and dragged the kids out of the car.

In less than two hours, we'd found bargains we couldn't believe. I bought new shoes for Ginger, two shirts for Scott, and a birdhouse I just couldn't live without. Barb made fun of me, but hey, it was hand painted (not sure by whom) and only cost a dollar. We made our purchases and headed back to the car. I opened the trunk to find it too full of the guys' junk, so we just loaded it all into the spacious backseat and threatened the boys if they bothered the bags.

"Hey, did you manage to get any of the liquid embroidery supplies that were on sale?" I asked Barb. We had discovered a new way to embroider our linens; no need for needles and thread, just use a handy little tube of paint that glides on with a ballpoint on the end.

"Yeah, I did. I got five tubes of paint for a dollar. Now that's a deal." I was feeling pretty smug at our thriftiness.

Coming back around the beltway, in the right direction this time, we hit a traffic snarl.

"Looks like some touch-up construction," Barb said and pulled a cigarette out of her purse.

A Virginia State trooper was making arm gestures at me. "Must want me to slow down for the construction," I said. I drove past him to see him flailing his arms in the rearview mirror still looking at us.

"Is he waving at us?" I asked.

Barb turned to look. "You know, I think he is." She frowned.

I pulled over onto the shoulder, and the trooper walked up to the window.

"May I see your driver's license and registration, ma'am?" These troopers were looking younger and younger every time I got pulled over. I reached for my purse only to remember I'd left it on the kitchen table. I figured all I was gonna need was my crisp twenty-dollar bill and nothing more.

"Geez oh flip, I left it at home, officer. I never knew I'd need it today!"

Barb already had the registration out of the glove box. She was getting good at this.

"Was I going too fast? I'm not sure what the speed limit is in this construction zone."

"Just stay in the car, ma'am. I'll be back in a minute." He leaned down to survey the occupants of the backseat.

The trooper walked back to his cruiser, and the questions began to fly. The boys were jumping up, looking out the back window and trying to see if he was bringing handcuffs.

"What did you do, Ellie? You think we were going too fast?" Barb finished lighting up her cigarette while she cracked the window.

"Not sure. I guess I might have forgotten to read the speed limit signs." I scratched my head and checked the rearview mirror. The cop came back toward the car, and for some reason that warm and fuzzy feeling was slipping away.

"Ma'am, this car's been reported stolen. I'm going to have to ask you and your passengers to exit the vehicle and stand aside in the grass." He pointed to the shoulder. "Away from the road."

"Stolen? But it's my car, I mean, my husband's car," I stammered.

"I'm sorry, ma'am, but I'm going to have to insist that all of you get out of the car right now."

Barb and I just looked at each other and gave the boys a you'd-better-behave look. We gathered ourselves as quickly as we could and found a place to sit on the hillside next to the highway, trying to get the boys out of the way of oncoming traffic.

"What in the world does he mean 'stolen'?" I asked, wringing my hands. I'd always had this fear of going to jail for something I didn't do. "Just like one of those old movies," I thought to myself and then said it aloud.

"What are you talking about?"

"Never mind." For once I was speechless.

The cops were going through the Cadillac with a fine-tooth comb. Why would it be reported stolen? Had Will bought a hot car? We'd had it for over a year. It figured that I'd be the one who was driving when the hammer came down and someone had to do hard time for buying a stolen vehicle. No wonder he got it so cheap.

The officer took the keys from the ignition and walked around to the trunk of the car. Oh no, not the trunk! I elbowed Barb and nodded toward the cop. She had that same "please don't lock me up" look on her face as I did.

"Do we get orange suits before they hook us up on the chain gang?" Barb asked.

The officer lifted the lid of the trunk. All I could see was his hand waving from behind the lid as he called for the other policeman to take a look. My heart almost beat out of my chest.

"We're going to jail," I said, scared to death. The two policemen walked back and towered over us as we sat on the hillside.

"Ma'am, we're going to have to insist that you ride along with us to the police barracks. Were you aware that the trunk is loaded with rifles and ammunition?"

"Well, yes, sir, I—"

"What about the kids?" Barb asked.

"You're just going to have to bring them with you. We can call someone to come and pick them up when we get there," the officer answered. "Please remain in the vehicle while we transfer the weapons to the cruiser." The trooper walked back to the trunk.

"I'm gonna kill those two. If these guns still work when I get home, then they can send me to jail for a real crime," Barb ranted, once the officer went back to his cruiser.

"Yeah, come to think of it, if we kill them, we get twenty years. If we don't, it's a life sentence!"

We couldn't help but laugh. The cops probably thought we were crazy. "Ellie, they have a cop car on three sides of us. There's not much of a chance we're gonna play Bonnie and Clyde on 'em." We'd just seen *Bonnie and Clyde* the week before.

"Officer, would it be okay if we brought our shopping bags with us?" Barb batted her brown eyes at the cop as we got out of Betsy to head to the police car. Those guys were getting younger every day. She still had it.

"That's probably a good idea," he answered. "So they don't have to be entered as evidence."

"Evidence? Evidence of what?" Barb asked, but nobody answered.

"We just need to take a look inside them first." He followed his protocol and put the bags in the front seat with him. We climbed in the back with the boys.

Our first experience with breaking the law. Looking out the front window through a cage.

"Wow!" Jay jumped up and down holding onto the cage and stomping his feet. Barb pulled him over onto her lap. "It's just like on *Dragnet!*" Barb shook her head, and I leaned my head back on the seat and wrapped my arms around Timmy. Maybe if I closed my eyes, I could beam myself up like on *Star Trek*.

The ride to the police station was a little subdued in between Jay's observations from "How fast will the cruiser go?" to "I have to pee!" We did get a few looks from other vehicles as we sat at stoplights. I wanted to tell them that we were just on a field trip, showing the kids how to be respectful to police and all...

"Yeah, we definitely win the Bad Moms award." I looked at Barb.

"Hanging with you is never dull, El." The cruiser pulled into the police station parking lot. The young officer opened Barb's door for her. Hey, she gets top billing wherever she goes, even jail. "I keep waiting for Allen Funt to jump out from behind his candid camera." Allen never showed.

The inside of the police barracks was pretty much like any movie I'd ever seen, dark wood floors and the sergeant's desk had a railing that sat up a foot or so above everyone else. The officer showed us to a bench along the wall across from the sergeant. We laid the shopping bags on the floor next to us.

"Here's my telephone number, but I doubt anyone's there right now. My husband's working," I said.

"Great, we'll probably have to sit here all afternoon waiting on Will and Jake to get home." Barb pulled her sweater across her shoulders. "Should we call Roberta to come pick up the boys?" She looked toward the boys, who were sitting on the floor, eyes big as watermelons, watching the activity in the police station. "If the cops have to put up with Jay very long, they'll lock us all up and throw away the key."

She must have read my mind.

"That jerk," I said, referring to Will. "I hope they throw the book at him!" I said, but didn't really mean it. Could this car have been stolen when Will bought it? Nothing added up.

"Mr. Reilly? Will Reilly?" the officer asked into the receiver. Strange, Will shouldn't be home already. *It's only twelve noon.* I raised my eyebrows to Barb.

"Yes, sir, we've recovered your car." He looked my way as he spoke into the receiver.

"Recovered his car? What does he mean 'recovered his car'?" I leaned over and whispered to Barb.

"Yes, sir. There are two women and two young boys who claim to know you. One says she's your wife, but she doesn't have any identification." He sat down at the desk. "Yes, sir. You can meet them here at the station. It's the Fairfax city barracks on Chain Bridge Road." He wrote something down as he listened to Will on the other end of the line. "Yes, sir, that's the one." He held the phone on his shoulder as he shuffled papers. "We also have a few other questions to ask you when you get here. Thank you, sir. Good-bye." The officer looked at me to see if I'd caught the gist of the sergeant's conversation, and when he realized I had, he sat down at a desk and began his paperwork. Yep, just like on *Dragnet*. The only thing that was missing was, "Just the facts, ma'am."

The sergeant turned his radio back up, trying to drown out the sounds of the kids, no doubt. Tom Jones sang, "What's New, Pussycat?" If he'd asked me that just two hours ago, my answer would've been so different.

Barb was trying to keep the boys as still as possible, without much luck. Jay was physically incapable of sitting still, and William was more than happy to follow his lead.

"It's gonna take them at least an hour to get here," Barb said. She had given the boys pens and paper to write on, but their interest was fading fast.

"Okay, boys, move over. Let me show you how it's done!" I sat down on the cool wood floor with them for a tic-tac-toe tournament. This should be a good way to calm my nerves. Problem was, they were both beating me. I'll blame it on the debut of my criminal record.

Officer Black, the trooper who hauled us in, began to soften as we waited for the guys to come. He found a deck of cards and played Go Fish with the boys until the phone rang, and he had to take a call. He returned with Pepsis for everyone, and it wasn't long before I realized that he had the hots for Barb, but as usual, she was clueless.

"How many children do you have?" he asked her.

"Three. I have a daughter who's thirteen."

She had always been unaware how her beauty affects men. Either that, or she just wasn't interested.

"Ellie, for God's sake, get off the floor!" Will's voice boomed from the door. I looked around to see that he and Jake had walked in and let the door slam behind them.

"It's either this or an orange jumpsuit and a cell, Will!" I said, and not for the first time, wished he were dead. I jumped up in time for Will and Jake to walk away and talk to the police officer.

"Yes, this is my wife and son. The others belong to him." Will nodded in Jake's direction.

"Why would you have thought the vehicle was stolen, Mr. Reilly?" the officer asked.

"Because I don't allow her to drive it!" he answered, with a you-haven't-noticed-she's-an-idiot-yet tone. "She has a hard enough time with the station wagon; no way she can handle the Cadillac." He gave him his you-know-what-I-mean look. "I came home, and it was gone. She doesn't even have a key." He looked my way in a lightbulb moment.

"If she'd remember to carry her purse, this whole thing could have been avoided," Will added, as if to place further blame on me for his inconvenience. My blood pressure was rising. So, this is what it felt like to hate the one you're committed to for a lifetime sentence. It was then that it dawned on me that I wasn't the one who was Catholic. I could get out of this. They can't excommunicate me! Another lightbulb went off, this time in my head.

"Well, Mr. Reilly," the officer went on to explain, "it wasn't just the stolen vehicle issue, but the interesting cache of weapons in the trunk that gave us the greatest concern."

Will and Jake looked at each other.

"Oh, those weapons!" Will said. "Those are just our target practice guns. We're members of the Berlin Rod and Gun Club. We go out to the shooting range just about every Saturday." He reached in his wallet and pulled out his gun club membership card. "It's easier to just leave everything in the trunk until the following week." He offered the card to the officer.

"Especially when you have kids around the house," Jake added, trying in a lame way to be helpful. Barb and I just looked at each other, shaking our heads.

The officer seemed satisfied with the explanation and began writing up the papers to get us jailbirds released, but not until he'd sufficiently lectured them. He went on about putting the guns away instead of using the trunk for a shed and how not to jump to a conclusion if his car wasn't in the driveway when he got home.

Barb and I just grinned at him from behind the guys' backs, and when they walked to the sergeant's desk, he winked at us. Hanging with Barb definitely had its perks.

The boys continued to play on the floor while the four of us adults hurled a myriad of one-liners at one another.

"What the heck were you thinking, Jake? Reporting the car stolen; that's just crazy!" Barb fussed.

"Barb, let's just get outta here, and then we'll deal with explanations."

"Ellie, this whole mess could have been avoided if you'd just carried your purse with you. How do you go shopping if you don't have a purse?" Will said. "Where'd you get any money, anyway?" He hadn't even gotten to the part about "Who did I think I was driving *his* car?" But he didn't disappoint.

Officer Black was now back sitting at his desk, and it was obvious he couldn't help but overhear our arguments. His shaking head gave up his poor opinion of Will and Jake's attitudes. I was beginning to realize that just maybe this was my "normal" but didn't necessarily have to be. I didn't have to do this anymore.

The trooper came out with the papers for us to sign for our personal releases. When all the ink was dry, Barb and I gathered up the boys, who had been playing in the shopping bags.

"What in the world?" Barb said as she looked at her hands, all covered in yellow and red ink from picking up the bags. She looked down in time to see the mess the boys had made with our liquid embroidery paint tubes. Not only had they given themselves tattoos but managed to break holes in the metal tubes, enabling them to finger-paint on the shiny hardwood floors beneath the sergeant's desk. Little puddles of yellow and red paint coated the floor swirled by their fingerprints.

"Geez oh flip," I said as my eyes followed Barb's to the foot of the sergeant's desk. Jake and Will were standing in the midst of the painted collage. They folded the papers, turned, and walked toward the door. "Guess we're gonna get jammed up again."

"Ellie, let's go!" Will looked back over his shoulder. Barb and I just looked from each other back to the sergeant's desk. There were yellow and red footprints marking the guys' exit. Barb and I gathered the kids and tried to make the great escape, but not soon enough.

"Sir! Mr. Reilly, Mr. Kincaid!" the sergeant bellowed. Will and Jake turned around.

"Yes, sir?" Jake asked.

"I suggest you two gentlemen find some rags and clean up this floor before you leave." He pointed to his new art deco wood floor. The guy's eyes widened as they realized what an unwelcome design they'd left behind. Before they could give the unspoken command for Barb and me to clean up their mess, the sergeant interjected.

"You ladies go on ahead; your husbands can handle this." He grinned and winked, and Barb and I smiled back at him. Sometimes there is true justice, or karma. Not sure which this was, but I was grateful either way.

We grabbed up the kids and ushered them to the bathroom to clean up and out of the station and back into the Cadillac. Betsy would have to bring the big guys home tonight. The sergeant had slipped me the key.

"Dear God, get us out of here before the two of them come barreling out after us!" Barb said as she reached in her purse for a cigarette and rolled down the window.

"It won't be fun when they catch up with us tonight. Which way do I turn here?" I was confused already and wasn't yet out of the parking lot. Two hours into the forty-five-minute drive, we were home. So, the beltway's a circle, huh? We discovered it takes a good hour and a half to drive it once, all the way around. The boys finally settled down and conked out in the backseat.

"Barb, I think I'm done." I got into the slow lane and stayed there. No need for another visit from a trooper today.

"Huh?" She threw her cigarette butt out the window and rolled it up.

"I'm gonna lose my mind if I stay with him much longer." I shook my head and tears slid down my cheeks. "I think the only thing I'll miss is hanging with you and Jake."

"Nothing has to change with us, El." She reached over and squeezed my arm.

"Divorce always seems to divide and conquer friendships." I wiped the tears with the back of my hand. "Just look at Roberta."

"I know, but that won't happen with us." She let a heavy sigh escape. A sure sign she was sad. I knew her better than she did sometimes.

We drove in silence awhile until we realized we were well past our exit. "Oh well, let's just keep going since the beltway's a circle. I don't know about you, but I'm in no hurry to get home!" We circled the beltway until our exit came up again. We pulled up in front of my house and woke the boys up and pulled them into the house for a rude awakening. Kids shouldn't have to listen to this mess. I made up my mind that mine wouldn't have to listen to it much longer. I think that's what kept me from really killing him.

We walked into my living room, and I sent the boys off to the kitchen for a snack. Will and Jake took turns ranting and raving about what a mess we'd caused. We'd already planned to just let them beat their chests in front of each other and then take 'em down a peg or two when we got them alone, so we did. Problem is, when Will shuts me down and refuses to talk, there's not much left to say. The Russian and US governments could take some lessons from us when it comes to Cold War tactics.

"How'd it go last night?" Barb asked as she dropped her purse on my dining room table. It was Sunday morning, and Will had carted the kids off to church. My two hours a week with no one but Timmy to care for.

"Typical. He showed off for Jake and then refused to discuss anything with me." I sat two cups of coffee down next to the coffee cake she had brought from Giant.

"You're kidding me, right?" She opened the pastry and cut a few slices. "After all that belly aching, he didn't want to talk anymore?"

"Yeah, just walked in, sat down in his chair, and ignored me the rest of the night." I took the larger slice. "How about you?"

"I listened to Jake awhile and then made him see how ridiculous the entire thing was." She shook her head. "Then a little make-up sex, and life is good again. He even agreed to watch the kids so I could go to the grocery store and stop by here to see you."

I looked down at the half-eaten pastry in my hand. Tears welled up, and I choked back a sob. Barb looked up and realized why I didn't answer.

"Oh, hon, I'm sorry." She put her coffee down and reached over and covered my hand with hers.

A little sympathy was all it took, and I lost my composure. I dropped my head on the table and sobbed.

"Yeah, we used to do make-up sex." I lifted my head and looked at her. "I got at least three kids that way." I dropped my head back down on my crossed arms. When the make-up sex goes out of a marriage, there's not much left.

"What am I gonna do, Barb?" I finally lifted my head. "No make-up sex is not a good sign!" I leaned back in my chair and wiped my eyes with a napkin she handed me. "I can't leave. How will I make it with all these kids to take care of?"

"I know, but you know what? We're gonna get jobs, right?" She picked up the Sunday *Post* and pulled out the classifieds. "See, there's plenty of 'em! To hell with these men and their money; it's time for us to make some of our own." With that, she pulled out a pen and started circling prospects.

We sifted through the ads and made a game plan for calls the next day. She took a page and left one for me. How did I ever make it without her?

After Barb left, I stared at the classified ads, and it was then that I realized that it had never been that important to me to be independent, nor did I ever really have a burning desire to be on my own. Having kids, I'd always been "needed" by someone, and that had given me the purpose that I'd thought was enough, and maybe in a good marriage that would have been. But the realization hit me after Barb left that the difference was that Jake truly loved and adored her.

The hurt of knowing that Will didn't love me like he should have cut to the middle of me, but at the same time, birthed a resolve to survive and make the best of the hand that I'd been dealt. Who knew? Maybe I'd find a few wild cards.

The mere mention of me getting a job put Will into orbit. It didn't make any sense since he was always complaining about not having enough money. I knew that the real reason was he was afraid he'd have to take on some responsibility for the kids.

"Don't think I'm babysitting while you're at work," he said. There it was, out in the open.

"Geez oh flip, Will. You think I'm delusional, or what?" I carried the last of the dinner dishes into the kitchen, grateful for a reason to exit the room. I picked up the receiver and dialed Barb's number. She had called earlier, and I'd promised to call back.

"Jake gave me this ad from his office today. It talks about applying to work at the Government Printing Office working nighttime hours," she said, and she began reading the ad to me.

"Hmm, we wouldn't have to pay for sitters if we worked opposite shifts from the guys. What kind of jobs are they?"

She began to read the ad, but all it said was "clerical positions."

"Well, we were kind of 'clerical,' right?" I responded.

"Yeah, if that's a term that applies to licking envelopes!"

Roberta was interested, too, and Barb made appointments for all of us to have an interview. Karen and Ginger were our built-in sitters.

I drove over to Barb's, dropped off Ginger and the boys, and picked up her and Roberta.

"What kind of qualifications do you think we need to have for this interview?" I asked Barb.

"Not totally sure. Could be typing or alphabetizing stuff, filing. Guess we'll just have to wait and see."

"Will said it's probably filing jobs." He had told me not to bother to apply, that I couldn't spell well enough and wouldn't qualify anyway.

"Well, we've got to try," Roberta said as she primped in her compact mirror. Always on the prowl, that one.

We nailed the interviews and by noon the next day were part-time federal government employees. Not bad for rookies! We could tell the guys were stumped, just couldn't figure it, but we were ecstatic and figured it was time for a celebration.

"What are you gonna wear?" I asked Barb.

"Heck, I don't know."

"You pick out what you want to wear, I'll come over Saturday, and we'll put it together."

Barb ended up looking like a million bucks in the pants and top we made. Kind of like Laura Petrie on *The Dick Van Dyke Show*, and she was every bit as pretty as Mary Tyler Moore.

I'm so grateful that we moved back here, but I think Will and I both knew from the start it would most likely be the beginning of the end of us. Neither one of us ever said it out loud, but we knew it just the same. We just couldn't live in the same house seven days a week. Our weekend marriage in Cambridge had been tough enough, but full time was giving us a run for our money.

Neither Will nor I said it out loud, but my finding the job at GPO was a godsend for our home life. Our hours were opposite each other and kept us from having to endure each other's company too much. Between his rifle matches on the weekends and my ushering the kids to their events, we only had to spend small amounts of time together. I soon discovered that working helped me to keep my mind off my troubles.

I'd been stuck in the onesies for so long but was starting to catch up and hit my stride. I wondered what the tensies would be like.

"So, where do you live?" Barb asked Darlene, our coworker, during the lunch break on our first night on the job. She and Barb had been paired up to bind new training manuals.

"On Carter Street in Radiant Valley," Darlene said as she pulled her Fritos out of the bag. She wore her hair short and blond. Only her hairdresser knew for sure...

I looked up from my tuna sandwich. "Isn't that near the community pool?" I asked.

"Sure is, right next door," Darlene answered. "How'd you know?"

"I live just a few blocks from there." I took another bite and reached for the saltshaker.

"Well, you'll just have to join our carpool," Barb said.

"Hey, works for me." Darlene looked up from her Pepsi.

"Are you married?" Roberta asked, looking at her wedding ringless left hand.

"Nope, divorced a few years now. I have two kids, a boy and a girl."

"Got out of the onesies, huh?" I asked.

"Huh?" Darlene frowned my way. We explained how if you don't get past the onesies on the first try when playing jacks, it could take years to catch up.

"Yeah, we finally got out of the onesies when we got this job," Barb explained. "Been stuck there awhile."

"How do you get to the tensies?" Darlene asked. We all just looked at one another, grasping for an answer.

"I guess you have to die to get there, 'cause none of us ever has," I piped up. "At least when it comes to dealing with men; we're stuck in the same ruts. Kinda like a hamster on a wheel."

"Well, there's strength in numbers, right?" Darlene asked.

"That's what they say." Roberta balled up her paper lunch bag and headed to the trash can.

Darlene fit right in and joined the carpool and was already a Tom Jones groupie. That's when we knew it was meant to be.

After a while, the outings with Barb, Jake, and the kids were about the only time Will and I spent more than an hour breathing the same air. His sarcasm became more and more bitter as the time went by, and before long, I was even dreading the picnics.

"Yeah, the potato salad was good, all right," Will answered Jake, when he complimented my cooking. "She gains at least a pound each time she makes it."

Even I was stunned at his cruelty. The silence was broken by the kids' voices laughing as they played hide-and-seek in the patch of woods next to the picnic tables. Jake just looked at him, turned, and walked away. I often wondered how those two stayed friends.

"What's wrong with him?" Barb leaned over and said under her breath as he followed Jake to the river's edge. The kids had come out of the woods and climbed onto the playground equipment. Jake and Will pulled out their fishing poles. Barb and I stayed behind to put the food back into the coolers.

"Just another cheery day in the land of Reilly." I cleared the paper plates from the table. "He's a lot better when Jake's around though."

"This is better?" she asked, and the look in my eyes gave her the answer she was looking for.

My relationship with Will died gradually, as I think most bad marriages do. I could blame it all on him, and for the most part, I do, but as Barb would say, it's time to "fess up." I knew six months into it that I shouldn't have married him, but by then Roger was on the way, and the cards were dealt.

Somewhere along the way I managed to find my confidence again. I think that day in the police station I realized that being stuck in the onesies was a choice, not a fate. Getting beyond the onesies was up to me and nobody else. Alone or together, happiness was my choice, and I chose to be happy.

It was a slow letting go, first physically and then emotionally, as we slipped away from each other. Each of us pretended it wasn't happening, but I knew in my heart it was over. Waking up slowly, only this time, to the death of my marriage. I had pretty much decided that as long as we could cohabitate semipeacefully, I could hang in there for the kids' sake. After all, a distant father was better than none at all, right?

"Did you talk to Roberta?" Barb asked over the phone. I picked up a runaway tennis shoe and threw it down the hallway in the direction of the mudroom. My poor telephone cord was worn from being pulled in every direction and would only stretch to the end of the hallway.

"Yeah, it looks like we're going. She won the contest."

Roberta had gathered enough signatures on a petition for some local politician and won four backstage tickets and passes to the Tom Jones concert at Shady Grove this weekend. He sure does have a good voice, and from what I can tell swings his hips as good or better than Elvis. The four of us (we now referred to ourselves as the "Tensies") had gathered at Roberta's and watched him on *The Ed Sullivan Show*, drooling and dancing all over her living room. I felt like I was sixteen again, although now that I think about it, I don't think I ever was sixteen.

"What are you wearing?" Barb asked.

"Not sure, probably just a pantsuit," I answered, preoccupied with a report card of Ginger's sitting on the kitchen counter I'd just picked up. *Egads, not so good.*

"Hey, I'll call you back. It's report card day, you know," I reminded her.

"Ugggh," she replied. Report card day with Jay was guaranteed to rock the Kincaid household. Jake tried so hard to connect with Jay, but it was tough. Holding onto that kid's attention was something that not even I had been able to do for more than ten seconds at a time. I don't know how anyone could expect a teacher to do it all day long.

❧

The Tensies were decked out to the nines as Roberta drove to Shady Grove near Gaithersburg for the concert. Aqua Net kept our hair immovable and lipstick was being blotted on a passed around Kleenex.

"I hear he's really hung," Roberta said.

"Is that what they talk about in that fan club you joined?" I asked.

"I heard it's just a sock," Darlene answered.

"All the better to 'sock it to me!'" Roberta laughed. Barb elbowed me as we sat in the backseat and rolled her eyes. We married ladies had been banished to the backseat. Barb had told me she suspected that Roberta had been messing around on Dick before they separated. She didn't have any evidence, just a gut feeling. My jury was still out, but I'd learned to go with her gut.

We pulled into our parking space at Shady Grove and walked into the concert hall. The stage sat in the middle, and it was a very intimate setting for a superstar like Tom Jones. The lights came up, and out came Tom, singing, "What's New Pussycat" and dancing like he'd never stop. Even in the midst of the concert frenzy, I was reminded of the afternoon in the police station.

The women responded to his charisma like teenyboppers at a Beatles concert, screaming and dancing in the aisles. Roberta was joining in like she owned the place. Her excitement was contagious, and while we didn't scream, the remaining Tensies did do some dancing in and out of their seats.

"Geez Louise, what are you doing?" I asked Roberta when I looked down to see her pulling a pink pair of lacy panties out of her purse.

"Sending him my best!" She held on with her left index finger and pulled them back with her right, letting it go like a slingshot. The panties landed at Tom's feet and the three of us slid down in our seats, but we shouldn't have worried, as a dozen other pairs flew through the air right behind Roberta's.

"Better duck—there's no guarantee they're clean!" I hollered to Barb and Darlene.

When the last of the encores was over, we wove our way through the crowd to the security guard and presented our backstage passes.

"Here they are, Joe," the guard hollered over his shoulder. A large colored man in a green shirt looked our way.

"Right over here, ladies." Joe directed us with his hands, waving toward the dressing rooms.

He ushered us behind the wall next to the stage. I walked behind Roberta, and Barb and Darlene followed close behind me. I could see Tom standing with his back to us, giving out autographs. Joe whispered something in his ear, and Tom nodded. He signed one more autograph and turned to face the three of us. His curly black hair glistened with sweat and a blue towel hung around his neck.

Joe made the introductions. "These are the ladies with tonight's backstage passes, Mr. Jones."

"Well, what lovely ladies they are, Joe." Tom's Welsh accent added to the swoon factor, and his brown eyes twinkled. His white shirt was buttoned only at the bottom. "Maybe I should button it up for him," Roberta whispered in my ear, but even I was too enamored to answer.

He stood in front of the makeup mirror with the big white light bulbs all around it, just like the ones I had seen in the movies. People milled around him, putting things away.

Tom had a gentleness about him as he posed with us for pictures. Of course, Roberta went first. It was embarrassing the way she hung all over him, running her fingers through the hair on his exposed chest. He took it well (what man wouldn't?). Darlene and I started to make cracks, and Barb just did her normal stand-in-the-background regal thing. Well, it worked because Tom had eyes for her as soon as he looked her way.

"Well, my princess, why don't you come on over here?" He motioned to her.

She was just so darned pretty, standing there in a red dress with her hair swept up on top of her head like royalty, and he obviously recognized it. She attracted them like flies without trying, even rich, sexy ones.

Barb smiled, looked down at the floor, and walked over. Tom put his arm around her waist and kissed her on the cheek, and Roberta shrank back and frowned. Roberta—the schoolgirl in her seemed to come out more and more lately.

I snapped a few pictures and after she began to breathe again, Barb grabbed the camera from me and told us to pose with Tom. Darlene, Roberta, and I stood next to him.

"And we saved the best for last, did we?" he winked at me, and I thought my knees would buckle. Barb snapped a few pictures, and Tom made a gracious exit, but not before he finagled another kiss from Barb as she blushed and shrank back.

"Yeah, the 'princess' managed to get two kisses!" I laughed as we climbed back in the car. Roberta put her car into drive and hit the gas a little harder than necessary.

We were still talking about the concert and backstage visit as she pulled off the Baltimore Washington Parkway. The neon Hot Shoppes sign blinked at us from across the road. We decided to stretch the evening out longer with a stop for some onion rings and a Pepsi.

As the waitress took our order and walked away, Roberta confided that it was official; she and Dick were separating. Barb and I didn't say much, but I know I could've read her mind that time.

"Yeah, Dick's moving out and back home with his mother until he can find a place." She took the last drag off her cigarette before snuffing it out in the ashtray.

"How'd you manage that?" Barb finally opened her mouth in between bites and sips.

"Make 'em miserable enough, and they'll go anywhere to get away from you," Roberta said.

It was strange to think that one of us would be divorced. We'd always had so much in common with our lives mirroring the other. Darlene had been the first one of us who was single, but we'd grandfathered that in when she'd signed up.

No wonder Roberta had been acting like she had. Her misery was a pretty well-kept secret. We knew they argued a lot, but with the hassles of raising kids and all, we all fought. And all this time, I thought I was the one with the lousy marriage.

Roberta and Dick separated and eventually divorced, and she continued to live with the kids up the street from Barb. Dick took their children on most weekends, giving Roberta some much sought after freedom. She still carpooled with us some of the time but began to hang with some other single women from GPO.

"Where's Roberta?" Darlene asked as she slipped into the backseat of Betsy. Barb rolled her window up as she put her cigarette out in the ashtray.

"She's riding with Shirley," I answered as I put Betsy back into drive.

After a few moments, Barb piped up. "Guess we ain't single enough for her these days."

Our contact with Roberta lessened, but we chalked it up to the single girl syndrome. We still went to several of Tom's concerts over the next couple of years, traveling to Atlantic City, New York, Baltimore, or DC, and lucky for us we weren't more than a few hours' car drive from any one location.

Barb and I made plans to take a bus trip to Atlantic City to see Tom in concert. Roberta and Darlene couldn't get off work, so it was just the two of us. Having daughters as built-in babysitters was well worth the cost of a new Rolling Stones album for Ginger and Supremes for Karen. The guys were happy to let us go. They had a Redskins game, so we'd never be missed. We cooked dinner ahead of time, so all the girls had to do was heat stuff up on the stove.

It was still dark as we drove into DC at Union Station, where the bus would meet us for our 6:00 a.m. departure. I parked Betsy, and we locked the car. "Looks like we're not the only groupies in DC!" Barb laughed when she saw the line of women getting on the bus.

"Yeah, but none of them can say that Tom called them 'princess' except for you!" I reminded her, and she grinned.

Barb loved the slot machines, and I must say I had fun teasing her about her gambling habit. At least now I knew she had a weakness. Me and food, Barb and one-armed bandits.

"At least when I buy a begonia I have something to show for it."

"You'll thank me when I hit it big!" She dropped three more coins in the slot. I shook my head and walked outside.

I strolled the boardwalk for a little while as she'd win, then lose, and then win some more. It was fun to hang out in the glitzy casinos and pretend we really belonged in a castle of sorts. Since Camelot had left town, there'd been very little hob-knobbing with royalty.

Tom didn't disappoint us, as we danced in our seats and a few times in the aisles. "What's New Pussycat" was the latest craze. By the time it was over, we were spent and both happy to crawl on the bus and sleep for the five-hour ride home. It would be about 2 o' clock a.m. by the time we got to the bus station in DC, and then we'd drive home from there.

We were snoozing pretty well when I overheard the bus driver talking on his CB radio. "Are you sure we should go in?" he asked. "Well, if you say so." He hung up the radio microphone and shook his head.

I wondered what he was talking about but was napping too well to really care. I opened my eyes to what seemed to be either a bad dream or a lousy movie. The next thing I knew, we were riding through the streets of DC, but the noise was deafening. People were shouting and running in all directions. It was a mass of humanity between the bus and the terminal.

Soldiers were everywhere with helmets and masks in front of their faces. They lined the streets of my nation's capital, scattered between burning buildings and vehicles with windows smashed. It was like waking up in the middle of a bad dream, only it kept on going.

"What the heck is going on?" Barb asked as she peered out the window. "It looks like we've been invaded!"

Before I could reply, the bus driver picked up his microphone to make an announcement.

"Ladies and gentlemen, I don't know how many of you know, but Martin Luther King was assassinated yesterday." There was an audible gasp from the passengers. When you're in a casino, not much news from the outside world penetrates. "Evidently, it sparked some rioting in our major cities like Washington and Baltimore."

"Riots?" I asked.

"Shhh!" Barb nudged me. "Listen!"

"I will be stopping in front of the DC bus terminal and the National Guard will be standing by to escort you inside the building. Please go where they tell you to go," He said. "In the meantime, I must ask you to bend over and keep your heads below the window line. We don't want anyone getting shot or hit by something coming through a window."

We looked out the windows of the bus to see cars on fire, windshields busted out, and stores in flames. It looked like Armageddon in the capital of the free world. Panic gripped me in a way I'd never known before.

"What the heck is this all about? Why would they riot? What good does that do?" Barb said with panic in her eyes. I pulled her down, and we sat on the floor of the bus in front of our seats with our feet underneath our chairs. We could feel the bus turn into the terminal parking lot, and the driver announced it was safe to stand up.

We grabbed our purses and held hands as we waited our turn to get off the bus. We agreed that wherever one went, the other would go, too.

"Now I know what they mean when they say 'the hair on the back of my neck stood up' because I think mine is," Barb whispered in my ear as we inched our way off the bus.

My heart beat wildly as we rushed from the bus through the human shield of a tunnel that the National Guardsmen had made for us to run through. I could hear people screaming and glass shattering followed by more shouts and cries. We made it inside the terminal, and once we gained our composure, we joined the other passengers that stood in line at the telephone booths that dotted the room. The soldiers herded us away from the windows. I now knew what it felt like to fear for my life.

"How are we going to get out of here?" I wondered out loud.

"Why in the heck didn't they tell us what was going on earlier? Why did they bring us all the way into town? You and I could have jumped out a few miles outside of the city and walked home for that matter!" Barb said.

We ducked at the sound of breaking glass from outside and dropped like bricks to the ground at the sound of gunshots. When the noise stopped, we stayed down on the floor, leaning up against the wall, out of the line of fire. We cried and held onto each other. We hoped.

The television set above a bank of phones droned on.

"Stokely Carmichael, leader of the Student Nonviolent Coordinating Committee at Howard University, led a peaceful march that turned violent in the nation's capital," the reporter stated. "Over twenty thousand negroes were rioting when it became difficult for the 3,100-person police force of the nation's capital to control. President Johnson called in 13,600 National Guard troops, and they were able to turn back the crowds just two blocks short of the White House."

We stared at the television. Nothing seemed real. There were tanks on the White House lawn and in front of the Capitol. Soldiers with machine guns were everywhere. This doesn't happen here, not in our city. I grabbed Barb's hand. Not in our country. I felt like I was watching the *Twilight Zone*, only this time, I was an unpaid extra.

"What is this world coming to?" I asked Barb. She just shook her head. For the first time since I'd known her, she was not picture-perfect in public. If I hadn't been so scared, I would have had a field day with her less-than-Barbie-like appearance.

"Why would anyone want to burn down their own city?" Barb asked me. We were full of questions that had no answers. "Why would they want to hurt us?"

I had no answers. No one did.

After a few hours of not hearing any gunfire or breaking glass, we stood in line at the phone booth to call home.

"Will?" I asked as he picked up the other end of the line.

"My god, Ellie! Where the hell are you? You were supposed to be back here hours ago!" he hollered. Forget asking if I was okay; it was obvious that I had interrupted his beauty sleep.

"We're at the bus station in DC. Can you come and get us? They won't let me drive the car."

"Ellie, they won't let anyone in or out of the city, and there's a curfew in place until further notice," he explained in his normal condescending tone.

"I guess we'll just have to wait until this blows over and then drive out when they let us," I said, resigned to more time under siege. "Tell the kids I love them." I hung up the phone and realized for the very first time that I truly didn't love him anymore. He hadn't even asked if I was okay.

Then it hit me. I might not ever see my kids again.

I hung up the receiver, and an empty feeling of fear and desperation landed in the pit of my stomach. I didn't realize that tears were streaming down my face. Barb was on the phone next to me explaining our dilemma to Jake. I stared across the room, slid down the wall, and sat on the floor, watching the madness going on around us. She slid down next to me with the phone cord stretching just far enough. She grabbed onto my hand and squeezed.

"Yeah, we're okay now that we're inside. The soldiers are doing a good job of guarding us." She listened to him on the other end and reached over to wipe the tears from my face with a napkin out of her pocket.

"Yeah, there's a kitchen here, and it looks like they're letting us have whatever we want. We're okay." She nodded at me as if trying to convince herself. "Sure, we'll call you when we're on our way home. Yes, we'll head out west toward Virginia when the time comes." She listened some more. "I love you, too." She stood up just long enough to hang up the receiver and ducked back down next to me.

"What's up, El?" She wrapped her arm around my shoulder. Without waiting for an answer, she reached over and pulled me close for a big one-armed hug. We just sat there terrified at the noise and craziness going on around us.

"I don't love him anymore, and he doesn't love me," I said. There. I'd said it out loud. There were shouts of anger from the street outside. "I just want to see my kids again."

"Oh, El, it's gonna be all right. We'll be with our kids in just a little while, you'll see." I leaned my head on her shoulder and closed my eyes.

I'd always been afraid of the dark, afraid to go to sleep without at least one light on. Now it was darkness instead of light for protection. Darkness blanketed the city with the exception of the golden glow of flames in the distance.

We made it through the night, napping here and there, using each other's shoulders for pillows. Barb woke with a stiff neck, and I rubbed her shoulders to try and loosen her up. Once it was daylight, the curfew was lifted.

"Ladies and gentlemen," the ticket agent announced over the loudspeaker, "if your vehicle is parked in the terminal parking lot, you may retrieve it now and head home." He went on to offer more advice on the best routes out of the city. Barb stood there taking notes on the back of a napkin. It was a good thing my navigator was with me.

We found Betsy and headed home. I followed the directions faithfully, and we were home by eleven o'clock that morning. It took a few hours to get there since Jake had made Barb promise to go home on the Virginia side of the beltway. He felt it was safer in case we made a wrong turn; we wouldn't end up in the bad part of town. A wrong turn? Us?

Jake met us at my house. Will stood there as I hugged each one of my kids until one by one, they wriggled away. I smelled each one's hair and recognized their scent from when they were little. I promised myself never to forget the fear of losing them or being lost to them as long as I lived.

I'd always known they were the light of my life, and after the last twenty-four hours, I knew for sure that living without them promised nothing but darkness for me. But I also knew for sure that even my children couldn't give me what I needed most.

CHAPTER 7

Barb
It's My Party and I'll Cry if I Want To

Rioting is not revolutionary, but reactionary because it invites defeat.
It involves an emotional catharsis, but it must be followed by a sense of
futility.

—*Martin Luther King Jr.*

Well, now we were career women. Who would've believed it? After several jump starts, Ellie and I were making our own dough in the form of a paycheck.

Not that the jobs or the results were all that glamorous. It was just more work for us, when we let ourselves think about it, but we decided it was worth it just the same. It was amazing that once I was bringing home some bacon of my own, Jake didn't seem to think that sharing a bank account with Will was all that important.

"Yeah, but now we can save the money together, Barb. We won't have to pay the bank fees." He put the newspaper down next to him on the couch.

"Don't worry, hon. I don't mind paying the fees on my own checking and savings account. I'll give you thirty dollars a week toward bills, and I'm saving the rest."

"Saving for what?" He leaned forward.

"What's it matter? Just saving." That was all he was getting from me on this deal. I'd had to learn that sometimes I just had to know when to put a sock in it.

I decided you could read all the books you wanted by the famous feminists—Gloria Steinem, Darlene Friedan, and whoever you wanted—but when you had kids and a husband, it wasn't as easy as all that. I'd learned to artfully maneuver my way through married life and with a little give on Jake's part for a change; we were doing better and arguing less.

"Geez, Jake, has the whole world gone mad?" I asked, standing on our front porch and gawking at the smoke on the horizon. It was a few days after Ellie and I escaped the bus terminal in DC. The television blared the latest on the riots that were just a few miles from our front door.

"Seems so." He stared at the sky. "Kids, go on back inside," he said as he held the storm door open. Karen and Jay ducked under his arm and retreated into the house.

"I know it's been a few years, but it seems as if since JFK was killed, nothing's been right anymore," I said. "I mean, it's only been five years since that, but everyone seems to be angry all the time. When's it going to stop?"

"It won't until something changes." Jake pulled me closer. He leaned back on the railing and pulled my back up against him. I always felt so safe when he did that, even with the sky gray with smoke.

"Like what?"

"Racism. Like it or not, it looks like our generation is the one that's going to have to come to grips with the colored and whites living together, without killing one another."

"But all these stupid ideas about bussing our kids to inner-city schools to make things 'equal' doesn't make sense either." I leaned my head back on his shoulder and stared at the sky. The smoky haze was starting to cover the sky over our home on Columbia Place.

Politicians were trying to come up with equitable solutions between the races ever since the Civil War, but this time it would be at the expense of our kids' education. Our kids were supposed to be the political "guinea pigs." Living in the suburbs of the nation's capital made us sitting ducks when it came to instituting a new policy of forced integration of schools.

"Will's thinking about sending Ginger to Elizabeth Seton, a Catholic girls' school. It's going to cost him a fortune to keep her from going to Fairmont Heights," Jake said.

"How can they afford that, Jake?"

"I guess Ellie will have to miss a few red-dot sales." He chuckled, but I cringed at the thought.

"And Will might have to sit out a football game or two."

"Touché." He kissed me on the back of the neck. "But what choice does he have, Barb? She can't go to school there. She'd never be able to stay after school for anything. I know it's not easy for Will to let go of that much cash, but he does have his priorities straight on this one." He defended him, even when he didn't need to. I turned and looked him in the eye.

"I think it's time we move outta here," I said.

"Move? Move where?"

"Surely you can't be serious? Just look in front of you, Jake. Look at the smoke." I pointed to the sky. "It's only a few miles from here. Where will the flames end up?" I was pulling out all the stops. "Besides, half our neighbors have already sold, and the coloreds are moving in! They've burned down their neighborhoods, and now they're moving into ours!"

Thanks to Ellie's influence, I'd changed my vocabulary, if not my prejudices. We'd already lost some selling power by procrastinating. "Maybe you want to live next door to them, but I don't."

He just stared at the sky, and I walked back inside, letting the storm door slam behind me for effect.

Within a few weeks, Jake was talking about relocating as if it were his idea. I'd learned that if I let him take the ball and run with it, things got done.

We put a realtor on it, and within a week we had a buyer for our house and a new house in our sights.

"This guy's a speculator, Barb." Jake ran his fingers through his hair and agonized over whether or not to take the offer that had been made on the house. It was a thousand lower than what we'd hoped for. "He's a slumlord."

"I don't care who he is, Jake. What color is his money? As long as it's green, that's all that counts. So what if he's an investor?"

Jake sighed, shook his head, and signed the contract.

We'd found a single-family three-bedroom ranch on the other side of Prince George's County, about seven miles away, two miles from Ellie. Now there's a bonus. We were all moved in before school started.

The kids settled into their new schools. Jake fashioned the basement into a family room over the first year we were there. Karen was twirling on the junior high school majorette squad and making new friends.

"Where'd you get the money for all these records?" I asked as I picked up the Beatles' latest forty-five lying on her dresser next to her record player.

"Oh, I've been saving my allowance," she mumbled and took the record away from me. I knew she was lying because the girl had never "saved" a dime in her life. It was an ongoing joke around the house at how money burned a hole in her pocket.

I worked on her for about two minutes before she cracked. It's not that my interrogation skills are that great; she's just got too big a conscience for her own good. She confessed that she and Ginger had a shoplifting routine worked out and had pulled their modified Bonnie and Clyde routine in probably half the stores in Capital Plaza. Jake hit the roof.

"You're taking every single thing back, young lady!" he ranted. He called Will, and together they walked the little juvenile delinquents from store to store returning the stolen goods—wallets, records, books, makeup. You name it, they had it.

That night when they got home, Karen went to her room, and Jake and I lay in bed talking. He described the terror in the girls' eyes as the proprietor of each store threatened to call the police or their schools.

"I think they learned their lesson," he said.

"Yeah, but just think about it if we hadn't figured it out. It might have been a really good Christmas." I chuckled, relieved that I wouldn't have to hide a file in Karen's next birthday cake.

And then she hit puberty. There should be a chapter of required reading on this before you have kids, but if there were, we probably wouldn't have any. What do I tell her about what's happening with her body without actually having to *tell* her about sex? I'm sorry, they didn't teach this one in home economics, and they should have. I was stuck in the onesies on this one, that was for sure.

So, I did what every good mom did and went to the drug store, bought a book called *All About Your Body* and gave it to her.

"Here, you like to read books, right?" I asked.

"Yeah, sure." Karen looked up from brushing Kelly's hair. Geez, she was turning into a young lady right in front of me. This just couldn't be. A few years passed, and she developed into what looked like a woman. Heck, she had a better figure than I did.

I dropped the book on the couch beside her and walked back to the kitchen and assured myself that if she had any questions, she'd ask. I bought extra Kotex pads and told her where I kept them, in the linen closet. Whew, that wasn't so hard.

Karen's life of crime seemed to be behind her. She did well in school and worked hard to stay on the honor roll. Her love of twirling and Jake's threat to make her quit if her grades fell was enough to keep her in line. The years went by, and before we knew it, she was in high school.

"Barb, we can't let her go to that school. It's not safe!" Jake worried. We had just received a letter that confirmed the rumor we had heard. Karen was being transferred to a different high school beginning in her junior year. Forced integration of schools was now a reality in our lives. Moving to a better neighborhood had bought us a few years but hadn't accomplished what we thought it would. Karen did luck out in that her new school was really no further away and not as scary as Fairmont, but there had been racial riots at Bladensburg, Jake's and my alma mater, the year before. We'd moved to the far end of the county but evidently not far enough to escape the clutches of mandatory bussing out of our own neighborhood.

"Dad, it's really not that bad. They said they expelled the kids who were causing the problems. I'll be fine." Karen put the letter back down on the dining room table. She'd already signed up for majorette squad tryouts. Jake sighed and ran his fingers through his hair.

"Well, let me think about it," he said and headed to the living room for the evening news.

"Ginger's hating the Catholic school. I don't think she's keeping up well. They're so much further ahead than the kids in public schools," Ellie said over the phone.

The federally mandated integration of schools had triggered a lot of change. People like us had bought homes in certain areas partly because of the good schools, only to find out that our kids were being bussed twenty-five miles in another direction.

"It seems like the only ones making out here are the private schools and the government!" Jake ranted at the dinner table. I reached over and took a piece of bread to go with my spaghetti.

"What do you mean?" I handed a piece to him.

"The private schools are making money, and the government doesn't have to pay to educate those kids." He took the bread and spread on some butter.

I agree that everyone should have a good education. So, why not bring the schools in the lower income neighborhoods up to snuff instead of bussing kids where they don't want to go? I just didn't get it.

It worked out okay for Karen since the riots and fights had run their course by the time she got there. She was sixteen years old, on the majorette squad, working part time at a coffee shop, and dating the captain of the football team.

Her grades were pretty good, but not as good as before she discovered boys, and never good enough to suit Jake. Ever since her second-grade teacher told him that she was "gifted," he expected so much from her. She'd turned into a pretty young girl and was a good combination of both Jake and me, if I did say so myself.

It was summertime, and it was time for our annual family vacation with the Reillys on Lake Erie. The best part of our little "beach barracks" was that there was no kitchen. We ate in the mess hall, and let me tell you, soldiers don't go without food, and neither did we.

Jake, Will, Roger, and Scott took part in the National Rifle Matches, so they had something to keep them busy. El and I were busy enough keeping an eye on Karen, Ginger, and the younger boys. For once, the girls were a bigger challenge than the boys. The base was crawling with testosterone, and for two teenage girls, it could be a dangerous combination. The problem was getting the girls to realize that, since they thought they'd died and gone to heaven.

Ellie and I trudged across the sand carting beach bags and kids, heading for the snack bar.

"Roberta asked me for a loan, but I didn't have it to give to her. I felt bad. I would've really liked to help. I guess Dick's not being very helpful since he moved out," I said to Ellie.

"Yeah, she came to me, too. Don't get mad, but I loaned her my tent money." We'd been saving for a bigger tent for camping at the beach.

"You did? Can she pay it back fast enough?"

"I guess I assumed she would..."

"You're a better woman than I am, that's for sure."

"Or just a bigger sucker."

"You make the call." I winked at her and walked faster, while the sand burned my bare feet.

Ellie and I had made the decision to go to the beach with the kids every year whether the guys could go or not. We couldn't afford to rent a cottage or hotel, so we'd decided to diversify and get into real estate, at least portable real estate. We'd already reserved a tent site at Assateague State Park, a few miles south of Ocean City, Maryland.

We made it to the entrance of the snack bar and dropped our stuff outside, grateful for the coolness of the overhead fans.

"Barb, will you keep an eye on William for a minute?"

She'd sat the two-and-a-half-year-old on the pool table next to the jukebox. The girls gravitated to the music machine and started dropping in their babysitting coins, selecting tunes. The little kids and I stood and pondered what I was not going to buy them, no matter how well they pled their case.

"Hot town, summer in the city, back of my neck getting dirty and gritty," the Lovin' Spoonful crooned over the loudspeaker.

Ellie came back from the ladies' room and picked up William off the pool table and walked away. I glanced back toward the pool table. No way. The little darling had left a deposit, nice and tidy. Tootsie Roll size.

"Ellie, where's his diaper?" I whispered in her ear. Her eyes got wide and looked to the floor. There it sat, under the pool table on the floor. I squatted down and picked it up and scooped William out of her arms. The kid was always stripping.

"You're cleaning it up. I'm not the momma!" I said and headed toward the ladies' room.

146

"But he did it on your watch!"

"I'll probably end up with racing stripes on my arm as it is. You'd better hurry up before someone sees!" I looked over my shoulder, and she rushed to the bathroom to retrieve paper to clean up the mess. I whispered to the girls to keep the hired help's attention diverted for a minute, and after cleaning up, we made a hasty retreat out the door. "I pity the fool that racks his balls on that table next!" Ellie laughed as we exited stage left.

"Man, we never had an opportunity like this when we were their age. Hundreds, no thousands, of guys to choose from," Ellie whispered to me later as we stood in line at the mess hall, waiting to get our dinner. You couldn't look ten feet and not find a male in his twenties checking out our girls.

As worried as it made me, Jake was in full panic mode.

"Barb, you've got to keep an eye on her every minute," he said as he grabbed his rifle to take to the match.

"Yeah, Jake, don't worry. I'm on it."

Well, we managed to keep the girls from getting pregnant, but it wasn't for their lack of trying. Ellie caught Ginger in the top bunk of their barracks with Melvin, a young soldier from Florida.

"I went to unlock the door, but it was already open, so I just walked in and flipped on the light. Covers and clothes started flying, and the little creep, well…maybe not so little," she said as she held her hands up indicating length, "jumped down, quickly introduced himself while dressing, and exited stage left." Ellie sat her coffee cup down and shook her head. Not wanting to ruin their vacation, she didn't tell Will.

"What did Ginger say?"

"Mostly 'Uh, uh, uh.'"

"You Reilly women are hot blooded, you know." A lot of help I was.

"Hmm, yeah, I guess I can't argue that one."

"Now I know why people resorted to chastity belts," I said to Ellie the next day as we sat on the beach. We kept watch over our flocks playing in the water, building sandcastles, and flirting with the lifeguard on the wooden raft floating about twenty yards out. That's where Karen had focused her attention the past few days.

My biggest ace in the hole with her was that she thought she was in love with Lee, the football player. So, I was counting on her conscience keeping her in check, and I didn't play fair, bringing Lee's name up at every opportunity, hoping that she wouldn't do much more than flirt.

Boy, it was weird when your kids began to date. First of all, I wasn't old enough to have a daughter that was marrying age. I got married a month shy of seventeen, so my theory was that she thought she's grown up. I know I did at that age. Geez.

I'm thirty-four now. When did that happen? It seems like I woke up one day and was almost halfway through the thirties to forty. Wow, was that a blow. But I must admit, sex had a new appeal to me those days.

I'm not sure what happened; all I know is that I couldn't wait to get the kids to bed at night. Of course, Jay is like a kid that just drank a pot of strong coffee and still, at the age of twelve, didn't like to sleep any more than he did when he was four months old.

Jake was enjoying my new interest in bedroom activities. I wasn't sure how long it would last, but he wasn't complaining.

El was good about occupying Kelly and Jay for an hour or so in the afternoon in between rifle matches for my daily tryst with Jake, and Keith, the lifeguard, diverted Karen's attentions.

After a few sunburns, bug bites, several picka-nickas, and lots of swimming, we packed up and headed back to Maryland. The guys didn't win first place, but each of them placed in at least one competition and wound up with a couple of little trophies, enough to keep the egos fed.

Ginger had a new boyfriend in Melvin, and Karen dumped the lifeguard in favor of her hometown boyfriend.

A few days after we got home, I was cooking dinner and decided that Kelly had been out of my sight a little too long. She was five, and a pretty good kid, but when it got too quiet, my mom radar went off. I turned the flame down on the macaroni and fried perch and headed toward the bedroom.

The linen closet door was open, and she'd pulled everything out of the bottom of the closet to get to the kittens that our cat, Maggie, had given birth to just three weeks before.

"Look, Mommy, she's letting me pet one!" Kelly looked up through her dark brown bangs while she held a gray and white kitten in her two hands.

"Yeah, I see that, Kel. Just be really careful, okay?" I reminded her. I began picking up the toilet paper, extra towels, and a few boxes of Kotex to put them back in the closet.

Hmm, why are there still three boxes of Kotex left? It doesn't look like Karen has used any...

That familiar, dreaded stuck in the onesies "you might be pregnant" feeling hit me, only this time, I wasn't the one that killed the rabbit.

For once, I wanted to be wrong. I prayed I was wrong, but knew in my heart that I wasn't. Why didn't I get her on the pill when I caught her and Lee in the living room? How stupid can I be? A knot in the pit of my stomach told me that my suspicions were right. The same knot that had shown up eighteen years ago when I worried that *I* was pregnant.

"Barb, quit blaming yourself." Ellie said as she turned into the GPO parking lot. That's what friends were for: telling you lies when you needed them most.

"El, I can't get out of this one. I should've taken her to the doctor before it needed to be for a pregnancy test." Guilt was following me wherever I went these days.

When I confronted Karen, she folded like a house of cards, confessing that she'd missed her period.

"We want to get married."

"Is that what Lee wants?" I asked. She assured me that he did and called him at work to let him know there was a command performance required in our dining room when he got off.

I have to hand it to the boy (hey, eighteen years old is still a boy, despite proof to the contrary); he never wavered about taking on his responsibilities. He'd changed his mind about going to college and was going to work in the family business as an apprentice bricklayer.

"Mr. and Mrs. Kincaid, I know this looks awful, but you have to know that I do love Karen." He started his please-don't-kill-me-just-yet speech and put his arm across Karen's shoulders. "And we were planning to get married in June when she graduated anyway."

Did he have to remind me that she was still in school?

We agreed to allow them to marry if she would sign up for night school to finish her high school education. It broke my heart that she'd miss the same things I'd missed—proms, parties, college, the list goes on and on. I guess it's true that if you don't learn from past history, you're doomed to repeat it. Why did she have to be the one to pay that price? My fault, all my fault.

I remembered the day I'd given her the *All About Your Body* book. Why didn't I do more? I knew what had happened to me. I guess I just thought lightning couldn't strike twice. Now I know that only applies to trees.

We all agreed that the wedding needed to be soon. Lee and Karen met with Lee's parish priest and set up the ceremony for a week from Friday. Can't waste time when there's a bun in the oven.

The two of us shopped for a wedding dress and settled on a semiformal knee-length dress and took it home to show Jake. He was disappointed and sent us back out to find a real wedding gown. His daughter might be having a shot-gun marriage (he did actually threaten to shoot Lee when we told him), but she was going to have a real wedding.

Karen and I headed back out for more shopping and found a pretty empire waist, embroidered gown that didn't require that I take out a loan.

An unexpected wedding, even a small one, can put a strain on a budget. Jake decided we'd just cash in some of the savings bonds we'd been buying through payroll deduction for as long as we could remember. Thank goodness for nest eggs.

"Are you going to get Ginger on the pill?" I asked Ellie. She picked up her Pepsi bottle and took the last swig. We'd gone to the beach for a quick afternoon of sunning ourselves at Sandy Point, the beach right next to the Chesapeake Bay Bridge.

"I don't know. I bought some rubbers and gave them to her," she confessed. "I even explained how to use them."

"Oh, do tell!" I asked, knowing I'd live to regret it.

"Well, I reached over to the kitchen counter and grabbed a banana…" She went on, and before we knew it, we were doubled over laughing in the sand.

The people on the neighboring beach towels started looking our way, trying to figure out what was so funny.

"It's...kind of..." Ellie giggled as she tried to explain to the lady on the next towel but just gave up.

By now, half the beach was giggling along with us but still didn't know why. Trying to recover, I picked up my little transistor radio and blew off the sand. Mama Cass sang "Dream a Little Dream of Me," and Ellie began to sing along. Man, I wish I could sing like that.

"Your voice actually sounds like Mama Cass," I said and straightened up the beach towel.

"Thanks!" She smiled, impressed with herself.

"It really wasn't meant as a compliment." We both knew I didn't hand out many of those, but she really did sound like Mama Cass.

"So, do you like the wedding dress you and Karen picked out?" El asked.

"Yeah, it's really pretty, but we still need to find a veil. We picked one out, but it cost almost as much as the gown!"

She thought for a moment, and I could see the wheels turning. Just the look in her eyes would give her away in a creative moment, almost like she was somewhere else.

"Don't buy a veil. I have an idea. Let me make it for her as a wedding present."

"Are you sure? We don't have much time," I said, grateful for the offer.

"Don't worry about it." For once I bit my tongue, remembering other times that she'd said those very same words. Getting lost, burned carpet, crabbing in the dark, the list goes on.

The day before the wedding, Karen and I sat at the living room table going over preparations for the reception that would be in our family room downstairs.

"The morning sun, when it's in your face, really shows your age. But that don't worry me none, in my eyes you're everything," Rod Stewart crooned from my radio in the kitchen.

Nice. I think he thought that was some kind of compliment to poor Maggie when he wrote this song, but if I were Maggie, I think I'd kick his butt.

There was a knock on the door and, without waiting for an answer, Ellie and Ginger walked in with William and Timmy trailing behind. The boys changed their minds and went back outside to find something to do. El walked into the dining room, holding a brown paper grocery bag.

"It's time for the unveiling," she said and handed the bag to Karen.

"Wow, is it my veil?" Karen asked, and Ellie nodded.

Karen reached in the bag and pulled out the white tulle with white flowers and a touch of green leaves nestled in the middle. She'd sewn a few white pearl beads throughout the netting. Karen held it up for all of us to admire. El had outdone herself this time.

"It's beautiful, Aunt El, thanks so much!" She jumped up and hugged Ellie. We all smiled and fussed over the handiwork.

"Well, let's try it on," El said and took the veil and placed it on Karen's head. The tulle raped down over her face to create the illusion of a bride. We all just stood there and stared.

"Well? How's it look?" Karen asked, confused that nobody had said anything. She headed to the living room to check out the nearest mirror. We all just stood and watched her.

It was then that reality knocked me upside the head. My little girl was getting married. When did she grow up? How'd I miss that? This was all happening way too fast...

"Wow, Kar, I can't believe you're really getting married." Ginger took the plunge and said what I was thinking.

"I know. It's just now starting to sink in." She stared at the mirror. She looked so cute wearing jeans, a T-shirt, and wedding veil.

"You're reminding me of when you and Ginger used to play bride when you guys were little," I reminisced. What's wrong with pretending anyway? When did that change while I wasn't looking?

She turned and looked at me, taking off the veil. "Yeah, I'd try and make the Menace walk me down the aisle," she said, "but he'd take off halfway down the hall, leaving me alone at the altar."

"You looked more like a nun than a bride with my tablecloth draped over your head, but I never had the heart to tell you." I smoothed her long brown hair with my hand, peeking over her shoulder into the mirror.

"Now you have a candle ring on your head. Who knew?" El said.

"A candle ring?" I took the veil from Karen to examine the flowers. Sure enough, the plastic flowers and green leaves were a candle ring with another flower glued in the middle to hide the hole.

"Wow, I would've never known!" Karen admitted, taking the veil back to see for herself. "You're something else, Aunt El."

"Just don't try and light the wick!" Ginger said.

"At least wait until you guys get to your hotel room after the reception," El instructed, and the laughing was on. Jake heard the commotion and walked up from the basement where he'd been doing some finishing touches to the family room.

"What's so funny?" he asked, but knowing he couldn't handle the joke in front of his now-grown-up little girl, we just kept on laughing.

"Now we know what to get her for a wedding gift, a candle snuffer!" El added, and we all raced past Jake toward the bathroom, just like always, elbows and knees flying, jostling for position and doing the cross-legged ballet.

Ellie and her crew headed home for dinner, and Karen left with Lee to see his relatives for a little O'Brien prewedding dinner. I was ready to collapse from all the excitement. I plopped on the couch and decided it was as good a time as any for the announcement as Jake read his evening paper.

"You're going where this weekend?" Jake looked out from behind his *Washington Post*. "The day *after* the wedding?" It dawned on him.

"To Ocean City. Ellie found us a three bedroom condo for seventy-five dollars for the whole weekend," I explained. I knew what the next question was going to be before he did.

"Who's going to watch the kids?" he asked.

"Well, I was hoping that their dad would volunteer. I checked his social calendar, and he doesn't have any rifle matches or football games or side jobs on the books for the weekend." I was ready for objections this time. Maybe I should go into sales. They say handling objections is half the battle.

"I checked with Suzie next door, and she's available anytime this weekend to sit for you if you want to go to the range or anything." I set the hook and waited to see how much resistance he'd give me. Since Karen was getting married on

Friday and would be away on her honeymoon for the weekend, the reality of the no built-in babysitter advantage was painfully evident.

"Who's going?" he asked. *Awesome, I'm not getting an argument. I must be getting better at negotiations, too.*

"Just the Tensies," I answered and he knew I was referring to Ellie, Darlene, and Roberta. It was going to be a great time. After a summer of swimming lessons, picnics, and getting ready for another school year dealing with registrations, doctor visits for updated shots, and putting on a wedding, I was ready for a break.

Jake relented after I gave him the "I really need a break after putting on a wedding" look as well as a promising nibble on his ear.

The wedding was simple but sweet. The church organist pinch-hit for us, and it came off without a hitch. The O'Brien family had eight kids, a few of them already married with families, so they alone filled up half the church.

After the ceremony, everyone drove back to our house, and our family room was transformed into a reception hall. Momma had robbed her gladiola garden, and the flowers gave the room a festive look. Karen chose the Carpenters' *We've Only Just Begun* for her first dance, and before we knew it, the cake was cut, the bouquet was tossed, and it was time for the honeymooners to hit the road—and the Tensies, too.

Karen and Lee headed to Cleveland, Ohio, to visit his grandparents since they couldn't make it down for the wedding and would be back in a few days so Karen could finish up school. Not much in the way of a honeymoon, but they were young and didn't know any different.

I was so ready for three days of privacy in the bathroom, no huge piles of laundry to even look at, no meals to fix unless I felt like it, and nobody to tap me on the shoulder needing something.

Ellie didn't fare as well as I did and ended up with a full-blown fight with Will on her hands, but she hung in there. Saturday morning we were on our way, if not bright-eyed, then bushy-tailed.

"Ready?" I said as I jumped into Betsy's shotgun seat in my usual navigational role.

"I was born ready!" She laughed and drove up the block to Roberta's house and blew the horn. "He was spoiling for a fight, but I blew him off." El leaned her head back and let out a sigh. "Ginger's there, for Pete's sake. I don't know why he cares if I'm not home. I doubt he'll really notice anyway."

Roberta jumped in the backseat and threw her suitcase in the wayback.

"How'd it go?" I asked, referring to her talking Dick into staying at the townhouse with the kids for her girls' weekend.

"Not bad. I rocked his world, and he stayed for the weekend," she confessed.

"That has to be weird," Ellie mused.

"Yeah, well, a girl's gotta do what a girl's gotta do sometimes, you know?" she asked, and neither of us answered. This was virgin territory for all of us. Pun not intended.

We pulled up to Darlene's house, and she was out the door and down the steps before Ellie could blow the horn. Her mother lived with her and was keeping her kids for the weekend. Now, that's a great arrangement.

"Ocean City, ready or not, here we come!" Darlene said as she slammed her door shut. The gabbing started and didn't stop until we got there three hours later.

"Wow, we made great time," Ellie said looking at her watch.

"Must be some kind of record. I don't think we made even one U-turn." I opened the door to Betsy's wayback.

"Must be my driving's getting better."

"Must be it's hard to get lost when you only have one turn to make since Route 50 dead ends in Ocean City." I guess I should just give her the compliment. "But then again, I have noticed you're learning your way around better." I sucked up.

We gathered our stuff up out of the car and, arms loaded, headed up the little wooden sidewalk that went in between our wooden apartment building that faced the ocean. We were on Sixty-Sixth Street, which was a good way north in Ocean City, but we were thrilled with our good fortune at finding such a place and at a great price.

Ellie walked behind me, and I could hear the flip-flop of her sandals on the wood. All of a sudden, instead of flip-flop, flip-flop, all I heard was flop, flop,

flop, boom! I turned around to find Ellie spread-eagle on the sidewalk, suitcase in one hand, sand bucket, shovel, and canvas raft in the other. She'd stubbed her toe, fought to keep her balance (hence the flop, flop, flop) before sprawling out behind me.

She looked up, lying on her belly, and grinned. "Bet you thought that was an accident, huh?" She pushed herself up onto her knees and brushed the sand off her hands.

Now, there are some things that will make you giggle and others that make you just plain belly laugh. Once I knew she wasn't hurt, this one was the latter. I didn't see it happen, but Roberta and Darlene did, and they were already laughing and crouching trying not to pee their pants.

"Are you okay?" I asked, crouching down to help, with tears rolling down my face.

"Yeah, I think so!" she said, joining the crowd and laughing with us.

"You'd make a better commercial for Coppertone than that little girl!" Darlene teased, pulling El's housedress down to cover her butt.

"What about a commercial for luggage and its durability!" Roberta suggested. "Maybe we should call Samsonite!" And with that it was a cross-legged ballet trying to get the door open to the apartment.

We spent the days on the beach doing our best not to get sunburned but not with much success. Ellie would hang in the water on the raft just about all day. The rest of us would take turns going in with her.

"Come on in, Barb!" She waved me in from past the first wave.

"No, thanks. I ain't going where the big fish live." I stayed put in my lawn chair. "Besides, I'm shark bait this weekend."

We'd take turns cooking meals and washing dishes. Of course, I made a big pot of spaghetti, and we just ate on that for most of the weekend. Once the dinner dishes were done, we'd do hair and makeup and head for the boardwalk.

Ocean City has one of the best boardwalks ever. It even rivals the famous Atlantic City in my book, except there aren't any slot machines. Carnivals, games, jewelry stores, T-shirt shops, souvenir shops, candy shops, ice cream, funnel cake, arcades, and just plain old people watching, you name it. We'd walk the boards and shop until our feet hurt, then sit down on a bench and just make fun of people as they walked by.

El walked into a souvenir shop as I sat outside on a bench eating an ice cream cone. I watched the seagulls dance in the sky while the ocean waves whispered in my ear. What a treat after such a hectic couple of weeks. I still couldn't believe I was going to be a grandmother.

I stared out at the ocean with the gulls flying back and forth, fishing for their supper. I could see Karen's expression the first time I showed her the beach when she was just a couple years old. I think it was the first time I'd ever seen pure amazement on anyone's face. She ran to the water, not the least bit afraid. She let the waves come up and cover her little feet, and I scooped her up just in time to keep the wave from knocking her down. This time, I'd been unable to scoop her up from the wave, and it knocked her down, or up, depending on how you looked at it.

Now I found myself wondering what she had been thinking these past few months. She'd only dated a few people before Lee and hadn't had much experience learning the ropes. Now the rope had pulled her in, and I prayed that Lee was half the man that Jake had turned out to be. Yeah, I prayed.

Darlene and Roberta had walked on ahead to check out another jewelry store. Ellie came out of the shop with a small bag in her hand.

"I'll be right back. I have to use the ladies' room. Save me a seat for when I come back."

I stared back at the water. The smell of Thrasher's fries with vinegar made my mouth water, and I made a mental note to get some on our way back to the car. My conscience continued to dog me. Maybe I'd been too young to have kids when I did. I must not have paid enough attention to what had been going on with Karen. I promised myself I'd do better with Jay and Kelly.

Ellie sat down beside me and draped her sweater over her lap, with her hand underneath.

"What's the matter? You cold?" I asked.

"No, just watch," she whispered, looking the other way.

"Watch what?" I looked from side to side.

"Shhh!" she warned. "Just watch me," she said in her not-so-normal drill sergeant tone, so I shut up and kept my eyes peeled—for what, I had no idea. As groups of people strolled by, she'd wait for them to just about get past us and she'd pull the sweater back just a little bit. She had a water pistol underneath, and she'd aim for their backs and heads, arching nicely so the victim looked up instead of over.

A young man walked by with a group of his friends. The water landed right on top of his head and instinctively, his hand reached up and touched the wet spot and then he examined the evidence. Seeing nothing but water on his hand, he looked toward the sky for a hovering sea gull or rain cloud. "Hmm," it was as if we could read his mind. He began scanning the audience for a culprit, but when all he spotted was middle-aged women sitting on a bench, with a half shrug, he walked on with a perplexed look on his face. Once out of earshot, we belly laughed.

"What in the world gave you the idea to do this?" I asked her in between victims.

"I dunno. I fell in love with Big Blue." She lifted up her sweater to show off her handgun, admiring the Ocean City sticker on the nozzle. "I couldn't resist. Here, use it wisely." She reached in the bag and handed me my very own red gun.

"Thanks, my favorite color!" I said and tucked the loaded red shooter under the jacket on my lap.

I waited for the next group to come by and aimed high at a baldheaded guy. His hand immediately went to his head, and then he looked at his hand to see if he had a bird deposit. He turned his head to the sky. Not a cloud or bird to be found. He kept walking, looking at his hand, but still not showing his girlfriend.

I bit my lip to stifle a laugh but lost it as soon as he was out of range. We kept on shooting as soon as the coast was clear. The drill was always the same, and that's what made it so funny. Reactions were, more often than not, predictable, and because we were always found innocent, it felt as if we were getting away with something sinister.

But the law of averages runs out on everyone, and even the most well-practiced sharpshooter was bound to get caught. We got busted by an innocent bystander. The couple sitting next to us on the bench caught on. The wife discovered our sinister plot and elbowed her husband and told him to watch. They played along with us and laughed for an hour.

Roberta took the opportunity to flirt with the men on the nearby benches as they caught on.

It was Sunday night, and we were leaving town on Monday after a few hours of beach time and packing.

"Come on, guys, let's 'pack it in,' pun intended," I said after one too many yawns. "You must not be making me laugh enough. I have to get some sleep."

"Yeah, I'm ready," Ellie said, and Darlene nodded.

Roberta was standing a few feet away talking to some fellow boardwalker. She wasn't ready to leave and was angling another way back to our apartment.

"You guys go on ahead. I'll catch up with you later," she said, eyebrows raised. We just looked at one another, not sure what to say. More uncharted waters.

"Well, okay," Darlene said.

"Do you have your key to the apartment?" Not waiting for her answer, I added, "How are you going to get home?" I asked just like the grandmother-to-be that I was. Did I say *grandmother?*

"Yeah, I'm good, and I can take the bus. It's only fifty cents," Roberta answered.

The three of us just looked at one another and shrugs won out in the end. We left Roberta there on the boardwalk and drove home doing some bus-stop drive-bys.

El drove slowly up Baltimore Avenue that ran parallel to the boardwalk. Folks stood waiting on the bus that ran every five or ten minutes on weekends. When she went slow enough, we could squirt someone and watch them try and figure it out when we were half a block away. We laughed the entire sixty blocks back to our apartment.

We parked Betsy and climbed the steps to the balcony of our apartment that overlooked the beach. It was a clear night, with nothing but stars and moon in the sky reflecting on the ocean.

When Darlene came back from the bathroom, we leaned back on the Adirondack chairs and just soaked in the sound of the waves and full moon shining down on the water. Yawns overtook us all, and we dragged ourselves up and back into the apartment.

"I'm hitting the sack. Whoever gets up first, wake me up," Ellie said over her shoulder as she headed to the bathroom.

"I'm right behind you," I said as I put away the clean dishes on the drain board. We heard the front door of the apartment open and turned to see who was walking in. There stood Roberta and her new friend, Jim, lipstick on his collar and all.

"Hi, Jim," Ellie said. Darlene and I just looked at Roberta like she had two heads. What's she thinking, bringing some man she doesn't know into our place?

"Hey, we decided to come here and get away from the crowd." Evidently, we were invisible. Roberta had had a few too many margaritas but not so many that she didn't feel the chill in the air.

"I think I'll just grab this blanket, and we'll go for a walk on the beach." She pulled the afghan off the couch. Relieved, we all nodded at that idea, and Roberta and Jim walked out the door and down toward the beach.

"Can you believe her?" Darlene said as the screen door slammed.

"Well, she is separated, you know." Ellie defended Roberta.

"Yeah, for three whole weeks." I shook my head.

"Hope she's on birth control," Ellie said.

"Yeah, now wouldn't that be a fun baby shower!" I grabbed the bedspread off my bed and sacked out on the couch and slept with one eye open until Roberta came back, alone. I pretended to sleep while she let herself in and headed to the bedroom she shared with Darlene. The mom in me won out as I got up to make sure she'd locked the door before I headed back to my room.

The rest of our time together was edgy. Roberta had crossed a line that the Tensies had never felt the need to establish. We'd always had husbands to consider until Darlene came along, and hers had been a preexisting condition for the Tensies. She had decided to remain single until her kids were grown, so dating had never been an issue. While sleeping with someone other than our husbands might have been the gist of some of our jokes, that was all it had ever been.

We got up early and hit the beach for one last dose of sun, sand, and ocean. It's funny how when a group of mothers are together, all heads turn automatically when someone called out, "Mom!" Our heads turned in tandem, even though we'd sworn off the role for the weekend. I was the lucky winner. Karen and Lee were walking across the sand toward us.

"What are you doing here? I thought you were going to Cleveland." I shielded the sun from my eyes.

"The car broke down, and by the time we got it fixed, we decided to turn around and come here instead. It's a lot closer and definitely more fun than Cleveland," Karen said as she stood over me.

"So, you've been here all weekend?" Darlene asked.

"Since Saturday afternoon," Lee piped up. "Karen wanted to come by and say hi before you left." Karen threw her towel on the sand and plopped down beside me.

"Come on, let's get in the water," Lee said to Karen as he pulled off his T-shirt and tossed it to the ground.

"No, I don't want to get my hair wet yet if we're going to the boardwalk later." She touched her hair. "I'll just stay here with Mom. You go ahead."

Lee shrugged, turned, and charged into the waves, diving past the first set. He hung in the water with Ellie and Roberta.

"If I didn't know better, I'd swear she was flirting with Lee." Darlene leaned over and whispered with regards to Roberta when Karen walked to the apartment to get a drink.

"I'm thinking the testosterone calls her name, no matter who it is." I shut up as the three of them exited the water and headed for the towels. Roberta's giggling and middle-aged strut was just about embarrassing. Darlene and I looked at Ellie, and her raised eyebrows let us know that Roberta's flirting wasn't our imagination.

Karen walked across the sand and handed Lee a Pepsi. "So, how's married life?" Ellie asked Lee.

"So far, so good!" he chuckled, and I cringed. The thought of my little girl sleeping in a bed with a man/child was more than I'd been looking for.

"We will be heading back late tonight." Karen piped up as if she knew she needed to change the subject. "I have school tomorrow." She was signed up for night school in her senior year. It turned out she was attending with many of her friends, as they elected to graduate that way instead of being bussed to Fairmont Heights.

We packed up the beach stuff and headed back for the condo. Karen and Lee said their good-byes and headed out to finish up their honeymoon. We loaded Betsy and headed west on Route 50 toward home.

Roberta never talked about Jim, and none of us brought him up. I figured she didn't want to hear my opinion, so I kept it to myself. We drove home digging into the Candy Kitchen fudge and Fishers caramel popcorn until we were almost sick before saving the rest for the kids.

(soft break)

Christmas came faster than usual that year, but we'd started Christmas shopping back in the summertime. We'd used layaway as our financing tool and insurance that they'd have what we wanted come Christmas Eve.

"Yeah, Kelly loved that Barbie we found for a dollar. You should have seen her face when she opened up the Barbie car. Thanks for pointing that out to me on that top shelf, El."

"No sweat." We were both in the middle of cooking Christmas breakfast and could tell someone else on the party line wanted to use the phone.

"We'll be over around four," I said and hung up. I was bringing dessert. Chocolate chip cookies, my specialty. Toll House and I were longtime buddies. Jake and I herded the kids into the car and headed to Radiant Valley.

We walked into a living room full of Christmas fun, toys, and boxes everywhere. I tiptoed around the partially constructed Tinker Toy houses to the dining room. "Here's the cookies!" I sat the cookie-laden red-and-green holly platter on the table.

My eyes gravitated to a new decoration on her dining room wall. "My goodness, where in the world did you get that?" I asked, looking at some wooden leaves hanging on her wall. I think they were "sconces" of sorts. And without waiting for an answer, I added, "Don't tell me; let me guess. Sylvia must've given them to ya, and this is her twenty-four hours on the wall?" Oh, when I get on a roll, I just can't stop. And my foot just gets deeper and deeper into my mouth before I even know it.

"No…I bought them at Zayre's. You know, that new department store out in Lanham," she answered, looking down at the carpet.

Realizing that I'd hurt her feelings regarding the differences in our tastes, I slid my arm around her waist.

Trying to recover, I said, "But they're the best-looking wooden leaves I've ever seen. And they really do go well with your dining room suite." I could see she was still not buying my insincere apology. See what I mean about deeper and deeper?

The kids sat around in a circle next to the Christmas tree and exchanged gifts. When they were done, they headed into the bedrooms to play. I insisted Ellie open her gift first, and she was thrilled with her new supply of liquid embroidery I'd found on the clearance table way down in the basement level of Hecht's last week. I'd also found this neat little basket with a folding lid that she could use for her embroidery supplies.

She took her time handing over my present, and I didn't understand her reluctance until I opened the shiny package. Matching wooden-leaf sconces, just like hers.

"Oh, they're just like yours!" I didn't know what else to say. My foot was so far in it was gagging me. She hugged me anyway. Will I ever learn to keep my opinions to myself?

The kids played with their Christmas toys, and we pulled out the cards and started playing Rummy. We played for a few hours, and after overdosing on cookies and fudge, packed it in before it was too late. The guys had to work the next morning, and El and I had lots to do before leaving for work the next night.

Winter turned into spring and the promise of summer. The cherry blossoms were out, and the Easter bunny was next on the horizon.

I hung up the phone after a strange call from Darlene. I walked into the living room where Jake sat reading. "So, I just heard that Will gave Roberta a ride to work."

"You heard what?" Jake looked up from his *Evening Star* newspaper.

"All I know is what Judy told Darlene," I walked closer and whispered, making sure the kids couldn't hear us. "She said she saw Will dropping Roberta off at GPO for work," I repeated. "Why would he be giving Roberta a ride?"

"How the heck would I know?"

I sat down across from him on the couch. "Come on, Jake!" I was not digging his pretending to not know. "You two can't go to the bathroom without the other one knowing!" When he didn't give it up, I huffed and headed for the kitchen. Time to burn dinner.

He knew something, I was sure of it, but his loyalty to Will got the better of him every time.

I'd noticed how Roberta had perked up every time Will had been in the room at the gun club dance last year but chalked it up to the alcohol and her need to be the center of attention. Now the signs were just about undeniable that something was going on between them. I wanted so bad to say something to El, but what if I was wrong?

I imagined talking to Roberta about her affair. Oh, I came up with some zingers, but again, I was afraid that I might be wrong, and then what? Maybe I'd learned something about keeping my opinions after all.

Our camping vacation at Assateague was coming up fast. I let Ellie talk me into tie-dyeing our tent some putrid shades of red, yellow, and green. We looked at the colorful portable condo we'd created for our maiden trip to the beach.

"At least the kids would know which tent was theirs, 'cause there surely won't be another one like it," I said.

I kept reminding myself that Assateague Island had beaches and sunshine. I tried to forget that it didn't have a toilet or running water, except after a short hike. And don't forget the ponies that are running around. I needed to have my head examined.

Jake and Will thought they were smart, allowing us to take the Cadillac when Betsy had to go in the shop for the week. Letting us take the Cadillac was a small price for Will to pay for a week of peace and quiet, and I let Jake know that they didn't fool us, not for a minute.

I had my suspicions as to why Will would want a week by himself. I felt like such a creep keeping this to myself, but I didn't want to ruin El's vacation either. What harm will a week at the beach do? I decided it could only make a girl feel better.

The kids "oooed and ahhed" as we drove over the Assawoman Bay Bridge to Assateague Island. The evening sun shone on the water, giving it a golden glow, and the sandy beach stretched along the shore with seagulls gliding overhead. Assateague was a barrier island that took a lot of the abuse that storms dished out so the mainland didn't have to.

"Look! There's some!" Ellie pointed with one hand as she drove with the other. She pulled the car over to the side of the road and stopped so we could gawk.

The kids were enthralled. "How did the ponies get here?" Timmy asked.

"Rumor has it that they were on some Spanish ships that wrecked offshore over a hundred years ago. They swam to shore, and here they are," I explained. We sat marveling at the wildlife, not just ponies, but deer and rabbits, too. When we realized this was something we would see over and over again all week, we drove on to find our campsite.

The island was green with mostly pine trees and dune grass growing everywhere. The campsites were on the beach side, and we'd gotten lucky being positioned fairly close to the bathhouse.

We argued over where to position each of the tents and proceeded to get out the instructions for putting them together. It wouldn't be long before we realized that neither one of us was good at "constructing" anything.

"I don't know about that, El. One strong wind off the ocean and that tie-dye tent is history." I had my hands on my hips with my head cocked to one side, sizing it up. She shrugged. It didn't look like the other tents in the neighborhood, and it wasn't just the color. There were fewer "wrinkles" here and there. We hadn't done a very good job of lining up the stakes to the loops on the base of the tent.

"Can I help you ladies?" The man from next door had taken pity on us. His wife stood at his side.

"Could you?" I replied with tremendous gratitude in my heart. He ordered us around for about ten minutes. When he was done, our colorful tent looked like the Taj Mahal to us.

"Thanks so much!" I said, shaking his hand. It was all I could do not to give him a great big kiss and hug for saving us from ourselves.

Our artistic efforts had livened up the little two-bedroom condo, not to mention the neighborhood. Every car that went by slowed down to take a look. The tie-dyed tent with the Cadillac in the driveway—now there's an oxymoron when you need one.

The kids were still running around at the playground as the work was temporarily finished. We soon discovered that with camping, the work was never done, and nothing was ever "finished."

The kids actually came at first call, not out of obedience but hunger. Our first camping meal of hot dogs and beans was ready and waiting. You would have thought it was filet mignon.

As soon as she was finished eating, Kelly headed back over to her first nature lesson. She'd found the sand colored toads that dotted the dunes behind our campsite. She went back to the box she had safely tucked them in.

"Hey, Kelly, look!" hollered Timmy. He had beat her to her froggy charges. Timmy stood a few feet from Kelly with a toad in one hand and a dinner knife in the other, pretending he was going to behead the ugly sand-colored fella. With his curly green locks from his tent-dyeing days and bright-blue eyes, Timmy looked like a little leprechaun demon.

"No, don't!" she shrieked. "That's Tony!"

And this was only day one.

The sun was beginning to set, and in their ever so casual way, the Assateague mosquitoes showed up for dinner and tried to eat us alive.

"Hey! The bugs are all over us!" William announced as we all swatted and jumped.

"Get in the tent," Ellie said, and into the tent we went. Before long, we were huddled together inside. As we looked at one another, we wondered what to do next. It was only six, and if we put the kids to bed this early, they'd be up before dawn.

"Now I know why everyone here has one of those tents with see-through screening on all four sides." Ellie zipped up the tent door behind her. "Did you notice they had their picnic tables and lounge chairs inside the screen?"

"We'll have to go buy one tomorrow," I said. It didn't take long before we discovered that you were either inside a tent, car, or bathhouse when the sun was rising or setting.

"It's not in the budget though," Ellie said.

"If we split it three ways, it won't be so bad," I calculated. "It's either that or we sit in a tent every evening for the next seven nights."

El and I headed to the bathhouse with the dirty dishes, and Darlene agreed to stay back on kid duty at the campsite.

We waited in line for our turn to wash and dry at the outdoor mop sinks behind the bathhouse.

"Here, I'll wash and rinse; you can dry and stack," I said in my not-so-bossy tone.

"Do you think it's true?" El asked me.

"Is what true?" I knew from the look in her eyes what she was talking about.

"That Will's having an affair," she said with no emotion.

I continued to wash the dishes, rinse, and hand them to El for drying. I let the water run, with the steam rising up between us. Her face was sad and resigned. For once, I didn't know what to say.

"I don't know, El. I just don't know." I poured more Ivory Liquid on my sponge. "What do you think?"

"I think it's true. You know he'd never have let me take his precious Cadillac except that he wants rid of us some kinda bad." She began drying the dishes.

We kept washing, rinsing, and drying until we were done. The line had formed again as more families waited their turn with more frying pans and coffee pots to clean.

"I don't know what I'm going to do. I guess it depends on how far he forces my hand. I don't have any money to speak of, Barb. I don't know how I'm going to support the kids on my own. We don't make nearly enough at GPO," she said, staring at the wooden sidewalk as we stepped back onto the sandy path. The wild ponies dotted the landscape and chewed on the sea grass while they waited for a camper to drop a hot dog.

"Don't worry, El; Will's gotta pay his fair share. I know it's not easy getting money out of him, but that's what lawyers are for," I answered, trying to pull some hope out of thin air. I knew we didn't want to talk about this in front of the kids, so I motioned for us to sit down on a nearby bench, clean dishes on our laps.

"Why did things have to change so much?" Ellie asked, staring down at the sand, not expecting an answer. "Our biggest worry used to be what color to make the candles next year."

"And who we didn't like that we could give them to," I reminded her, and a grin sneaked its way to the corner of her mouth. "How'd you know that I knew?"

"I've watched you beat yourself up all day for not telling me. You know how you chew your gum extra hard and hum a little louder than normal."

"Who? Me?"

"Yeah, you. Well, I'm not gonna let it bother me this week. We've worked too hard and have earned a full week at the beach." She stood up. "Come on. What'd you bring for dessert? I know you have some chocolate hidden in those duffel bags." And of course, I did.

I called Jake from a phone booth at the bathhouse after I knew he was home from work on Thursday. I closed the booth door as fast as I could to keep the pesky mosquitoes, a.k.a., Maryland state bird, on the outside.

"Hey, how was your day at the beach? Did you have good weather?" he asked.

"Sure did. How was work?" I asked all the normal questions.

"Fine, just fine." He wasn't giving me anything to work with here.

"How are Will and Roberta doing?" I took the plunge.

"What?" he asked, trying to gather his thoughts, but I was too quick for him this time.

"You know *what*!" I finger-painted in the condensation on the window of the phone booth door and leaned my head down against the glass.

"What do you mean, Barb? Why are you interrogating me?" he asked. A good offense was his best defense, but I was ready for him this time.

"Did he give her any more 'rides to work'?" That was all the explanation I was giving up.

"I don't know what you're talking about," he argued, letting me hear what he sounded like when he was lying. Big mistake.

"Oh, I think you do, and just know this. He needs to keep the whore put away until Ellie can get out," I instructed, knowing that Jake had influence over Will. Jake and the Catholic Church was as good a combo as any for knowing right from wrong. Jake was the most honest and trustworthy person I knew. If we had to rely on Will's decency to give Ellie some space right now, I knew I needed to enlist Jake's help.

"Listen, Jake." I took a deep breath. "You owe Ellie and the kids some support here." No, I wasn't above using the kids as pawns in this one.

I'd played what I was going to say to Jake over and over in my head. Like warning him that he'd be looking for a place of his own if he didn't reach in to help El and the kids, but Jake's sense of right and wrong did triumph his desire to ignore the problem. I didn't get much of an argument, and by the time I hung up the phone, I was sure he'd work on Will. Ellie was going to need some financial help to get out on her own. Jake was the only person on earth who could get Will to part with a buck—and we both knew it.

"Okay, Barb. I'll see what I can do, but we really shouldn't get in the middle of their problems." He tried one more time to bow out.

"If you wanna talk about being in the middle, Jake, you can take it up with Will and Roberta." I pounded on the glass window of the phone booth. "They're the ones who put us here!" I surprised even myself at my resolve.

"Does she know about Roberta?"

"I don't know for sure, but she knows he's messing around with someone." I looked over my shoulder to make sure nobody could hear me. "The marriage is over, and now she needs our help." He backed off, and we managed to hang up on a civil note.

I stood in the phone booth, staring into the Assateague twilight. The glow of a lightning bug revealed the mosquitoes that waited to feast on my arms. Glad that I'd brought a jacket, I pulled it on. I opened the folding door as it creaked in reply. The young mom from the campsite next to us smiled as she walked past me to close the booth door as fast as she could with the hopes that the mosquitoes would follow me down the road instead of her into the booth. The jacket proved enough of a deterrent that the pesky skeeters didn't give me too many issues.

I walked back to the campsite and sat down for an evening of cards and laughs with Ellie, Darlene, Karen, and Ginger. I was sad for Ellie but excited for her at the same time. I knew she'd be all right. I think part of me envied her soon-to-be independence. It was time for her to get outta the onesies for good.

CHAPTER 8

Ellie
This Diamond Ring Doesn't Shine for Me Anymore

Citizen Control of Police Is Aim of Panther Plan

Oakland, Calif.—The Black Panther party plans to organize a national campaign for community control of police.
Panther Chairman, Bobby Seale, said at the conclusion of a party con-ference today that the Panthers and a coalition of about fifty national committees will fight fascism by working to get city charters changed to permit communities in the city to organize and control their own police forces.
Seale said that the Panthers will no longer try to fight capitalism with black capitalism but with a campaign to control the lives of people in black communities by harnessing the police force...

—The Evening Star, Washington, DC, July 21, 1969
Waterene Swanston, *Star* staff writer

knew that my marriage was over, and it seemed to be easier when I thought about leaving, but I just didn't know which way to go. It was obvious that Will was not going to make the first move and go anywhere, so it looked like the kids and I would have to leave. I think he felt that I would look like the bad guy if I left, and I knew he'd hang on white-knuckled to anything that was price tag worthy.

What a mess. How did it get like this? I couldn't imagine raising the kids on my own, but then it dawned on me that I did it when we were in Cambridge, and they were a lot smaller then. When is it easier for them? Did it ever get easier for them? I hoped so.

Things were so expensive in the DC area. There was no way I could stay right here unless I moved to an apartment complex that wouldn't be good for the kids. I decided we needed to move a little farther outside the beltway. I'd heard it was cheaper in Charles County, but it meant a longer drive to work.

I also considered changing jobs. I wasn't 100 percent sure, but the Roberta–Will thing was starting to heat up, and I knew I couldn't hang in that kitchen. Barb had suspected it, but hadn't said anything, so I'd let her off the hook and brought it up. We'd taken the kids to Sandy Point for a day of cooling off in the Chesapeake.

"Yeah, I heard about Will driving Roberta to work a few times while we were in Assateague. Her car broke down, and we weren't there with the usual carpool," I said, watching Barb to see her reaction. It was obvious that she'd heard the same thing.

"El, I so wanted to tell you the rumor but didn't want to cause a ruckus in case there was nothing to it."

"I confronted him," I said. My lip betrayed me with a quiver. We sat on a beach towel watching the kids play in the waves. I dug my toe in the sand, working to cover up my other foot. Cover up the ugly truth with sand.

"When?"

"Right before we left to drive down here. He was busy patting himself on the back for letting us use the Cadillac in Assateague. I couldn't take the smugness anymore." I could feel my stomach tighten just thinking about him and Roberta. They were probably together right now.

"He admitted they'd been having an affair for the past three months. I just didn't know it was Roberta for sure until this week. It all fits now. I really got stuck in the onesies on that one, kiddo."

"We all did. That lousy slut. Now that I know it's true…" Barb reached in her beach bag and pulled out her Pall Malls and lit one up. "What did he have to say for himself?" She blew out the smoke, stood up, and motioned for the kids to come back down the shoreline to the beach in front of us. She sat back down next to me.

"Not much, just that he's decided that he wants a divorce and thinks he's in love with her." My voice lowered. Just the sound of the words out loud made me nauseated.

"In love with her? He actually used the word *love?*" Here we go, my girl was ticked off now. Barb ranted quietly so the neighboring towel dwellers couldn't hear. "He wouldn't know 'love' if it hit him in the face! He's had the love of his life sitting next to him for the past twenty-plus years!" She looked from the ocean to me and wrapped her right arm over my shoulder and pulled me next to her.

We just sat in silence, watching the kids play in the surf. I was so grateful for her right then I didn't care if Will walked off a ten-story building. I leaned my head on her shoulder as more than twenty years of tears fell. She reached in the beach bag, and since it was the best she could do on short notice, pulled out a peanut-butter-and-jelly-laden wadded-up paper towel. Sometimes no words were the best ones.

We both cried, not so much for my marriage but because we knew things would change between us, too. What would our families do on holidays? It wasn't going to be easy going on double dates anymore with Roberta on Will's arm. And Barb was so mad at Jake over Will's indiscretion, it wasn't doing their relationship any favors either.

"I'm so sorry, El," Barb said over and over, and stroked my hair.

"I'm sorry, too," I sobbed. "You're the best friend anyone ever had. I don't want to lose you, too."

"I don't give a damn what Jake says, nothing's gonna change."

"I'm sure it'll be fine," I lied, and we were both okay with that. Sometimes Denial could be a welcome companion.

I could see other sun worshipers looking at the two bawling women huddled together on a towel.

"We'd better straighten up, or they're gonna start talking." I nudged her, and she looked to her left. A husband and wife were trying not to stare at our nose-blowing.

"I'm sorry to dump all this on you. I know you're upset that Karen's gone." Lee had decided they would move to West-by-gone-Virginia to live. He was starting up a business with his brother-in-law. Barb had had a meltdown but seemed to be rebounding.

"Yeah, it was tough to swallow. I just wanted to go scoop her up before she could leave." She drew circles in the sand with her finger. "Especially after she had the miscarriage." This time, I handed her the used paper towel. Karen had miscarried three weeks after her wedding. "It just seems so unfair that she's given up so much for so little, and I can't change anything." She leaned her head on my shoulder, and I leaned back.

"We're a fine pair, aren't we?" I asked her. "Here we are fretting the end of my marriage and the beginning of Karen's."

We stared into the face of Fate that day. Fate that refused to move out of our way, refused to give up its hold on Karen and let go of me. I'd tried to befriend Fate, but it had constantly double-crossed me. As friends, Barb and I had gotten closer than most sisters. As women, we'd grown into adults that we sometimes didn't recognize. We'd grown up, wanting to be mature and responsible, but in the process, discovered just how hard it could be when you got kicked out of the onesies and into the real world.

We stared at the water and remembered there were kids we were supposed to be watching.

"Let's go in and dunk the kids. Pretending to drown them always makes me feel better." I tugged on her arm. "Last one in's a rotten egg!" I said and crawled to my feet. I reached my hand out and pulled her up off the blanket. We ran toward the water and splashed our way over to the kids.

We played in the Chesapeake Bay shoreline for the rest of the afternoon. The bay bridge was off in the distance, and an occasional barge would chug by heading for the Baltimore harbor. Sailboats glided by in the breeze, looking as carefree as I wished I were. Every now and then a motorboat would whiz by, giving us a wake to rock on with the canvas rafts.

A jellyfish sighting was the only thing that was able to chase us out of the water. Fear of the sting was enough, and we plopped back down on the towels and blankets. I pulled out what was left of the peanut butter and jelly sandwiches, and we chowed down. Kelly and Timmy irritated each other, showing just how tired they were. We weren't past the Naval Academy exit on Route 50 before all of them nodded off to sleep.

"I could have stayed on that raft till dark," Barb said as she rolled her window down a crack to light up a cigarette now that the kids were snoozing. "I can still feel myself rocking."

"Yeah, me too." I rocked the steering wheel back and forth to emulate the rocking of our imaginary rafts, and we giggled. "I thought about hitching a ride to China on one of those barges but wasn't sure they'd take kids. What really stinks is not wanting to go home."

Will and I had become very good at avoiding each other. Except for weekends, there was only about two hours a day where we had to be in the same space. There was about an hour and a half in the evenings before I left for work, unless he could think of a reason not to come straight home from work, and about a half hour in the mornings while I was getting the kids off to school and he was leaving for the office.

The next morning, Darlene called Barb and me to say she'd found an ad for help at District Photo. I think the two of them were just saying they wanted out of GPO, but I suspected they were just trying to get me away from having to face Roberta and the affair every day.

The ad was for clerical positions. We had turned out to be pretty clerical the first time.

We all three applied and all three got hired. This time, clerical meant developing film. Hey, I always said I needed to learn a trade.

"You're *what?*" Will said, looking up from his plate of roast beef and mashed potatoes. That was one way to divert his attention, tell him I was quitting my job. The money was drying up, all his massed wealth, just a dream, no more glitz for the girlfriend.

"I'm tired of GPO and will be going to work at District Photo. There's no future being part time at GPO. This is still night work, so it won't change anything for you." I reached for the salt and pepper. "I just need a change."

A change without rumors of you and your little whore, I thought as I looked down on my plate of food. Then it dawned on me that I was just making it easier for him, but by now, I didn't care. If easier for me meant easier for him, then so be it.

The three remaining Tensies (we'd officially kicked the hussy out by building a campfire in Barb's ashtray and burning her in effigy) began a career in photography development. Working together in a dark room could be dangerous for women with sick minds. My fear of the dark didn't help either.

"I have a real knack for developing film," I told Ginger and Karen as we began our second card game of pounce for the night. Karen had come home for a long weekend to celebrate her birthday. Barb filled up our glasses with ice and Pepsi. Will had a side job (is that what you call it?) this evening, and Jake and Lee were at a little league game with Jay.

"But Mrs. White didn't quit GPO with you guys? How come she didn't quit, too?" Ginger asked.

I wasn't about to touch that one. I glanced up at Barb as she walked into the room, and I jumped up, making the excuse that I had to run and get an extra deck of cards out of Betsy's glove box so Barb could play, too. Sometimes a girl has to run for cover.

"Thanks for leaving me there for that one," Barb whispered as I shuffled my cards.

"What on earth do you mean?"

"You know!"

"Oh yeah, you'll have to let me know how you did with that handoff." I dealt the cards. Later, when the girls were in the kitchen making popcorn, I insisted on knowing what she'd told them.

"Oh, El, don't make me tell you. I'm afraid you're not going to like it much."

"Geez, give it up, Barb." I looked over her shoulder to make sure the girls were still in the kitchen. "What'd you say?"

"I just told them Roberta preferred to stay at GPO since we weren't talking to her because of her affair."

"You what?" My stomach did a summersault.

"What did you want me to say? I didn't tell them she was messing around with Will, I just said she was messing around and we didn't approve."

"Hmmm, not bad for short notice." I cleared the table to make room for the popcorn as we continued our pounce marathon. We played and laughed and accused one another of cheating. Barb won this round, but only this one. They packed up their cards, and we cleaned up the popcorn and Pepsi leftovers. Barb and the kids headed home, and Ginger and I retreated to the living room.

"When's Dad coming home?"

I walked over to the TV and turned on *The Tonight Show*.

"He should be here soon." I plopped down on the couch next to her. Will's recliner remained ominously vacant.

"So, we're really gonna move out, huh?" Ginger looked at me. She'd turned into a long-legged beauty with dark auburn hair. What had happened to my red-headed freckle-faced ten-year-old?

"As soon as I can get the money together, we're on our way." I reached over and put my hand over hers. "I'm sorry, Ging."

"Sorry? Why are you sorry?"

"I'm sorry that I'm breaking up our family."

"Mom, our family was always better when it was just us in Cambridge." She leaned her head on my shoulder. The laughter from Johnny Carson's monologue filled in the lull in our conversation. I realized that she was right. While I'd found a sister in Barb, a full-time life with Will had threatened to choke the life right out of me.

"Besides, maybe a new school is just what I need. I just can't hang with the girls at Elizabeth Seton."

I'd been worried about Ginger's high school education. The mandatory bussing had truly messed up her high school experience. She never did like school very much to start with and struggled with some of her subjects. The Catholic school was way too tough for her, and I was hoping when we moved to Charles County that things would get better. That county had not been mandated on the bussing yet, so she'd be able to get more involved.

Ginger walked over to the corner and picked up her guitar, the one I'd given her for her twelfth birthday. She sat back down next to me and started strumming and humming. I chimed in, and we sang our personal rendition of "California Dreaming." Well, Waldorf wasn't California, but it was a far better dream than the nightmare I'd been living in Radiant Valley, that was for sure.

Ginger was a talent, and I'd known it ever since she was taking curtain calls on the back porch in Cambridge. She gravitated to the guitar, even though my first love was the piano. I think it was the style of music in those days, more guitar-friendly. She had an awesome voice and a real knack for drawing in a crowd. I was sure my girl was going to have a chance in show business.

As we finished the song, we heard a car door slam. Ginger looked out and her shoulders slumped. "It's Dad."

We both got up from the couch and headed for another part of the house.

(soft break)

"You won't believe this," I said over the phone the next morning as I dried the last dish from the night before.

"Try me," Barb answered, sounding preoccupied.

"Will coughed up five hundred dollars for us to find a place with." There was no response on the other end of the line for a few seconds.

"You're right, I don't believe it. What'd you do, rob his wallet in the middle of the night? How'd you dust off all those cobwebs without waking him up?"

"I don't know, but it seems as if he's gotten a dose of reality and realizes what a dog he's been all along. Truth be known, he probably knew it would take me six months to save up enough, and he can't wait that long." I took a deep breath. "But I don't care why. Not anymore. All I know is the kids and I are out of here the first of the month." There, I had said it out loud, and it made me feel better.

"Since Roger's engaged and Scott is already on his own, I only have to worry about finding a place big enough for me, Ginger, William, and Timmy."

"Wow," was all she said. The anchor of reality made my heart sink. We'd known I would move out and move on, but we also knew things would never be the same. Divorce dictated that, didn't it?

"I'm going out to get boxes now," I said. "One thing Betsy's still good for is hauling boxes. I think I need to think about a new car pretty soon though. Don't know if Betsy's up to a commute from Waldorf. I feel like I'm getting ready to bury a loved one just saying it." I rambled. "I know I don't have a place yet, but I want to get a jump on the packing. There's a lifetime of things to go through."

"Hey, Jake's got a rifle match tomorrow. You want me to come over and help you pack?" she asked, and I didn't waste any time taking her up on her offer. I wanted to spend as much time as I could with her before I left Radiant Valley.

"That'd be great. Let me know when you're coming, and I'll have the coffee and donuts ready to go." And with that, we hung up.

I looked around the kitchen and into the dining room, the place where my kids had spent the past ten years growing up. The marks on the kitchen doorjamb begged me not to go. The little hash marks that I'd artfully carved into the wooden frame that measured the height of Ginger, William, Scott, Roger, and finally Timmy, with their names and dates next to each, brought back memories.

"What the...?" Will had asked as he noticed the nice artwork on the door-jamb. We had moved in two months earlier, and the kids and I had put on the first set of marks the first day we moved in. It had taken him that long to notice.

"It shows each of the kid's height. We can do it every six months or so. They're growing so fast." I put down the wooden spoon I'd been stirring the macaroni with on the stove. I reached over and glided my finger over one of the marks.

"I can't believe you did that, Ellie!"

I jerked my hand back.

"I worked hard to buy this house, and you're carving into the walls?" he barked, and without waiting for an answer stormed off to the living room, *Washington Post* in hand.

Such warm memories. How would I ever bring myself to leave? I sat down at the dining room table, not trying to stop the tears. I mopped them up over and over with the used napkin I had in my hand. I looked at the clock and figured I had another thirty minutes before any of the kids would be home from school.

I stared into space as memories of snowball battles in the backyard and hot chocolate parties to warm the kids and me up after sled rides down our hill in Radiant Valley flooded my mind. Tie-dyeing the Assateague tent in the yard and digging candle wax out of the carpet before Will got home put a surprise smile on my lips. Then there were the Christmases eating Barb's chocolate chip cookies that threatened to break a tooth with every bite.

I looked up on the dining room wall to see the wooden leaf sconces and laughed out loud.

"You're right," I said to an absent Barb. "They *are* ugly, and they'll be my parting gift to Will…and Roberta."

I'd been praying for a way out of this marriage but hadn't anticipated being sprung so soon. I was scared of being on my own but more scared of staying with him. I decided it was time to go when I started daydreaming about his demise. Now he wanted out as badly as I did, and five hundred of his precious dollars was proof enough of that.

The good thing about memories was that I could take them with me. I resolved to carry them in my heart and make lots of new ones. Moving back here from Cambridge had helped me to learn to stand on my own and realize my need for independence from sadness.

I admitted to myself that when Momma died, I latched on to Will for someone to love and love me back. Well, the "love me back" part didn't work out too well, but in the process, I'd learned to love myself. I discovered that I could make a living if I worked hard. I could put groceries on the table without stealing a steak. I'd found a way to take care of my kids and me.

I didn't take part in the bra-burning marches in DC, but I had learned that as a woman, I could make a difference, a difference in my own life and in lives of those I loved the most.

CHAPTER 9

Barb
I Am Woman

On to Mars Suggestion Voiced Again by Agnew
At the Smithsonian Institution's aviation museum, later (Spiro T.)
Agnew, VP of the United States, in a CBS television interview, said
again he thinks the United States should go to Mars before the year
2000...Astronaut Frank Borman, who has become a sort of liai-
son man between the White House and the $24-billion Apollo
program, said President Nixon does not necessarily agree
with Agnew..."

—*The Evening Star* staff writer, Washington, DC

We were working in the dark room, feeling like real photographers.
Ellie was sitting on one side of the machine, feeding the film for
Mrs. Parson's dog show pictures through the developer, and I was sitting
on the other side facing her. She really did have a knack for this, despite her
fear of the dark. Darlene was at the table, stuffing the envelope with Mrs.
Parson's vacation pictures.

This was more entertaining than binding government books and pamphlets
at GPO. Vacation pictures, golf outings, holiday events, and sometimes amateur
porn were enough to keep us giggling every night.

Jake had fussed about me giving up a government job for this, but sometimes loyalty outweighed benefits. Besides, I pointed out to him that I couldn't

be held accountable for my actions if I had to be around Roberta five nights a week. At that, he dropped the subject.

One Thursday night, Darlene was making up her usual stories about the people in the pictures as she'd stuff the envelopes, and we rolled on the floor laughing.

Something kept tickling my ankle. At least I hoped it was tickling and not crawling.

"The attorney said"—El caught my eye with that one—"I need to add up all my expenses and provide copies of our past tax returns before they will come up with a child support figure." Now I knew there was something crawling up my ankle and on toward my knee.

"What the!" I jumped up from my seat. It was dark, and I couldn't find my way back to the light switch fast enough.

"Don't turn on the light! You'll ruin the film!" Ellie said.

"You're right, but there's gotta be a snake or something in here. It keeps trying to crawl up my leg!"

With that, Darlene came to my rescue, finding the light switch. Tough luck for Mrs. White's dog show pictures.

Light didn't bring out the little critter or whatever it was that had molested me. I rushed out to the front desk and insisted our boss come in and investigate. Poor Mr. Potter must have thought I was nuts.

"We were rolling the film through, and something kept creeping up my leg inside my pants. When I felt it on my knee, well, that was it!"

Poor Mr. Potter. He crawled under and behind desks, pulled out file cabinets, bent down under tables, and moved the photo machines, but nothing turned up.

We had no choice but to turn out the lights and go back to work. I wasn't excited about it, but having no proof of my molester, we went back to work on Mrs. Black's second roll of, this time, vacation film.

"That does it; I quit! The darn thing just crawled all the way up my leg." I jumped up and headed for the door.

"No, don't!" Ellie said. I stopped in midstep and turned to see her silhouette in the dark room. She held a semistiff piece of negative film. It was about six feet long and by pointing it downward, when it touched the floor, the end curled upward in a V shape. The more she pushed it toward the floor, the more the end crept upward. Right up my pant leg. I'd been had.

The girl ain't right. Even living in a marriage that held no smiles, she'd managed to have a good time, whether it was in a dark room or a dark relationship.

I was starting to feel a little sorry for Jake. He didn't approve of what Will was doing, but he didn't walk away from him either. The whole situation was beginning to take its toll on our relationship.

"Barb, you can't expect me to drop Will as a friend just because he's making a mistake. You wouldn't do that to Ellie." I knew that was true, but couldn't help myself.

"Just don't bring him over here, Jake. Don't expect me to pretend there's nothing wrong." After a while, we learned to avoid the mention of Ellie and Will, but the unsaid "remember-whens" hung in the air between us.

We'd have to come up with a Plan B for weekends and holidays. Our two families were fractured, and none of us knew what to do.

"I've found a place in Waldorf that's big enough for the five of us," Ellie said as we finished up the dog show pictures. "We're moving in next week."

"Wow, that's thirty miles from here, El."

"Yeah, I know, but it's all so expensive in this area, I had to go out a little ways."

That weekend, Karen and I helped her pack for the move.

Karen had had a miscarriage three weeks after her wedding. She and Lee moved away to West Virginia when I wasn't looking. He'd taken a job in a family business, and before I knew it, she was living four hundred long miles away. This weekend, she was home for a visit.

Watching your kid make life-changing decisions is the toughest part of being a parent. And I had thought it was the two o'clock feedings or making sure they had their homework finished.

They waited for a year after the miscarriage to start a family and now had a baby girl. Yep, I was a grandmother at thirty-eight. When Karen asked me what I wanted the baby to call me—Granny, Grandma, or what—I thought for a moment and answered, "Barb" but settled for "Grandmother."

"Do you want the paper plates?" I held up a leftover stack from our last outing.

"I doubt he'll be going on any picka-nickas. The way I look at it, I'm entitled to half of anything in these cabinets, Barb. Just take it from there."

I went out to the car to grab my cigarettes. El had agreed to let me light up instead of taking a break alone outside. I reached in and grabbed the Pall Malls and headed back inside the house. Walking up the sidewalk through the chain link gate and into the yard, I realized it would be one of the last times I would walk this path.

As I reached for the handle of the storm door, I heard El and the girls singing the old Rosemary Clooney tune she'd taught them when they moved here from Cambridge:

"Ain't a gonna need this house no longer,

Ain't a gonna need this house no more,

Ain't got time to fix the shingles,

Ain't got time to fix the floor..."

I let go of the door handle and lit up. They don't need me messing up their harmony. A tear stung the corner of my eye. As happy as I was for her—I really was, I tried to convince myself—but I was sad for us. The four of us, El and Will and Jake and me, had shared so much of our lives together for the past ten years. Everything had changed thanks to Roberta.

I could hear Momma saying, "If you can't say anything nice," but right now, where Roberta was concerned, all bets were off. Besides, that was the nicest thing I could come up with, and I'd had plenty of notice this time.

Thanks to Will, the creep. Thanks to Fate, that evil monster. I tried to be happy for Ellie but couldn't help feeling sorry for myself. I never realized before just how much I loved the way my life was and I selfishly didn't want it to change, but I wanted Ellie to get out of the onesies of unhappiness once and for all.

"This old house is getting feeble,

This old house is needing paint,

Just like me it's tuckered out,

But I'm getting ready to meet the saints!"

They crooned like a bunch of Rosemary Clooney hillbillies.

I snuffed out my cigarette and walked back in. We cried some and laughed a lot all day long as we loaded the boxes with memories.

Ellie and I were packing up the contents of her china cabinet in the dining room. I reached up and pulled down the school pictures of the kids she had framed on the wall. I looked at the wooden leaf sconces and then to her, unsure of what to do.

"Don't worry; he can keep them," she answered without my asking. "I already decided Roberta deserves 'em."

"Cool, does that mean I can wrap mine up and give them to him for Christmas?" I asked. I had hung my matching set in my foyer as a pledge of allegiance to my friend. It had been the only way I could figure to get my foot out of my mouth that Christmas night long ago.

"Sure, you've paid your dues on that one, kiddo."

Christmases and Easters would never be the same again, and the unspoken words hung between us as we finished packing the dining room.

It wasn't long after Ellie and the kids moved out that it became common knowledge with all our friends that Will and Roberta were dating. The thirty miles between him and Ellie turned out to be a blessing, although she and I were too far apart. We did get to catch up on things at work, but it wasn't the same. Working at District Photo had been a good change, but we all knew we needed to find jobs with a better future.

The three of us applied for daytime jobs with the federal government. The nights were wearing on us, and we wanted some normalcy with daytime hours. Darlene and I got jobs with the National Weather Service as—are you ready for this?—secretaries. Those typing classes had paid off. We were working 7:00 a.m. to 3:30 p.m. Monday through Friday. No more nights!

Ellie changed her mind at the last minute and decided to go back to the Government Printing Office and the night shift.

"I can't believe you can even think of going back there," I said to Ellie. Roberta still worked the night shift, and Ellie was walking wide-eyed back into the situation.

"I can make more money with the overtime I can get there, and I need their benefits. I didn't need the insurance when we went to District Photo 'cause I was on Will's, but something tells me that's not gonna be the case once the ink is dry on the divorce papers.

"It works better this way. Ginger's home with the boys at night, and I can sleep while they're in school." I sat at the dining room table and held the phone to my ear with one hand and a glass of Pepsi in the other. "I'm there when they leave for school and when they get home," Ellie said.

There was no sense beating a dead horse. I just wondered how she was going to keep from beating Roberta up on a nightly basis.

"I think Darlene and I might drive out to see you on Saturday, if you're gonna be home," I said.

"That would be great!" she said and we hung up the phone after she recited directions to her new place. The irony of taking directions from El didn't escape me, but I kept my mouth shut for once and made a mental note to pick up a map of Charles County.

Jake was insecure about my friendship with Ellie now that she was "single." Go figure. I'd given in to him on a lot of things, that's how we'd stayed married, but I knew this one was a deal breaker for me. I'd decided that if he expected me to give up my friendship with El because she was single, he'd better think twice. I tolerated his friendship with Will as long as he didn't try and mix Roberta into my life. I was not going to allow him to dictate boundaries of my friendship with Ellie.

"It's a right at the light coming up; that's number five," Darlene said as we navigated our way through Southern Maryland. I was driving my dad's Chevy Vega. Momma had given it to me when he died the previous year. The ugly green color and lack of power steering that made it drive like a mini-tank was compensated by no loan to pay off. My father had finally given me something besides a game of cat and mouse.

We pulled up to the curb in front of several mobile homes.

"Which one is it?" Darlene asked. I leaned over the steering wheel, trying to see the house numbers.

"There it is." I pointed. "I'd know that pink flamingo anywhere." I pointed to the tacky bird lawn ornament she'd bought in Florida when we drove down to visit my cousins two winters ago. Of course, she didn't think it was tacky, but being the loyal friend that I was, I'd clued her in. We climbed out of the mini-tank, and El walked out the door and down the steps to greet us.

"El, I love your yard! This is great! And look at this nice big deck, too. You've gotta love it here!" I said as I hugged her tightly. She was beaming. No one would ever know the grief she'd spent over making this decision, but once she had, she never looked back. As always, my El was making the best of the cards she'd been dealt.

"Where are Ginger and the boys?" I asked. I hadn't seen them in several weeks now.

"Ginger took them to the movies. She and Jimmy were going anyway."

"Wow, an afternoon with no kids, how'd we manage that?"

"It took us a few years, but I think we've started to figure it out." She laughed that contagious laugh of hers and looked more radiant than I'd ever thought possible. We'd just finished the tour she'd given us of her new home.

"Buffy loves it, too." She beamed as she bent over to pick up her little cream puff of a dog.

"Yeah, I'll bet she misses Will." I smarted off, remembering how mean he was to her little pooch.

"What's this?" Darlene asked, pointing to a potted plant in the living room. The only plants I've ever had were plastic, but Darlene was a green thumb.

Ellie's face took on a sheepish grin.

"Why, it's a houseplant. I think it's some kind of palm," she explained.

"Well, maybe the big one is, but this smaller one is definitely not the same type of plant." Darlene bent down to examine. She was a houseplant guru who tended, repotted, and cajoled her plants. I cajoled my plants, too, right into the trash can. Being a plant in my house was signing up for a slow death.

"And since when did you become an arborist?" I asked.

El's sheepish grin turned into a big smile. "Well, let's just say it's 'home grown' and leave it at that."

I was still clueless, but Darlene was catching on.

"Ellie, you're growing pot?" Darlene looked up at her.

"Well, let's just say a seed fell in and made the best of it." Ellie tried to recover, but she was in too deep. She reached up into a kitchen cabinet and pulled out what looked to be a cigarette of sorts. I was still in the dark, and then it hit me.

"Ellie! I can't believe you're smoking dope! What if you get caught?" I said, mouth wide open.

"Who's gonna catch us?"

"Us?" I looked at Darlene, but she was already taking the cigarette from Ellie.

"Hmmm, no kids for the afternoon. Why not? Come on, Barb; let's give it a try," Darlene coaxed. "I haven't done it in years." She grabbed the doobie.

"Isn't pot against the law?" I asked. I could just hear Jake roaring now as he came to the police station to pick me up. Again.

"Only if you sell it! Here, take a hit," El said as she took a drag, held her breath, and passed it my way. I looked at her like she'd grown a second head.

"Take a puff and hold your breath as long as you can before you let it out." Ellie pushed it into my hand. "And stop with the 'I don't know how you could do that' look. You're the smoker here, for Pete's sake!" She sounded like Miss Connie on *Romper Room*. Maybe pot was how Connie handled twenty-four-year-olds every day with a smile on her face.

I took the joint (boy, I'm finally a bona fide hippie) and held it up to my lips, taking a drag. I braced myself for I don't know what, inhaled, and held my breath as instructed. I passed the doobie (wow, listen to my expanded vocabulary, would ya?) to Darlene.

"How...long...do I hold?" I asked like a good doobie student, trying to hold in the smoke. Hmm, Miss Connie has Do-Bees doesn't she?

"You're doing fine. Just hold it as long as you can," El answered.

Within twenty minutes, we were all sprawled out on the living room floor with the couch pillows in tow.

"I don't think I can walk," I confessed, reaching down to feel my legs.

"Oh, you're okay. I thought that the first time, too," El said, trying to sit up Indian style.

"The first time? How many times have you done this?" I asked, but Darlene managed to change the subject on me.

"So, when's the divorce gonna be final?" she asked Ellie.

"Looks like sometime in April, just six months to go." She stood up and walked in the kitchen. "Can't come a day too soon for me. I hope he marries Roberta the next day."

"They deserve each other," I said as I struggled to my feet, not sure they would go in the right direction.

"They deserve worse than that!" Darlene followed us.

"I can't think of anything worse than being married to Will," El said.

"You ought to know," Darlene said.

"Hey, El, got any chips?" I opened the kitchen cabinet.

"There's so much more to life than I ever realized," Ellie said.

Didn't she hear me? I'm really hungry.

"My marriage was killing me, and I never knew it."

"Yeah, I know what you mean," Darlene said.

"Hey, let's be gentle. I'm still living in that married world, you know." I opened the kitchen cabinet, looking for calories. "What do you have to eat?"

I was being ignored. "The kids are so much happier. We don't have to wait for the six o'clock cloud called Will to come home." She stared at the window. Her right hand reached over and rubbed where her wedding band used to be.

"Are *you* happy?" Darlene asked and sat down at the kitchen table.

"Happy doesn't describe it, but I think I am." She smiled like I hadn't seen her smile without the presence of laughter in so many years.

"So, how's Karen and the little princess?" El asked. I was the proud grand-mother of a beautiful baby girl, Nellie.

"They're doing good," I said, checking the freezer in hopes of chocolate ice cream. Nothing but hot dogs and frozen potpies.

"What's the baby going to call you?" Darlene asked.

I thought about it for a minute and answered, "Barb." I grabbed my tummy. "Did you hear that?" I asked wide-eyed.

"Hear what?" Ellie replied, wider-eyed.

"My stomach growling! Do you have any food or what? You know how I get when I'm hungry!"

"You aren't hungry; you just have the munchies," Ellie said as she pulled out a couple of Hershey bars and three bottles of Pepsi.

189

"Call it what you want, just hand 'em over and nobody gets hurt. Geez, El, what happened to your steak supply? The only thing I saw in the freezer was hot dogs and potpies," I asked.

"Well, I can't afford steak. I can hardly afford hot dogs anymore." She poured oil into a pot on the stove for a popcorn binge.

"You never 'afforded' it before," Darlene said as she opened her candy bar.

"Yeah, well, when I moved out I figured that I'd better quit with the sticky fingers. Didn't think Will would bail me out if I got caught once I was on my own."

"Didn't you think we'd come to your rescue?" I clasped my hands to my chest.

"I know how tight Jake is with a buck. You might have a problem when it came time to put the house up to raise my bail."

"Yeah, but I could always have baked a cake with a file in it." I handed her the canister of popcorn kernels and she sprinkled them into the pot, poured the oil, and put the lid on.

"You forget, Barb, I've tasted your cakes." Ellie slid the pan back and forth on the stove while she held onto the lid. The kernels started to make that delicious popping noise guaranteed to make my mouth water. "Besides, I realized it was wrong, even if the stores were ripping us off and wouldn't miss a steak or two a week." She reached up and grabbed the salt from the cabinet. "It makes me feel proud to open the fridge and realize that I've bought and paid for everything that's in it, even if it is just hot dogs, eggs, and baloney!"

The Mamas and the Papas crooned from the radio on the window sill, "Dream a little dream of me."

"Sweet dreams till sunbeams find you, sweet dreams that leave all worries behind you," Ellie chimed in. Darlene and I joined her, and I was reminded why I stick to humming. These two made me sound like Minnie Pearl.

"Stars fading, but I linger on, dear." Sounds of popcorn hitting the lid on the pan tinkled in the background. We put our arms around one another's waists, watching the stove, swaying back and forth, and waiting for the sound of the popping to stop.

"So, Ellie, how long you been a pot-smokin' hippie?" I asked as we sat back down in the living room with our Pepsis and three brown paper lunch bags full of hot salty popcorn.

"Not long."

"Define *long*." I shoved a handful of popcorn in my mouth.

"Anything over six inches," she said as she held her thumb and index fingers apart maybe two inches. We dropped the popcorn, giggling all over ourselves and making cracks about Jake, Will, and men in general. The sight of three Clairol hair-dye pot-smoking junkies rolling in the middle of her living room was a Kodak moment I was grateful no one captured.

I gathered my composure enough to ask, "Are we still going to Assateague next summer?" I wasn't sure she'd still want to go.

"You betcha! The Tensies-minus-one live on. We've got reservations, right?" El said.

"Sure do." I said.

We munched on the popcorn and sipped our Pepsis while we talked for what seemed like hours, telling stories that made us laugh and cry, remembering our grown up growing pains. The afternoon sun and the tree outside the window made a playful shadow as the wind picked up outside.

After we'd eaten ourselves into next week's calories, we dragged ourselves off the floor and stretched like cats. We didn't get far, and plopped onto the sofa.

"Hey, guess what? I'm not afraid of the dark anymore," Ellie said.

"Yeah, right." Darlene laughed.

"No, really! I had this dream a few weeks ago. I was in the backyard, and the sun went down. All of a sudden, I realized I was alone outside in the dark. I started feeling all frightened and scared like I always do, when I noticed a glow coming from under the trailer." She propped a pillow up behind her.

"A little fairy flew in front of me, kinda like an angel, and whispered that I didn't need to be afraid anymore. That even when it was dark, she was there. She told me to just 'wake up slowly,' and I'd be fine."

Chills ran up my spine as I realized she was serious, and she continued.

"I opened my eyes in the darkness and just laid in bed. Waking up slowly, like we used to talk about, remember?" She looked at me.

"A fairy, huh? Tinker Bell or maybe an angel?" I asked, but I knew better than to giggle. The look in her eyes told me she was serious this time. "Waking up slowly." I sighed. "I haven't thought about that in a long time."

"Sounds like you've been smoking too much of this stuff!" Darlene tried to add some levity, but El didn't laugh.

"You're serious, aren't you?" I asked. I knew just how afraid of the dark she'd always been. I used to wonder if maybe that was why she worked nights, so she could sleep in the daylight instead of the dark.

"It's hard to explain, and saying it out loud sure doesn't make it sound believable, but it sure was real. It's one of those dreams that just stuck with me," El said.

I reached over and hugged her.

"Hey, a hug?" She looked at me in surprise.

"Yeah, must be this stuff you made me smoke."

It was so clear how at peace she was. A serenity I'd never noticed before. And to think I'd been so worried that she'd go into an even deeper depression when she got out on her own. I was wrong on that one, and sometimes it was just plain good to be wrong. Single life must have set her free. Part of me couldn't help but be jealous.

She had decorated her new home in her usual fashion, with lots of color. Pink in the kitchen and orange and greens in the living room.

"You would have made a great flower child," I said.

"It's never too late!" El laughed. "I don't even have much of an appetite anymore. Unless I smoke this stuff, of course. But it's like food isn't even a big deal for me right now. Look how loose my pants are." She pulled at her waistline to show several inches gone.

"Ellie, that's great!" Darlene said.

"Your face is thinner, too," I added. "But you've always been a beauty, no matter what you weighed."

She started confiding that she'd met a man that lived in the neighborhood and that they'd become fast friends.

"Frank's smart and funny. We can talk for hours on end." She propped her elbow up on a pillow. "The only time Will ever had anything to say was when something didn't go his way," she said.

"Frank, huh?" I said out loud, not meaning to. Darlene and I just looked at each other with eyebrows raised. El had mentioned him on the phone, but now he had a name.

"There you go, thinking the worst again!" Ellie threw a pillow and hit me square in the face.

"Worst of what? What do you mean, 'again'?" I said and tossed it back at her.

"We're just friends, for real. He's a widower and just buried his wife of twenty-five years a year ago. We've been out to dinner a few times, and he's great with the boys. He brought them kites and even checked over their homework. I doubt Will ever even touched one of their school papers."

We waited around until 4:00 p.m., hoping to see Ginger and the boys and sobering up from our smoke-induced stupor. I had to get home to cook dinner.

"Give Ginger and the boys a big kiss for me. Speaking of kisses, how are Ginger and Jimmy? Are they still talking about getting married?" I asked as I gathered my purse and keys.

"Oh, they're horny as a couple of toads. Jimmy wants to get married. They haven't set a date just yet, but it might not be that far off." El opened the door, and we walked out onto the deck. "Their hormones tend to rage about the same time ours did. Imagine that." El shook her head.

"I have no idea what you're talking about." I winked at her and continued toward my car.

"Wow, it doesn't seem like we're old enough to be talking about our kids having sex," I said.

"Yeah, Grandma," Darlene said.

"That's 'Grandmother' to you, my dear." I elbowed her. "You'll be joining me soon enough. Besides, being a grandmother is the closest thing to hitting the tensies I've ever done." Nobody was more surprised than me to find that grandmotherhood was such a kick.

I hugged Ellie and whispered how much I missed her.

"Next week is Halloween. What are you guys gonna be?" Ellie asked.

"Barb's just got to pull her broom out of her closet, and she's all set. No need for a costume." Darlene laughed, and I shoved her toward the car.

"Yeah, I know, but you'd think she'd be ready for a new broom by now," Ellie chimed in.

Why do I continue to take this abuse?

"We're having a Halloween party at the office. I'm thinking Roberta might show up dressed like…never mind," Ellie said, catching herself. Even now, she couldn't dish it out to Roberta like she deserved, but I could.

"She needs to dress like the whore she is, and Will can drop her off in the Cadillac just like her pimp would," I said, and we had one last laugh before we headed home.

Darlene and I gave her one last hug and climbed into my mini-tank.

"Are you sure I'm okay to drive?" I hollered to her as I rolled down the window of the green bomb.

"For you, it's probably an improvement." She waved backward over her shoulder as she climbed the steps on the deck. Darlene and I pulled away honking the horn and giggling our way out of the neighborhood.

"Boy, I hadn't realized just how much I'd missed her," I admitted as I cracked the window and lit a cigarette.

"Wow, our girl's making it on her own," Darlene said as we turned onto Route 301. I turned up the radio when Tom Jones started howling, and we headed back to the other side of the beltway.

Yep, I think this time she's out of the onesies for real.

CHAPTER 10

Ellie
Dream a Little Dream of Me

Faith is taking the first step even when you don't see the whole staircase.

—*Martin Luther King Jr.*

The life I carved out for myself and the kids turned out to be the best thing I could have ever done, not only for me but for them, too. At first, I felt guilty for taking them away from Will. After all, he was their father, but then I'd think about the happiness that we found there in that little mobile home, and everything made sense.

Handling all the bills was one of my biggest challenges. Money and I were not what you'd call close friends. Maybe "casual acquaintances" would have been a better description. We visited with each other, but Money and I were never on a first-name basis. He never liked me very much. This I knew because he never stuck around very long. I think that was what scared me the most about being on my own, trying to keep track of him.

Despite Will's frugality and stinginess, I always knew that there was money to pay the bills. But I also knew that when I moved out, I would have to pay my own and try to get Money to hang around a little longer, but he never did. It worried me, but I managed to learn to control my spending, pay the bills first, and have fun with the rest.

It was strange that with all the added responsibility of being on my own, I had found a sense of freedom I never knew I could have. It was hard to put into words, but even with being on a tight budget, I'd never been happier. Pillow fights with the boys when I was tucking them in and eating in the living room if we felt like it; little things that Will would have fussed about or just not permitted were now the norm.

I could read in bed and not bother anyone or buy a flower at the nursery and not have to worry about a verbal browbeating in front of the kids. I could talk on the phone as long as I wanted and with no party line. It was the best two bucks a month this girl ever spent, a private phone line.

"Hey, Mom!" Timmy called to me and knocked me out of my state of melancholy. I turned around from unpacking the leftover box of dishes to see him lined up against the corner wall between the eat-in kitchen and the living room.

"Yeah?"

"You need to mark my height on the corner of the wall." He stood up straighter. And so it went. We christened our new home with names and dates for each of us, me included.

The kids and I had our picka-nickas on Saturday afternoons when the weather was good. Ginger's boyfriend, Jimmy, came when he could and was great with the boys, playing ball and pushing them high on the swings. We missed the Kincaid family, and sometimes Barb and the kids came with us when Jake was at the rifle range or working on a side job with Will. We still made time for "making skies" after we ate, lying down on the picnic blanket, staring at the sky.

"There's a couch with a dog sitting on it, and if you look over there, you can see his TV." William pointed to the sky. Making skies together was what we did best.

"That's not a TV, it's a box of Cheerios. See the *O*s?" Timmy argued.

The kids used their imaginations, and it became a competitive activity for us during the picka-nickas. Ginger kept score for the two little ones, making sure that one would win one week, and the other the next. She was such a natural mom.

"When do you think you and Jimmy will get married?" I asked as we lay there trying to make skies after the boys had grown bored and run off to the playground. I liked Jimmy, and they seemed to fit well together. He certainly seemed to be in love with her.

"He wants to, but I want to wait awhile." She leaned up on one elbow. "Maybe later in the summer after graduation."

She'd turned from a carrot-top, freckle-faced little girl into a slender, long-legged beauty with shiny auburn hair. I would have said she was the spitting image of me, but she did have Will's height and olive complexion. She had gleaned the best from both of us.

"I love the way things are right now. I love Jimmy, and I love being together with you and the boys." She sat up to make sure they were within our sight. "I hate to say it, but I don't miss Radiant Valley very much."

Every other Sunday, Will would come by and pick up William and Timmy. He took them to church and out to lunch. It was a shame that we had to move out for him to spend time with his kids.

I made Will agree not to bring Roberta around the kids, at least not until our divorce was final, and that wouldn't be for another six months. The pain and anger of knowing that Will loved another woman, and an ex-Tensie, had finally started to let up. It only took me a few weeks of living on my own to realize that the two of them had done me a favor. It was as if they had opened up the door to the cage and let me out.

Meeting Frank made me realize that life had possibilities for me. He'd filled a place in my days that I didn't know was empty. When we first started to date, we'd take the boys everywhere we went—to dinner, the movies, even a pickanicka once in a while. We managed to have a few dates on our own, and last week, after going to the movies to see *The Godfather Part II*, we ended up back at his house alone. His girls were spending the night with a friend, and Ginger was home with Timmy and William tucked in.

"Sue sure made a nice home for you, Frank." I picked up a wooden frame with a family vacation photo. Frank's arms surrounded his girls and his late wife, Sue, as he stooped down to pull them closer to him.

"Yeah, she was quite a gal. A great mom, too. I hope you didn't mind coming here, Ellie."

"No, not at all. I want to know what your life was like. Is like." He reached over, grabbed my arms, and pulled me close. I could smell the Hai Karate aftershave I'd given to him for his birthday the week before.

"It's better now than it's been in a long time," he said and stroked my hair. I don't know when the last time anyone did that to me was, or if anyone ever had.

We stood in the living room just hugging each other, and he started kissing me with a tenderness I'd never known from any man. We fell onto the couch and explored each other like teenagers on a second date. Somehow we'd found our way to his bedroom where, thankfully, he'd removed any remnants of Sue. There was nothing but Frank and me there. We lay next to each other and talked for hours. We laughed, cried, and shared our deepest secrets.

I laughed to myself that the Tensies would never believe that nothing sexual had happened.

"I have a strong faith in God. I know He's what got me through losing Sue," Frank said. He went on to explain how he found God in his life. "He was there all along, I just didn't know it. Prayer built my faith as I saw the answers unfold. You're the answer to my prayers, El." He pulled me closer.

I didn't say much, but knew I wanted what he described. I prayed a silent prayer that I could find this peace he talked about.

I fell asleep in his arms, and when I woke, I felt like I'd slept for days. His arm was around my waist, and I realized that we must be "spooning." It made me grin to myself as I remembered nothing but Will's back all the years we'd shared a bed. And at that moment, I willed myself not to compare Will and Frank again, good or bad. I stayed in the bed and was as still as I could be and didn't want the world to start up again. When Frank woke, he leaned over, laced his fingers in mine, and whispered in my ear.

"I'm falling in love with you, El."

I lay there letting the words soak into me. With a smile on my face, it was a surprise that tears slid down my cheeks. I was mourning the death of my marriage and celebrating my future at the same time. I held on tight to Frank's hand.

I thought about the past few months. I'd had so much fun with Barb and Darlene last weekend. I giggled when I thought about what their reaction would be when I filled them in on the last twelve hours. I swiped the tears away before I turned over toward Frank.

He pushed the hair out of my eyes and whispered, "What's so funny?" He tugged on my shoulder and rolled me over until I faced him.

"What's wrong?" he asked. A worried look crossed his face. One renegade tear had hidden in the corner of my eye and had made the great escape down my cheek when I rolled over to face him. He reached over and wiped it away with his thumb.

"Nothing's wrong; everything's right. Really right," I answered, and kissed his cheek.

We lay there waking up slowly together and giggled that no one was going to believe we slept together and nothing more.

"What time is it?" I asked when I realized the sun had been up for a good while.

He reached for the clock on the nightstand and turned it toward us. "8:15."

"I'd better call Ginger and let her know when I'll be home. Will should be picking up the boys for church, so they'll be gone for a few hours."

Ginger teased me. "Yeah, Mom. You guys just stayed up playing jacks all night. I know. Did you get past the onesies?"

"Ging, I know it looks bad, but," I stammered, sounding school girlish, "well, anyway, I'll be home in a little while. Try and make the boys think I'm sleeping in my room until they leave with your dad, would ya?" I rolled back over to find that Frank had left the room. I stood up to go find him as he walked back in the room with a tray of breakfast goodies.

"Get back in that bed, young lady." I sat back down on the bed, my ladylike mouth hanging open, not knowing what to say.

"Okay," was the best I could manage as he placed the tray on the bed between us. Coffee, English muffins, Del Monte fruit cocktail, orange juice, and best of all, a handful of black-eyed Susans positioned in a mason jar. "Why, that's the best bouquet I've ever seen."

Frank blushed. It was obvious that Sue had trained him well. Hey, being with a man who someone else broke in was good with me. She'd done a far better job than I had, that was for sure.

We ate and talked, ate some more, drank coffee, and talked some more. That day, I decided that the only way to get to know someone is to wake up slowly together. Not sitting at a breakfast table, not getting dressed for the day, just hanging out, soaking in the conversation as the day peeked through the curtain.

Frank shared how he liked to watch old movies on rainy Saturdays and ride a bike on sunny ones. He talked about how much he loved his girls and struggled getting over losing Sue but being strong for them.

"I sent them to stay with Sue's parents in Connecticut for a month in the summer after she died. While they were gone, I was finally able to cry and mourn the way I'd wanted but couldn't while they were home." He choked up, but just a little before going on. "By the time they came home, I was afraid I'd just burst into tears at the drop of a hat like I'd done when they were gone, but it was as if all the crying had helped to heal me. Helped me to be stronger for them." I nodded and took another bite of my English muffin.

"I think spending time with Sue's mom and dad helped them grab a hold of Sue's past, giving them something to hold onto in the present," he looked at me as if to say he was sorry for thinking about her. I picked up the tray and sat it on the floor.

"It's okay." I wrapped my arms around his neck. Turned out I was good at reading a man's mind. "It's okay," I said as I hugged him tight. His tears found their way to my heart.

I fell in love with Frank that day, and now I know why they call it "falling in love." When you fall off a ladder, you're unable to stop yourself, you can't help what comes next, and you hit the ground. When I fell in love with him, it was for all the right reasons, and this time when I hit the ground, I landed on my feet.

I thanked God for my second chance. I knew that marriage was supposed to be a lifetime commitment, and I felt bad about that, but I also knew in my heart that everyone made mistakes and He was a God of love.

I had been prepared to stay with Will. I managed to be happy enough with my kids and friends to keep me going, but when he wanted out to be with Roberta, it had hurt just enough to push me out the door. It was as if I'd been given a "get out of jail free" card, and I used it the first chance I got.

I thought back to the struggles that Barb and I shared over the years, how we talked about waking up slowly and how much we treasured it; how few opportunities we had to greet the day on our own terms as moms, housewives, and working women.

Now I knew I'd been waking up slowly all along, like the caterpillar that had spun her cocoon and went into hiding only to come out and discover that she no longer had to crawl along on her belly.

I remembered the times when I felt that I had to crawl on my belly to stay out of Will's way to keep the peace. It dawned on me that I'd been hiding in my cocoon from the truth of my marriage, of who I really was. No more crawling for me. I'm out in the open, flying high every day.

When Barb and Darlene came by last week, we had such a good time talking and laughing, just like old times. Well, almost. We were now officially potheads. Who knew?

I'd missed Barb so much. Our friendship was one of the biggest casualties of my marriage breakup. As I looked back, I knew that she was what kept me sane when the rest of my life was shriveling up. The afternoon with her and Darlene made us realize that the more things changed, the more they stayed the same.

Barb's marriage was hitting a rough patch because of Jake's friendship with Will, but I told her she needed to cut him some slack. He and Will were brothers except for genetics. Jake couldn't turn his back on his brother, even if he was wrong. Jake wouldn't be Jake if he did.

Halloween came, and I was as excited as the boys. I resurrected my Millie the Clown costume for the occasion. Her wig was a little crunched from being crammed in a plastic bag for the last few years, but nothing a little Aqua Net couldn't fix. I replaced a few of her ruffles and even had to take the seams in a little.

I put the costume on and took the boys trick-or-treating before I left for work. They ran from house to house, and Ginger stayed behind handing out

Tootsie Rolls to the little ones who came to our door. When we'd hit just about every home in the park, we headed back.

The phone was ringing as I walked back into the living room with pillowcases of candy. I pulled off my curly rainbow-colored wig and picked up the receiver.

"Hello?"

"Hey, El," Barb said on the other end. She was returning my call from earlier in the day. I'd wanted to tell her about my night with Frank. "Are you leaving for work yet?"

"I'm going in late, so I have time. Just got back from trick-or-treating." I sat down on a kitchen chair after checking to be sure the kids were all outside. I went on to tell her all about my night with Frank. "I am just so lucky, Barb," I said. "I hit the tensies when I found him."

"Luck has nothing to do with it, El. You deserve to be happy."

"But there's one thing that's changed," I said, surprising even myself.

"What's that?"

"I have this sense of not being alone anymore, even when Frank's not around." I twirled Millie's orange and blue hair with my finger. "It's more than not being afraid of the dark, like I told you about when you were here."

"Hearing voices?" she joked. "They have meds for that, you know."

"No, not like that." I pulled the wig's curls straight and let them spring back into place. "It's like God is with me all the time, giving me peace."

"How'd that happen?"

"I think it's been a gradual thing, not a big epiphany or anything, but Frank explained a lot to me." I grasped for the right words. "He talked about how God has been a big part of his life."

"That's great, El." I wasn't sure she meant it. I recognized that little hitch in her voice when she wasn't sure about something.

"Don't worry; I'm not joining the Holy Roller club or anything."

"Just so long as you don't roll away too far," she said, just as the boys bounded into the house. We said our good-byes, and Ginger and I got the boys ready for bed.

As I packed my lunch to take to work, I thought about my conversation with Barb. I knew she didn't "get it," but I'd try and explain it better later. It was like getting a great deal at a red-dot sale; I wanted her to know and share in the great deal I was getting.

We had always joked about making it to the tensies. Geez oh flip, don't look now, girls, but I think I just scooped up all the jacks in one swoop.

CHAPTER 11

Barb
Alone Again, Naturally

I know God won't give me anything I can't handle. I just wish that He
didn't trust me so much.

—*Mother Theresa*

llie sat across the table from me, looking better than I'd ever seen her. She picked up the silver teapot and poured us each a cup of her special blend.

"I can't get over how good you look," I said and stared at the shiny teapot and then back at her. "The single life is sure treating you well." She grinned in response.

"Where'd you get this?" I asked as I reached over to trace the raised scrolling outline on the pot. But she beat me to it and moved it away as if I might break it. She smiled.

"It's shiny even if you can't touch it," she said and caressed the teapot.

"Must have been Frank," I thought out loud, and felt a little hurt by her evasiveness, but she wouldn't tip her hand. She ignored my comment and stared at me.

"You have to listen to me," El said. Her gaze held me and muted my normally sassy response.

"Okay," was all I could muster. I stared at her over my teacup as I took a sip and set it back down on the saucer. The white sweater she wore had what looked to be little pearls sewn into the fabric. It had a shimmering effect that set off the auburn highlights of her hair. Miss Clairol must have come out with a better shade, and she'd definitely gotten a raise to be able to buy such a pretty outfit.

"It's all okay," she said. "Don't feel sorry for me."

I picked up my teacup and shrugged.

"Why in the world would I feel sorry for you?" I took a sip of my tea, looking over the rim at her. "I mean, you've got a great guy and kids that love you, and if you lose any more weight, you'll give Twiggy a run for her money." I let go of one of my famous heavy sighs and got ready to chatter some more.

"There's not much time. You have to hear what I'm saying," she whispered, and leaned forward.

"Why are you…" I looked over my shoulder as a soft breeze came up from behind. There was nothing but the closed storm door behind us. "…being so mysterious?" I asked and leaned forward in like fashion.

"Here and there you can feel it coming, just don't feel sorry for me," she said.

"What?" I asked and thought she must have felt the wind, too. I saw a look in her eyes I'd not noticed before.

The phone jolted me awake, and I opened my eyes. I shook off what must have been a dream as I reached up and turned on the bedside lamp. I crawled over Jake for the phone. "Why don't I just move this over to my side?" I muttered. He could sleep through World War III.

"Hello?" Why do people always dial the wrong number in the middle of the night?

"Barb, it's Will."

"Will?" Jake stirred and twisted toward me when he heard Will's name. He reached for the phone, and I handed it to him, as I assumed Will wouldn't have anything more to say to me in the middle of the night than he would in the daylight. We hadn't spoken to each other in months other than the obligatory hello over the telephone when he called for Jake, at which I did the automatic handoff of the phone with my "it's him again" roll of the eyes.

"Hey, what's going on?" Jake mumbled into the receiver. "She was? Is she all right? Oh my God…"

We were both sitting upright by now, and the suspense was killing me.

"Okay, I'll be right there. You hang in there, buddy." Jake hung up the phone.

"What in the world is going on?" I pushed my wild woman hair out of my eyes and focused on him.

He looked at me with an uncertainty I'd never seen in his eyes before. "What happened?" My stomach twisted, and I somehow knew that I didn't want to know.

"Ellie was in a car accident on her way to work last night."

"What? Is she in the hospital? What happened?"

"Some drunk hit her broadside as she was going through a light." The look in his eyes was one I didn't recognize.

"What hospital's she in?" I jumped out of bed and reached for my robe. "Where'd they take her?" He just looked at me speechless. "What?" I almost yelled. Jake shook his head and tried to pull me back on the bed, but I pulled back.

"She didn't make it to the hospital, Barb." He ran his fingers through his hair. My stomach hit the floor. "She died at the scene."

"What? No way! I just saw her last weekend and—" I remembered how we laughed while we were stoned. Was this my punishment for smoking dope?

"El's dead?" the words hung in the air between us as we just looked at each other. I fell to the floor and landed on my knees. Jake reached down and pulled me up next to him on the bed. We held on to each other closely as I cried. I looked up to see that his face was wet with tears, too. Why that surprised me I wasn't sure.

"Ellie!" I called her name, half expecting a response. "The kids, where are the kids?" I asked. Jake turned away, grabbed a towel, and wiped his face. My stomach twisted again as my thoughts turned to Roger, Scott, Ginger, William, and Timmy.

"They're okay. They're with Will. He went and brought them home with him as soon as he found out."

"Great, just what they need. Poor babies." Whatever popped into my head came out of my mouth. For once I wasn't censoring my thoughts for our relationship's sake. I'd gotten better at biting my tongue over the past few months, just trying to keep us both from being so defensive or angry all the time. The Reilly breakup had, at times, threatened to break us, too.

We both grabbed yesterday's clothes and got dressed. After I put on my shoes, I sat on the edge of the bed, staring into space. She's not really gone. She can't be gone forever, God. "Please, God," I prayed, knowing it was too late but did it anyway.

Before I knew what he'd done, Jake had called his father and made arrangements for him to come over and stay with Jay and Kelly. I picked up the phone to call Darlene. There was no easy way to break the news to her.

"I'll meet you there as soon as I can," Darlene said as soon as the hysteria subsided for her a little, and we hung up. It was a comfort knowing she'd be there. Dealing with Will was not going to be easy for either one of us, but there's strength in numbers, even when the Tensies just shrank from three to two.

"I can't bring myself to call Karen," I said to Jake. "Should we call this early?" It was as if I was frozen on the side of the bed. Jake picked up the phone and dialed Karen's number as I went into the bathroom.

"Honey, it's Daddy. I have some bad news." Jake went on to give the now-canned version of El's death. I couldn't bear to hear it again. I shut the door, sat on the toilet, and cried even after the tears ran dry.

No more Betsy! No more picka-nickas, no more red-dot sales, no more sand between our toes or making skies. I never before realized just how much a part of me she'd become and could only wonder how much of me she took with her. She not only made me laugh but also made me see the good in everyone and everything. I was a lonely, scared kid with two kids of my own when I'd met her. I was afraid to take any chances, to step out of the onesies. Now what?

"Why Ellie, God? Why not Will? Nobody likes him anyway," I informed Him. How'd you make a mistake like this? How'd you let this happen? Her kids need her." Every time I thought of the kids, I broke down again.

Now I knew what "Only the good die young," meant.

"Guess I'll be around awhile," I said out loud. After my private temper tantrum, I realized I could be treading on thin ice. I'd questioned God's authority and lack of judgment. I knew it wasn't prudent, but I couldn't help it.

"Are you ready to head over to Will's?" Jake tapped on the bathroom door. "Dad's here to stay with the kids."

I opened the door to see Jake's eyes red and puffy and realized he'd been in the bedroom doing the same thing as me. I hugged him again and didn't want to let go.

"She can't be gone, Jake. She can't be gone!" He stroked my head and reminded me that we needed to get over to Will's and help with the kids. Tears that I thought had dried up came pouring out again.

I walked down the stairs to the kitchen where Jake's dad was making coffee in the kitchen. He turned when he heard me walk in. Bill was tall with a distinguished graying moustache and a crumpled shirt. It was obvious he had jumped out of bed and dressed in a hurry to get here, although a crumpled shirt was the norm for this single older man.

"I'm so sorry, Barb," he said as he hugged me. He was the dad I'd never had, and I'd never had the need to let him be one until now. He stroked my hair and let me cry some more. "Don't worry about the kids. You go on over to Will's." I hugged him again and grabbed my jacket. Jake was at the front door waiting for me.

We plopped down in our yellow Galaxy. Jake started the ignition. "The Lion Sleeps Tonight" wheema whacked out of the radio into the predawn air. He reached over to turn it off, but I touched his hand and shook my head. We sat, staring out the windows.

Flashes of Ellie and Ginger singing into their wooden spoons in the little kitchen of her Cambridge cottage flooded me. The song washed over me like a tranquilizer. "A wheema whack, a wheema whack," the Platters crooned. Never again would I see a wooden spoon and not want to sing into it. Never again would I hear this song and not want to make a U-turn. Never again would I hear her voice. Out loud.

"Jake, it's like she's here," I said, staring through the windshield as he drove through our neighborhood to Radiant Valley.

"I know." He reached over and covered my hand with his.

"I was dreaming about her when the phone rang." I pulled out a cigarette and cracked the window. "She was trying to tell me not to feel sorry for her." The tears showed up again and didn't stop until we pulled up in front of Will's house.

It was almost daybreak when Jake opened the storm door and we walked into Will's living room. Not Will and Ellie's living room, just Will's.

Will, Ginger, and Jimmy were sitting at the dining room table. Roger and Scott sat in the living room and stood up to give us hugs. William and Timmy just sat next to each other on the couch, staring at nothing. Captain Kangaroo gave instructions for building an alphabet wall to Mr. Green Jeans on the television, but no one paid attention.

Ginger pushed her chair back with her legs, ran over, and threw her arms around me. She buried her head on my shoulder and cried. "I'm so glad you're here, Aunt Barb. Mom's gone!"

Her shoulders heaved, and her auburn hair clung to the tears on her face as she pulled back and looked at me. I cried with her and pulled her hair back behind her ears. Leaving the others behind, I took her hand, and we walked out the side kitchen door.

There was a chill in the early morning November air. Daylight was just peeking out over the plum tree, the tree where Ellie had spent countless hours talking with her kids.

Ginger and I sat on the low-lying branch and stared at the side of the house. I could hear the radio in the kitchen playing the McDonald's jingle, "You deserve a break today, so get up and get away," thinking how odd it was that the rest of the world didn't stop just because ours had.

"She said she had a really fun time with you and Darlene last week." Ginger picked up a twig and started to snap it into pieces.

"Your mom had fun no matter what she was doing or who she was with."

Neither of us could say much without breaking down, so we just sat quietly in between comments and crying jags.

"What should I do, Aunt Barb?" Ginger asked, eyebrows raised.

I brushed her auburn hair out of her eyes. I immediately knew what she meant but didn't want to let on. "Whadya mean, hon?"

"Should I move back in here and help Dad raise the boys, or should I marry Jimmy?"

"Ginger, I don't know. Only you can answer that." She was such a mom to William and Timmy because of the odd hours that El had worked. My adult self knew she couldn't walk away from them now. She'd discover that for herself and didn't need me to tell her.

"It's too soon to make any big decisions. Just take it one day at a time." I handed her another Kleenex. "Karen's flying in later this afternoon," I said, trying to make her feel a little better. I could see Jimmy peeking out the screen door, trying to decide if he was needed or not. He decided not and went back inside.

Ginger started crying again. "I always thought we were just like you and Mom. Always tried to be."

"You're so much like your mom. So loving and pretty. So funny and a practical joker." I turned and looked at her. "Remember the time you, your mom, and Karen went to the drive-in movies? You dropped Karen off, and we thought you'd left."

She nodded and half grinned.

"You knocked on the door and hid in the bushes, scaring us half to death." My words hung in the air, but she didn't notice my poor choice of words.

"Yeah, you got us back though when you turned on the sprinkler and soaked us." The laughter choked us as our tears jerked us back to reality.

When Jimmy peeked out the door for about the fifth time, we figured it was time to go back in.

As I walked through the house, I found it hard to believe that El didn't live there anymore. Even though she'd been gone from the little house in Radiant Valley for months, there were still signs of her everywhere. From the plum tree in the side yard to the upside-down wallpaper in the bathroom to the ugly wooden leaf shelves in the dining room. She was everywhere.

Seeing the shelves brought that Christmas flooding back. "Remember?" I looked at Jake and pointed to the tacky wooden shelves on the wall. He grinned and nodded.

The matching set was still there. Ellie and I would never be a matching set again. My bookend was gone. My other shoe. My right hand. My sister. Reality splashed me in the face for the umpteenth time that day.

I sat down at the dining room table with Jake and Will and remembered dozens of candles in milk cartons cooling on every spare spot in the room. Will looked up at me, his eyes red-rimmed with a shell-shocked, hollow look.

"I never wanted her to die, Barb. I did love her." He looked at me. "I still do."

"I know." I had nothing prolific to offer but reached across and covered his hand with mine and surprised even me. Despite the soured marriage and affair with Roberta, he was still Jake's dearest friend and the closest thing to a brother he'd ever have. He and Ellie had shared a life together for twenty-five years, and there was no way to deny any of that.

"You couldn't know Ellie and not love her," I added.

The house slowly filled with friends and relatives who tried to find a way to be helpful. The dining room table gradually loaded up with casseroles and baked goods. The phone rang, and I picked up the receiver.

"Prince George's County Hospital's on the phone for you, Will," I said as I handed him the phone. None of us could figure why the hospital would be calling. Will had already identified El's body, and she'd been moved to the funeral home.

"What? Where is he now?" Will asked the person on the other end of the phone. "Well, I guess I'll wait here for him to come home. Thanks for calling." He walked over and hung the receiver back on the wall. He scratched his head and looked at Jake.

"I guess Scott went to the hospital. He threatened to kill the drunk who was driving. He's in ICU, and it sounds like Scott caused quite a scene."

"Good for him. I'd like to get my hands on him myself," I said. Roger volunteered to hunt Scott down and bring him back to the house. I was sure he was grateful for the chance to escape the awful details that were dumped in our laps. Details like morgues, funeral homes, caskets, limos, and burial plots. Heck, she was young and not old enough to worry about finding a final resting place. I knew that the only place she'd ever wanted to rest was somewhere with her feet planted in the sand, definitely not in the dirt.

Karen arrived midafternoon and offered to stay behind with William and Timmy during the first funeral viewing. Will had taken the boys earlier in the day for a private viewing but didn't think they needed to go through hours of stress on top of that.

"Mom, I just don't know what to say to them; they're so young," Karen said, wringing her hands. The eczema on her hands was broken out worse than ever. It seemed that nerves activated the rash. She'd gained weight since moving to West Virginia. I didn't suppose there was much to do besides eat in that godforsaken place but managed to keep my opinion to myself.

"Just talk to them about everyday things. If they want to talk about their mom, they will." I touched her hand. "Your hands look sore."

"Yeah, it seems like every time I come home, they break out."

Every time she came home, Lee gave her a hard time. I'd heard them arguing over the phone during her previous visits. He was probably afraid she wouldn't return. It was becoming obvious to me that there was trouble in River City, but that would have to wait for now.

I felt as though I was watching my life through a telescope, like it wasn't really happening to me. My partner in crime was gone. Gone. Just plain gone. Darlene and I sat together in the living room, trying to make sense out of any of it.

"Do you believe in heaven?" I asked Darlene.

"Yeah, I do. I don't know if it's the harp and cloud thing, but I do think we go on to a better place. Let's face it, Barb; there's got to be something better than this." She picked at the little balls of fuzz on her sweater. Her normally perfect hair was disheveled and flatter than normal. I didn't even have it in me to tease her. El would've been disappointed in me.

"We're down from four Tensies to two, you know," Darlene said.

"Yeah, I thought about that. I don't think I could survive the onesies again, so you'd better take good care of yourself." I picked up my teacup from the coffee table. "I've been thinking that she really didn't go that far away." I looked at Darlene out of the corner of my eye to see if she thought I was losing it. Feeling safe, I continued. "I feel like she's right here with me, telling me it's all right, but it can't be all right. Nothing's 'all right' anymore."

"I know. It's like she's whispering to me. You felt that, too?" She looked relieved. We just looked at each other and realized we didn't need to say more.

We didn't have to talk. We both knew we were right but were afraid to say it out loud any more than we already had.

Bits and pieces of what must have been the dream I'd shared with Jake came back to me slowly. I stared at the teapot that sat on the table.

"I think I was dreaming when the phone rang last night," I remembered out loud. Ellie's pearl-laden sweater stood out in my memory. "El and I were drinking tea, too, I think." I looked back at Darlene.

"Yeah, dreams can be weird sometimes," Darlene agreed.

"No, it was more than that…" I put the teacup down. "She kept saying, 'Don't feel sorry for me' and 'It's all okay.'" A chill ran up my spine.

"Wow," Darlene said as she stared back at me.

"She said, 'Sometimes you feel it coming.'"

Darlene's face went white. "Barb, that's too weird." She grabbed onto my hand and squeezed.

"Yeah, funny I just now remembered the rest of it." We sat and stared at the teacups.

"Maybe we're not really down to two Tensies. Hmm, we'd better watch out." I looked over my shoulder. "Will would love nothing better than to help Jake get me committed." I snapped back to reality.

"Yeah, then I'd have to start dating Jake and hanging out with Roberta," Darlene quipped.

"I think the padded room is the better choice of the two." I punched her in the arm.

"Me too!" And we broke into giggles.

Jake walked into the living room with a "what's going on?" look on his face. We looked at him and burst out into guffaws and rolled back on the couch. The more we tried to hold it in, the more we lost it. He shook his head and went back to the dining room.

Tragedy kicked me in the gut, but Ellie's humor was still standing.

Before we buried Ellie, Ginger decided to move back in with Will and help raise the boys. Ellie's sense of duty lived on in Ginger, and as Sonny and Cher would say, "The beat goes on." I worried out loud to Jake and Darlene about her choice but knew in my heart she would have done it no other way.

I'd not been to many funerals, but the ones that I'd been to were for older people who had lived long lives. At least they both seemed like they'd had enough time. I realized then that time was something we never had enough of; the clock could wind down without our even knowing it. It wasn't like in a football game with a scoreboard to tell you when the game's over or if it's a tie and you get to have overtime.

Why couldn't El get some overtime? I would have given anything to have just fifteen more minutes with her. One more crabbing excursion, fighting over a random crab, or one more late night raid at Hungry Herman's.

The four of us sat in Will's living room, waiting on everyone to finish dressing so we could leave for the final viewing and burial.

"Remember when Karen fell in the water down at Deale Island while we were crabbing?" I elbowed Darlene. Karen and Ginger looked at each other and smiled. It had been a night of firsts. We strolled down Memory Lane until everyone was ready to go.

"She always said that if she lived long enough and ended up in a home she was going to start eating poorly, smoking, and drinking heavily," I said.

"Eating poorly? Now there's a novel idea!" Darlene said.

"Barb, we'd better get going," Jake said as he picked up his car keys. We pulled ourselves off the couch, buttoned up our coats, and headed for the car. The drive to the funeral home was a quiet one.

We pulled off Georgia Avenue into the funeral home parking lot in the Vega. The muffler or lack thereof on the mini-tank announced our arrival so that everyone in the parking lot turned and looked our way, Roberta included.

"What's she doing here?" I blurted.

Ginger began to cry again.

"This is ridiculous, Jake. You'd better get that witch and Will out of my way!" I ranted. "Jake, you'd better tell Will to keep her away from me and Ellie's kids!" I pulled out a cigarette and a pack of matches. He didn't waste any time jumping out of the car to head me off at the pass.

"Some people just don't have any sense," Karen added and grabbed Ginger's hand. "Just ignore her. Let's go," she said, and I followed. This must be what it's like to want to kill someone. Now I knew how good people ended up in jail.

Momma pulled up in her red Cutlass. She opened the door and joined us as we walked across the parking lot.

"Did you see who I saw?" Momma asked as we hugged. She was so tiny; I always wondered if I was really her kid.

"Yeah, Jake ran over to run interference," I answered. "Why does she continue to amaze me?"

Roberta spotted us and slithered into the funeral home as inconspicuously as any hussy trying to be a lady could.

I took one last puff off my cigarette and snuffed it out on the pavement with my foot. Intuitively, Darlene and I swept Ginger and the boys into the waiting room next to the funeral parlor. Other than the private viewing, they'd never even been to a funeral before and weren't sure of what to do. None of us were.

I stooped down to look William and Timmy in the eyes. "Boys, I know this is tough for you, and if you don't want to go inside, that's okay." I looked from one to the other. "Your mom is just lying there. If you want to go see her, you can." I tried to keep from crying, but a renegade tear fell down my cheek. I brushed it away with the back of my hand.

"That's okay, Aunt Barb, we want to see her again," William assured me. Ginger walked over between the two and grabbed the boys' hands. I stood up and kissed her on the cheek, and they walked away toward the coffin.

Will walked over and stood behind Ginger and the boys at the casket, with his back to us. His shoulders heaved.

Jake and I walked into the funeral parlor and sat in the chairs until Will and the family had said their good-byes. When they walked away, we got up and walked up to the pink casket.

When my eyes saw her, my heart skipped a beat. I recognized the white sweater with the pearls woven into the threads. I remembered that I had seen the sweater in the dream when the phone rang a few nights ago.

Jake put his arm around my shoulders, and I shook. I didn't cry, I just shook and couldn't stop. Reality splashed me in the face as I realized I would never see her again, at least not on this side of heaven. I felt my heart beating. I barely resisted the urge to turn on my heels and run. Until now, Ellie's death was something we'd talked about the past few days; now it was real. I heard a whimper behind me and turned to see Darlene. She stood alone, crying.

I looked at Jake, and he nodded. I walked to her, and together we held hands and stared at Ellie.

"Remember I told you about my dream?" I asked her, and she nodded, tears streaming down her face and leaving a trail in her makeup. "Well, that's the sweater she was wearing," I said, not believing my own words. Is this what a nervous breakdown is like?

"I thought Ginger said she'd never worn it yet, that she'd gotten it for her as a birthday present," Darlene said, objecting to my delusion.

"Yeah, I know, so let's make this our little secret," I whispered to Darlene. I leaned over the edge of the casket to her ear. "It's all okay," I said, but I didn't believe it. Was I just trying to make a dead friend feel better? Better to keep that one to myself.

We turned and walked back to the chairs and sat down.

We just sat there and stared at El while the room filled up with people. When I looked up, it was standing room only.

"Wow, look at all the people," Darlene whispered in my ear. "I guess it shouldn't surprise us. You couldn't know her without caring about her."

The piped-in organ music groaned in my ears.

"This music has got to go," I said.

"You're right; she'd hate this," Darlene said. "I'll go see what I can do about it."

Ginger and Karen walked over and sat down next to me. I was still shaking and afraid to stand up. I wondered if this was what it felt like to almost faint. Voices seemed to float around me, there was a slight ringing in my ears, and my hands were tingling.

The sad organ music stopped, and a different sound came over the loud speaker. "You'll never know…just how much I love you." But it wasn't Ellie singing the tune this time, it was Rosemary Clooney. "You'll never know just how much I care." Ginger looked at me, and a small smile tipped the side of her mouth. It was like balm to my soul to see her smile, to see anyone smile.

"That's better," she whispered, and we all nodded in agreement. How Darlene ever pulled that off, I couldn't figure. The sound of Rosemary Clooney's voice warmed me like an old familiar blanket and sent chills up my spine at the same time.

Darlene, Momma, and I enjoyed a little sick comic relief as we watched people's reactions when they discovered that Roberta was sitting behind Will in her miniskirt.

Karen walked over. "Let's hit the ladies' room and get outta here," she said. Momma and I followed her, but Darlene stayed behind to greet a coworker. We took off out of the parlor and headed down the hallway to the restroom.

"She's too old for that outfit," Momma said to me as I came out of the stall. "She should know better, Barb. Some people are just plain uncouth." Momma never said a bad thing about anyone, but Roberta proved to be too much for her southern belle rules of etiquette.

"I know, Mom, but Ellie was right when she said, 'You just can't fix stupid.'" I buttoned my pants.

I came out of the stall, lit up a cigarette, sank down into a wingback chair, and stared across at my reflection in the mirror. "Yikes, look at my hair." Before I could reach in my purse for a comb, Karen beat me to it, smoothing my bouffant.

"Why don't you get a blow-dry style?" Karen asked. She'd tried to talk me into it before. "It would be so much easier, no more curlers, a lot less Aqua Net."

"Nah, too short for me. Besides, I'm stuck on poufy."

"I can't believe Roberta showed up here," Karen said.

"I guess I shouldn't be surprised at anything she does. The kids don't need this. It was bad enough that Ellie had to see her every night at GPO, and now she's got to put up with her at her own funeral. Unbelievable," I said.

Momma's eyes widened as she looked over my shoulder. I looked in the mirror and was shocked to find Roberta standing there. Talk about timing.

I left my ladylike self sitting in the chair, and before I knew it, I was on my feet with Roberta backed up against a bathroom stall door. We stood inches apart, and her beady little eyes were now anything but "little."

"Who the hell do you think you are, showing up at El's funeral?" I hissed. She just stared at me, and for the first time I could ever remember, had nothing to say. Her face went white. I could feel my heart beat in my throat.

"Well?" I stepped closer.

"Will and the boys need me here," she fumbled.

I blinked, not believing my own ears, when she added insult to the injury.

"And Ellie was my friend, too!"

I stared at her and shook my head. How'd she fix her mouth to say that? I let out a half laugh, half screech and barely recognized my own voice. "Friend? You call yourself a friend? You were a slut in high school and still are! I warned Ellie about you, but no, she wouldn't listen. She kept sticking up for you."

I stepped a little closer, with my hand poised for a good swat at her cheek. She skulked backward and must have thought she was up against a wall, but the stall door wasn't locked. The door swung open and she fell onto the toilet, swinging her arms and catching nothing but air.

"I'd flush you, but you'd just clog it up!" I turned and walked over to the sink, feeling good about my desire to kick her while she was down.

The door to the ladies' room opened again.

"What in the world?" Darlene said as her eyes went from me to Roberta. The hussy smoothed her leather miniskirt over her thighs and slithered between us out the door.

Rosemary Clooney made fun over the Muzak speaker: "Sisters, sisters, there were never such devoted sisters, never had to have a chaperone, no sir! Lord, help the sister who comes between me and my man!" I was sure El was running the show here, or at least the music.

"You okay?" Darlene asked.

"Depends on how you define 'okay,'" I said and plopped down into the chair.

Ginger walked in. "What the heck happened? Roberta came out of here like a bat out of hell."

"You missed it! Mom let her have it. I thought she was gonna flush her for a minute," Karen said.

"Now, that would've been worth the price of admission!" Ginger said. "Thanks, Aunt Barb." She walked over and hugged me.

"I was getting ready to smack the rouge off her fat cheeks when she fell back into the stall." I hugged Ginger and smoothed her long auburn hair and held on.

"Yeah, she was in half swing when the stall swallowed her up and she fell onto the toilet," Momma said. "I'm thinking she wet her pants." This from the one who taught us all to be a lady, not to bite our nails, always prefer crystal to cut glass, and wear gloves while gardening. But the girl could get down when it was needed.

"Barb, you should've hit her when you had the chance!" Momma added as she put her red lipstick back in her bag and snapped it shut as we walked back to the lobby.

"I don't know about you guys, but I can't go back in there," I said. The thought of saying good-bye to El was too much.

Jake stood next to the funeral director, who looked at his watch. Evidently, we'd overstayed our welcome.

We all looked through the doorway at Ellie lying in the funeral parlor. Will's mom, Sylvia, leaned over Ellie and fixed her hair. Sylvia's necklace dangled over El's chest as she feigned concern over her almost-former daughter-in-law's appearance.

"Doesn't she normally wear her hair parted the other way?" Sylvia asked Will, and he shrugged.

"Look at her, pretending to care about Ellie," I said. "Makes me sick."

"I can just see El reach up and snatch that necklace right off her scrawny neck if she leans over her again," Darlene whispered and Sylvia did just that. We looked at each other and remembered how Ellie had no use for the catty old witch. The vision of her scaring the bejesus out of the old biddy was like laughing gas.

We broke into belly-hugging guffaws. Will and Silvia looked at us like we should be shot, and maybe they were right, but the image of Ellie grabbing a hold of the old broad was almost as good as the real thing.

"Barb, what's going on?" Jake asked as he walked up.

I looked at him, giggled, and shook my head. I wiped the tears away again.

"Come on, Barb. Roberta came out of the bathroom crying. What'd you say to her?" he asked.

"Not nearly enough." I walked past him and out of the funeral home, unable to say one last good-bye to the queen of the Tensies.

CHAPTER 12

Barb Against All Odds

*If death meant just leaving the stage long enough to change cos-
tume and come back as a new character...Would you slow down?
Or speed up?*

—*Chuck Palahniuk*

*M*emories can be your best friend or your worst enemy. Living in Prince
George's County was a constant reminder of the way things used to
be and never would be again.

"Kelly, put that back, hon. I already got some Oreos."

She shrugged and put the bag of cookies back on the shelf. I always thanked
my lucky stars with her. I figured I must have paid my dues with Jay, and God
knew I couldn't handle two hyper kids in a row.

It had been a few months since El's accident; I still couldn't bring myself to
say that she died. Accident sounded better, less permanent, less lonely.

I continued to load the belt with groceries. After paying the checkout girl, I
pushed the cart toward the automatic doors and almost ran into the backside of
a lady who was picking up her groceries after her bag had broken. I bent over to
help her gather in the renegade cans.

"Here you go. They should double-bag canned goods!" I said as I handed her
some stewed tomatoes.

"Thanks," the familiar husky voice said, and I stiffened when I realized I'd bent over to help Roberta. She froze in place, her beady brown eyes wide, eyebrows raised. I immediately wished I'd taken the opportunity to run up her backside with the grocery cart. Hindsight, how come it never shows up fast enough?

"Don't mention it." I just stared at her, and my heart beat so hard I could feel it in my head.

"Barb, I wish we could, I mean, do you think—"

I pushed my cart around her thunder thighs and exited stage right as quickly as I could.

I thought twice, stopped, and turned back to look at her to give her a tongue lashing but took one look and felt the old familiar hatred again. I now knew how people killed in the heat of passion.

"Believe me, Roberta, you don't want to hear anything I've got to say." I turned and pushed Kelly and the cart out to the parking lot. Driving home, I had visions of her lying flat on the shiny grocery store tiles with my cart tracks on her back. I daydreamed about the witty comebacks I could have made to make her feel like the traitorous witch that she was.

"I can't do this anymore." I slammed the bag of groceries on the dining room table.

"Do what?" Jake asked and looked up from his *Washington Times*.

"I can't live in this town and be responsible for my actions. I ran into Roberta again."

Jake sighed and rolled his eyes.

I made up my mind. I'd find a way out of this county.

"Does she still have any hair left?" he said.

"It's not funny, Jake. That house I told you about in Howard County is still for sale."

"Be real, Barb. You really want to move?"

"Look, we can make a thirty-thousand dollar profit on this house and only have to finance thirty. And we'd have three-and-a-half acres instead of a 'lot' in a subdivision."

He got up and turned off the television as we headed to bed. Hmm, I wasn't getting anywhere. It was time to make it his idea.

"By the way, are you going to put in a garden this year?" I asked. I knew that it bugged him that there wasn't enough sunlight in our shady backyard to grow a decent tomato.

"I don't know. I might take them up on it at the lab and rent one of those garden plots again." He pulled up the covers, and we snuggled.

You can grow a big garden if we move to Howard County." I put in the hook: "And buy a tractor." It was time to start reeling him in. Guys loved tractors, didn't they? Anything with a motor and wheels was good enough bait. "Didn't you say that Sonny lives out that way? Wouldn't it be nice to live close to him and Maryann?" *Shut up and let him think, Barb. Just be quiet.*

"Well, now that you mention it." Jake paused and ran his fingers through his hair. Now I knew I was getting somewhere. We both realized it would be a healthy thing for our marriage if he didn't live right around the corner from Will and Roberta, but neither of us was willing to say it out loud.

"You want to go look at this house the realtor called about? It's about a forty-five-minute drive to work. We could go on Saturday."

"That's a long drive every day, Barb." He shook his head. I pointed out that since I'd gone to work full-time as a secretary at the National Weather Service, we could carpool.

"Well, I guess it wouldn't hurt to drive up there and see." He kissed me on the cheek. "Don't think we're going to buy something just because we're looking."

Timing was everything, so I set the hook and pulled him up over the side of the boat, but I wasn't above letting him flop around a bit before I reeled him in. Saturday morning, we drove the hour to Sykesville. Once we were past the Beltway and Route 95, it was nothing but farms and rolling hills. I asked myself if I really thought I could live this far out, but the good kept outweighing the bad.

"I'm not sure I like it enough to move way out here," I said out loud, without meaning to, but that reverse psychology thing was my new best friend. We pulled up in the driveway and walked around the four-acre home site. He was already envisioning his garden and riding around on the tractor. *Green Acres*, Eva Gabor, and me. I could see the resemblance.

And so it went. By the end of the weekend, we'd put our house up for sale and signed on the dotted line for a new home in Sykesville. And that, girls, is how you do it. Make it all his idea.

Country living was an adjustment but a good one. Jay and Kelly's schools were smaller and had more parental and community involvement. They adjusted fast. Jake and I had a hike to work every day, but it was worth it. The drive gave us time to talk, really talk. Jake was excited about his vegetable garden, and I even thought about trying my hand at canning. Did I say *canning*?

It had been almost a year since El died, and I didn't hear much from or about Ginger in those days. My only line of communication was through Jake, and I found it was better if I didn't mention Will. Since Karen lived in West Virginia, she didn't hear from Ginger as much either. Karen did say that she'd finally moved out of Will's and in with Jimmy, leaving the boys behind.

Jake and Will still worked on side jobs together, and once in a while they went out for an afternoon of target practice at the gun club. One Saturday morning I was making a second pot of coffee when Will knocked on the door.

"Hey, Barb. Is Jake ready to go?" he asked.

"I'm not sure. Come on in," I said, not knowing how to get away with slamming the door in his face. I walked down the hallway as he waited in the kitchen.

"Jake, Will's here," I announced as he finished drying after his shower.

"Okay, tell him I'm coming," he answered, with a worried look in his eyes.

"You'd better hurry up. I can't be held responsible if you leave me in there with him for more than a minute or so." I turned on my heel and headed back down the hallway. I hadn't spent any time alone with Will since way before Ellie died.

I walked back into the kitchen. Will had made himself at home and was sitting at the counter.

"Your new place is nice," Will said, looking out the back window.

"Yeah, we like it."

My instincts and claws both came out at the same time.

"By the way, Will." I couldn't help myself. "Did Roberta get that new position working for Mike Carlson? Gretchen told me she was leaving and that

Roberta had applied." He took the bait. I'd heard through an old friend that Roberta was jockeying for a promotion and this time not on her back.

He raised his eyebrows, probably surprised that I was offering up everyday conversation. I yanked on the hook.

"She doesn't know yet. They're supposed to make the announcement next week." I considered whether to yank twice or let him swallow the hook whole. I decided whole was better.

"Really? Because I heard Sue Cartwright got the job."

"No, I don't think so. Roberta would've told me."

"True." I said and started reeling him in.

His head tilted to the left, letting me know that the hook was in place.

"I hear it's hard working for Carlson." He was out of the water, flopping a little bit, but held on.

"Why is that?" He was off the hook and on my plate.

"Gretchen told me she left 'cause he was forever trying to get her in bed." Let him wonder how Roberta was gonna handle him.

Will just looked at me, not sure how to react. Having to reply, he offered up, "Really?" Now that was original.

I turned on my heel and headed down into the basement to flip laundry loads. No person had ever let me down as much as he had, and considering my childhood, that said a lot.

I reached in the dryer and pulled out a towel and started to fold. I stared at the folding table, our old kitchen table that we retired to the basement when we moved to Howard County. The yellow Formica and silver edged trim was still shiny. I thought about the many times Ellie and I had sat drinking coffee or Pepsi, tuning out screaming kids while plotting our next excursion or moneymaking scheme here at this table. It wasn't until I was finished folding that I even noticed the tears falling down my cheeks. Would they ever stop? I realized I missed not only El but Will, too. I missed the vacations, the crab feasts, and the gun club dances.

Jake opened the basement door and called down the steps. "I'll see you around five, Barb."

"Okay, bye!" I called back.

I wiped the tears away with a towel and wondered if it would ever get better, when the phone rang. I picked up the receiver that Jake had just installed next to the washer and dryer for me last week. Gotta keep the wife happy while she's folding laundry. It was Darlene.

"You ready to go yet?" she asked. We were going shopping and out to lunch.

"Yeah, I'll be leaving in fifteen minutes. See you in a bit. I had some fun torturing Will this morning. I'll fill you in when I see you." I hung up the phone.

I thought more about my run-in with Will as I sat at a red light on the way to Darlene's. I knew he and El weren't in love the way they should have been, but why did he have to have an affair with Roberta? If he could have only waited, none of this heaped-on hurt would have had to happen. But then I realized that if the affair hadn't happened, El would never have had the happiness of her last few months. But then again, she wouldn't have been living in Waldorf and driving through that intersection on Halloween either. The what-ifs were still piling up.

Ellie had deserved to have someone who loved her for who she was, someone who relished in her laughter and grabbed onto the ride, because whoever's life she was in, it was guaranteed to get bumpy. At least she'd found Frank before she checked out.

Frank had been devastated when El died. He'd attended the burial but had stood in the back, and we didn't know he was there until it was over and we saw him walking out to his car.

"Frank!" Ginger had called out, and ran to meet him.

"Oh my gosh, it's Frank," I said.

"Who's Frank?" Jake had asked.

"Ellie's friend. I'll be right back." I walked over to join Frank and Ginger. He was medium height with sandy brown hair and cuter than El had described.

"I still can't believe it," Frank said as I walked up. His eyes were red-rimmed, so he fit right in with the rest of us. I put out my hand to shake his.

"I'm Barb Kincaid. You must be Ellie's Frank."

"Yes, uh, at least I used to be. She talked about you a lot."

"Well, you know she sometimes exaggerated." I smiled at him. It felt good to smile, but the pain on his face reeled me back into the sadness.

"Yeah, well, she loved you like a sister. I do remember her saying that."

"Aunt Barb and Mom were like Lucy and Ethel, only more dangerous!" Ginger said.

"Frank, thanks so much for bringing El so much happiness so quickly," I said, surprised at my openness with a stranger, but any friend of El's...

"She was easy to love," he said. "I just can't believe she's gone." He broke down and sobbed. Ginger and I each hugged one of his shoulders and tried to comfort him for a few minutes. We gathered our composure for what seemed like the hundredth time.

"Why don't you come over to Scott's for the wake?" I asked, but he shook his head.

"No, that wouldn't be right."

"No really, Frank," Ginger said and handed him a tissue. "Dad's going to his house with you-know-who. You have to come."

And so he had. Most of the crowd drove over to Scott's house and congregated in his family room. We'd reminisced about Ellie and all the crazy things she had done. Everyone had a story, and Frank was no exception.

"Did she ever tell you guys about the time..." He'd gone on to describe his first adventure with her in a car, trying to find her way to the drive-in theater in Charles County.

As I sat at the red light reminiscing, I fished around on the seat until I found an eight-track tape of Tom's greatest hits. There was nothing like a little "Green Green Grass of Home" to make me feel better. Tom and I harmonized the rest of the way to Darlene's house.

Darlene jumped in the car, and I began to tell her about my conversation with Will.

"He didn't know whether to crap or just turn and run!" I said, wishing I had it in me to laugh, but all I could feel was sadness. "At that point, I just turned and walked down the stairs. That's when you called." I purposely left out the part about my crying jag.

"Ellie would've been proud, kiddo." She pulled out the sale ads and turned off Tom. We plotted our assault on the new Landover Mall, a red-dot sale at Hecht's, and a white sale at Woody's. It didn't get much better than that, except we were one tensie short.

Since we'd shopped through lunch, we stopped and ate an early dinner at Peter Connell's Italian Inn on the way home. I packed up the leftover pizza for Jake's dinner, and we walked back out to the car.

As I drove through Radiant Valley toward Darlene's house, there was a detour from road construction, and we found ourselves forced to drive up Denmark Drive, Will's street. There it was, Roberta's car, parked right in front of his house. I slowed down, and we just looked at each other.

"You thinking what I'm thinking?" Darlene asked.

"Depends on what your ammo is," I answered.

"I have mustard," Darlene answered.

After we made sure no one was looking, Darlene and I took turns spooning the mustard up under the handles of Roberta's car door. One of us would keep a lookout and the other would do the spooning. It was hard to do that upside down and not get the evidence on you.

"Hey, hurry up!" I said as I got back in the car. Darlene finished up her finger painting and jumped in beside me. We licked the mustard off our fingertips as we put the lid back on the mustard jar. "Yuck, if it tastes this bad by itself, why do we smear it on otherwise good food?" Darlene grimaced.

I pulled the car past Will's house and pulled over to look back. We couldn't have timed it any better.

"Hey, she's coming out of the house." I looked in the rearview mirror. "Here." I positioned the mirror so we could both see.

Roberta walked through the gate of the chain link fence and dug in her purse. She pulled out her keys. She unlocked the car door with her right hand, held the packages with her left, and reached under the handle to open the door. She didn't notice the mustard until she reached up to brush her hair from in front of her face. With that, she saw the yellow smear on her hands and had a perplexed look on her face as she looked down at her hand.

Before she could put her purse and packages down, she'd managed to get it all over her coat. Darlene and I rolled in laughter watching Roberta's angst unfold in the rearview mirror. Roberta wiped her hands as best she could and got in the car.

We could see her reaching to find hoped-for napkins in the glove box.

"Look! She's licking her fingers." Darlene giggled.

"We should've used the hot sauce instead!" We laughed until our sides hurt and Roberta gave up and went back in the house to clean up. I put the car in drive, and we made a clean getaway.

I pulled into Darlene's driveway and followed her inside to use the bathroom before driving the forty-five minutes back to Howard County.

"Did Roxie tell you about the new project?" Darlene asked as I picked up my purse and keys.

"Yeah, she's not real happy about it." Roxie was our new boss at the National Weather Service.

"She found some more racial slurs written in the bathroom yesterday," Darlene informed me. Roxie was colored and the best boss we'd ever had. Working for her had opened my eyes to a lot of things. El would've been proud.

"So, was it you?" I asked, teasing her.

"Yeah, but I borrowed your red marker to point the finger your way," Darlene jabbed back.

"No, really, I wonder who's doing it." I grabbed my car keys off her coffee table.

"Don't know. Roxie thinks she knows, but she's not saying." Darlene followed me onto her front porch.

"See ya at work." I waved as I walked back to my mini-tank, and she waved back. I hopped in the car and headed back to Howard County. I was getting used to the drive, and it didn't seem so long anymore. One and a half times through Tom's eight track and I was home.

I parked in our driveway and reached in the back for my shopping bags and the pizza box. Jake was sitting in the family room watching University of Maryland football. I was tempted to tell him about the mustard caper but thought better of it.

"Did you say you were going somewhere with Darlene next Saturday?" Jake asked. I nodded and looked up from putting away the groceries.

"Sorry, Barb, but I don't think you can go. We've been invited somewhere," Jake said.

"Really? Where?" I closed the kitchen cabinet.

"We have something to do I forgot to tell you about," he said, shifting his weight in the recliner and running his hand through is hair. Translation: "I've been putting this conversation off for some time."

"What?"

"Well, uh, Will's invited us to something on Saturday."

"Well, issue resolved because I'm not going to see Will on Saturday. I don't care what the reason is."

"Then you won't mind if I stand up for Will and you're not there?"

Stand up proud? Stand up straight? Then it dawned on me.

"You've gotta be kidding!"

I'd always thought the Will-and-Roberta thing would burn itself out. I'd played it out in my mind that he'd dump the traitor and I could forgive Will for letting his little head tell his big one what to do. We'd all three be friends again. I could help raise the boys, and things would be okay for once. I was sure that it had hit him by now, but this proved I was wrong. I knew it was hard to second-guess a guy's sex drive, and I should've known better.

"They're getting married at two o'clock Saturday."

"Married?" I repeated the word as if it were a four letter one. "What's he think, he's going to make an honest woman out of her?" I slammed down the carton of eggs. It looked like we were having scrambled. "You can't make honest people out of traitors, Jake!"

"Barb, it's his life."

"Bully for them. Oh, I get it." A lightbulb moment. "He's waited a wid-ower's year for mourning. What a guy! He deserves her—heck, they deserve each other." I closed my checkbook and put it back in my purse. "I can't believe he's really going to make this permanent, but if he is, you'll have to witness it on your own." I walked to the basement door. He pulled on my arm, but I jerked away.

"Leave me alone, Jake! Just leave me alone." I headed down the basement steps and slammed the door behind me.

I pulled the leftover laundry from that morning out of the dryer and threw it in the basket. I felt so alone and missed El so bad it hurt. I hurt for me, I hurt for her, and I hurt for her kids. I hurt for Jake because it was a shame he had to have a best friend that he couldn't bring home. I dropped a quarter on the floor, and it rolled under the old kitchen table. I knelt down and reached under the chair and grabbed the money. Instead of standing back up, I leaned my head down on the chair and let the tears escape. I cried like I hadn't in almost six months.

"Oh, Ellie, I miss you so much! God, why did this have to happen?" I begged him for some kind of explanation. I laid my head on the seat feeling the coolness of the vinyl.

"Praying seems to be more effective when I'm on my knees," I remembered Ellie saying. What was that all about? Then I remembered the day we prayed over the spilled wax on her dining room carpet. What the heck, I was already on my knees.

I prayed to God that day in my basement. I prayed that he'd help me to pull myself together and help Jake and me get through this. I was sick of being angry all the time.

I asked that somehow I could forgive Will for the damage he'd done to people with his selfish decisions. I didn't think my marriage could survive the resentment that had collected in me if I didn't.

I'm not sure if it was my imagination or what, but my animosity did seem to lessen after that day. I even found myself telling Jake that it was okay for him to stand up for Will but that I still couldn't bring myself to go. He understood, and after that, we learned to artfully dodge the subject of the newlyweds.

When Jake and Will worked side jobs together on Saturdays, Will would normally wait in the car while Jake got out the door. But this particular Saturday morning, he came inside to help Jake carry a box of equipment for their job out of the basement. Before they could make their great escape, the phone rang, and Jake picked it up. It was a customer calling about some electrical work, so he stretched the cord and walked into the dining room to talk.

I looked up to see the same person I'd known before, the one who was married to the best friend a girl ever had and now married to Roberta. My lip quivered for just a mini second. It was the first time since their wedding that we had been alone.

"Oh, hey, Will," I stammered, unsure of whether to offer him a cup of coffee or poke his eyes out. I thought I'd just have to see how far this adrenaline rush would take me.

"Hi, Barb. How've you been?" he answered, trying to figure if I was gonna swing or spit.

"Uh, okay I guess. How are the kids?" Why did she have to die and not him? I just never understood and never would. Lucky for him, that one hadn't been left up to me. God, you helped me with Jake, but this might be a bit much to ask…

"The boys are good. William's birthday is next week. He'll be ten."

"Wow, it doesn't seem possible. He's ten already," I repeated, letting the ten-year span sink in. Ten years ago seemed like a lifetime for a moment and then a blink all in the same few seconds. I had a glimpse of sitting on the highway with El and the kids waiting for the ambulance. I'd tried to keep Jay from playing in traffic and still make sure she wasn't about to squirt the baby out on the asphalt.

My, how things had changed. I grinned, and it was obvious that Will didn't know what to think and he looked at me hard, trying to read me like he used to.

There had been times in my life when I didn't particularly like my brother or approve of my sister. Seeing Will again made me want to look over his shoulder to see El coming up the rear. The only thing coming up his rear would be Roberta. But it was then I realized that he was Jake's brother, and you don't disown a brother for making a stupid decision.

The "not knowing what to say" feeling was gone, and reality splashed me in the face again. That slow ache in the pit of my stomach came back. Would it ever go away for good? I had to know.

"Do you ever think about Ellie, Will?" I asked, looking out the kitchen window.

I stood with my back to him and stared at the white tenant farmhouse on the back of our three-and-a-half acres. We'd just left it there since we didn't have the money to tear it down. We told ourselves that it added character at no extra charge, so we used it for storage and a conversation piece.

"Sure I do," he said, shocked that I'd bring her up, but what else was there for us to talk about? Roberta? I doubted he wanted to go there.

"We had a lot of good times," I reminded him.

"I miss her every day," he said.

"You do?" I turned and looked his way. He was staring down at his hands on the countertop.

"Yeah, and it's hard to talk about with just anyone. We grew up together. You couldn't know Ellie and not love her. You know that, Barb." He glanced up at me and then back down at the counter.

"What's Ginger up to?" I asked, realizing that I had let him off the hook, not meaning to.

"Oh, she's living with Jimmy. She's been there about six months now, but I don't hear from her much." I slid a cup of coffee his way, and he picked it up. "Timmy and William spend a lot of time with them on the weekends."

He needed to take his not-so-new wife's advice. Years ago, when we were interrogating Bobby and Jay about who set the golf course on fire, I could still hear her saying, "Think before you speak, son, think before you speak." She had said it over and over in front of the fire marshal. She warned her kid what to say and not to say, and at the same time tried to hang mine. And now she was raising Ellie's boys. I found myself feeling angry all over again.

Jake hung up the phone and looked at the two of us.

"Ready to go?" Jake asked Will.

Good timing, boys.

❀

Spring came and Jake's garden grew to new heights. It was an acre in size, and by the end of summer, it produced enough tomatoes to make spaghetti sauce for ten years. I called Jake's aunt Sadie and took lessons over the phone on how to can vegetables. Our summer weekends were full of tomatoes, green beans, and corn. I was a regular Betty Crocker, apron and all.

"What's that?" I asked Jake as he walked in the house. He placed a large shopping bag on the dining room table and opened the china cabinet drawer to retrieve scissors and tape.

"Huh?" he said as he turned around, obviously surprised that I was home. I'd dropped my car off for repairs, and Darlene had brought me home. If he's saying "Huh?" he's looking for a good line. He ran his hand through his hair. Oh geez, here we go again. "What are you wrapping?" I asked.

"Oh, this is just something for Will's birthday. I got him a new set of binoculars. Want to see?"

"Yeah, Jake, like I'd want to see Will's birthday present! And what did you do, win the lottery?"

"No, Barb, we just finished up the Cooke's side job and made some extra for wiring the garage, too." The rage in me bubbled to the surface once more. Jealousy was my ugly sidekick.

"Well, at least Will is lucky enough to have another birthday. Oh, and his and Roberta's anniversary should be coming up soon. What are you going to get him for that?" I practically screamed. Losing my temper was not the norm for me, but this time, I couldn't control it. Every angry thought, every sad moment, every longing for my best friend took over.

I reached over and threw a coffee cup against the wall, seeing it crash into a hundred pieces. *Hmm, that felt good.*

"Barb, what the?"

I picked up a crystal vase that he'd given me for Christmas and let it fly and smash into the same wall, joining the coffee cup on the floor in like fashion. I briefly wondered if this is what they called a "nervous breakdown" but quickly decided that I didn't care. All those prayers in the basement seemed light-years away and of no consequence. All that mattered was the anger that bubbled up and out of me.

Jake took a step toward me, but this time I threatened to make him the wall as I chucked an iced tea glass and it smashed on the wall beside him. He stepped back.

"Barb, I'm sorry, I didn't mean for you to see the present. I didn't think you were home."

"Oh, and that's supposed to make it better? Doing everything behind my back?" I screamed.

I picked up the next thing I could find and looked in my hand. It was a red ceramic cardinal on a pedestal, the last birthday present El had given me. We'd gone to Jake's aunt's ceramic shop on a Saturday and spent a few hours painting green ware. She'd surprised me when I unwrapped my present a month later to find the red bird that I'd admired when she painted him. I could still hear her giggle when I opened the box.

I stood frozen. The tears stung the edges of my eyes and warned me that they were about to break loose. I looked at the mess that I'd made on the kitchen floor. Jake stood and stared at me as if he didn't know who I was.

I leaned back on the refrigerator and slid down to the floor, holding the cardinal. I sobbed and clung to the bird. I felt Jake's arm slide around my shoulders and pulled me close. His hand held my head, and I buried my face in his chest.

When I had choked out every sob I had, I looked at him and saw he'd been crying too. It was then that I realized he missed El, too. He was caught in a snare he hadn't set and didn't know how to get out of. We sat on the floor next to the refrigerator for over an hour.

"Sometimes I know I'm getting over losing her, and I feel guilty. I feel like I shouldn't feel better about it. I feel like *someone* needs to really mourn her, really miss her, and get mad for her. Her kids can't because of Roberta, and her husband won't. It's like I just can't let her go." I cried some more. Jake held me and made some of his own confessions about missing Ellie and missing me.

"It's like I have this cut, and it's full of glass and rocks," I tried to explain. "I just put a bandage over it but didn't pull out the glass and rocks by dealing with what happened. It keeps getting worse; know what I mean?"

"Yeah, I guess I do, and I think you're right. Nobody's talking about what happened. None of us knows what to say." He held me tighter.

We sat awhile longer, and piece by piece, Jake helped me pull out the rocks and glass.

"Am I having a nervous breakdown?" I looked him in the eyes. The green eyes that I always knew would look after me.

"I don't know about the nervous part, but by the looks of things, the breaking thing could be an issue." Jake said. We laughed at the mess I'd made and cried over the lost days of family vacations and picka-nickas with the Reillys. We giggled at the silly things El and I had done, and he told me he understood how I felt.

"Barb, I just don't know what to do sometimes. I try and keep my friendship with Will under wraps because I know it hurts you. Maybe I should just back off from Will."

I thought about his offer. This could make things a whole lot better, but I knew in my heart, it could also make them a whole lot worse.

"No, you don't have to dump Will." I kissed him on the cheek and hugged his neck. I pulled back and looked him in the eye. "Just Roberta."

He grinned.

I looked down at the red bird in my hand, and I knew in my gut that El would want me to get past this. It was time to pull the pieces of glass out of my heart and let it heal for good.

"No, you don't have to do that. It'll be fine," I assured him. "Maybe I should just throw a fit more often. It sure made me feel better." He pulled me up off the floor.

"I don't know if we can afford it," he said as he looked down at the mess I'd made. He pulled me close, kissed me on the cheek, and hugged me tight. I knew he was what I needed. As much as I'd needed El as a friend, I needed Jake even more.

That day, I started to pull the rocks and glass out. It hurt, sliver by sliver, but it was then I finally started to heal. I knew El was still there. She'd shared herself with me all those years, and her love and laughter had rubbed off on me. She'd shown me how to be a better woman that I ever would have been on my own without her.

I learned to carry her with me just by not forgetting. It was as if she hit me over the head from the other side that day. My heart still ached because there was no way I could reach in and help her kids. Roberta was the wicked stepmother, a typecast role if I ever saw one. Roger and Scott were grown and building lives of their own, the younger boys would most likely adapt, but Ginger was the one I worried about the most.

After Ellie died (it seemed that I filed everything in a pre-and post-Ellie folder in my head), and when Ginger had to move back in with Will, all she could do was put a Band-Aid on her hurt. No one wanted to help her pull the rocks and glass out, so when she did heal, I knew there would still be a lot of the pieces inside her, a lot of unresolved grief.

Karen said she was becoming more and more distant, and she suspected Ginger had gone from using just pot to other drugs and lots of alcohol. Her Band-Aid was getting bigger, and all we could do was sit back, watch, wonder, and pray.

I walked outside to water my flowers on the back porch. A cloud covered the sunshine that had scorched them all day long. "You Are My Sunshine" was gone, and this was no passing cloud where I knew the sun would come out on the other side. Ellie's sunshine wouldn't be peeking its way back into my life, and I had to come to grips with the shadow she'd left behind.

CHAPTER 13

Barb
Dream a Little Dream of Me

*I've learned that people will forget what you've said, people will forget
what you did, but people will never forget how you made them feel.*

—*Maya Angelou*

Years go by, and it's true; time goes by faster when you're busy raising
kids and pulling your hair out. My fiftieth birthday reminded me of eating that big Hershey bar you get in your Christmas stocking. You eat one piece,
then another, and before you know it, you've only got a few bites left. Then
there's the bellyache. That's what turning fifty is like, a big kick in the gut. You
wake up one day and wonder how you ever got that old.

Raising kids, paying bills, cooking, cleaning—now there's a good time, but
the past twenty-some years offered a lot more than that. I'd just turned fifty (I
know, it was hard to believe, especially given how great I looked) but had to
admit I'd had a good run, and it wasn't over yet.

Ginger moved to Jamaica just a year after Ellie died when she and Jimmy
broke up. I had reached out to her many times and just couldn't connect. It
was as if she'd hidden herself away from everyone. Karen said when she caught
Jimmy cheating on her, she just up and left with only a quick phone call telling
Karen she was on her way to the land of flowers, blue water, and reggae.

Karen managed to get down to Jamaica for a visit a year or so later, but I
got the impression it didn't go very well. She said they had a good time, but I

don't think she and Ginger were able to find a lot in common. She wouldn't talk much about it, and that alone said a lot. They did continue to talk via airmail envelopes every so often, but one can tailor what is talked about on paper much better than in person. I think Karen preferred not to know, but she also talked about how much she missed her. It turned out we had both lost our best friends, one to eternity and the other to the drug culture.

Ginger stayed in Jamaica for over ten years singing in bars and, I assume, partying.

"Have you heard anything about Ginger lately? Did she move back yet?" I asked Jake. We were sitting on the back deck burning some hamburgers on the grill.

"Will said she just got back on Saturday." Jake stood back; trying not to let the smoke from the burgers hit him in the face.

"Wow, after ten years in Jamaica, I hope she does all right." Visions of dreadlocks and a Rasta man's baby on her hip had danced in my head from time to time, but she still had no children.

"Well, it's her second rehab graduation." He scooped the burgers up and put them on the plate I handed to him. We sat down at the picnic table, and I doled out some of my not-so-famous homemade potato salad. We went on to talk about Karen and Kelly, comparing notes to see who knew what about whom.

We danced around the subject of Jay since we weren't sure we really wanted to know what he was up to. He'd gone through a few relationships and one short marriage, lived in several states, and worked odd jobs to survive. His lifestyle worried us both. We wondered what we could have done differently, but realized that we had to let go and let him go his own way. Even if it wasn't "our way."

There were days throughout the years when I felt I'd never get over losing Ellie, my self-selected sister. Sometimes the tears would hit me over something silly like a memory of folding towels while holding the phone on my shoulder listening to Ellie plan our next get-rich-quick scheme. I'd find myself crying silent tears so Jake or the kids wouldn't hear me sobbing from the inside out.

There have been times when I could have sworn she was sitting right next to me. An event or memory would trigger her voice in my ear. She'd taken up residence in my heart long before she'd checked out, and when she did, she moved right into my dreams. I wrote down the dreams, whatever I could remember. She never came to say hi without reminding me that it was "all okay."

I'd made it a habit to write down the dream in a little notebook I kept by my bed. When I needed a slice of her wisdom, I'd open the pages and read, trying to capture her humor or compassion to help keep me straight.

When the Old Man (guess I should refer to him as my father, huh?) passed away, Momma and I reconnected. Once he was gone, I didn't have to worry about my girls being left alone around him.

Momma and I traveled to Las Vegas and Atlantic City together since we were genetically connected slot-machine junkies, and I contributed to her delinquency by encouraging her to become a Tom Jones groupie.

Momma turned out to be a world of surprises. I would have never guessed that this ninety pound southern belle would have turned into such an avid football fan. We watched the Redskins together as Jake narrated and taught us all about the rules of the game.

"I can tell when it's time for a field goal," I said.

"Yeah, how's that, Barb?" Jake asked.

"They pull up the net behind the goal line." He shook his head and laughed. What was so funny?

After a few years of television tutoring, Jake and I started going to the Redskins games together. It turned out that sex wasn't the only thing that kept him happy. If your marriage is fading fast, learn all you can about football, girls. It works like a charm.

Jake bought Will's season ticket from him when the old boy got too cheap to fork over the money every fall. I suspected that Roberta wore him down about being gone most Sunday afternoons, but that was okay with me. They deserved each other. *Did I say that?*

Jake's dad passed away a few years ago after a bad car accident. He'd been in great health, and I think he would have outlived us all if that hadn't happened. Another good person, gone.

About a year ago, Momma decided it was time to sell the old house on Cheverly Avenue once she had given up her driver's license and was worried about living on her own. The steps and large yard were just too much for her to deal with, so she moved in with us.

Jake had started building an apartment in our basement for his dad, but he'd passed away before it was finished. We offered to finish it for Momma, but to our surprise, she didn't want the privacy and moved into our third bedroom. She was only with us for a year when she died from emphysema. Before we knew it, both of Jake's aunts passed on, and that entire generation was gone.

But I've decided that you don't lose someone you love without God giving you someone else to care about. Enter grandchildren. Karen and Lee moved back from West Virginia with their daughter, Nellie, and Kelly a boy and a girl. I decided that if I hadn't gone through the agony of raising my own kids, I wouldn't have had such fun with the next generation.

And so it went. I was "Grandmother" or as Katie, Kelly's daughter eventually crowned me, "Fairy Grandmother." Watching the years pass by seeing my grandkids grow up enabled sixty to sneak up on me unannounced.

Grandmothers get to be Santa Claus every day, and yard sales were the perfect enabler for Grandma Claus. Having grandchildren had allowed me to validate my shopping habit, and yard sales could make me look like a champ without having to take out a loan. They're this poor girl's dream. I can only imagine the fun El and I would've had together making Saturday morning raids on other people's junk.

The hazards of growing older seem to increase with every passing year. Hazard number one: forgetting seemed to be an acceptable flaw once I passed fifty. "Oh, I forgot" seemed to be a built-in part of my everyday language. While it might have been okay with everyone else, I refused to be the feeble little grandma. That is where I got my passion for list making.

As a result, I had lists to manage the lists. I had a list for the grocery store, a list of what to take to Vegas and/or Atlantic City, a list of what things to check before I left the house, and a list of what bills to pay when, and that was just the short list. And when we got a computer, it enabled me to store and change my lists with the click of a mouse.

Hazard number two: the lines and wrinkles. Crow's feet might have added character, and gray hairs counted as points for stress-related issues, but sagging skin, jowls, and a thick crinkly neck, those didn't count for anything except bad genes. I didn't get flirted with anymore unless the old geezer was over sixty and didn't yet know he was harmless. So, I had a facelift.

I thought Jake was going to blow a cork. "Why would you want to do that, Barb?"

"Why not? I can't stand the way my neck looks. I've aged twenty years in the last two."

"You're still beautiful to me, babe." He slid his arms around my waist and hugged me from behind, but the bathroom mirror didn't change its tune, and unless I resigned myself to seven years of bad luck compounded every time I crushed one, I had no choice. I used money I had inherited from Momma and knew she would have told me to put all the coins in the machine for one last pull anyway.

Hazard number three: complaining. This seemed to be something that came naturally once I entered my sixties (yep, I passed yet another decade). *Entitlement.* That was the word. I'd worked too hard and endured too much bad service to put up with anything less than perfection. I had to admit that not having much of a memory aided in my quest for perfection from everyone else. It was tougher to remember when I was less than perfect.

Waking up slowly happened more often after sixty, and I found that after years of absence, Ellie came to visit in my dreams more frequently when I hit rollover stage two in the daylight hours.

In the last dream I can remember, Ellie and I were sitting on a rock in the middle of a daisy-filled meadow watching little kids play. They weren't our kids, the best kind.

"Hey, you're letting the gray show." Ellie touched my permed hairdo.

"Yeah, after a while you lose the race and get tired of supporting Miss Clairol." I found a way to change the subject. "Wow, that butterfly is really moving fast." I pointed to an orange and black Monarch that was headed our way, skirting the tops of the flowers.

"Sometimes you can feel it coming," Ellie said.

"Feel a butterfly? Hmm." I tilted my head.

"No, not the butterfly."

"What do you mean by 'feel' then?"

"It's all okay," she answered, and Jake nudged me. I rubbed my eyes and looked at him.

"What's that about a butterfly?" he asked and pulled the bedspread over my shoulder.

"Huh?" I said, only half awake.

"You were talking in your sleep. You do that a lot lately."

"Must have been dreaming." I rolled over to get out of bed but first grabbed my notebook to jot down what I could remember.

The phone rang as I put the pen down, and I reached over to pick it up. It was Darlene. We took turns calling each other once a week to share the long-distance charges since she'd moved three hours away. She'd married a realtor several years ago, and they were living right outside of Ocean City, Maryland. She loved living near the beach, and she and her new husband, Joe, seemed well suited for each other.

Karen and Lee had managed to stay married, probably thanks to Nellie. She was able to get him to move back to the DC area and escaped West Virginia after seven years. She began a career for herself as a receptionist for a property management firm and now sells real estate.

Jake and Will stayed friends, and just because of geography, their contact lessened. Somehow, it all seemed to work out.

I enjoyed my job as a secretary at the National Weather Service in Silver Spring. At first I had a tough time adjusting to my new boss, Roxie. She was a black woman, and I had a chip on my shoulder, assuming that she was the result of all the affirmative action garbage going on these days. It turned out, even if it was, that was okay.

Roxie proved to be a great friend, and while she didn't take Ellie's place, she certainly filled a void. I learned a lot from Roxie and not just about government red tape. She showed me that black people aren't all out for a handout. That it's not true that they can't be of any value unless they can catch a football for the Redskins.

Roxie took me to lunch one day and poured out a confession. What is it about me that pulls the secrets out of people?

"Barb, Joy and I are more than just friends." She looked up from her bowl of beef stew. I just stared at her as the significance of her statement eluded me. She was responding to my question about whether or not she was going to take our coworker, Bob, up on setting her up on a blind date.

"What do you mean?"

"Joy and I are more than just roommates," she went on to explain. Boy, you have to love those lightbulb moments.

"Oh." Boy, I can be prolific, can't I? This homosexual issue was becoming more and more of a water-cooler topic these days, but I'd never heard Roxie's name associated with it. Probably because she was so feminine and dressed so well. I mean, gay women all wear work boots and slick their hair back, don't they?

"Are you okay with that?" she asked me, not sure what to think about my lack of response.

"Okay?" I wondered how to stall and keep my response from becoming a reaction. "First the black thing and now this." My sarcasm always was my escape mechanism, and this time was no different. "You sure do give a girl lots to get used to, Roxie!"

"I know, Barb," she said, reaching over and patting my hand with hers, "but you've adapted really well so far!"

"Yeah," I stumbled. "Just don't tell Jake. He's insecure enough with me working around a bunch of men as it is. Don't need his homophobia to kick in!"

Sometimes I thought Ellie was up there somewhere just orchestrating what it was she thought I needed to know. I learned lessons that I knew she would have shown me herself. I'd come to the conclusion that it was better to have a coach from your invisible corner than not have one at all. But she should have warned me about that bike ride.

I'd decided that I needed to become more athletic not long after we moved to Howard County (the middle-age rump was starting to chase me), so knowing that I hated to sweat and wasn't competitive enough for sports, I decided to take up bike riding. So, every evening, Kelly and I would jump on our Huffy's (a good name for a bike, given the huffing and puffing it inspired in me) and hit the road. Until I fell and hit my knee.

I'd battled arthritis in my hands for years but muddled through. When I fell on that bike and hit my knee on the pavement, it was a catalyst that turned into arthritis. I fought the pain with cortisone shots for years and did my best not to whine. Finally, the doctor talked me into a knee replacement, and—voilà—I felt so much better.

Since I wasn't coordinated for bike riding, and I'd heard that swimming was good for arthritis, I decided we needed a pool. So, much to Jake's chagrin, I contracted someone to dig a swimming pool in our backyard. I'd been saving money for years, and now I had decided what to spend it on.

"So, how's the pool coming along?" Karen asked over the phone.

"Hmm, the pool and I are in the dog house." I looked out the kitchen window at the big yellow backhoe that was becoming a fixture in my backyard.

"What do you mean?"

"Well, they hit rock." I turned away from the window. "Evidently, there's lots of rock on our property."

"Isn't that their problem?"

"Nope, it's mine. There was a 'rock clause.'" And so it went. My $10,000 pool was now costing more like $13,000, but I would have cut off my left ear before I'd admitted I'd made a mistake to Jake. I sucked it up and dug a little deeper into my savings.

Oh yeah, then I signed up for swimming lessons at the Y. Nothing like a little cart before the horse, but no matter; it was all tax deductible for medical reasons. Gotta love loopholes.

Before long, it was hard to tell the pool had ever been my idea. Jake became the best pool party host you could ever want. He learned to balance the water and vacuum up the sand and leaves. I had always fantasized about having a pool boy, and now I had one.

Within a few years, I had the second knee replaced and wasn't riding a bike again but managed to maneuver my way around yard sales like a pro on Saturday mornings. Karen would often drive over and spend Friday night. I'd drag her out of bed to hit the road by 7:30.

Because of my two artificial knees, I was able to take an early retirement at the age of fifty-seven. There was no more getting up at 4:45 and heading out for an hour drive (two if it was snowing) to work.

The irony wasn't lost on me how years ago Ellie and I couldn't wait to get out of the house and get jobs. Now, thirty years later, I couldn't wait to stay home again. I'd get up with Jake and get him off to work in the mornings and enjoyed my time alone. I'd finally found the time to clean out all those avalanche cabinets that before then I'd open and stand back to clear the way for the onslaught of teetering pots and pans.

One Tuesday morning while Katie Couric was giving me my morning news about a monkey that made the great escape from a zoo, I began pulling out old record albums, feeling guilty that I wouldn't throw this stuff away. I had piles on the floor to keep, save for later, read right away, give away, and even managed one for trash.

I reached my hand all the way back to the rear of the dark cabinet and felt a stack of what seemed to be papers. I pulled the stack out to realize it was a bunch of my dream journals that I had kept for years after Ellie died. I sat down in my recliner and spent the day reading and reminiscing. I laughed, I cried, and then I laughed again. She came back to me again through the pages of half thoughts and dream particles. Butterflies, pearls, "you can feel it coming," and "it's all okay," being her constant themes.

"It's easy for her to say, she's in heaven," I said to Sugar. I'd taken to talking to dogs a while back. I'd discovered that my white German shepherd, Sugar, understood me as good or better than anyone. Sugar's ears perked up, and I could hear a car pull into the driveway. I shuffled the notebooks into a pile and laid them on the counter.

I opened the door as Jake walked across the driveway. He walked in and kissed me on the cheek as he went by.

"What are you reading?" He picked up one of the yellowed spiral-bound notebooks. I reached over and gently took it from him.

"Oh, those are just those dream journals that I've kept all these years."

He ran his fingers through his hair and looked at me. Uh oh, that telltale sign of trouble on the horizon...

"It looks like I'm going to have to take that early out." He reached down and patted Sugar on the head.

He began to talk about retirement, not because he wanted to, but the Naval Ordinance Lab was relocating a lot of its offices, and his department was to be a victim of the federal government downsizing. He was sixty-four (when did we get this old?) and was offered an early retirement package. Even with the dangling carrot, he didn't want to do it.

"When?" I asked as I sat down on the kitchen barstool and dished out dinner.

"Next month," Jake said as we each hovered over a plate of my now famous spaghetti. It had taken forty years to perfect, but hey, better late than never.

"Why can't you move with them?" I asked.

"They're downsizing the staff. I think I'll have to take the early out offer they gave me. It looks like I'll be retiring in the fall."

I tried not to choke on my pasta. I'd gotten used to my time alone during the days. No kids, no coworkers, no husband to wait on. For the first time in my life, I did what I wanted, when I wanted. My time was my time. Now it would be "our time." So, El, how come I didn't see this one coming?

Kelly threw Jake a retirement party, and all of his friends were there, Will and Roberta included. I managed to be civil and, thanks to Kelly's large house and big yard, didn't have to say much to either one. Some people are like rashes; they keep coming back.

And so it went. Jake continued to work his electrical business and even worked one day a week gratis for the government, just glad to be needed. We started to travel together, going on a Caribbean cruise and a couple of jaunts to Atlantic City and down to Ocean City when we felt like it. Life was good.

And after only a few months, Jake got sick. It started with a dry cough, and after a few doctor visits and tests, he was diagnosed with esophageal cancer. He'd quit smoking thirty years before but still blamed it on the cigarettes. I think he was probably exposed to something while working at the naval lab. I was still a closet smoker and had officially quit five years ago but still fought the urge and lost the battle a few times a week.

Jake and I lay in bed talking about the future. My future alone without him. I'd selfishly guarded my alone time before and after he retired but never wanted it to be all day, every day.

"Barb, you know I've always loved you, right?" He turned over slowly, pushing his favorite feather pillow up under his head. He was covering all his bases this time.

"Yes, Jake, I know," I answered, letting a tear slide down my cheek. He reached over, wiped it off with his thumb, and we held onto each other.

"I'm sorry for things I've done that hurt you," he said. I knew he was referring to his friendship with Will and a suspected brief affair with a secretary, but I let him off the hook. "There's nothing to apologize for, Jake," I answered. "Neither one of us has been perfect," I admitted, but that was all. I wasn't going any further than that. My warts could stay right where they were. Hidden.

The kids reached in to help while Jake was sick. Jay cut grass, Karen planted flowers so he could see them outside the living room window, and Kelly, living the closest, came by every chance she got.

Kelly's kids were a constant silver lining to this otherwise gray cloud that we now lived under. It was amazing the ray of sunshine a simple hug or smile from an eight-year-old could bring to either one of us. Jake went through surgery, chemo, and radiation. His treatments ran the gamut as we grasped on to any type of hope the medical community could offer.

I would sit in the living room in the middle of the night as he slept and as the reality of his departure and my unavoidable widowhood hit me, I visualized what my life would be like on my own. I'd always wondered what it would have been like to be a single chick, but being alone after sixty wasn't exactly what I'd had in mind. It seemed that Jake and I had worked so hard to get over the rough spots, and now that the time to kick back and have fun was here, he was heading to the other side without me. I knew I'd be okay. I had the kids and grandkids to get me through, and there was always the occasional trip to Vegas or Atlantic City on the local blue-hair bus…but it turned out that I had only wanted to hit the jackpot with Jake by my side. Who knew?

Hospice was such a help to me during his last few weeks. It was a tough decision for him to let go of the feeding tube, but we'd come to grips with the fact that he wasn't going to recover. No one had told me out loud that what it amounted to was that he would starve to death.

Watching someone die wasn't all that new for me. Momma got sick and lingered for a while with emphysema and died in her sleep. But Jake was only sixty-five now, not seventy-eight.

Jake's friends, including Will, were a great help to me as we drove back and forth to Baltimore for radiation treatments and doctor visits. Will was retired now and came to drive Jake to his appointments a few times a week, giving me time for a needed nap or trip to Wal-Mart.

Like it or not, I was indebted to Will for his help, and as Jake's health declined, Roberta was in the mix. She was a Bible-toting churchgoer now and wanted to make sure Jake had his ducks in a row. Hey, who was I to argue spiritual integrity?

I heard Will's car pull up in the driveway. Jake was in bed, where he spent most of his time lately. I walked to the door to let them in. Will's hair was mostly white now, but he was still handsome. Roberta had taken up where I'd left off with her support of Miss Clairol. It's funny how I aged slowly and she did it all at once. That's what happens when you don't lay eyes on someone for twenty or so years. Then it dawned on me that she was probably thinking the same thing about me. But I reminded myself that I was one facelift ahead of her, at least as far as I knew.

"Hey, you guys. Thanks for coming," I said as I stood back for them to walk in. Sugar sniffed their pant legs, recognizing the scent of their dogs. "Jake's in bed, but I think he's awake."

"How's he doing today?" Will asked. The frown on his face made me want to cry.

"Not that good, I don't think, but it's hard to tell. He's not having 'good days' anymore," I explained, and looked at Roberta.

"I'm so sorry, Barb," she said. "But it is good to see you."

"Thanks," was all I could muster as I led them down the hallway to our bedroom that now doubled as a hospital room. Jake had turned down the offer for a hospital bed, preferring to stay in our old king-size. His medications and medical supplies had taken over the top of my nightstand; along with the cd player Karen had brought to give him some entertainment.

"Jake, Will and Roberta are here," I said quietly as I nudged his shoulder. He opened his sunken eyes and turned his head our way. He'd lost over one hundred pounds and some of his hair in the past year, and the smaller he got, the less he looked like Jake and the more he looked like his dad.

"Hi, Will." He took a labored breath. "How you doing, Roberta?" A worried look crossed his face and he turned to see if I was homicidal with her in the room. I winked at him letting him know it was okay.

"We're fine, Jake," Roberta said and stepped toward the bed. With that, I left the room to let them visit.

That old familiar hole in the pit of my stomach returned. The hole that I'd been living with for a year since Jake had been ill. With Roberta's return, I recognized it as the same emptiness I'd felt when Ellie died, but this time I refused to allow anger to partner with my sorrow.

"How are you doing, Barb?" Roberta asked. Jake had fallen asleep, and the three of us sat at my kitchen counter eating tuna sandwiches I'd made while they visited with Jake. I'd grown accustomed to cold sandwiches since the smell of food cooking made Jake sick to his stomach.

"As good as I can. Thanks to Will and Randy. They've been a big help getting Jake to his appointments." I rambled. "Kelly comes by most days, and Karen and Jay come down on the weekends."

We continued with the small talk until we finished with lunch, giving updates on each of the kids. Ginger was out of yet another rehab and working in the fish market of a local grocery store chain. Timmy, William, and Roger were all married with children. Scott had remained a confirmed bachelor and Roberta's kids were all married with kids as well.

Once they said their good-byes, I stood on the porch and waved as they backed out of the driveway. Sugar stood at my side and nudged my hand. I reached down and stroked her soft white fur.

"Either I've forgiven her, or I'm just too old to care anymore, girl," I said to Sugar. "I'm not sure."

I walked back in the house to take a nap while Jake slept. It reminded me of the baby days when I'd learned to power nap. It's like riding a bike; some things you just don't forget how to do. I closed the family room drapes, took the phone off the hook, and leaned back in my recliner.

I woke with Sugar nudging my hand with her wet nose.

"What's the matter, girl? You need to go out?" I put my feet down and stiffly stood up. I walked toward the kitchen door to let her out, but she walked back toward the bedroom and stopped to look back at me. I just stared back at Sugar, unable to move.

I knew before I walked into the bedroom that Jake was gone. His chest didn't rise and fall anymore. He just lay there.

"Jake?" I said, half expecting him to answer. He'd been so sick for so long, I'd expected him to die before, but he'd always hung on.

"Jake?" Like I could wake him up.

I lifted up the covers and slid in next to him. I held him.

"You're cold," I said and reached down to pull up the comforter over both of us. I held him close and stroked his hair down. The tears came and I clung to him.

I thought it had hurt when I lost Ellie, but when I'd lost her, I had Jake. When I lost Momma, Jake was there. He'd been the one constant in my life since I was fifteen years old.

"I'm glad you don't hurt anymore." I stroked his hair. "I'm glad you don't hurt."

I held him and remembered burning his breakfast, laughing when he spilled oatmeal in his lap, and shopping for our first grandchild's first Christmas together. I thought about how he helped me keep it together when Kelly eloped and the time we went on our first cruise, and he pretended to know how to speak Spanish wearing that silly sombrero he insisted on buying.

I tried not to feel sorry for myself, but it wasn't happening. Not this time.

"Give Momma and Ellie a kiss for me." I gave him one last directive for old time's sake. *And your dad, Aunt Sadie, Aunt Frances, Uncle Maggie, and so many of the people we've loved together.* At least he wouldn't be alone. And it dawned on me that for the first time in my life, I really was.

I lay there next to him in bed for one last time and sobbed until there were no tears left. When I felt as if I'd wrung out my soul, I slid out of the bed to see

Sugar's head resting on the other side of the mattress. I covered Jake back up and leaned down to kiss his cold cheek one last time. He was gone.

He'd gotten stuck in the onesies of cancer, but made the leap to the tensies without me.

CHAPTER 13

Barb
Wind Beneath My Wings

The litigation mounts over the so-called 'JFK papers,' which allege all kinds of sinister ties among President Kennedy, his putative lover, Marilyn Monroe, and the Mafia. The documents sparked a federal grand jury investigation after ABC News branded them forgeries last September.

—John Carmody, *Washington Post* Staff Writer, Friday, January 9, 1998

*F*all would have been my favorite season if it hadn't been for winter being its next-door neighbor. The leaves trickled to the ground as a prelude to the ice and snow. Now that Jake was gone, I wasn't sure just how long I'd be able to hang on to our country home with all of its demands. At least with the onset of winter, the grass could self-groom, and I could hire someone to plow the driveway when it snowed.

Jake had been gone five months, and I was adjusting. Adjusting to one load of laundry a week, a gallon of milk going bad every two weeks before I remembered that I didn't drink milk, and no one but Sugar to talk to during most meals. Sugar and I had just finished our breakfast, and I was putting the dishes in the dishwasher when the phone rang. It was about the time of day that Karen would call from her cell phone on her way to an appointment first thing in the morning.

"Hello?" I answered.

"Mrs. Kincaid?" the voice on the other end of the line was familiar, but I couldn't pinpoint it.

"Yes?"

"Aunt Barb, this is Ginger," the woman said. "Ginger Reilly."

"Ginger! It's great to hear your voice!" Now I knew where the familiarity came from. She sounded just like Ellie.

"I've been back from Jamaica awhile now. Sorry I haven't called before this, but I'm working at Giant, and they keep me hopping."

"No need to apologize, hon. It's just great to hear your voice." Or your mom's voice. Shades of hours on the phone with Ellie flooded me. Ginger and I made the normal small talk, and I struggled to pay attention to her answers while the familiar sound of Ellie's voice lured me down Memory Lane.

"I called to get Karen's address. I want to invite you guys to Dad's seventieth birthday party next month." And so it went. We talked awhile longer about her time in Jamaica and new job at Giant. I knew it had to be a letdown for her to give up her singing, but she didn't complain. It seemed she was happy to be back.

"I can't believe Dad's gonna be seventy." She coughed and continued. A smoker's cough that I'd come to recognize. "We thought we'd better give him at least one birthday party before he croaks!"

I laughed, not at what she'd said, but that she'd said it in true Ellie fashion. "You sound just like your mom." I paused and swallowed hard. "In more ways than one."

"Now there's a compliment!"

We talked awhile longer as she gave me the lowdown on the boys and Will. I kept her talking as long as I could and enjoyed hearing the echo of Ellie.

I called Karen to let her know the date of the party, and we made plans to go.

"You won't forget, right?" I asked, knowing how many different directions she was always going.

"Nope, I've already written it in my calendar." She assured me every time I felt the need to ask.

Ginger's call intrigued me over the weeks leading up to the party. It seemed as if everywhere I turned, there were reminders of the times when the Kincaid and Reilly families were like one. Vacations, dances, picka-nickas, and just plain burning dinner while talking on the phone, stirring a pot of noodles with a baby on my hip.

The weekend of the party took its time getting here but finally did, and Karen's friend, Sue, met her at my house for the weekend. Sue lived in Pennsylvania, and my place was a good halfway meeting spot for them. We piled into my white Taurus station wagon and left early enough to hit some yard sales on the way to Roger's house for Will's party.

After a few "will you takes" and loading up the back of the Taurus with much-needed junk, we followed Ginger's printed page of directions.

"She must take after her mother," I complained as we made our third U-turn trying to find the right street.

"Yeah, Mrs. Wrong Way lives!" Karen agreed as she turned the car around. Something told me that Mrs. Wrong Way never did die. Not from what I'd heard on the phone that day a few weeks ago.

"Aunt Barb!" Ginger said and threw her arms around me as I walked into the house. "It's so great to see you!" She hugged me for a second and looked up.

"And Karen, when did you go blond?" She let go of me and bear-hugged Karen.

"When the gray started winning the war." Karen laughed. "When did you start looking so much like your mom?" There, it was out in the open.

"You think so?" she asked. It was eerie seeing Ellie walking and talking. Ginger was taller and had a little bit different nose, but other than that, Ellie's clone stood there laughing and joking. The age and weight she'd picked up made it so, and that old familiar playfulness mixed with sarcasm was hard to miss.

"I can't believe nobody's ever told you that," I blurted, and then realized that it was probably just like it was for her twenty-some years earlier. Nobody talked about the dead wife in front of the current wife, especially when the current wife was the ex-friend of the dead wife.

We walked in and continued the reunion. The boys were all there with their families. I'd seen Timmy over the years by employing his talents as a home remodeling contractor. He and Ginger were the two that most resembled Ellie. Roger and William favored Will, and Scott was a combination of them both. Scott had remained a bachelor all these years.

"Rumor has it that Roberta has asked Dad for a divorce," Ginger confided to Karen, Sue, and me. "He told Roger that they might be splitting up."

"Hmm, there's no being stuck in the onesies on this one. She must have another man. A woman doesn't leave her husband at our age unless she has options," I said. *This might turn out to be fun.*

Will and Roberta showed up. Will seemed genuinely surprised by the party. He was definitely shocked to see us.

"Barb, I can't tell you how much it means to me that you guys came." He pulled me aside. "It's great to see you," he added. I could see the pain in his eyes. "I miss Jake so much."

"I know." I gave him a hug. *What has gotten into me?* "Ginger was thoughtful to think of us," I answered, looking across the room to see her and Karen laughing and posing for pictures. "It's neat to see them together again," I said.

He looked their way and nodded.

"It sure is. Seems weird that Jake's not here, too," he added, with tears welling up in the bottom of his eyes. "I'm sorry." He tried to recover as I handed him a napkin, and he wiped his eyes. "He was like my brother, you know."

"I know, and I'm thinking he is here," I tried to console him. *Wait a minute; ain't I the widow?*

I watched Roberta and Will to try and see if there was any truth to the rumor, but she was putting on a good front. There was something else that hadn't changed much.

The party wound down but only because of the clock. Ginger and Karen clicked just like they did when they were five years old playing jacks on the back porch in Cambridge. Before we drove away, we had agreed on a home movie party in my living room on the following weekend.

"So, what'd you think?" Karen asked.

"About what?" I answered.

"You think Will and Roberta are splitting up?" she asked as we rode toward my house.

"Oh, I'm not sure. Neither one of them were tipping their hand, but one thing I know for sure," I said. "She ain't leaving him without having someone waiting in the wings, that's a fact. Not at her age."

"Well, Ginger has a great theory." Karen threw out the hook.

"Yeah, what's that?" I nibbled on the line.

"If they get divorced, you and Will could get married, and we'd finally be real sisters!" Karen reeled me in. We giggled all the way back to my place at that one.

The girls all showed up on the following Friday night. Ginger brought shrimp and vodka. *So much for rehab.* Karen brought desserts.

"The only thing missing are the crabs," I said, overwhelmed at trying to fit everything in the refrigerator. "And your mom," I added, looking over at Ginger.

"She's here. I just know she is, Aunt Barb," she answered.

I'd told her to drop the "aunt" and call me Barb, but it wasn't happening. There was just something wrong about a forty-four-year-old woman calling me "aunt." I felt something wet on my neck as I stooped to make room on the shelf of the fridge. I reached around and wiped off the water and looked at Ginger.

"Recognize this?" she asked, holding up a squirt gun in her hand.

"Big Blue!" I laughed. "I haven't seen him in years!" I grabbed the gun from her. He was one in the same and still had the "OC" sticker on the nozzle.

"Yeah, and as you noticed, he still works!" She pointed to my wet hair on the back of my head.

"Has he had much of a workout over the years? Your mom almost got locked up the last time." I trailed off, not knowing if I should continue.

"'The last time' what?" she prodded me.

"Well, the last time we were in Ocean City together, we found a really good perch," I remembered, and began to tell the story of our life of crime as the memory tapped me on the shoulder.

We talked, laughed, cried, and laughed some more. You couldn't talk about Ellie without laughing about what she'd said or done. Squirting tourists on the boardwalk, showing up a day late for the Coast Guard picnic, crabbing until two in the morning, stealing paperweights from the White House—there was never a dull moment.

We settled in the family room after ravaging the steamed shrimp. Karen popped the tape in the VCR. I had taken all the old eight-millimeter home movies and had them transferred onto videotape. The movie was shaky and fuzzy, but that didn't keep the constant warm breeze of memories from sweeping over us.

"Look at Scott. He really did look like Howdy Doody." Karen laughed.

"Wow, Aunt Barb, you sure were a looker," Ginger said and then tried to recover. "Not that you're not now, of course."

"No matter, my looks packed up and moved out a while back. Now I'm just left with a wit and wisdom that makes me smarter than most everyone I know."

"Wow, there's not a lot of shots of your mom, but whenever she's there, she's always laughing and joking around," Karen said to Ginger. Ellie had always been self-conscious about her weight and managed to stay out of the way of the camera a lot, but every once in a while, we'd catch a glimpse of her.

"Yeah, she made everything fun."

"Look at William crying," Karen said. "I remember that. The monkey at the zoo stole his little Matchbox car."

"Yeah, that kid was always crying about something," I said.

"He still whines a lot." Ginger laughed. "His wife always says he's her third kid."

"That's true about most men." I gave them the benefit of my wisdom. It wouldn't be nice not to share. "I think that was the same vacation when he pooped on the pool table."

"Yeah, he was always dropping his drawers and pinching a loaf wherever he wanted." I handed Ginger a paper towel. "Your mother tried to make me clean it up, but I bolted on that one."

"Yeah, and William thinks he's better than us now that he lives in Mount Airy!" Ginger took a sip of her Pepsi. "Turned into a regular yuppie snob."

"Really?" I asked and looked at Ginger. "You thinking what I'm thinking?"

"Do you have any toilet paper?" Ginger asked, and before I could answer, Karen piped up.

"Are you kidding? You're talking to Barb, the queen of Scott tissue, that is." Karen headed down to the basement and retrieved a four pack.

"Hey, let's leave him a little gift," Sue said as she picked up the pumpkin I'd bought for Kelly's kids to carve for Halloween the next week. I grabbed a black marker and started scribbling: "That's what you get for pooping on the pool table!"

We piled in the Taurus, and I drove the fifteen minutes to Mount Airy. After a few U-turns (Ginger had definitely inherited El's non-sense of direction), we found William's house, and I stopped the car a couple of doors down and turned off the lights, leaving the motor running.

"You guys go ahead, and when it looks like you're done, I'll pull up closer and you can hop back in," I instructed. "I swear, if I didn't know better, I'd say your mom is sitting right next to me." I looked at Ginger, who sat beside me in the dark car.

"Are you kidding? She'd already be out of the car and wrapping up the first tree!" Ginger whispered as she hopped out and quietly shut the door.

I sat watching my daughter, Ginger, and Sue crouch behind the bushes and trees of William's front yard, wrapping Scott Tissue around tree trunks and branches. Ginger got creative and wove it around the railing of the front porch. She quietly sat the pumpkin on the welcome mat. I scanned the lights of the neighbors, and it seemed as if everyone was sleeping.

When they'd covered almost every branch in the yard, I pulled the car up slowly, leaving the headlights off. Thank goodness for a full moon. We drove back to my place, strung out on adrenaline, as if we'd pulled off a major heist.

"I wonder if he'll know it was us because of the pumpkin," Karen said after a too-late second thought.

"Nah, he was just a baby, and I don't know that he ever heard about it," Ginger assured her.

"Well, he's your brother. You're the one with the most to lose," she answered. We pulled into my driveway and headed into the house and straight to bed. It had been a while since I'd been awake at 2:00 a.m., except for when Jake was sick. My back hurt more than usual, but hey, what are a few aches and pains in the scheme of things?

When I put my head on the pillow, I grinned.

"Well, El, it seems as if you're right. It is 'all okay,'" and it was. After a twenty-some-year hiatus, the Tensies were back in business.

❀

My back had been bothering me ever since I'd taken the trip to Ocean City with Karen.

During our trip, my fanny pack, the wallet on a belt I carried instead of a purse, hurt my back, but I chalked it up to the constipation that I constantly battled.

The week after we toilet papered William's house, I decided it was time to go to the doctor to check it out.

I made an appointment with Dr. Bridges, and he decided to run some tests. My symptoms of back pain, constipation, and swollen ankles were enough to draw his concern.

When Dr. Bridges said that he wanted to put me through some tests to "rule some things out," the first thing I thought of was those pictures from my last trip. The pictures made me look old, but it was more than that. I had that grayness, that pallor that only a sick person has. I'd seen it many times when I would take Jake to his treatments.

Here and there you can feel it coming, El had said way back when. She was right. Sometimes you just know it's coming. You know the other shoe's about to drop, and this time, right on your head.

I argued with God awhile until I decided He already had his mind made up. I figured that Jake and I must be like salt and pepper, bookends, or a good worn-in pair of flip-flops; one's no good without the other.

I cried long and hard for a few days all by myself before going back to the doctor for the test results. I'd suspected for a while that something bad might be wrong. My side hurt, but I thought it was from lifting Jake too much when he was sick and not sleeping well on the futon after he got really bad. After the first visit with Dr. Bridges, I could tell from the look in his eyes that he suspected the worst, whatever that was.

Sugar was there with me as I cried, screamed, threw stuff, and cried some more. I would have bet that dog knew everything that was going on. The thought of going through surgery, chemo, and radiation was more than I could take. Sugar and I had grieved Jake together, and now she was going to be an orphan. And so were my kids.

I'd made it clear to my kids that I wasn't to go "six feet under." I wanted to be cremated. I wasn't gonna rot in some box. I'd go out charbroiled, sitting right next to Jake on the hillside.

I told myself not to be so pessimistic. I'd read all the articles about how your attitude was half the battle with cancer, but I just had this feeling. Did I say cancer? I didn't know for sure that what it was, but after watching Jake get sick, there was just something all too familiar. Maybe if I labeled it "Cancer" with a capital *C*, I'd give it the respect it thought it deserved and it would fade away with my imagination. It just seemed that the awful cloud that came to visit a year and a half ago when Jake got sick never left. The cloud was still there after Jake died, and at first I thought it was just depression hitting me, but this turn of events whispered in my ear that it wasn't.

Jake's death and the reality of my own illness forced me to reckon with my own spirituality. I'd never been a churchgoer, but I believed in Jesus and the Trinity, and even the most evangelical people will tell you that's good enough. If Billy Graham and the Bible said so, it was good enough for me. I'd only gone to church a few times as a kid, but the time I went with my girlfriend, Susie, was my last voluntary visit.

"This is Barb." Ten-year-old Susie from up the street had introduced me to Mrs. Barker, the Sunday school teacher. Susie had invited me to attend church with her that Sunday. We'd had a sleepover at her house.

"Well, hello, Barb, welcome. Come on in!" Mrs. Barker's blue eyes lit up. "Have a seat at the table, girls." She'd motioned for us to sit next to each other at the far side. The other children turned and looked at me. One or two recognized me from school, so I didn't feel so out of place.

I enjoyed the lesson about Noah's ark and we colored some pictures and Mrs. Barker talked about the upcoming summer vacation Bible school. The class munched on juice and vanilla wafers while we listened to the rest of the story.

When the adult service was over, we were dismissed, and Susie and I walked out to the front of the church to find Susie's parents. When they weren't there, we headed back to the Sunday school rooms.

"I figured you didn't know who she was," the lady with the red hat said to Mrs. Brown, Susie's mother. "She's one of Howard Carter's kids. You know, the man in the neighborhood that got arrested for soliciting a prostitute!"

"Oh my goodness, no!" Mrs. Brown's hand flew to her mouth, and Susie and I stood behind her in the doorway to the classroom. "You mean the man that was just convicted? I read it in the paper just yesterday!" she exclaimed.

"One in the same," she assured her. "They fined him $50."

"I knew you'd want to know. You're not going to allow Susie to play with her anymore, are you?"

I'd heard my parents arguing behind closed doors a lot over the past few months before and the word *solicit* was used once or twice. I'd heard the whispers of the kids at school and felt them shunning me. But Susie had been different, like none if it mattered to her. I was her friend, and she hadn't cared what my father had done. Until now.

"I should think not!" she said. Susie tugged at her mother's elbow, telling her that the little pictures with big ears were right behind her.

I didn't know what *solicit* meant, but I knew it wasn't anything good. I knew enough to know I should be embarrassed and ashamed, and I was. I looked from the ground to Mrs. Brown, to Susie, and back to the ground again, wishing I were invisible.

"Susie, we have to go home now. Perhaps Barb should go on back to her house, too," she suggested, not looking at me as she picked up her black shiny purse and grabbed Susie's hand. The lady with the red hat looked at me out of the corner of her eye as if I were going to do something awful before making my exit.

I ran out of the church and cried all the way home. I ran and ran until I thought I wouldn't be able to breathe anymore. I almost ran right by my house until I caught sight of it on the hill. I stopped and stared.

There were lilies growing everywhere on our poorly maintained lawn. I compared the sight to that of our neighbors with tidy little boxes of flowers instead of lilies that, if left unattended, would take over a yard. I even hated that awful orange color of wild lilies. Momma always cut them and kept the house filled with the fragrant flowers, but to me, they made us look like we were poor and unkempt. To this day, I hate the sight of lilies.

That day, I hated the sight of our red brick house on the top of the hill. I hated everything about that house and the people inside. Why did I have to live here? Why did my father have to do something wrong? Why did I have to get punished for what he did?

After that, Susie wouldn't talk to me anymore. The lesson they'd taught at Sunday school about loving your neighbor and forgiveness didn't apply to me. I cried myself to sleep every night for a week without anyone hearing. I mourned the loss of my friend and the loss of my innocence. I made a pact with myself never to get close to anyone anymore and never to go back to church, where the mean people hung out. Trust was not in my vocabulary. Until Jake. Until Ellie. Until now.

Getting sick forced me to face God again and more than just in a prayer. I knew things wouldn't be over for me when I ended my time here. I knew that He would walk me through this valley of the shadow of death once more, just five months since my last visit, but I didn't have to be happy about it.

I'd always found that the best way to deal with anything was to do it alone first, and then it's easier to face everyone else. It's kind of like riding a bike or learning to skate. Fall by yourself the first few times, feel sorry for yourself, and wait for the hurt to subside before you face anyone. It turns out that finding out you're going to die is pretty much the same.

Don't feel sorry for me, I remembered Ellie saying to me in my dream on the night she died. *Don't feel sorry for me.*

I cried and yelled and cried some more. Where did everybody go? Jake, Ellie, Momma, the list just went on and on. Why didn't you just take me with you? Why do I have to do this alone? I stood in the middle of the living room, poor Sugar circling me, looking up in bewilderment. "Pray." That's all I heard. "Pray."

So I did. I crawled down on my knees, the two artificial ones. Strangely enough, it didn't hurt this time. I bent my head onto the seat of my recliner, and Sugar stuck her wet nose next to me on the arm of the chair.

Over the years, I figured that if I didn't have time for God, He didn't have much time for me. I always thought I'd save the prayers for when it really counted. It looked like this was one of those times.

I hadn't prayed much during my life. At least not on my knees. Well, there was that time with Ellie and the candle wax, and then again in the basement...

"How do I do this, God?" I prayed, not sure I was doing it right. How do I deal with dying alone? I know I have the kids, but they all have lives of their own. It didn't take me long to figure out that this being single at sixty-two years old wasn't all that it was cracked up to be. Heck, I'd only been single for five months. I was just getting used to being alone, but this was more than I'd bargained for.

Then the words I'd heard Billy Graham say on television in the middle of the night back when Jake was sick came back to me. I'd been flipping channels, and even *The Tonight Show* was a recent repeat. I'd put the remote down during a commercial, waiting to see what would come on next, and walked to the kitchen to fix a glass of tea.

"You say you can't relate to God as your father? Why do you think that is?" the reverend said, and I stopped in my tracks, just listening. "Did your earthly father desert you? Perhaps he couldn't relate to you or treated you poorly," he said in his soft southern drawl. "Or abused you."

I walked back and sat in my recliner and listened to the preacher speak to the thousands of people in the auditorium. He wore a wide blue tie, showing that it was a repeat of a show that had been taped probably twenty years earlier.

"Just know this," Billy said with his blue eyes staring right at me, "God is your true Father. The one who will never leave or mistreat you. He's always there in the middle of a traffic jam, in the middle of the night, in the middle of your living room."

"God, you know I believe in you. I always have." I closed my eyes and prayed. "Please help me now, help me die. I can't do this alone." I laid my head down next to Sugar's and cried.

When the tears dried up, a peace surrounded the room and my spirit and filled me with what I can only describe as a flowing tide. I was engulfed with peace I'd never felt before, an assurance that I was going to be okay. I wasn't alone now and somehow knew I wouldn't be again. Can this be God? Am I dead already? No, my head is starting to hurt from all the tears, so I know I'm not in heaven.

I stayed there until I knew for sure I wasn't just "covering my bases" because I was dying. I felt Him there; I knew He was for real. I talked to Him like a long-lost friend. Like Ellie or Jake was sitting right here next to me.

"I'm sorry that I never went to church," I whispered. "But I'm guessing you know why." I lifted my head to find Sugar still lying beside me. As soon as I moved, she nuzzled her head under my arm again.

"We'll be okay, baby. It'll be fine," I said as I hugged her big white furry head.

I quit feeling sorry for myself that night and stopped being mad at God. I realized that we each have a time to be here, and there comes a time when the gig's up, and it's time to look forward and not backward.

At least the girls have their husbands and families. Karen's life had always seemed to mimic mine, but I hope she gets to skip this chapter.

Jay is too much like my side of the family. He inherited the alcoholism that my brothers and father suffered from. Karen thinks he has this attention deficit disorder, and I'm inclined to agree. He won't get help for it, so he'll continue on the road of self-destruction, and there's nothing I can do about it. He's forty going on fourteen.

Kelly is married with two children, and when I think of them, I'm tempted to break down again. Her two kids spent so much time with Jake and me. We loved every minute of it, but now it looked like they were going to lose both of us.

I've had a good life but still managed to feel sorry for myself once in a while. Getting married at sixteen did away with many choices I might have had, but it also gave me my freedom, without which I would have been destined to dodge the Old Man's attention for a lot longer. It wasn't long after the Sunday school class incident that I personally discovered what *solicit* meant.

Jake turned out to be a good husband and father. I found that sticking it out paid off when the kids grew up and moved away. We became friends again. Best friends. Watching Jake die was grueling and just plain awful. We'd grown up and old together.

Ellie had at least one advantage over me in checking out early like she did. We all remembered her being forty-two years old with just a few crow's feet, an occasional appointment with Miss Clairol, and having had just dropped a bunch of weight. Oh well, she always wanted to look better than me, and I guessed this time she would. I had twenty years of worry and wrinkles on her, but I preferred to think of it as wisdom. At least that's what I'd tell her.

Thanks to Ellie and Jake, I think I'd turned out to be a better person than I would have been without them. At sixty-two, I now know that you don't get that many good people in your life and certainly not any better than those two. I'd been missing Ellie more in the last two years since Jake's illness had set in than I had for many years. I knew she would have been there with me every step of the way in my living nightmare.

When I think about saying good-bye to people for good, I fall apart, and I can't let that happen. If I lose it, how will my kids make it through? Sometimes I wish I was the type to tell people what they mean to me, but they'll just have to let memories speak for themselves. I'm not going to be breaking down and crying so that people will feel sorry for me. There's nothing to feel sorry about.

I remember wise words coming out of the mouths of the older generation before me, but at the time, I was too stupid to appreciate them: "Youth is wasted on the young." Now I know what they meant. I woke up one day and realized my days were numbered. Just like one of my birthday cards said this year, "Life is like a roll of toilet paper, the closer you get to the end of the roll, the faster it goes." True enough.

I learned that love is what matters in this world. Without love, we have nothing, and I've had lots of it. Love made me a wealthy woman.

It seems that I finally have a checkout date. No time for one last trip to Atlantic City or one more dip in the ocean. No more Redskin games or ballet recitals. No more yard sales and—unless I have to make a deal at the pearly gates—I said, "Will you take...?" for the last time.

I wonder if there are slot machines in heaven. Sure hope so, 'cause I plan on cashing in when I get there. I'm not so sure I'll qualify for a halo, but I'm counting on at least a crooked one. No more stuck in the onesies for me, it's time for the tensies and this time, for good.

Made in the USA
Lexington, KY
27 June 2017